Mercy of a Rude Stream

Other works by Henry Roth
Call It Sleep
Shifting Landscape
Mercy of a Rude Stream: Volume I
A Star Shines over Mt. Morris Park

Volume II: Mercy of a Rude Stream

A DIVING ROCK ON THE HUDSON

H E N R Y   R O T H

St. Martin's Press | New York

MERCY OF A RUDE STREAM, VOLUME II: A DIVING ROCK ON THE HUDSON.
Copyright © 1995 by Henry Roth. All rights reserved. Printed in the United States of America. No part of this book may be used or reproduced in any manner whatsoever without written permission except in the case of brief quotations embodied in critical articles or reviews. For information, address St. Martin's Press, 175 Fifth Avenue, New York, N.Y. 10010.

Endpaper and title page photograph of rifle team courtesy of 1924 DeWitt Clinton High School Yearbook.
Part One photograph, page 1, © 1994 by Sara Stemen.
Part Two photograph, page 61, courtesy 1924 DeWitt Clinton High School Yearbook.
Part Three photograph, page 253, courtesy 1928 City College of New York Yearbook.

Pages 81 through 97, chapter IV, Part One, first appeared in a different version as a short story, "The Vanished Bus Line," in *Blue Mesa Review*, No. 5 (Spring 1993).
A brief passage from chapter XIII of Part Three appeared as "Impressions of a Plumber" in *The Lavender*, 3, No. 3 (May 1925), pp. 5–9, and later in *Shifting Landscape*, 1987 and 1994.
Pages 114 through 119, chapter VII, Part One, will be excerpted in *Three Penny Review*.

Design by Jaye Zimet

ISBN 0-312-11777-9

First Edition: February 1995

10 9 8 7 6 5 4 3 2 1

2405-3265
8/00

For Felicia Jean Steele

THE FAMILY OF IRA STIGMAN

Ira's Mother's Family Tree

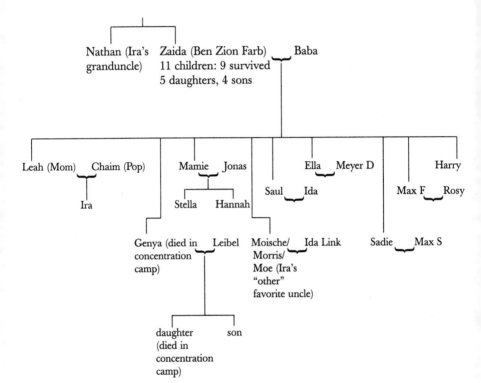

Nathan (Ira's granduncle)

Zaida (Ben Zion Farb) 11 children: 9 survived 5 daughters, 4 sons — Baba

Leah (Mom) — Chaim (Pop)
Ira

Mamie — Jonas
Stella   Hannah

Saul — Ida

Ella — Meyer D

Harry

Max F — Rosy

Genya (died in concentration camp) — Leibel

Moische/ Morris/ Moe (Ira's "other" favorite uncle) — Ida Link

Sadie — Max S

daughter (died in concentration camp)   son

⌣ Married

┬ Children

THE FAMILY OF IRA STIGMAN

Ira's Father's Family Tree

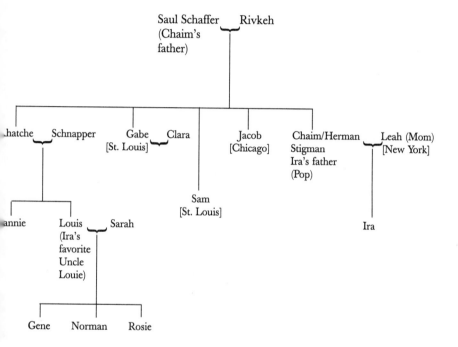

With profound acknowledgment for the
work of my devoted agent, Roslyn Targ,
and Robert Weil, editor supreme.

CONTENTS

In every cry of every Man,
In every Infant's cry of fear,
In every voice, in every ban,
The mind-forg'd manacles I hear.

—William Blake, "London"
From *Songs of Experience*

PART ONE

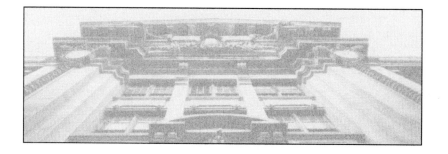

STUYVESANT

I
_____

In the winter of 1921, after completing a year in their newly initiated
junior high school, Ira Stigman and Farley Hewin began attending
Stuyvesant High School. It was downtown, on the east side of the city,
and because attendance at the school was far in excess of its capacity,
two overlapping sessions had been instituted: an earlier one for up-
perclassmen, and a later one, beginning before noon, for freshmen
and lowerclassmen.

The new Lexington Avenue IRT subway line had recently been
opened, and Ira took that to school, getting on at 116th Street,
changing at 86th, to be whisked downtown past two express stations
to 14th, and then walking east the few blocks to the high school.
With what schoolboy joy he and Farley would greet each other in the
late morning when each by different routes or different trains, taken
at different stations, by some magic art would arrive at the same
street corner simultaneously. What windfall of happiness Ira felt.
Soon, he would have to share these walks to school with others: soon,
an admiring entourage would grow up around Farley, would fall in
step with him. Still, no matter how many trooped along, when he
spied Ira, Farley always waited for him to come to his side, a clear indication of whom he had singled out for his chum. Ira reveled in the
security of that knowledge.

For it was almost as if Ira had divined it, as if his intimation of destiny were truly inspired. At the end of calisthenics in the gym class the second week of school, a short track event was held, a sixty-yard dash diagonally across the gym floor. In the first heat, a compact, heavy-thighed youth scurried into first place, in another heat a scrawny young black sprinted to the finish line ahead of the pack. Who placed first in the heat that *he* was in, Ira didn't know, only that he trailed as usual. And then came the heat in which Farley competed; he won easily. With competition winnowed down to finalists came the deciding heat. The winners of the preliminary trials were pitted against one another. Grinning in secret complacence at the foreknowledge he alone possessed, and yet with heartbeat quickened, Ira watched destiny unfold. The black youth darted into the lead ahead of the pack, ahead of the heavy-thighed boy, who was in front of Farley. And then the miracle that only Ira expected took place. Those amazing, hammering strides of Farley brought him abreast of the others two-thirds of the way, and propelled him into the van at the finish—first across the line!

It was scarcely an exaggeration to say that Farley became a celebrity that very afternoon. Admirers trailed him to the subway kiosk that same evening after school let out, and Ira, Farley's closest friend, became a notable by sheer contiguity.

In the next few weeks, Farley was relieved from regular gym exercises and given intensive training during free periods to fit him for the hundred-yard dash. At the end of September, the first of the high school interscholastic meets was held at the Armory in uptown Manhattan. Farley was entered, and won the silver medal for second place. A newcomer, a freshman, one with the barest minimum of training, inexperienced and untried under the strain of intense competition, he was hailed as sensational. His performance was featured on the sports pages of all the metropolitan newspapers. The new "Stuyvesant High School Meteor," the sportswriters saluted him.

In the meantime, Ira, in his laggard, groping fashion, despite his pride in Farley's achievements, his pride in being Farley's best friend, was chafed into vague recognition that he was unhappy in Stuyvesant: he wasn't suited to the place. His sloppiness, his ineptitude with tools, his incompatibility with material precision, his aversion to the strict, the mechanical—he could no more define what troubled him than he could define a cloud. It was more shape than thought, an undulant image, like the face of the shop teacher, quizzically watching Ira's clumsy use of the scratch gauge on a piece of lumber. The shop teacher said "pattren"; Ira said "pattern." At a later date, Ira might have attempted an epigram about Proteus encountering Procrustes, but that shirked coming to grips with the plain facts of what was wrong with him.

Undoubtedly his discontent stemmed from the sheer unsuitability of his temperament, aptitude, and background for the kind of technical training Stuyvesant afforded. His inability to adjust, his dilatoriness in conforming to a new regimen, the unaccustomed late hours of freshman attendance, all seemed to give substance to a sense of having veered away from potential, strayed from some dim affinity. His first month's grades were abysmal, much worse than Farley's, whose were respectable by comparison. Ira failed in every subject except English.

Lord. Ira realized how in this eighth decade of his life, little in so many ways the adolescent juvenile he portrayed, or strove to re-create, resembled the "normal" youngster of that age and period. The differences were too many to go into, but the greatest difference, perhaps he deluded himself, was in the matter of his way of mooning about the opposite sex, about females.

His mind was already seared, his mind was already cauterized. He didn't have to dream about romance, enlarge on it with all the tender frills and streamers that in the fancy of others his age composed the fringes of the youthful crush. He never had one—well, perhaps at the very outset of the fateful spring of his twelfth year, when he experienced—for how short a while—the first vague, diffuse writhing within him of infatuation for Sadie Lefkowitz. She was the sister of two delinquent brothers, one of whom was shot while holding up a crap game; the other barely escaped with his life after falling from the roof to the awning of the big Third Avenue German butcher shop from which he was trying to steal whatever he could get his hands on. Sadie lived in the tenement three doors east. She had rosy cheeks; she wore her long underwear tucked into her long black stockings (and, when last seen, was an usherette in a movie house, and for hire). But

Sadie was that token, as it were, to furnish him with some notion of the adolescent yearning for its idol.

"*Sweet Adeline, my Adeline,*" the Irish and Italian half-grown youths his age sang at night before the lighted window of Biolov's drugstore near the corner of Park Avenue, harmonizing above the muted rumble of trains, "*each night I pray that you'll be mine.*" Ira was much further along than most of them were, much further in wickedness, evil, unspeakable evil. And such self-awareness did what to him? It barred him from the exercise of run-of-the-mill, of street-average thrills. "G'wan," Petey Hunt prompted in his tough, side-mouthed, Irish way, encouraging Ira to make his move toward plain, freckled Helen standing in the tenement doorway of a summer evening. "G'wan, ask her for a lay. We all laid her. She'll give ye a lay."

"No." Ira shrank back.

Already undone. Always on that same amber screen, Ira would see enacted the moment when the irrevocable wrenching of his life began, the unutterable, shattering ecstasy that twisted his being out of shape, forever. It was like that experiment Mr. Goldblum had conducted in the eighth grade to demonstrate to the startled class the pressure of the atmosphere. Suddenly the shiny gallon can crumpled—everlastingly out of shape. He had done it; it had happened: the smooth, regular container became deformed.

What had happened to him was cross-grained, unnatural, a ruinous deflection. It was the blacks who had taught him just how awkward he was, the blacks he was to work with as a laborer on WPA projects. He would tell himself the same thing later that he was telling himself now. In the natural course of things, of slum life, of slum vitality, slum venery, when Mrs. G, Jewish, deserted by the ultra-Orthodox husband she couldn't abide, leaned on her broom in her shift and, wan and forlorn, gazed at him from her window across the street, across the street and a flight up from the sidewalk, like his. That was when a black kid of fifteen or sixteen, his own age then, might have gone over on blatant pretext to put his hunch to the test.

But you couldn't. Ira argued with himself: you couldn't. You would have had the spunk knocked out of you by Pop.

Yes, but when did this ruinous deflection occur? Not before his parents moved to Harlem in 1914, but afterward. Why blame Pop—or blame Pop alone? Think of what disaster Mom contributed, the very bane itself.

Blame them? Yes and no. Blame, try to fix it on anyone; it slides off. The crux of the matter is or was—and we are back at it again—that severance from folk, that severance from homogeneity that—beatings by Pop or not—would have allowed multiform exit, multiform access to the diversity in unity of the surrounding milieu.

In the primitive typescript which he had written in 1979, Ira had set down the following:

"The tried and true, or should one say, the trite and true figure of speech to describe the function of what is to follow is that of the keystone; without it, the subsequent narrative tumbles to the ground. And yet, it is this particular and essential keystone that for a long time I sought to substitute for with a makeshift. In other words, that I stubbornly balked at using because of its shameful disclosure of the character of friend Ira Stigman.

"I have been three days debating with myself, consenting one day, refusing the next, and in the end, consenting again. My acquiescence, I believe, is not owing to scantiness of fictive ingenuity in finding plausible expedients that would still preserve the integrity of the arch. But militating against such subterfuge, unfortunately, is that in the preceding account, I prepared for the introduction of the genuine article, prepared for it so strongly by the prominence I accorded my bosom companion, Farley Hewin, my cheery, staunch refuge from ruined Jewishness, that, in spite of my self-recrimination, the logic of the commitment brooks no departure from veracity."

II

Worsening the situation of his bad grades, literally disastrous for him, was the fact that Ira in this new school kept losing things—his possessions—invariably because of inattention, carelessness, failure to keep strict guard over his property. And the moment his vigilance lapsed, the articles disappeared; they were appropriated, stolen. His entire briefcase, as his book satchel was called, the new walrus-hide briefcase Tanta Mamie had bought for him as a graduation present, which he had treasured unused until he went to a "real" high school, the briefcase and its contents, books, notebooks, mechanical drawing aids, all disappeared. He came home blubbering, anticipating the storm of recrimination such loss would provoke. And it did. Mom and Pop volleyed the cost of replacement at each other—and at him. Only his sneakers hadn't been taken, for the simple reason he hadn't packed them into his briefcase that day, because there was no gym. So it went, even afterward, when his briefcase was replaced: sometimes a protractor would be taken, sometimes a compass, sometimes a ruler. And always he kept losing his fountain pens, one after the other, all those presented him at his Bar Mitzva, and even the Waterman that Max bestowed on him later, a unique fountain pen with a retractable gold pen point. All, all went, purloined the minute he left them unguarded.

School attendance became sown with pitfalls, nightmarish at times. Every hour, every day, contained its start of anxiety, frantic search, rancorous reassurance—and too often the savage anguish of loss. Worries over his possessions thudded into his inattentiveness, and his inattentiveness seemed to become ever more habitual, an invincible caesura of consciousness . . . goddamn dope, forever daydreaming, woolgathering. Bad enough, but the fantasizing was far worse, his cunning conspiring to fulfill his fantasy. It was like a thickening shadow across the delight he felt being in the same school with Farley, a thickening shadow blotting out the vicarious glory of being Farley's boon companion. He began to steal.

In vindictive fury at first, after he rushed back from the hall at change of class, to find his fountain pen gone from the groove on the desk in which he had left it—only a minute before! His last and only fountain pen! Lousy bastards, sonofabitch bastards! He'd get even. He'd snitch someone else's pen. Frig him, whoever he was. . . . And what a cinch it turned out to be! Nothing to it. It was so easy, he'd get another one. Never have to worry about fountain pens anymore. Once you did it, had the nerve to do it, once was all that you needed to learn the knack; at the beginning of the gym period everyone divested himself of his jacket, changed shoes for sneakers, and went out on the gym floor to begin calisthenics. Ira loitered behind. Brushing, as if by accident, against a nearby jacket, exposing the inner breast pocket, brought to light the clip of a fountain pen. It took only an instant to extract, and in an instant the pen was his— his, and slipped safely into his own pants pocket.

"And thus he became predator." Ira read the words of his first draft, the yellow typescript beside him: became! He could feel the grim sneer that bent his own lips: he became a predator from that day on. Ira appended the text: "Indeed, it seems to me not in the matter of fountain pens alone, but as if their theft was symptomatic of the metamorphosis the entire psyche was already undergoing."

Ah, yes, the point I was about to make, Ecclesias, and then forgot, as often happens to the writer, and probably more often to the aged one; so that the intended aside seems like a luxury, a self-indulgence. I once wrote a novel, as you know well, Ecclesias, when I was young.

—Yes?

And the poor little nine-year-old tyke was victimized by the society around him, by forces in the environment around him, the good little nine-year-old tyke I might have written.

—Wasn't he?

Yes, of course. In the novel. But the reflection is a false one; it's quite distorted.

—Perhaps. But let me ask you: why do you say that?

I say it because it is false to me, to the one I am, to the one I actually was.

—At the time of writing?

At the time of writing, yes. That's exactly the point—I think of Joyce's Dedalus here, and of Joyce himself—censoriously as usual: trying to formulate my chief objection, and to test it against the evidence: that what I found most objectionable in Joyce, most repelling, was that he had brought to an extreme the divorce between the artist and the man; not merely brought to an extreme; he had flaunted it, gloried in it: the icon of the artist detached from his autonomous work, disavowing moral responsibility for his creation, paring his nails with divine indifference. Joyce had amputated the artist from the man. What baloney.

But to my point, the writer I was imagined, given trifling variations of detail and time, that he was faithfully projecting, enacting, faithfully engrossing himself in his milieu, nay, faithfully representing himself in relation to his milieu. Do you follow me? The guy really believed he was purveying the truth, realizing actualities.

—Do you deny that the writer was victimized?

But not in that way! He was part of the process. And it is his part in the process he unconsciously suppressed, unconsciously omitted, and hence the picture is distorted. I can say the same thing another way: the writer was under the delusion that he was portraying truth, but in fact, he wasn't.

—How do you know he is now?

I don't—with any absolute certainty; only the relative certainty that I have at least taken into account, born witness to, hitherto ignored relevancy.

—Could it be at the expense of art? Could it? You are silent.

I don't know.

The theft of the fountain pen led to the theft of another, and still another. Their acquisition conferred on Ira something akin to freedom, a new kind of freedom, unwonted freedom from concern: not only from that shudder of alarm over whether he had or hadn't taken his fountain pen with him when he changed classes, and would now have to pay the penalty for his neglect (even if he did, there were more where those came from); but the freedom accorded by callousness, the license that sprang from callousness, callousness that dispersed the thought of the unhappiness he brought the one he had despoiled, callousness that bartered sympathy for power, that toyed with depravity.

And then came the inevitable, the inevitable in its devious way. Came the day when in the breast pocket of one of the jackets that he brushed against was clipped a magnificent fountain pen, the upper barrel glistening in silver filigree. Silver! Vine and arabesque! He clawed at it; it was his.

His!

For a long while he kept his superb trophy hidden in his favorite cache, the dusty floor underneath the lower drawer of the built-in wardrobe in Pop and Mom's bedroom, kept it wrapped up in a piece of brown paper bag beside its run-of-the-mill mates. The round knobs on the dingy-white drawer, the dark maw within when the drawer was pulled all the way out, the accumulated dust on the floor whereon his fountain pens were secreted became accomplices of his stealth, abettors of his crime. The preciousness of his unique prize, the silver-filigreed Waterman, continually glided through his mind, continued to twine about it, like the silver filigree around the barrel of the pen.

On a sunny weekend toward the end of March, he and Farley lazed together in the sandy-carpeted mortuary—once again reinstated as the Hewin family parlor—lazed and chatted about the track meet Farley was scheduled to compete in next month. He felt sure he would place. Coaching and practice had greatly improved the two things in his running that most needed improving: his start and his stride. He had already been unofficially clocked in the 110-yard dash in the awe-inspiring time of 11.6 seconds.

Every now and then, Ira would wind up the phonograph, put on "Mavoureen" with John McCormack singing, and, paying only token attention to Farley, drift off into enchanted reverie under the spell of the Irish tenor and his mellifluous brogue. Clipped to the inner breast pocket of Ira's jacket was the silver-filigreed fountain pen. He had brought it with him. Why? Because it was safe to sport it on weekends, with no school, and no owner to claim the beautiful object as his, not Ira's. Because the pen tantalized Ira's consciousness so continually, he had to wear it—even if he didn't display it. He had to wear it concealed or he had to give it away, because what was the fun of wearing it concealed?

Farley was talking about Hardy, the black youth who always came in second to Farley at workouts. "You never saw anybody eat the stuff he does," Farley laughed. "You know, Irey, he'll eat a hot dog, mustard and sauerkraut—and an ice cream cone all together." Farley stopped speaking when Ira drew the pen out of his pocket. "Hey, that's nifty."

"Here, have a good look at it." Ira extended his arm and brought the pen within Farley's reach.

Farley rotated the barrel, admiring the filigree. He admired it, frankly, just as Farley would, without envy, happy in his friend's possession of something so handsome and so costly. "Hey, never saw anything so nifty, Irey!" he congratulated.

And with that suffusion of affection, of blood swamping the brain, Ira presented Farley with the pen. Oh, no. Farley tried to return it. He couldn't accept it. It was too valuable, too beautiful, to be given away. But Ira insisted; he wanted Farley to have it. That was why he had brought the pen with him today. One of his rich uncles, a jeweler, Ira fabricated, had given him the pen, and he wanted Farley to have it. He himself had a satisfactory, plain Waterman—which he showed Farley. No need to have both. He wanted Farley to have this one. In the end, Ira persuaded him to accept it. For Farley, appreciation paled the hue of his blue eyes. In spoofing ritual of exchange, he tendered Ira a new yellow pencil from his father's supply. For Ira, the moment was like a rush of vertigo: immense joy danced in his head—but it was immense joy suddenly bonded to a wraith of qualm; it was immense delight in Farley's pleasure at receiving the gift—but coupled with a specter of foreboding.

Excused from participating in calisthenics, and the other activities of the triweekly gym program, Farley had been appointed "monitor" of the gym class. Each student occupied a preassigned spot on the gym floor, and Farley was accorded the privilege—or the honor—of checking off the attendance on a chart on which names corresponded to spots. Grimacing in broad, familiar wink at Ira, who grinned back in acknowledgment of his special status, Farley came through the columns of students as the short, burly gym instructor barked the tempo of the drill. Ira was checked off on the chart, and Farley went on. . . . A minute later, he was back, his features furrowed questioningly, his blue eyes darkened with seriousness.

"Hey, Irey," he said in a subdued tone, "there's a guy up front in the next row, says it's his pen. It was yours, wasn't it?"

"Sure it was mine. He's crazy!" Ira blustered.

Farley left. In another minute he returned, even more serious this time. "He says he's going to the office if he doesn't get it back. Do I give it back to him?"

Ira's world began to buckle, to crumple into a shapeless wad. He felt his very being wobble about and lurch, abandoned by any guidance, bereft of any center. Still he persisted, clung stoutly to the untruth, to the integrity of his lie bound in the integrity of his gesture of friendship to Farley.

God Almighty! Some kind of wholly irrational, wholly impossible urge clamored within Ira as he typed: I'll barter. I'll swap you the next ten million seconds, any ten million seconds of my life, for ten seconds of lucidity way back then, ten seconds of caginess, ordinary, garden-variety common sense. How could anyone be so goddamn preordained to do the wrong thing?

"No. He's crazy! It's my pen."

"You sure, Irey?" Farley's tone of voice and countenance both pleaded loyally on Ira's behalf. "I can give it back to him, and that's all there is to it."

Farley went away again. A few minutes later, the young gym instructor who was Farley's coach came through the lane of students. He had the silver-filigreed pen in his hand, and was trailed by a tall, delicately built, steady-eyed youth with an olive complexion.

"Will you come with me," the young instructor requested of the dazed, the benumbed Ira.

All three left the gym, climbed the flight of stairs to the main floor, and entered the office of the assistant principal, Mr. Osborne. After explaining the nature of the dispute, the young gym instructor placed the fountain pen on Mr. Osborne's desk, was thanked with a grave nod and relieved of further stay.

Ira knew his doom, the inexorable, irreversible doom that had befallen him—nay, nay, invited to befall him.

The pen, asserted the youthful classmate quietly, had been given him on his graduation from public school by his father. Even in the void drained of reality, the lineaments of the other's good breeding were manifest. He could bring his father to school and prove the truth of what he said.

And Ira, now nauseated to the very soul with guilt, with the dread sickness of the abject felon, asked to speak to Mr. Osborne alone. Mr. Osborne was a large, kindly, unpretentious man in his fifties, corpulent with sedentary life, and with a fine, wide, pale brow. He asked the other student to step outside the office, to wait outside the door.

A few more seconds, and Ira was alone with the assistant principal, alone with him—and with the portraits of former administrators on the wall. Ira broke down completely. Poor automaton, poor nitwit, Ira mocked himself: with what easy resolution history could be revised: he needed only to have asserted that he found the pen on the cloakroom floor near the gym, in the hall, anywhere, concocted anything plausible—and very likely gotten off with no more than a stern reprimand for not turning in lost property. And since he had implicated the most promising track man who had entered Stuyvesant in all its history, the whole matter might have been glossed over with a show of severity.

But no, Ira burst into tears and confessed all: he had stolen the pen from the other's jacket pocket in the gym cloakroom. How many such thefts had he committed? Mr. Osborne asked. Three or four, Ira lied: he didn't know. Mr. Osborne meditated gravely, came to a conclusion. The youth waiting in the hall outside was called into the office. He was handed the fountain pen, and at the same time directed to report back to the gym. Blubbering Ira was left alone with a thoughtful Mr. Osborne. Patiently, soberly, he listened to the delinquent's tearful lamentations of having been robbed of his own fountain pens, robbed of his briefcase and all its contents, of everything he left behind on a desk, even a little assignment book. He had given the fountain pen as a present to his best friend.

Pathetic lump of sniveling juvenile, Ira could imagine later what he must have looked like to Mr. Osborne. Nor was it difficult to surmise what went on in the other's mind: how best to dispose of the case before him, determine the fairest thing to do about the dripping clod of doleful adolescence. In the end, Mr. Osborne informed Ira that he was excused from classes—and from school—that he was to bring his father to Stuyvesant tomorrow, to bring him to the same office he was in now, the assistant principal's office. Mr. Osborne would then make known the decision he had reached in the case. Meantime, Ira was to leave all textbooks now in his possession in the secretary's office next door, and bring with him tomorrow all other textbooks belonging to the school. He would write Ira a pass that would permit him to pick up his belongings and leave the building. Mr. Osborne issued his instructions with sober compassion, but with firm authority.

Ira obeyed. He gathered up his belongings in the gym cloakroom, changed to shoes outside the secretary's office, deposited his textbooks on her desk, where a pass was waiting for him. Then with an unnaturally light briefcase, as if all its former weight were inside him now, he pulled on his light topcoat, handed the door monitors his pass, and stepped out into the changeable March day, into the fresh breeze against his face. Overhead, before him at the street's end, a regatta of shining clouds veered toward him between high buildings.

Doomsday. Doom everywhere. On street and edifice, the pall of doom, on vehicle and pedestrian and storefront, in passing sounds of the city the knell of doom. In every step, in breath and heartbeat. Crook. Thief. He had been caught. Too late now to regret deeds done or undone: to have kept the pen concealed, steadfastly, not made a gift of it to Farley, maybe sold it to somebody, outside the school. Waddaye say? Five bucks? No? Then three bucks. All silver. And with one of the dollars for her. Okay? Huh? Okay? Easy, instead of this—oh hell, forget it! Why hadn't he claimed he had found it? Under a bench in the gym—anywhere?

Too late, too late and irrevocable. With his near-empty briefcase, a taunting reminder, dangling from his hand, he walked west, half cognizant of the direction he was taking, distracting remorse with motion, ruffling it with New York's changing scene. Where was he to go? The Lexington Avenue subway at 14th would take him home—

too soon, too soon to mourn in futility in the kitchen, too soon to sit *shiva* over climax of woe with Pop's return from work. Ira was sure he would be expelled—why else had he been asked to hand over his schoolbooks, and bring the rest tomorrow? And what had Mr. Osborne said? "You're not bad habitually, but this stealing of student property has to stop." Expelled. Wish to Christ he had gone on with the rest of the grammar school graduating class, gone on to work, to a job, become a *pruster arbeiter,* as Mom said. If only her obdurate ambitions for the improvement of his lot weren't so indomitable. Or he so willful, so incorrigible, so rotten. Right away finding comfort in the dollar he could flaunt. What if he were working, making a dollar like Sid or Davey or Jake who had moved into the block? What then? Oh, too late, too late. Ira had been caught stealing—from another fellow in high school. Caught stealing and confessed, confessed and about to be expelled. It was altogether different from stealing on a job. You'd be fired. You'd get another job. This was different: the pen wasn't the company's, wasn't nobody's; it belonged to somebody, to another. And now you wouldn't be just fired. Mom would scream in Yiddish, *Oh, a veytik iz mir!* You've wrecked, broken your career. And he had lied to Farley, his best friend, and now Farley knew it.

Ira turned north on Broadway, the bustling continuum of the thoroughfare streaming by his fluctuating woe. Uptown, aimlessly walking. So you get fired. Pop got fired. So he went to the employment agency, and now to the union hall, the Waiters Local AFL, number, what was the number? Number two. Get the *New York World,* Ira counseled himself: look in the Boy Wanted ads, Young Man Wanted, as long as it didn't say Christian only, Protestant only. But this, expulsion from high school, all of destiny balanced on this. You could feel it teetering on its fulcrum the second time that Farley came around and said, The guy says it's his. One tiny grain would have changed the whole future, a single word: yes. You wouldn't even have had to say it was his. Just: yes. But he had lied to his best friend, and was trussed up by his lie: "My uncle gave it to me." No, no, no! It's his, it's his, Farley. Give it back to him. I'll explain later. And because Farley was a sensational track star, the sports pages said, once the pen was restored to its owner, all would have been overlooked, forgotten. So easy. So easy. But then he would have had to say, I lied to you, Farley. I—I found the pen.

Walk.

Through the crowded, noisy, fitful avenue, past indifferent landmarks, the Flatiron Building, past hectic intersections, Herald Square, Times Square, onward plodding: Columbus Circle, dully recognizing the changing character of the neighborhood, from commercial to apartment house, from utilitarian building to ornate, many-storied, multi-balconied edifice. At 96th Street, he quit Broadway, turned west toward the Hudson, entered on the lofty viaduct above the riverbank. On the paved paths down below—mothers, nursemaids, tending prams, the infants in them so snugly, colorfully bundled against the variable, brisk river wind. Strollers. That man twisting his mustache tighter, the way Mom twisted the end of a thread before addressing the eye of the needle. How enjoyable was every sight and sound, if every sight and sound didn't drag a lead weight after it. Look at the water of the broad Hudson, choppy, whitecaps nicked out of the cold gray river by the wind.

The Palisades across the river, with the huge Domino Sugar clock on the face of the bluff, giant hands telling the time: between 3:45 and 4:00 P.M. He could imagine the clock like a vast branding iron, every moving minute, every trailing hour, searing into his memory. He had walked until his legs had grown sluggish, bare hands grown cold, fingers cramped gripping the useless near-empty briefcase. He sat for a while on the green park bench, rested just long enough so that when he got to his feet again sinews had stiffened, joints ached. He trudged on. The sun slanted, abandoning the cliffs to long shadows, shadows that whetted the breeze to a cold edge. It would soon be lamplighting time, soon be gloaming. The paved walks below had all become deserted, a bare, desolate net of dim paths of pavement thrown over the sloping, darkened lawns that separated the empty, silent river below from the auto traffic on the viaduct above, the viaduct where he plodded. As if hoarding the waning light, the steel tracks of the New York Central freight lines gleamed on their dull gray beds of gravel, metallic streaks dividing river from land, the river that lapped against the massive blocks of granite, sustaining the railroad bed, blocks dumped higgledy-piggledy into the water.

Just a few years ago, he had gone swimming there with the Irish bunch in the street, gone in all innocence, in the years of trust and innocence. They wouldn't let the other few Jewish kids on the block come along.

"We don't want youse Jew-boys wid us," Grimesy snarled at Davey, Izzy, Benny. But him they had accepted. Why? Why had they let him go with them?

And afterward, when they had dried off, and put their clothes on to go home, a cattle train full of steers passed, the animals lowing behind the bars of their rolling pens, rolling toward the abattoir downtown. They threw rocks at them, the bunch of Irish kids did, at the parched beasts on a sweltering afternoon on their way to be killed. Ira had felt a pang, then. Always thoughtless cruelty became unfunny; the glee leaked out of it as if he himself were the butt of it, the victim. He couldn't help it. Maybe because of Mom, maybe because he was a Jew.

There was the path, there, upstream, that they used to take; you could barely see it now, serpentine through the dead grass, under leafless yet feathery-thickening trees, there; it reappeared like a slash down the steepest slope to the railroad tracks. Oh, he had gone that way a dozen times: nine years old, ten years old, eleven years old—when was the infantile paralysis year? Swam and soaked the disease-preventive camphor balls Mom had tied in a little bag about his neck. He should never have grown older. The words came out in English out of the oft-heard Yiddish with their malicious twist: "*Zolst shoyn nisht elter vern.*" And now, too late, he would leave the viaduct to take the same path again: *Zolst shoyn nisht elter vern.* . . . There it was, just as when he was nine and ten and eleven. Follow it. . . . Follow it through the grass, down the slope, not so steep as it looked, across the clean, shiny tracks on the ties on the gravel, across the shiny tracks unfazed by the frowning ties on the busy gravel . . . crunching footsteps to the tumbled river-rocks where the water dyed their margins darker than the dry granite above. Sun sheared off now, lopped off by the Palisades. Domino Sugar clock; what time was it as he made his way? Past the secluded, jagged little pools of water in the crevices of the giant jumble of rock. Here was the flat rock off which everybody dove. Flat rock, diving rock, curl your toes around the edge and belly-whop into the cool river. "An' no wires, or nothin' underwater to get tangled in," said Feeny, and everyone agreed. What had he done? What would happen to him now?

He couldn't think, that was his trouble. So he would be expelled from Stuyvesant; so his good name would be ruined. So he would be known as a thief, as a *goniff*. He alone knew that before; now it would be known by all. . . . And what if, what if he also knew, it were also known, that he had been caught too, committing something worse than theft, an abomination? As it well might be, but a single slip. Then throw your briefcase into the water now. Forestall everything: if he threw his briefcase into the water, he'd have to jump after it to get it back. And then? He wouldn't have to think about anything anymore. Sure, the water was cold, gravel-color cold. It would sting. But if he took a deep breath, a real, tired deep breath . . . in the water . . . it might all be over . . . before the water got through his clothes . . . his secondhand topcoat, his secondhand jacket. What was there to be afraid of? He might not even feel it. Anybody could slip off a rock in the river, even a flat one . . . like this . . . just swing the briefcase into the restless, dented water, as far as you can, into the water, rippling all the way to the gloomy Palisades. Come on. Soon be dark, and no more nerve. If he could only think. *Yisgadal, v'yiskadash, sh'mey rabo,* the mourner's chant, was that how it went? What did it mean? That's how it sounded. Pop would sit on a wooden box, the way he did when his father died, after he learned about it in a letter from Europe, slit the buttonhole of his vest with an old Gem razor blade, and sit on a box, sit *shiva*. And Mom, Mom, Mom! Wait—

Wait: now he knew. The river had just told him. He didn't have *seykhl* enough to discover it by himself. It didn't matter. It was true. No, it wasn't loony; it was true. If it wasn't true, then nothing was true; and if nothing was true, what difference did anything make? But here he was, standing with his briefcase on the diving rock on the

Hudson, with his briefcase to throw in the water before it was night-time. Why would he be standing here if it didn't make any differ-ence? If nothing was true? Then something was true. Here he was, at day's end living; in a moment to drown.

He turned around on the block of stone, turned his back to the river. So now suffer. Everything. The outcries at home. The expulsion from school. The shame. That was only the outside, the outside wreckage. What he was, what he already was inside, he would have to bear. He didn't know what he meant, only that the agony would be worse, and he had chosen to bear it, bear the havoc of himself, the only thing true. . . .

He climbed up toward the paved, lonely, darkling lanes, went un-derneath the viaduct, went on toward Broadway, into motor-din, store-light, headlights, human cries; he plodded south. It would be a long way to 119th Street, a long way to Park Avenue. But that was nothing compared to what lay in store for him. Just a long hike compared to what waited at the end . . . just a long hike—nothing, compared to destination. . . . Yes, what was anything compared to himself?

III

An hour later, Ira trudged home. It was after dark, well after dark, and long after even a belated arrival from Stuyvesant's second session might have warranted. A moment he stood in the hallway under the transom light, and then numbly opened the kitchen door: perceived the blank window shade drawn full-length down the window on the other side of the room; perceived the green oilcloth on the kitchen table, the silly, little-figured red apron hanging from the rim of the black iron sink; perceived the gas-stove burner on; green-painted ice-box with alarm clock on it and box of household matches, green-painted icebox in the corner of green-painted blistered walls next to the bedroom door where the mop handle leaned. And Pop seated at the table, and partway through supper, his dog-brown, worried eyes lifted to Ira as he entered. Heard Mom exclaim in relieved Yiddish, berating, "A plague take you, Ira. Where have you been since school let out?"

Followed at once by Pop's sardonic "Uh-huh! I can see by the crestfallen nose on his face something's gone wrong for him again."

Words clotted in Ira's throat; speech jammed. He crossed the room, took the mop handle from the corner, and handed it to Pop.

"Are you crazy?" Pop turned pale.

Passage had to be forced, passage for confession, his covenant with the river: "I was caught stealing a fountain pen. Another boy's fountain pen. The—" Ira hardened himself for retribution. "The assistant principal wants you to come to school with me tomorrow."

But instead of retribution, Pop threw the mop handle down. He looked, he was—could it be?—stricken close to tears. He threw the mop handle down, and fled from the kitchen into the gloom of the bedroom. Strange, the merest mote of a revelation formed in Ira's mind: Pop wasn't as strong as *he* was. Pop couldn't mete out what his son was ready to endure. Soft inside. So that was what he was?

"I think I'm going to get kicked out of school." Ira spoke stolidly, stood stolidly. "They took away my books. They want me to bring the rest tomorrow."

"*Oy, a brukh af dir!*" Mom drove the execration home with a fierce nod of her flushed, broad face. "Get buried, won't you! For all the torment you cause us! Dolt! Clod!"

And as suddenly as he had fled, Pop was back. "I hope to see you dead!"

"They were stealing from me!" Ira broke into wailing lament. "They stole my new briefcase, all my fountain pens."

"*Dummkopf!* If you're not smart enough to keep track of your own belongings? Whom are you deceiving?" Mom flung at him. "Others also have briefcases, have fountain pens. And who knows what else? And still they manage to keep them! Choke on your excuses!"

Pop heaped rage on rancor. "I hope you rot out of my sight! Rot! And this child I nourish? May flames char him to cinder. This thief I pamper?" He turned savagely on Mom. "It's all your fault. It's all your doing. You send him to high school. Hah! I would send him—you know where? To dig in the ground. To lay turf. For that he's suited. And may he lie under it!"

"*Oy, vey, vey!*" Mom groaned, stooped, stooped to pick up the mop handle. "Blunderer! Great ox! Oh, you're nothing to me but grief!"

"Send him to high school! She needs, she craves, a learned son. Nah! You have him: as learned as a canker. I told you!"

"You told me. Good." Mom opposed Pop's vindictiveness with her own anguish. "Can you say anything more than that? May a black year befall him. Oh, my grief!" And to Ira, "Yes, stand there like a post. *Got's nar.* Take off your hat and coat and sit down. How did they discover you were a thief?"

"I stole a silver fountain pen from a rich kid, from a rich kid's pocket. And I gave it to Farley. He went around with it in the gym. You know: where we go—for exercise." He lamented in English: "The gym. And the kid—he saw it. He wanted it back."

"Then why didn't you give it to him?"

"Don't know. I told Farley it was mine. I gave it to him."

"A fool," said Pop. "You see? A fool ought never be born. A fool should be stomped on! You idiot! Why am I so cursed? With her for a mother, with him for a son."

"*Gey mir in der erd.*"

Ira sobbed.

"Weep! Now you weep?" Mom said bitterly. "It would have been better had your eyes fallen out, your hands fallen off, before you stole the pen. And what do they want of you now? The pen was returned, no?"

"Yeah, but I told you already. I told the assistant principal I stole it. He wants Pop to come to school."

"*Ai,* be torn to shreds!" Pop bared his teeth in a fresh outburst of tortured rage. "Only be torn into shreds! *Ai, yi, yi,* to shame me further! To tell me I have shit for a son. For this I have to take time off from work to learn what a wretched dolt I've raised?" He swept the saucer of compote away from him. "Here. Feed this to your next husband!"

"Why do you say that to me?" Mom's throat mottled angrily. "I haven't taught him the ways to righteousness a thousand times? How many times have I shown him how a good Jewish child behaves? If a demon possessed him, what do you want of me?"

"Go. Enough. Speak to the wall. He's yours, and yours he remains. One thing he'll soon learn: what it is to be a crude breadwinner. Every day, every day, to go to work, to a job, to a boss, to labor for a pittance. Let him fill his own craw. He doesn't deserve anything better than that; he never has. You've fattened a gross sloth, and now you'll both find it out. Who knows, with toil he may scratch up a seed of wisdom."

Followed a long grievous silence, while Pop, grim-faced, taut, made an effort to peruse his Yiddish newspaper, sigh-groaned audibly, irregularly, again and again. . . .

"When did you eat last?" Mom asked.

"Me? I don't know. Before I left for school. Ten o'clock. The bulkie you gave me."

"I would feed him." Pop flapped the newspaper. "Chopped sorrows."

"What you would do I already know," Mom retorted.

"I'm not hungry," said Ira.

"No? I'm sure. Even your spectacles are stained. Go wash your unhappy countenance. I have pot roast and gravy on the stove. The noodles are already cold." Tears came to her eyes. She snuffed, went to the sink and blew her nose. "*Noo?* What are you waiting for?"

"I have to go to the toilet."

"Then go."

He entered the shadowy bathroom, held the door open until he located the dangling light pull, and as he tugged it, heard Mom say before he shut the door, "So he's a fool. But a child of indigence he is too. And of sorrow. Even if it were a golden pen, it doesn't matter. He's my child."

In the green-painted bathroom, against one shiny, uneven wall, stood a small chest of a dozen tiny drawers that Biolov had been about to discard, and Ira had retrieved; against the other wall stretched the long green-painted bathtub in its casket of matchboards. Ira lifted the chipped toilet seat, and was surprised at how little he had to urinate; after all, he had been weeping—the odd notion occurred to him—all those hours of roaming. He yanked at the toilet chain, tugged the light pull, and returned to the kitchen.

"And where were you straggling all this while?" Mom held the loaf of heavy rye bread against the flame-flowered cotton cloth of the mussed housedress covering her deep bosom, while she applied the gray carving knife with its tarnished concave blade toward herself through the thick crust. "All this time. When did you leave school?"

"I don't know. Gym is the first period. That's all I went to." He could feel appetite revive. "Maybe nearly one o'clock."

"And all that time roaming. Go to the sink."

"I didn't want to come home." Ira removed his glasses, smeared soap on his face, cupped hands under spouting cold water, wiped face on towel, wiped glasses. "I walked, that's all."

"And where?"

"Why are you asking stupid questions?" Pop interjected. "You'll have to pay the cobbler for his shoes. Then you'll know."

"True. And his father is also a man of means." Mom set the thick-hewn slice of bread before Ira, who began devouring it ravenously. "Wait, I'll cut some meat."

"I didn't know where to go, that's all." Ira tore away a mouthful. "I walked by the river. On Riverside Drive."

"And why Riverside Drive?"

"I don't know. It was by the river."

"Aha! I understent. You went by the water."

"By the water," Pop scoffed, brown eyes hard with animus. "Immediately he's leaped in. How the woman submits to his contriving."

"Chaim, let me be," Mom said quietly. "I haven't woe enough? And you haven't fear? Whom are you deluding?" She met Pop's set gaze with her own—until he looked away. And then she hacked at the meat in the pot, conveyed a chunk to the plate, tilted the pot to spoon gravy to cover the slab of meat, added noodles.

"Here. Eat." She set the plate down before Ira—and again confronted Pop. "He's my child. He may die for his *golem*'s brain, and the suffering he's causing me. And you as well. He gets it from you, after all. Let's tell the truth," she challenged him, "how did you steal out of Galitzia the first time?"

Pop put down his newspaper, thrust forward a startled, tense countenance toward Ira. "Look what she scratches out of the dirt! What has the one thing to do with the other?"

"I'm asking you."

"*Gey mir in der erd!*"

"You filched the passage money to America. True or not?"

"Kiss my ass."

"From your father. From his wallet."

"Go drop into your tomb."

"There!"

"She throws that up to me—how I quit Galitzia. How else was I going to leave? I had no money. My brothers were in St. Louis. I wanted to go, too."

"Well?"

"Whose money was it? You horse's head! My father's, no?"

"But you did steal it."

"*Gey mir vidder in der erd!* How else was I to get it?"

"*Oy, vey,*" Mom sighed. "When you returned to Austria, were you hanged for your misdeed?"

Pop wagged his head at her irately. "Would God I had never returned! A demon sent me back to Galitzia. To her! To you! The devil sent me back. But what—if fortune fails you, what can you do?"

Mom seemed too spent for anger. "Believe me, if fortune failed you, it failed me." She sat down, speaking calmly. "What would have been the harm if I hadn't suited you? I would have been an old maid. Ben Zion would have married his other daughters under me. As if he had any other choice. Sooner or later the Lord would have sent me a fat, sleek Jew of a widower, with a fine beard and a great paunch and a houseful of children. What would I have lacked? Do you want some more noodles? My pitiful son."

"I want some more bread." Ira chomped.

Mom stood up. "And what time does your father have to be at the school tomorrow?"

"I think maybe ten o'clock. Mr. Osborne comes in. He's the assistant principal."

"I'll have time to finish a breakfast serving," said Pop. "I'll slip away between breakfast and lunch." He nodded, addressing Ira. "Thank you for your thoughtfulness."

HENRY ROTH

And Mom, bringing Ira another slice of bread, added, "Throw yourself at his feet. Implore his forgiveness. Tell him you're the poor son of impoverished parents. You saw the silver pen. You snatched it. You couldn't help yourself. Never again will you be guilty of such foolishness. You can speak English. Then speak. Plead."

"He had to own a fountain pen." Pop rested elbows on the open sheets of Yiddish newsprint on the table. "Haven't I seen a hundred times *yeshiva* youth in the subways, pale, famished Talmud students going to the *yeshiva* near where I work? And what were they carrying in their hands? A plain bottle of ink. A steel pen in a wooden holder. Only this princeling had to have a fountain pen. Without it he couldn't learn, he couldn't record wisdom. And not only to have one fountain pen, but another to give away. You hear?"

"*Shoyn farfallen*," said Mom. "Enough torment." And to Ira, "If you're not allowed back into the school, what will you do?"

"I don't know."

"You'll come home."

Ira shook his head sullenly.

"You'll come home," she repeated. "No one need know. I don't want you roaming the streets." She sat down again, studied him with meditative eyes deep with sadness. "May God help you tomorrow with this *assistant principal*"—she assayed the English words. "May He help you indeed. But if not, if you're cast out of the school, that's not the end of life, you hear? You're a dolt, and you've learned a terrible lesson. Only don't lose your will for your career."

"Career," Pop echoed. "Keep filling his head with nonsense. He needs a career like I need an abscess. You'll see his career, and you'll see your dead grandmother at the same time, Leah."

"I can still hope," Mom said. "What else can I do but hope? You're his father. Do you wish to see him wholly destroyed? Nothing to become of him?"

"Ira has already given me good tokens, good signs of what to expect. Do I need more? And pray, spare me your questions." He averted his face, drawn again with inner torment. "I can assure you he is a fool."

"In truth. But who had the silver pen, and who didn't? Would the other need to steal one?"

"You're altogether clever. Would the other be the clod this one is? In his home tonight, fear not, the other's parents are rejoicing. And well they might: not only have they recovered a treasure. Their son showed wit; he showed judgment. He wasn't going to let the opportunity escape to recover what was his. There's a son."

"*Dolt*," said Mom. "May your heart ache as mine does. A little compote? I know you're fond of stewed pears."

"Yeah. And another slice of bread."

IV

Ira knew where he was at. He let the spate of memories flow through his mind: oh, those first years in rural Maine, in Montville with his family, his beautiful, young M, the two boys, in the latter half of the forties at the end of World War II. The ditch he dug in which to lay the copper tubing from the brimming, truly—how should one say—sylvan, precious pool of spring water on the hillside, to the kitchen sink. The half-stick of dynamite at the end of his pickax, half-stick of dynamite skewered harmlessly on the pickax point. Stop. Stop. The hardships, especially for M, the quasi-romantic impracticality of it all. But they had been together then, young relatively, though he was already forty by that time. But together! The hillside, crowned with stout rock maple trees, leafless at the close of winter, the sap gathering, the syrup making. Why did some things in the past become so much lovelier than they were, even as the ugly became hideous? One had to lower the sluice gate on the bygone somehow, or be swept away by the flood of reminiscence.

Ah, Ira hadn't even slept well last night. He had admitted to his friend and rheumatologist, Dr. David B, that in order to overcome the pain and lethargy of rheumatoid arthritis he frequently had to resort to ingesting a half-tablet of the narcotic Percodan. Dr. B remarked that he resembled Charles Swinburne in that respect. Swinburne too had depended on drugs to sustain his muse. And of course there was De Quincy and there was Coleridge, both of whom became addicted to opium. The effect of the half-tablet, the "high," the elevation of mood inspired thereby, was brief, but enough to overcome his inertia, and that was usually enough to enable him to proceed from that point on. The drowsiness that sometimes followed could be overcome by taking one or another of the proprietary caffeine tablets. The million vagaries, gestalts, that occurred to him during these times of lethargy were also valuable, Ira mused.

Wakefulness thudded brutally against the compassionate swaddling envelope of sleep; wakefulness pounded by reminders, hard and edged, that cleaved through oblivion into consciousness that it was morning. The bedroom airshaft window framed a gray slurry of daylight. Pop had already gone to his breakfast-luncheon stint. He would meet Ira in front of the school at ten o'clock. Ira was to wait there for him. . . . He dressed, in tense, apprehensive silence, ate the buttered roll Mom served him, gulped down his sugared mix of coffee and boiled milk in the dismally familiar stark kitchen. The backyard light over the uncurtained top of the window presented the gray washpole preening washlines in the blue baleful sky of March. Cruel aubade and foreboding fanfare ushering in the dread of the coming crisis. With Mom's injunctions almost unheeded, scarcely penetrating the density of his fear, he readied for school much too early. Better to patrol the sidewalk in front of Stuyvesant than stay in the house knowing what Mom felt, looking at her grief-harrowed face. He had only one book to return, the English grammar.

"You're not to stray blindly about," Mom enjoined before he left.

"When?"

"Afterward. If ill fate takes over."

"No, you told me that ten times."

"You promise? Swear."

"I swear. Ah, Jesus, leave me alone."

"I implore you. You know it would destroy me."

"I won't destroy you. I'll be home."

"Have mercy on your mother, Ira."

"Yeah. Yeah. G'bye." He left. . . .

Immune to the March day, he moved toward the Lexington Avenue and 116th Street subway station, moved on joints all but fused with anxiety: moved through and by and into an unreal, gritty, pitted world, a world with only a single channel open: via three bright streets to a sallow subway platform, and then via stale train atmosphere downtown. Only local trains stopped at 116th Street. He got on the first to arrive, and stayed on it all the way: to stall, to wear down oppressive time, to segment it with local stops, with change of passengers to churn the haunted lethargy. Then came the walk from 14th Street to Stuyvesant, and the restless wait. He had gotten to the rendezvous more than half an hour early. He paced . . . on the quiet sidewalk in front of the school building. . . .

And there came Pop, in workaday coat, features sharp and strained under the brim of his weathered gray felt hat, his nose capillaried as it was when he left for St. Louis. Ira tried to smile in grateful greeting, was rebuffed, left dangling, downcast before Pop's glare. Ira led the way into the school, past the monitors at the door, explained with dull indifference that left no doubt that Mr. Osborne had ordered him to bring his father to school.

Into the scholastic atmosphere, made strange by Pop's presence, through corridors inset at times by an open classroom portal, through which blackboards glimpsed, and hands driving chalk . . . a hand rolled a map down, the flat, tinted world like a window shade.

The two climbed the short flight of stairs to the main floor, heard gym activities remotely below. Trailed by Pop, who muttered, "Wait a second," Ira paused before the door of the secretary's office, stepped inside, and laid the English grammar book on the nearest desk. Mr. Osborne's office was next. Ira entered, in the van of Pop, and waited the second of the two to be recognized.

"Come right in. Please!" Mr. Osborne stood up. Big frame, not corpulent, fleshy, his large pale countenance and brow tinged with warmth and sympathy. His whole approach was cordial, his hand outstretched in greeting to Pop. "Mr. Stigman. I'm pleased to meet you."

"Yeh, t'enks. I'm gled too." His words clipped with extremity of tension, with nervousness, Pop shook hands with Osborne.

"I brought my other book, and left it." Ira indicated the secretary's office.

Mr. Osborne nodded, beckoned soberly to a chair. "Won't you sit down, Mr. Stigman." He motioned again. "Do take your coat off."

"No, no. I don't need. T'enks." Pop sat at the edge of his seat.

Mr. Osborne sat down. His whole attitude bespoke moderation: thoughtfulness, tempering, from the way his large hands were clasped on his desk to the creases on his brow. "I'm sure you know what's happened?"

"Yeh. I know." Pop's nod was dreary.

"I find it very—" Mr. Osborne opened his hands, lifted them slightly, let them fall. "Difficult. Unpleasant—very—to deal with a parent about a subject of this kind. I'm sure you understand—I'm a parent myself. But it's my duty to do so. Your son stole another student's property. A fountain pen, a rather valuable one in this case. If that were the only time he stole anything, gave way to temptation, one might—" Mr. Osborne bent his august brow in weighty deliberation as if seeking, but then freed himself from quest, "one might take a different view of the matter. Condone. You understand, Mr. Stigman?" And when Pop made no reply other than pinch his face up even more: "But this was only one of such acts Ira's committed: acts of continued and deliberate theft." His brown eyes rested on Pop in sincere pain.

Pop glowered at Ira. He began to snivel.

"And yet he's by no means a criminal. Not by any means. I can tell by his behavior, by his remorse. I can tell by your attitude, by his parents' attitude. He's been brought up to know the difference between right and wrong. There's no question about that in my mind. He obviously knew he was doing something wrong."

"I won't do it again, Mr. Osborne," Ira wept. "I swear I won't do it again."

"I'm quite sure you won't."

"So can you give me another chance? Please?"

"That's exactly what I can't do." His deliberation lent emphasis to quiet negation. "That's the reason I asked you to bring your father to school: to explain to you, Mr. Stigman, just why it's in your son's—it's in Ira's best interest to end all connection with Stuyvesant High School. To attend a high school somewhere else, a different high school, where none of this is known."

"I'll give him high school." Pop nodded ominously. "I'll give him. He'll get it yet, Mr. Osborne."

"No, it isn't punishment that we're after," Mr. Osborne strove earnestly, speaking with controlled gesture. "God knows, Mr. Stigman, he's already inflicted that on himself to no small degree. No, the thing I'm trying to explain, Mr. Stigman, has nothing to do with punishment. The thing I hope I can make clear is why he no longer can attend Stuyvesant High School. That is why I wished to speak to you personally. So there would be no misunderstanding. It's not punishment that concerns me here. Protecting Ira, protecting his future, is of far greater importance than punishment. He has involved another student in the theft, an outstanding athlete, by the way. The boy whose pen Ira stole now knows who it is. The word will certainly spread. All the others who've lost property, and I assure you that, unfortunately, they've been no small number, will suspect Ira, and you can imagine the consequences for him. His position here will become impossible. He simply can't stay here. . . . And," Mr. Osborn sat up, grave and irreversible in judgment, "it's in his best interest not to stay in Stuyvesant."

"Yeh," Pop agreed, his brown dog eyes full of woe, meeting Mr. Osborne's a moment, then sweeping to Ira's. "*Geharget zolst di veren.*"

In their peculiar-shaped cravats, wing collars, like Mr. O'Reilly's, like Pop's when he married, the former administrators looked down from the walls, in their repose forever captured in oil, their heavy watch chains undulating through Ira's tears.

"Please, let's have no misunderstanding on that point," Mr. Osborne said. "We're here to protect all the students. To protect Ira as well."

"No, no, I understent. I understent good."

"Then I can only repeat: as of this hour Ira is no longer a student of Stuyvesant High School. In a word—and a very harsh word it is indeed, Mr. Stigman, I'm sorry—he's expelled."

Ira sobbed.

"However, let me say this." Mr. Osborne rocked the blotter holder on his desk, studied the green underside incuriously. "In order that there be nothing against his record of this disgrace—because of the kind of boy he is—obviously not wicked—and the father he has—I've asked that his record card be removed from the files, and destroyed. He'll have no record of shame to live with. He's only

been here two months, fortunately, and we can wipe the slate clean—
with very little loss—with respect to time spent here at his studies."

"Yeh. Yeh. I see you a—you a kindly man." Pop bobbed in grievous praise. "T'enks. He should—ah!" he despaired of Ira. "*Aza lebn af
dir!*" he flung at him.

"You can start anew in any high school of your choice," Mr. Osborne mediated. "You need never mention Stuyvesant High School."
He stood up, jotted soberly on a pad, tore off a slip of paper, tendered it to Ira. "Give that to the monitor at the door." Then he extended his hand to Pop, who had also gotten to his feet. "I don't
need to repeat how painful this has been—for me as well as you."

"Yeh. T'enks. More I don't got—I don't hev to say. I'm sorry I
make you so much trouble. I'm sorry I got such a son." Pop nodded
brusquely. "I'm, I'm—just a vaiter. A vaiter in a restaurant. On my tips
I try to send him to high school. You see how it helps."

"Don't give up hope, Mr. Stigman. We're not dealing with a habitual delinquent here. Your son isn't a criminal. Misguided, yes,
but not a criminal." Mr. Osborne spoke as all three moved toward
the door. "The way the entire thing came to light proves it. Actually,
it's a rather incredible thing." He stopped at the door. "Goodbye,
young man. I suggest in the future you try to control your impulses.
Do you understand what I mean when I say 'control your impulses'?"

"Yes, sir."

"You've already caused your parents immense suffering. And
yourself as well. I hope you profit by this lesson."

"Yes, sir."

They left the building . . . walked in utter silence west, almost as if
they were strangers; their common unhappiness, the son's blame
and shame, the father's wrath and contempt, served as repulsion
against the weak bond of their kinship. . . . They walked until they
came to the small park, Stuyvesant Square Park, on Second Avenue,
where there they parted. Pop's restaurant was located farther downtown. Ira's destination nowhere, for the time being.

"Thanks, Pop," Ira quavered.

"T'enks it would be indeed," Pop answered in stony Yiddish, "were I to see you buried."

The ultimate, the epitome of rejection, Pop turned his back and walked off: the short, slight man in his black overcoat strode away, neither deigning nor able to communicate anything except his utter estrangement.

Alone, this terrible ordeal having ended, the outcome settled, Ira felt his constricted spirit expand again. He sat down on one of the park benches to assay his release, to scan the landscape of his dishonorable freedom. It seemed boundless, and equally shapeless. All he could discern about it at the moment was its sensation. The air was cool, variable, sunlit, terminally March. Overhead, tattered clouds jostled silently under luminous blue serenity. And under them, buildings, windows, and on the ground, people, pedestrians and vehicles, figures in motion or at rest.

Some kind of stage in his life had ended; that much he was sure of, but who could define it? He couldn't. Ended. Ended, as if a perverse destiny were fulfilling itself. Yesterday was mortal, yesterday, at the Hudson River's edge, had come to an end. He perceived something was in store, an earnest outcome for this anguish. But what? How was it that others' lives, Maxie's, Sid's, moved along in predictable, in sensible ways, toward a future with a label? His didn't, and he didn't know how to make it move that way.

Impulse. What had Mr. Osborne said? Self-control. He didn't know how to make his life happen in a self-controlled, sensible manner. And he paid for it. He hadn't wanted to go to junior high school, but he had listened to Mr. O'Reilly, and stayed in P.S. 24—and met Farley. And he hadn't wanted to go to Stuyvesant; he'd wanted to take a general course, like that given by DeWitt Clinton—but he had followed Farley. He didn't know what he wanted, that was the trouble.

Others knew what they wanted. Most wanted to make money, to be a success. He didn't. The other Jewish guys on the block were ambitious; he wasn't. That was the trouble: something had zigzagged within him, caused an irreparable quirk, made him a *lemekh*, a bungler, a freak. And now he had to find out how to deal with that kind of quirk, take it into account, try to fit life together again, if it could possibly be fitted together. Sometimes he had a feeling he stood in a large, clean, airy room where marvelous, nameless, intricate machinery was working out his destiny—in secrecy.

Under the opposite benches, sheltered by the green slats of the seats, small, grimy mounds of melting snow still lingered. Last refuge of winter, they seemed, crouching under the green benches, grimsprinkled winter brought to bay by the spring thaw. The matted lawn on the other side of the pipe fence back of the benches glistened sodden; the trees were feathery with buds; the breeze felt cool and rinsed. All footprints of pedestrians from wet to dry on the paved walk. Bark of trees so damp and swarthy, and building rooflines stretched tight. That was springtime. And this was he, Ira Stigman, sitting here, kicked out of high school. He felt an urge to commemorate the date in his small homework assignment book. He drew it out of his breast pocket, along with an indelible pencil. No fountain pen on his person today. He touched the point with the tip of his tongue, and wrote in purple letters. March 23, 1921: "The Devil laughed today."

And now, he'd better get up and leave the park, he counseled himself, leave, before somebody early on his way to the second session recognized him. He had promised Mom he would come home right away, as soon as the calamity came to an end, and it had come to an end. He stood up. He began walking toward the 14th Street subway station.

For whom had he suffered? And to what end? Jesus, that was strange: to think you had suffered toward some end. He knew he had suffered—because he was a sap. Wasn't that enough reason? No. It wasn't enough. That was river's message, gray river saying the same thing with a million choppy tongues all the way to the Palisades below the Domino Sugar clock—saying the thing that saved his life on the diving rock on the Hudson. It wasn't reason enough. He didn't suffer just because he was a sap. He made life live inside him. Only he could weave among a thousand people window-shopping, drift past the store windows, coats and hats and dummies, among living people, jabber-jabber, shuffle-scrape, in coats and hats like dummies too in living flesh and skirts that moved, and toot-toot and honk-honk and ding-dong auto and trolley din, and to him it meant something. That was the answer. Because he was alive, different.

Alive, different, all the way to the angle corner of Broadway, Union Square Park, where the cop blew his whistle, and whipped traffic through with his arms; alive, different, until he reached the dark kiosk, and went down the stairs with the horde. He'd never really figure it out, dope. But that was the answer. Vile and rotten and different. Why? Look at the way his mind could stretch out in all directions—in every direction away from himself, and bring it all back, and bring it to life inside him. Who else could do that who just got kicked out of Stuyvesant High School?

V

That was to be the original ending of Volume I of *Mercy of a Rude Stream,* so he had signified on the disk on which he kept a skeleton outline of the contents of the sections into which his work was divided: of necessity, according to the capacity of his computer. It was now four days since he had returned home from surgery, as it was termed these days (instead of an operation), to repair the hernia. He was almost back to normal, in body and mood, thanks in great part to M.

How he had marveled about this mystery, her, yes, impregnable devotion to him, while he was still in the hospital, chafing, fretting unduly at the colloidal personality of his average American roommate, his cheap, plastic tastes, his inane mental content, his preference for the sintered sham, for the gilded and gelded, with a wife like him, and friends as well, the TV programs he was addicted to.

He hated them instead of pitying them—that was the difference, that was where he was wanting, and M was not. He hated them because he wasn't one of them, he supposed (he had mulled about the matter for hours on end). He wasn't one of them. He was an everlasting Falasha, as he had written in his journal. Well—the miracle was that M loved him so, this daughter of the same dominant society that he detested for its banality, and that detested him, he was sure, with equal intensity for his alien views, elitism, his alien response to their mass-produced, disposable values. M loved him, cared for him, tended to him, looked after him with such solicitude—and such wisdom. She wasn't the only one in this *goyish* world of the Western Diaspora whom he respected, even formed deep attachments with—by no means—there were dozens, and not only intellectuals either—but her he worshiped, "this side of idolatry," worshiped her as devoutly as a flawed, fluctuating soul could worship another fallible, human being, could worship his mate of many years. She had awakened in him affirmations and compassions that dispelled the lethargy of his habitual cynicism, his alienation, restored him to a wider humanity, and who could tell? Her constancy and devotion might have been the spiritual catalyst in effecting that qualitative transformation in himself, a regeneration of personal commitment that was instrumental in the birth and growth of a wider personal commitment: his partisanship for his own people in Israel. Ironic too . . . she was not Jewish. . . .

Volume I. Finished. Done with. He had thought about it this morning, as he showered, breakfasted, and the rest, and he wished he could set down, or rather formulate, the thought as it first occurred to him: with the same pristine lilt of wording. But he was rarely able to do that, to remember the exact form of the advent of the thought, unless he had the means at hand, and the impulse, to jot the thing down at the moment of occurrence. He had not had either. So—the insight had gone unrecorded (no new experience for writers); he would now have to grope, cumberously, toward an approximation of the original formulation. It was to the effect, or bore within itself the incipient realization, that his "creative" days were done— no, that wasn't quite it; *that* he had recognized for a long time. The central point was that it was not his attempted innovations of narrative that were of interest to people; his endeavors in that respect had undoubtedly long since been dealt with by others—and surpassed. He simply hadn't been around when all this was happening. People, the reading public, were interested in him, to the degree they were, not because they expected exceptional literary output from him any longer, but because they were curious about the vicissitudes he had undergone, vicissitudes marked by an element of freakishness.

He should have known that from the first, but as usual was slow to apprehend; it had taken him all of Volume I to perceive it. What had happened to the author of that anomalous classic of Lower East Side childhood, as certain critics referred to it? That was the meaning surely of the frequent requests he received from journalists and others, freelance writers, for interviews. They reflected a degree of public curiosity regarding the extraordinary hiatus of production that was the dominant feature of his literary career. They sought information from him and about him on which to base hypotheses as to the cause. He wasn't prepared to advance any, since he was the last person in the world equipped with the necessary intellectual, philosophic, social apparatus to do so.

And not to forget, though he would be better off if he did, the letter he had received yesterday from David S of the *Washington Post,* a very sincere letter, requesting an interview; and his own decision not to grant it. Interviews preyed on his mind in anticipation, for fear that he would reveal the extent of his unfamiliarity with modern literature, his absence of profundity, the skimpiness of his critical faculties. Interviews took more out of him than they should, or were worth. Besides, he had already been done, well done, and as he would like to say, though he would probably veto the inclination, overdone. Most likely, though, his most compelling motive in denying the request for the interview was his desire to preserve the integrity of the unexpected turn his writing had taken, or was about to take, unexpected acknowledgment of the individual he had been, and still had to abide with.

"No, I'll conduct my own interview, Ecclesias," Ira muttered as he proceeded to SAVE the working copy he had already typed on the screen. Some faint but promising notion had crossed his mind as he did so; faint and remote, but at his age (and before), the faint, rare notions had to be retrieved at once, hermetically enclosed, or they volatilized. . . . Had the elusive, the evanescent thought been simply that he would soon be dust? He didn't know; it wasn't able to get him back on track anyway. But how he plodded, how he shuffled as he walked the length of the mobile-home hall to the kitchen. There M, her piano practice over, stood with bent head in faded pink variegated apron over blue shirt, paring vegetables to go into the Belgian cast-iron orange enamel stew pot—how beautiful her lofty brow under gray hair. He plodded, shuffled, he who had once been just like—how repelled he was by quoting that snobbish, evasive Jew-tweaker—TSE-TSE. No, Ira thought: old Bert Whitehouse in Norridgewock, Maine, a scad of years ago while he was writing his novel in 1933, had said it just as graphically in his way as Eliot had in his: "Once I could scale a four-rail fence one-handed; now I stumble over an inch-thick board on the ground."

And why should the public at large be interested in the inventions he might have to offer now? They represented anything but contemporary configurations; they were those of a half-century ago. This was a different age, and demanded—and needed—new interpretations and new judgments made from the vantage of a fifty-year gradient. It would take another century or more to disclose the proximity, the near-contemporaneity, of the seeming gap.

From his fifteenth year to his nineteenth, from his expulsion from Stuyvesant to—and perhaps beyond—his freshman year at CCNY. The facts here were very good. He knew he could recall with fair accuracy many facets of that period, some charged with dreadful meaning, some no more than diverting reminiscence. He was Mr. Editor. He was boss. He'd get on the linear choo-choo, and bowl along to the provisional terminal, no, the provisional hub, a junction point, in railroad parlance. How could he—that was it—delete, shorten, condense? What did he have here?

"It is as difficult to set down," he had written, "as difficult to set down as it is to recall the proper sequence of the farrago of events in the months succeeding my expulsion from high school. I returned to P.S. 24—"

And here Ira paused, paused and shook his head. These half-truths, half-truths he was forced to labor under, forced himself to labor under.

—Well, then, who are you? Editor or contributor?

Both and neither, Ecclesias. I know this is the time of my deepest undoing; I grow drowsy with the numbing dolor of it. This is the time. This is the time. All things apart from this are like so many streamers, mere fringes, fronds—

—Not quite, not quite. Among them are also life-determining episodes.

Yes. But the main thing is that it was during those years that I tore apart the ligatures, my psychic ligatures, sundered them irreversibly. The spring was pulled beyond its intrinsic elasticity, its constant, never to resume its original form. God, how one can ruin oneself, be ruined; it's inconceivable.

—*Alors, mon ami.*

VI

So back to P.S. 24 Ira returned. One of his aims, he was quite sure, was to obtain a transcript of his record in grammar school, and especially of his year in junior high school, since he would have to present this as credit toward continuation of high school. Ira Stigman had been expelled from Stuyvesant for fighting (that became his standard explanation, and strangely, no one questioned it), and his records had been destroyed. He needed them to enroll in another high school. Secondly, he appealed to crippled, mock-bellicose Mr. Sullivan, because he had once had such a high opinion of him in his English class (and such a low one in bookkeeping), for help in finding a job. He met Ira's appeal, or better said, his prevarication, with charity, and even with some indignation at what he regarded as summary punishment for so commonplace an offense. He wrote a letter of recommendation to the head of a small law firm whose books he kept. And on the strength of it, Ira applied for the position of office boy, either that day or the next—and he was hired.

Mr. Phillips, his new employer, gave the impression of being a reasonable man, even-tempered and deliberate, with a trait of smoothing the sides of his long straight nose between thumb and forefinger. He invited Ira to sit down at a desk and write a letter of application for the position. He found the letter satisfactory, except for one flaw: Ira had spelled his name with only one "l" instead of two. He would have to be much more careful in the future to note such details as this if he expected to satisfy the exacting requirements of a law firm, Mr. Phillips stressed.

But he was a washout as a law-firm office boy. Without more ado: a lamentable washout. A ludicrous failure. He could not even get a message straight over the telephone; in his anxiety and apprehension he couldn't even hear straight; he couldn't distinguish spoken words. Also, it was a rare occasion when he found his way to the right courtroom, the right session, the right hearing at the right time. Rare as rare could be. *Shlimazl!* Pop was right. And if by some stroke of luck he did follow instructions correctly, did get to the right courtroom at the right time, then he mooned past the announcement of the case for which he had been sent there for the express purpose of asking for postponement or deferral. Mr. Phillips smoothed the sides of his long nose a fortnight or two; his junior partner fumed, tutted, growled something about a chump. And Mr. Phillips's secretary was wracked by puzzling hysterias. . . .

The firm moved its location to new, more commodious quarters. The entire office decor underwent a change: the stout old friendly oak filing cabinets and the grainy yellow oak desks were replaced by sleek, coffee-colored metal. Along with that change came a change of office boys. Another youth took Ira's place, a youth of about Ira's age, but slender, large-eyed, knowing, a little amused, a little condescending. He reminded Ira of the fellow student from whom he had stolen the silver-filigreed fountain pen. Mr. Phillips explained that the newcomer was to take Ira's place beginning the next week. Ira was a good boy, Mr. Phillips affirmed, but not suitable for work in a law firm. He was sorry, but he would have to let him go.

To tell the truth, Ira wasn't too unhappy. He found the work boring, devoid of color and encounter, of the tangible tartan of the city's aspects he loved to contemplate. Except that he would have to go home and tell Mom that the source of his nine dollars per week had dried up, he felt more relieved than regretful at being fired. He knew he was just too much of a mope to cope with the job, with the abstractions he already perceived composed most of it.

So ended his brief untenable and tenuous association with the law, lawyers, and the legal process. He resolved never again to work in an office of any kind. It was enough to be a boob without having to cringe in humiliation of having others discover the fact.

If only there weren't so many interruptions, Ira mused, so many distractions in the life of the narrator. He could go on from episode to episode in a tale told autonomously from end to end. (His old complaint; was it pretext or legitimate?) Distractions were too many for him, or too beguiling, or he—his will—was too weak to resist. Once it had been strong enough, once it had, when he wrote his one and only novel.

He had managed to exclude distractions and involvements for as long as four years, until the opus was done. Ah, youth—and he had had a plethora of distractions and involvements. Sexual often, though not always: a love affair that went to hell; and that *pas de deux, de trois, de quatre*. And illness too had interrupted, but again, not for long. He had then clung tenaciously to his narrative, which was something he could no longer always do. And, dear reader, as Jane Eyre would say, and a whole swarm of other literary narrators of fiction, in the good old days when ye scrivener snuggled up to the reader, dear reader, if you don't like it you can lump it, whatever "lumping it" meant. Dear reader. There might not ever be any readers, dear or otherwise, though he made every effort to preserve means of communication with them, future means of communication: those floppy disks wherein he addressed Ecclesias. Dear reader.

But then, those were not the days, and these were, when he spent, or rather wrecked, an entire day, with a gut gone haywire—or perhaps he should say, spent altogether too many of them that way, recuperating from various surgeries or miasmas of mood and malaise, all or most of them, very likely, payments or penalties, retributions from excesses of the way, way back. But then too, and that perhaps was the worst of it, in that long past when he wrote his youthful "classic of Lower East Side childhood," he hadn't tried to pry off and peddle segments of the novel, as he did now, still hoping to make an impression on modernity (and garner a few bucks while he was at it), and in consequence, hadn't received the rebuffs he did now, and likely deserved, from various and sundry well-thought-of periodicals.

His stuff was now old hat, and for all he knew, stereotyped as well. But the rejections brought him face to face with the fact that he was an old man of seventy-nine, and his literary wares those of a seventy-nine-year-old man, waning and wanting, and perhaps pathetic. Be better, more dignified, if he shut up, maintained an air of remote reserve, because that way his deficiencies would remain unexposed. Good idea.

Well . . . As he wrote his literary agent: he would refrain from submitting further fragments of his writing. It was all or nothing now, and if it was to be all, then it would have to be posthumous. *Eheu fugaces, Postume, Postume, labuntur anni.* . . .

Roving again in the vicinity of 14th Street, on the east side of Union Square Park, passing by the ornate facades and arched windows of the lofts and office buildings of the time, he glanced at a BOY WANTED sign posted on a doorway: Inquire at the Acme Toy Company Upstairs. Again he found what he so lackadaisically sought, and was all but afraid to find: a job interview. The blowsy, stertorously breathing, cigar-puffing Jewish proprietor behind his mussed desk in his small, cluttered office was Mr. Stein, he informed the young applicant. Mr. Stein appeared to be in his late fifties. Beside him stood his son, Mortimer, a tall, dark young man in his twenties, who scrutinized Ira through the slits of intolerant brown eyes.

Together, they quizzed Ira, at the same time as they briefed him about what they expected of him. Did he intend to go back to school? Experience had already taught Ira the answer to that one. Oh, no, he assured Mr. Stein, he had quit school for good. They needed somebody all year round. They needed somebody who was quick to learn, somebody with a good head, because they had a big inventory with hundreds of different items in different bins, and somebody who was wide awake and honest and careful. Ira gave them Park & Tilford as a reference, stressing that he had learned the location of hundreds of items down in the cellar. Of course, the P&T store uptown had closed, and he was out of a job. His half-truth bore some weight. And further, they wanted somebody who was not afraid of a little hard work (pronounced "ard-vark" by the owner). Oh, no, not he.

Although the son remained darkly skeptical, the father hired Ira: "Vee'll geeve you a chence," he decided. The wages would be eight dollars and fifty cents a week, payable Saturday afternoon.

That first day he worked there, that first day he was hired, was already Saturday. Then he had been led into a contradiction again: payday on Saturday; and if so, why hadn't he been paid? Had he worked too short a time, or wasn't Saturday payday? Answer he could find none. Only that the few cents with which Mom had supplied him to go job-hunting, now that he had found one, he expended on buying lunch, and skimpy enough it was. When time came to hie him home, he had no carfare—and as usual was reluctant to ask. Why? Too deeply submerged in the past to fathom now. One nickel. Did he fear refusal? Did it mean to the kid that he was betraying some kind of weakness in having made no provision for a subway ride home? Did it deflate his seemingly sturdy self-reliance, hint at schoolboy dependence? God knows.

The kid hoofed it all the way from 15th Street to 119th Street. Over a hundred blocks in a straight line: five miles, as they reckoned it in New York, and this at the end of most of a day's work. The hike didn't hurt him, of course, borne along on those young, resilient legs, legs wearying only toward the end, the last few blocks of pavement over which he forged ahead with the single-minded resolve of a homing pigeon. He could see himself in the kaleidoscope of passage, in the shade of buildings in the late sun of late spring, see his straining face among the other innumerable faces and figures limned for an instant on the storefronts he strode past, as if progressing along a system of ill-reflecting mirrors. And turning the corner, at last, around the Phoenix Cheese Company's wholesale depot at Lexington Avenue into familiar 119th Street, his own sleazy street, his shelter, his home.

Why did he remember chiefly the unpleasant, the disastrous incidents connected with the job, Ira queried himself, the all-too-frequent mishaps of which he was the cause? Why was he so intent on proving he was a *shlemiel*? For no other reason than that he was. It was not a case of his protesting too much; he simply was. Ah, yes, wonderful: *Ses ailes de géant l'empêche de marcher.*

Who was to know that? Strangely enough, his blunders and casualties infuriated the younger Mr. Stein far more than the father. The senior Mr. Stein seemed not so much amused with Ira as always on the verge of being amused: what antic would he furnish next? It was Mortimer who made life miserable for Ira, made him so continually ill at ease that he virtually guaranteed Ira's commission of some egregious slip, which in turn vindicated Mortimer's rancor as it stoked further cause. Ira broke unbreakable dolls. He stepped into whole cartons of fragile Christmas-tree baubles. Immediately after, he spied the older man at his desk wheezing alarmingly with averted face: "Die insurinks vill pay for it," he said indulgently to his son, who, Ira supposed, wanted him fired at once. "My madicine dey don't pay for. So—de *yold* is better *vie* madicine."

But Mortimer was not to be appeased. One afternoon, returned from lunch, when he was at his most sluggish, Ira was called on to help Mortimer unload a big case of teddy bears. And while Mortimer stood high above his helper, one foot on a stepladder, the other on an upper bin, Ira tossed him teddy bears to stow away at the very top tier of the shelves. And Ira's aim astray more than once, Mortimer had to catch himself and the teddy bear at the same time. Suddenly, as Ira bent over to get at the bottom layer of teddy bears, whack! a teddy bear bounced off his skull. No teddy bear could ever make an impact that hard by merely being dropped—of that Ira was sure. It had to be aimed and hurled—deliberately and with maximum force. And even though Mortimer, high on his perch near the ceiling, served up a conciliating smile and an unconvincing "I'm sorry," Ira resolved to quit. That Saturday he did, without notice.

Ah, what it would have been like, Stigman—Ira let his head loll back—without the canker, susceptible to all phases of existence, unaware, or scarcely, of the poverty, of the penury and the squalor all about you? What else did the kid know, besides what he perceived, what he discerned within the confines of the slum his milieu? Mostly those things that books told him, the too often insubstantial library-world, at a far remove from his own. Still, the mind did open sometimes upon literary avenues, and some were feasible, might reward the traveler for his journey.

We go this way only once, said Thoreau; and he, Ira, had all but gone to the end of that way already. Nonetheless, it was a privilege to reconstruct the route, and on a computer. Could Ira repress that, that which now strove for utterance? No, he couldn't. It was the consequence of his having taken a half-tablet of Percodan, Percodan, which always tended to make him loquacious. Millie M, Marcello's wife, had given him *Jane Eyre* to read, the first and only Brontë novel he had ever read—and he could hear the quality of her prose pulse in his. A hundred and forty years ago she lived. She died in childbirth, but she spoke to him now, her spirit still alive and vital, toiling at the same craft, speaking through the medium of the same craft, speaking with a fine, vibrant woman's voice over a span of a century and a half, relating what it was to be alive then, imparting a sense of life through all the fuddy-duddy tags of religiosity, gothic implausibilities, supernatural folderol, bursting through Freud and the grave, through custom, culture, ethos, to impart a sense of the young woman of her time to an old man of his. And now look ahead—he thought—look ahead 140 years. Say *Kaddish* not only for your grandchildren, but for your great-grandchildren; rend your garments now, sit humbled by bereavement, sit *shiva*—which you never have done for the living—in a word, mourn for the unborn, for the departed of the future.

In that utterly changed world of 2125, with its changed mores, changed ambience, changed awareness, will any look back at you? Look back from a humanity whose nature you can scarcely guess at now: more extraordinarily different probably than Jane Eyre's world was from yours. Still, the only holistic world they will have to look back at will be such as this, through all the lame and ludicrous anachronisms—this mélange of fact and fiction. A hell of a lot of difference a misplaced year is going to make 140 years from now. Indeed, Ecclesias, if you wish to know, you have much to be grateful for in this digression. Not only because it relieves the heart, but it illuminates mortality in continuity, or continuity in mortality, reconciles the soul, yes, a very little bit, the human soul to its fate. So, let this be an indefinite interlude. . . .

VII

He had earned enough money for Mom to buy him his clothes for the coming school year: a few pieces of underwear—BVDs—socks, a pair of cheap shoes, and enough secondhand outergarments to last until he again brought home wages next summer. And how unabashedly she haggled with the secondhand clothes dealer on 114th Street, flushed with indignation, holding up to the light the seat of the touted pants to exhibit the worn fabric—heedless of the shopkeeper's disclaimers and Ira's cringing complaints. With his raiment provided, Ira felt excused from further responsibility for his own welfare until next year. Food and shelter, a bed to sleep in, he took that for granted; it was his by virtue of his parents' obligation—or really, Mom's obligation, since she was so dedicated to his getting an education. The carfare too, the dime she tendered him every day for transportation to and from high school, he felt equally complacent about. Hadn't he contributed sufficiently to his present source of supply when he worked in the summer? Apparel was the one thing that—to his way of thinking—didn't accrue naturally in the household, demanded supplemental cash, cash from the outside, cash that it was his duty to earn. And he had earned enough to defray the cost of secondhand raiment. He had discharged his duty. And as soon as he believed he had done so, he felt he was entitled to quit the job, to loaf with clear conscience.

So with bathing suit wrapped in a towel to form a small bundle, and the bundle tucked under his arm, Ira strolled west through 125th Street's shopping mart, its string of one-story shops, west, under the Sixth Avenue El, west, to the soaring, dark 125th Street subway overpass, and under it all the way to the St. George's ferry slip at the Hudson River shore. That was as far as shank's mare could take him. From there he had to board the ferry, which cost a nickel, and ride to the other side of the river, the New Jersey side at the foot of the Palisades. A highway ascended to the Palisades, but partway up, an avenue branched off through a residential section, and here he would hike north, above the river and parallel to it, hike along a narrow sidewalk by comfortable homes set back on sloping lawns, under the shade of trees in the full leaf of late summer. And now and then note a house rising in quiet affluence from curved, paved driveways where motorcars were parked.

America, flourishing, prosperous, where modish women in picture hats pulled on long white gloves as they walked to their automobiles. Almost without benefit of words, but as if thoughts were clouds imbued with meaning, he would mull on the imponderable gulf that separated him from everything he beheld—and was enchanted by— that separated him, the immigrant, from the American-born, the Jew from the gentile. Oh, it was more than just that, Ira would ruminate. To be the kind they were you had to come from the kind they were a long, long time. Always. No old Jews with whiskers, no Shloime Farb with his forked gray beard, clearing his throat luxuriantly as he bent over the Torah scrolls, Shloime Farb in top hat on *Shabbes*, no *cheder*, scant as the memory was, East Side pushcarts, babble of Yiddish, *matzahs* and Moses in the *Haggadah* engraving clubbing the felled Egyptian taskmaster. This world had no warm Yom Kippur after-noons strolling past the ground-floor synagogue, no feeble old Jews in their shrouds prostrating themselves in atonement—scary—noth-ing to flaw the wholeness of the kind they were who lived in those well-kept homes beneath the trees where he walked. And worst of all, he was sure, he was sure, no secret canker had already begun to mar the contented wholesomeness they seemed to possess,when he saw them clipping the hedges about their neat, elevated lawns, or seated in vivacious conversation opposite each other in their swinging gaily striped chairs. No. Their heartiness, their soundness, removed them.

A mile or so he would ramble thus along the tree-lined avenue— until he came to a painted arrow that marked the entrance to a path downhill whose other end opened on an artificially sandy beach. It was a privately owned swimming area on the Hudson, complete with dressing room, lockers, and a diving platform extending into the river. A fee of ten cents was charged for the use of a locker; other-wise, admission to the dressing room was free. There, Ira would change to his two-piece bathing suit, deposit his clothes in an out-of-the-way spot outdoors, walk to the sandy beach, and swim out into the "clean," pleasantly brackish depths of the wide Hudson estuary. He was a good swimmer. His roly-poly build, so often disadvanta-geous in land sports, served to advantage in water. He would swim out to the rusting hulks of the Liberty ships, quondam military trans-ports during the Great War, now idly tugging at the moorings in mid-stream. Airplanes, pontoon planes, were often anchored partway between the rusting ships and the shore, and Ira would hang on to a strut or guy wire for a breather. And once, while he was perched on a pontoon, a navy patrol boat churned up, and an officer ordered him to clear off. He did, but in his haste to comply, he dove off—and struck his head against something solid, was stunned, but managed to stay afloat until he recovered enough to swim back to shore.

Alone, so rash and alone, and often far from shore, from rescue, had he been the victim of serious accident, or been seized by cramp, he would certainly have drowned. And always in those spasms of momentary panic, when he imagined some Leviathan under him, or bucking the combined flow of river current and outgoing tide, when dry land seemed unattainable, he always thought of Mom: he shared in her inconsolable grieving for him.

"Why do I let you go?" she said to Ira more than once, so often that her words would remain fixed in his heedless mind. "I don't know myself why I do. I let you go because you have to learn about America. You must learn alone, because help you I can't. Neither I nor your father." And she would laugh ruefully. "Mrs. Shapiro chides me that I'm like a *goya*. 'You have a heart of stone,' she says. 'A stony heart like a *goyish* mother.' She doesn't know. If I lost you I would fall lifeless. I go about numb until you come home."

Too late to enroll in the current term, Ira had enrolled in the summer session of the night high school—at the very same large gray school building he had passed so often—and would again—on his way to and from the Lenox Avenue subway station on 116th Street. Second-year English, his junior high school record entitled him to take, second-year Spanish, and elementary algebra. After oppressive, sultry, electric-lit classrooms, sauntering through 116th Street, the crosstown trolley thoroughfare and the Jewish shopping equivalent to goyish 125th Street. He would saunter along with other working youth, as if he too were on his own as they were, and not just temporarily thrown in with them, bantering, chatting—about what? Classes, courses, jobs.

Ira could recall one exchange distinctly. He was sharply reproved by a gentile student—already a young man, several years older than he was—for some facetious remark he made impugning Calvin Coolidge. Ingratiating himself, as usual, when with gentiles, by recourse to mild Jewish denigration, he said humorously that Jews called Coolidge "Koilitch," which was the Yiddish word for stale *challah,* day-old Sabbath loaf, because it was so dry and colorless. His night-school classmate's rejoinder was prompt and pointed: Jews of all people had no business making light of the man who had led the country into its greatest period of prosperity. "Look at the way business is booming," he averred. "And who's getting the most benefit out of it? The Jews. That's the trouble with them. They don't know when they're well off." He was so emphatic in his condemnation that Ira made no reply.

Booming business. Commercial, industrial, financial prosperity. Exactly the things that had the least meaning for him, that he didn't give a damn about. But Ira couldn't tell him that. Such values were part of his fiber, as an American and as a white-collar worker, a clerk striving to get ahead. He would have been outraged if Ira had told him he didn't give a damn about Prosperity and Booming Business and the buoyant stock market. He would have called Ira a Red, a Bolshevik, one of the mangy, rabid, bewhiskered guys in cartoons in the Hearst newspapers who rushed wildly about wielding round bombs with fuses ignited. He would probably have told Ira to go back where he came from, or go back to Russia.

VIII

From the day of his expulsion from Stuyvesant, Ira continually thought of Farley. What did Farley think of him now? Could he, Ira, make amends? How could Ira get in touch with him? Did he dare get in touch with him? Had Farley told his parents? Ira yearned to see him. It was after his job in the warehouse, loading compartments with toys, had come to its inglorious end, though still a month before the close of the school year, on a clear, fine Saturday afternoon in late May, that Ira made his way to the Armory on upper Broadway where the high school interscholastic track meet was to be held. It was the last interscholastic track meet of the school year. Advance notices of the meet had been featured in the sports pages of all the metropolitan newspapers, especially by the *World*, which carried the most Boy Wanted ads. Farley's name figured often, as the one runner who could seriously vie for first place with the reigning star of the 100-yard dash, the junior from Utrecht High in Brooklyn, Le Vine. Anonymous among the first bands of students surging from subway to Broadway, Ira made his way to the Armory. He knew just where to sit—to obtain the best view of the finish of the one event he cared about. He sat at the very end of the Armory, where the finish line of the 100-yard dash was clearly visible from the first few rows of seats in the balcony above the track.

He arrived early, on purpose, paid his twenty-five cents admission, hurried upstairs to choose a seat in the first tier, the tier next to the tubular brass balcony barrier. In a little while, the bulk of the crowd began to pour in, ebullient, colorful high school youth, hailing classmates, waving school pennants, striding over the stiles of seat backs to join friends—carefree, as he was not—gregarious, boisterous, outgoing, all the things that he really was not. More than a little furtive, troubled lest one of his former classmates might recognize him, perhaps, even, if he was there, the very youth whose silver-filigreed fountain pen Ira had stolen, stolen and bestowed on Farley, the silver-filigreed fountain pen now resting securely in its owner's pocket. No. No one seemed even remotely conscious of his presence. He was safe, secure in his commonplace aspect, secure in his lackluster nonentity.

He watched with pleasant indifference the first events of the track meet, the padded ten-pound shot thudding on the Armory floor, the high jump competition in mid-Armory, the running broad jump, watched with almost euphoric lack of partisanship the race over the low hurdles, the 440-yard run—won by a mature black student from DeWitt Clinton, Ira noted, with prodigiously developed thighs; the mile run, won by somebody with a Greek name and a pedestrian stride, whom Ira remembered from the last track meet. And then came the trials for the 100-yard dash. At the remote starting line, Ira saw no sign of Farley. The heat was won easily by Le Vine, the gold medalist who had bested Farley the last time they competed.

He might have been Jewish, though his name was spelled as if it were French, or altered to look French. Slender, dark, graceful, he walked with triumphant, springy step from under the balcony where he and the other sprinters disappeared into the end zone after crossing the finish line.

It was in the fourth and penultimate heat that Ira thought he described Farley: that firm gait, sturdy figure without tension, dull-blond hair—and the big *S* on the shirt of his track suit. A cheer went up while the distant runners crouched, leaned forward. The far-off pistol cracked. Up the sprinters reared, and running. And how swiftly they neared, looming forward out of a hundred yards away, swiftly! In mid-distance, one runner took the lead: Farley. Through the din and cry and yell of the crowd he sped, so controlled his stride, his feet hammering out long paces on the boards, his small bony fists clenched, his blue eyes burning fixedly. He won his heat—Ira's best friend once!—he won as handily as did Le Vine, perhaps more handily. In silence Ira beheld him emerge from under the balcony: into a great swell of cheering; and smiling a little, open lips in deep breath, chest rising, he walked back on springy track shoes to the starting line.

The high hurdles were run, and the finals of the 220-yard dash. Ira watched idly. Till once again, Le Vine, with the conspicuous orange *U* on his chest, Farley, with the *S* on his, and others, finalists in the 100-yard dash, were warming up at the far end of the Armory, practicing starts, exploding from a crouch into a swift tattoo of feet. They were summoned to the starting line. There they crouched, as if all their weight rested on, was perched on, not their feet, but only their fingertips. The crowd hushed, became a nap of faces, pennants, figures, a tapestry covering the long oval of the balcony. The starter raised his pistol—and one of the finalists broke away. He returned. Once more the line of runners stood up, jigged tensely, drummed toes on the boards. Once again called to their marks, and set—the pistol cracked.

Five sprinters, all hammering the wooden boards with precise, disciplined, superhuman stride. They seemed abreast midway, then strewn apart. Then clearly in the van Le Vine, leading with smooth, even stride; he seemed to glide. And at his heels, trailing obliquely:

Farley. And then they looked abreast in the same plane, Le Vine and Farley. They were abreast. As though the dynamism of the heart drove, not mere training, or inculcation, but the inherited stamina of ages that would not be denied, Farley took the lead. Five, four, three strides from the finish line Le Vine contended, in agony and in vain striving against those pistons of flesh and bone of his rival pounding the floor a stride ahead of him. In vain Le Vine hurled himself writhing at the tape. Farley had swept it away.

The Armory reverberated to the roar of the crowd. Ira felt his eyes fill with tears. Farley came out from under the balcony, breathing hard, with unassuming smile. The other runners filed after him, Le Vine, panting, unable to mask the frown of the bitterness of defeat.

"Farley!" Ira could no longer contain himself, his finger swiping like a sickle at the tear under his eyeglasses. "Hey, Farley!"

Farley looked over his shoulder, stopped in stride: "Hey, Irey!" He took a step back toward the balcony. No mistaking the gladness of his mien, his voice. "Hey, where you been?"

"No place." Suddenly the focus of curiosity of those about him, Ira felt as if he had been snapped out of obscurity into fame. Farley was his friend, after all, his pal for all to see, his pal was the fleetest runner in all the high schools of New York. Acknowledgment of his status by those about him condensed into fixed appraisal.

"Come on down," Farley called.

"Nah."

"C'mon!"

"Now?"

"Sure. Right now."

"They don't let you, till it's over."

"Who said so? Come on."

Farley disappeared under the balcony. Hastily and deprecating, cynosure of fellow spectators, Ira made his way up the stairs to the exit midway of the aisle, and then, uncertain with trepidation, with confusion of feelings, he descended the stairs leading to the Armory floor. A uniformed policeman waited—permissively.

"Hey, Moran, that's him," said Farley.

Just being addressed by Farley brought a flush of pleasure to the

middle-aged cop's face. Bits of perceptions, notions, swirled through
Ira's mind: contrast, heavy wool blue uniform, scant track suit; unity
of the Irish; pride of the Irish; avuncular admiration—the freedom,
the sheer naturalness of the deep-breathing sixteen-year-old victor.

"Hey, why didn't you come around!" And an instant later, "Come
on. Let's go. I gotta get my sweat suit on."

"Where?"

"Over to the other end."

They had been clinging to each other's hands.

"I can't go."

"Why not?"

"I can't. You know why."

Farley understood. "Listen." He jogged in place. "Soon as I can
I'll meet you outside this door. It's right near Broadway. Okay? I'll get
my medal, and scoot out. Gimme about half an hour. Okay?" He was
already trotting toward the starting line.

"Do you want to go back up or do you want to go out now?" the
cop asked Ira.

"No, I'll go out."

The cop swung open the heavy side door of the Armory, held it
open on the sunlit throb of the street, surveyed the outdoors until Ira
passed, then swung the door to. Isolated, happy, glowing with reprieve, Ira waited next to the building. Waited. . . . For all his happiness—the realization grew as the minutes went by—it would never be
again the viable friendship it once had been. That was a thing of the
past, but still rich with affection, rich with reminiscent bloom. And
what joy to see Farley, to see him run and win, to share in his triumph.

And now, there he was! To see him in person come out of a door
at the other end of the building, see him and hear him, stride up,
blue-eyed, bareheaded, his light voice raised in familiar greeting,
small canvas duffel bag hoisted in breezy approach.

"Boy, didn't I beat it outta there? They wanted me to hang
around for more pictures of me and the coach. But I said I couldn't.
I had to skiddoo."

"Yeah?" Ira could feel the glow of his own happiness.

"Let's mope home, all right?"

"Oh, sure. That was wonderful. Boy. Watching you."

"I knew I'd beat him this time."

"They give you the medal already?" Ira asked. "It's real gold?"

"Yeah. Wanna see it?"

"Do I?"

Farley opened the bag as they walked, found the small, neatly wrought box among his track togs, opened it, displayed the colored ribbon and the rich gold disk with its raised athletic figure reaching out for a laurel wreath.

"Boy!"

"Nifty, huh? I did it in eleven two."

"Boy!"

"If I had a start as good as his, I bet I'd do it in eleven flat. Maybe better."

"Eleven flat! Wow!"

"He gets away in a flash. Like Hardy, that black guy in school who eats hot dogs and ice cream at the same time. Remember him? He got away like a rabbit. But I caught up with him."

"Yeah."

"The coach kept me practicing against him. Making me try to catch up with him sooner."

"Gee, it was wonderful."

They talked, talked tirelessly, without let, talked whole city blocks behind them, the long crosstown blocks as little noticed in their immersion in each other as the short downtown blocks. They talked about everything, everything that had happened since they separated: school and law office, training and interscholastic meets, hopes, intentions, expectations, two months of news and information tumbling chaotically out of each one's mouth. Farley had been on the point of moping over to Ira's house to find him. Why hadn't he come around? No, he'd never told his parents. "What d'you think I am? I told 'em you had to go to work."

"Oh. So they don't know."

"No. Nobody knows. O'Neil, my coach, knows. Couple of others. Gym teachers. And the guy. I see him every gym period. Marney. He never says anything. Why didn't you tell me the pen wasn't yours? You coulda got away with it. Easy." Farley was so matter-of-fact, casual, forgiving. "All you had to do was say you found it."

"I know. I know. Don't I know."

"What'd old man Osborne say to you?"

"He said everybody would—everybody would hear about it. I had to quit Stuyvesant for my own good."

"Nah! Nobody even knows, nobody in the class. Nobody ever said anything to me."

"He said there'd be others—"

"What d'you mean?"

"Other fellas lost fountain pens."

"Other fellas? You mean—" Farley turned his head in midstride, his blue eyes puzzled. "What the hell got into you, Irey?"

"I don't know."

But he did, or thought he did, at least in part, but all of it was too, too snarled now, too unspeakable, yes, not merely the stolen briefcase, stolen fountain pens, straightedges, and protractors. No, too far gone . . . driven into the self, remorseless and cruel and incorrigible, his stealing of the fountain pens only part of the forbidden he felt within himself, only part of the corroding evil. Stealing was easily overcome; he might never steal again, never really steal from another person. He had the power of choice. The other was amalgamated, was fused with bodily rapture, with a name never to be named. The other he couldn't refuse.

Ira and Farley rounded Madison Avenue. And there was the church, and a block south of it, the Hewin Funeral Parlor.

"C'mon in. I'm hungry. What about you?" Farley invited. His lips squirmed. "And thirsty, wow. A sandwich and a glass o' milk."

Ira balked. "I better not."

"I told you I didn't say anything."

"No?"

"They don't know anything about it," Farley stressed. "My mom's asked about you lots o' times. 'What happened to your Jewish friend who was so quiet and shy?' She likes you."

"Yeah? What did she say about the pen?"

"You mean I didn't have it anymore? I lost it. I'm tellin' you, Irey. Come on in."

They went in together, Ira following diffidently through basement gate and hallway, into the kitchen.

"You're quite a stranger." Always so joyless-seeming and resigned, nunlike Mrs. Hewin regarded Ira through gold-rimmed eyeglasses. The heavy down above her upper lip curved with her mouth in a rare smile.

"Yes, ma'am. I had to go to work."

"So Farley told me. But not all the time. You don't work all the time, do you? You don't work every day?"

He hadn't reckoned with quick, unsettling Irish wit. "No, ma'am." He delved for a plausible reply, unearthed a sorry one, a bedraggled one. "I didn't think I should—bother Farley. I'm working. He's going to high school."

"Oh, pshaw! I've yet to see anything like that bother Farley. The only thing I've known to bother Farley is that he can't drive one of the limousines."

"I can, too," Farley protested.

"Of course you can. Ever since you were ten." She turned to Ira. "I was so sorry when Farley told me you had to go to work. I know how much you wanted to go to high school. Do you like the work you're doing?"

"My job? No. First I worked in a law office. But they fired me already. I was working in a toy warehouse until about a week ago."

"Oh." So faintly amused, the heavy down on her upper lip was all the more conspicuous. "Why did they fire you at the law office? Did they think you were too honest to make a good lawyer?"

"No, ma'am. I—I guess I wasn't smart enough."

"Tush! Are you ever going back to high school?"

"I'm going at night."

"You are?" She studied him appreciatively. "I'm glad to hear it. Pity is it takes so long to get a diploma in night school. You'll be a grown man when you graduate."

"Well, maybe I can go back."

"To Stuyvesant?"

"No, ma'am. To some other high school."

"Mom, can we have a sandwich?" Farley interposed.

"Supper is in a little while. As soon as Katy and Celia get home. They've gone with Sister Wilma to the aquarium."

"I'm hungry now, Mom. So is Irey."

"You are?"

"Yeah. You didn't even ask me how I made out at the meet."

"Oh. Of course you did well."

"Yeah, but I won a gold medal this time, Mom. I came in first. I beat Le Vine."

"Oh, you did?" Her hand rested on the icebox latch.

"Wait'll you see it." Farley opened his canvas bag, drew out the little wooden box.

Footsteps could be heard coming down the stairs.

"Show it to your pa, too."

"Hey, Dad, what do you think o' this?" Farley queried as brushy-mustached Mr. Hewin entered.

Mr. Hewin paused, glanced at the medal on its white satin cushion, continued on his way to the kitchen sink. "You win that?"

"Yeah. I placed first, Dad."

Lifting his eyebrows to signify acknowledgment of his son's achievement, Mr. Hewin turned on the faucet, washed his hands. He was probably embalming a cadaver upstairs—for he turned away from the sink, lingering only long enough to dry his hands, while he surveyed his son with preoccupied approval. Then he went upstairs again.

So undemonstrative, Mrs. Hewin, so matter-of-fact, Farley's father. Ira thought of how Mom and Pop would have behaved in a similar situation—if he had brought home a gold medal, if he had won a gold medal—for anything. All the *mazel tovs* that would have poured out, and the blessings and praisings of God. Even Pop: "*S'iz takeh gold?*" His features kindled by the yellow disk: "*Azoy? A bisl nakhes!*" How different. And, yes, what did Le Vine's parents do or say to console him in his defeat? Jewish surely, with that twist of disappointment contorting his face: Jewish, but a different breed from his own Galitzianer kind. His parents already Americanized, not like Mom and Pop, but *gants geler,* as Mom would have said: yellow-ripe—like the parents, Ira was sure, of the fellow whose silver-filigreed pen he stole, or like those of that smart aleck who displaced him in the law office. Different already. Mrs. Hewin brought out a platter of meat— a large pale platter, on which rib bones showed above red beef already carved.

"Can we have some milk, Ma? Irey worked up an appetite, too," Farley prompted. "Didn't you, Irey?"

"Not—yeah. I mean only a little bit." Ira's mouth watered.

"I told you I could beat Le Vine, Ma," Farley reiterated placidly. "He came in second this time."

"It was wonderful, Mrs. Hewin." Ira tried to hold fervor in check, in keeping with everyone else. "I sat at the finish line. I—gee! The way Farley ran."

Mrs. Hewin turned from making sandwiches to look at her son. "I suppose you'll be all over the newspapers."

"I talked to reporters."

"You did?"

"All kinds o' reporters were there. You didn't see those bulbs pop, Irey—me and O'Neil together?"

"No. I was outside already."

"Wow! Thanks, Ma."

"Gee, thanks, Mrs. Hewin!"

"Do you think you can wash your track suit now?" Mrs. Hewin filled two glasses with milk. "That and your sweat suit. We can already smell when you're coming."

"You can't wash them, Ma," Farley objected plaintively.

"I can't? You'd be surprised."

"Aw, no. You wash all the luck out of it, Mom."

"That wouldn't be all you washed out of it. And don't you air all the luck out of it too, when it's out in the yard hanging on the line?"

"Luck doesn't air out, Ma."

"Oh, no? Faith, and what if it rained?"

"Ma, you can't wash it; that's all I know."

"Can you wash your hands?"

"I guess so."

Mrs. Hewin put the bottle of milk back in the icebox, followed by the platter of meat, while both youths washed their hands at the kitchen sink. She wet her lips, seemed to form words silently a moment as she closed the icebox door. "I wouldn't want you to lose."

"I'm not going to lose, Ma."

"No?"

Farley swigged a draft of milk. "I know I'm not. All I got to do is keep on training. I can get that gold medal every time."

How little sentiment she allowed herself to dole out: just a kind of pensiveness, a slight swelling out of bosom as she regarded her son. "Well, if you're going to stay with your Aunt Maureen in New Rochelle, could you wade out in the water with them on?"

"Aw, Ma!"

Later that same evening, when the two went out, and walked over to the lamplit street next to the church, Farley's friends were there waiting to meet him. A few of them had been to the track meet too, and had seen Farley triumph in the 100-yard dash. St. Pius Academy hadn't even placed. Still, when he displayed his newly won gold medal, even the owl-eyed Malloy, who had been so antagonistic before, forgot resentment in his unfeigned enthusiasm. "Hurray for the Irish!" he cheered at sight of the trophy.

Absolved, Ira basked in the glow of Farley's victory. Absolution and victory. And yet, it was to be the last such totally intimate restoration of their friendship. They would join together again, after track meets, in which Farley now regularly placed first—except for the initial meet following that summer's vacation, which he had spent in New Rochelle, swimming: "Softened my muscles," Farley explained. But he beat Le Vine in the next meet, and never placed second again while in high school. "Schoolboy wonder," the sportswriters called him. He was surrounded by new friends, droves of them, out of whose circle he never failed to single Ira out with his cheery greeting, "Hey, Irey."

Still, friendship thinned, not because of Farley's growing fame and number of admirers, but as the bond of interest between the two attenuated. They diverged—inevitably. Reunions became less and less frequent, and more and more transient: an exchange of greetings followed by congratulations offered for his almost routine victories. Ira attended track meets less and less often. Soon to be a student of DeWitt Clinton High School, he would have no reason for going but to watch the performance of a rival of his own school, a Stuyvesant runner, and one who came in first with unfailing regularity. Ira could read about it in the sports section of the following Sunday's newspaper. He ceased going. . . .

P A R T   T W O

D E W I T T   C L I N T O N

He had lost a whole semester when he entered DeWitt Clinton in September of 1921. He could no longer expect to graduate from high school with the February class of 1924, but with that of June. At least, though, he was back in high school again. It was a bleak time for him, without close schoolfriends, without close friendships of any kind, chastened by the ordeal of expulsion. He was humbled by a growing awareness of his inadequacies, amounting almost to stupidity, his slowness to grasp instruction, compared to most of his classmates, above all his inability to cope with abstractions, whether delivered orally in class or appearing on the printed page. And always contending with, always succumbing to, his vile cravings, cravings that preempted studies, ousted and routed concentration, cravings bringing terror and anxiety in their train, perpetual shadows inexorably etiolating his youthful spirits, his normal appetites, his readiness for diversion, his cheerfulness.

A smear of dreariness, Ira harked back in cheerless recollection. And worse to come, psychologically, and soon. Well, no need to anticipate it. It would arrive, flaw him irreversibly, rend integrity, with that *little rift within the lute,* he echoed the Tennysonian snatch. Had a lot of truth in it, sardonic snatch aside: a fifty-year widening, for example, made the music moot. No hurry, no hurry. That little rift within the lute that would make junk of any second novel. *Immobilité de junk,* as Rimbaud never said. But what would he do with it? Ira already found himself wondering. With one of his characters disallowed, disavowed, invisible. The thought came to him that he could excise material from his future writing, writing many, many pages hence, and inject it like a geologic dike extraneously into a different strata. No, it would never do. Let it be, let it rest. When that time comes, do what you can. You've enough to do rendering a straightforward account, without trying to skate on your ear. You're not clever enough.

Though he made no close friends in school, he drew nearer to Jewish acquaintances, new and old, on 119th Street. The street had changed in character over the years, since that day in 1914 when he and his parents had moved in—as he had changed from that pugnacious little East Side Jewish kid then to his present indeterminate Harlem self today. The street had in the intervening years become largely Jewish—with a Jewish grocery store in the middle, a kosher butcher shop across the street, a tailor shop too that was Jewish. A new candy store had opened in the middle of the block. In the back of it, strident pinochle games took place. And on the corner and around it on both sides along Park Avenue a Jewish greengrocer, Jewish butter-and-egg store, a Jewish hardware store, notions, and other minuscule Jewish *gesheftn* of that sort. Those Irish families who hadn't quit the neighborhood before the influx of Jews, who had chosen to stay on and live in tenements predominantly Jewish, had retreated to the block of red-brick, three-flight cold-water flats near Lexington Avenue. Next to the five-flight tenements of gray brick and brown, under their imposing eaves, the short block of red dwellings looked dwarfish indeed; and they were old as well, perhaps the oldest houses on the street, judging by the intriguing iron stars each had on its front, ornamental bolts at the end of massive iron rods that were concealed between floors and yoked opposite walls together.

—Ah, Stigman, Stigman. Fourteen years you resided there. Couldn't you have simply chronicled the changes that took place in the street? Vicissitudes of vicinity. There's a high-flown title for you. Fourteen years spent in polyglot Harlem, as against a few years on the homogeneous Lower East Side—which you warped out of shape anyway by the neutron mass of your later experience. Ah! Documented that motley squalor, that poverty: stoop and hallway and roof, street and cellar and backyard; and the sort that lived there, and when. Ah, what more did you need? There was a mine there for the literary man: see the Irish kids in their confirmation suits, white ribbon on their arm—wasn't that what the little gamins wore? See Veronica Delaney in the pride of princess-loveliness with her mincing gait and black beauty spot on her chin. And the box-ball games, and the rubber baseball games, and kids climbing down the sewer for the lost ball, or up, all the way up one of the cross-braced pillars, and over into the New York Central trestle, the overpass, daring the exposed third rail for the sake of a ten-cent rubber ball.

—And the mock-Homeric street-gang fights and the brawls, and the thousand, thousand sorrows and predicaments and situations. Mr. Maloney, man of 250 pounds or more, plodding heavily up the stairs. He was foreman of a street repair crew, and when the tenants downstairs raised too much of a row, he tapped the floor with a sledgehammer. And the poor Jew-girl—Cuckoo-Lulu, the Irish kids called her, lived on the ground floor back, flaunted a bedraggled rusty fox-fur on her neck in mid-July. Easy lay, easy flighty lay, even for you to muster up predatory courage to take advantage of, and you would; except that her father was already far gone with melanoma, his face a gruesome misshapen cinder block or lava boulder. And you would. Despite that. Except that Mom perceived your intentions—and for the first time, her face suffused, lectured you on the dreadful uncleanliness of women, and the dreadful diseases they could transmit to the unsuspecting male.

—Poor Mom, taking all the blame, as women had done since Eve. And you still would, despite that, entice—Cuckoo-Lulu. But her family suddenly moved away. So instead, you studied ways to augment your guile, improve deception beyond Mom's detection.

"O Lulu had a baby.
She named him Sunny Jim.

She put him in a pisspot
To loin him how to swim.
He sank to the bottom
He floated to the top.
Lulu got excited
And grabbed him by the—
O what a lulu!
Lulu's dead and gone."

—What a delicacy, that song by half-grown micks. . . . Oh, where were you, Stigman? On every flight of scuffed-linoleum, brass-edged steps of the stairs you climbed were stories (pun), were tales (pun again), hundreds of them. There was even a local newspaper, a house sheet run by an elderly Irishman—the *Harlem Home News*—into which to delve for "copy," if you had an iota of initiative, were willing to do an iota of research to exploit: whole volumes of prose awaited the turn of your hand.

No use, Ecclesias. You know full well where I was.

—Alas, yes.

It was a period then when of necessity Ira sought the company of the Jewish youth his age whose families had moved into the area, and those who still lived in the same block, like Davey Baer. Davey had graduated with Ira from P.S. 24 and gone to work as an office boy and wore a fashionable tight, white, removable stiff collar that pleated his scrawny neck into accordion folds. And Davey's younger brother, Maxie, now also earning wages, looking much like his older brother, swarthy and slight—and one of the group. They, and other Jewish youth, more recent arrivals on the block, or in the immediate neighborhood, became, as it were by default, Ira's provisional companions during that barren, that grievous period. Izzy (who became Irving) Winchel, with blanched blue eyes, a hooked nose, had aspirations of becoming a baseball pitcher. Utterly unscrupulous, the nearest thing to a pathological liar, and phony as a three-dollar bill; his arrant cribbings and copyings still hadn't saved him from flunking out of Stuyvesant. He did peculiar things with words: mayonnaise became maysonay, trigonometry trigonomogy. Maxie Dain, short of stature, quick, alert, well-informed, best-spoken of any in the group (perhaps because his family had moved here from Ohio), ambitious, an office boy in an advertising firm, and Ira was sure a capable one. Maxie Dain's father, blocky and affable, owned the new candy store, whose rear was depot for card games. Jakey Shapiro, short of stature and motherless; his short and cinnamon-mustached widowed father had moved here from Boston, married svelte Mrs. Glott, gold-toothed widow, mother of three married daughters, and janitress of 112 East 119th.

It was in her abode, in the janitorial quarters assigned her on the ground floor rear, that seemingly inoffensive Mrs. Shapiro set up a clandestine alcohol dispensary—not a speakeasy, but a bootleg joint, where the Irish and other *shikkers* of the vicinity could come and have their pint bottles filled up, at a price. And several times on weekends, when Ira was there, for he got along best with Jake, felt closest to him, because Jake was artistic, some beefy Irishman would come in, hand over his empty pint bottle for refilling, and after greenbacks were passed, and the transaction completed, receive as a goodwill offering a pony of spirits on the house.

And once again those wry (rye? Out vile pun!), wry memories of lost opportunities: Jake's drab kitchen where the two sat talking about art, about Jake's favorite painters, interrupted by a knock on the door, opened by Mr. Shapiro, and the customer entered. With the fewest possible words, perhaps no more than salutations, purpose understood, negotiations carried out like a mime show, or a ballet: ecstatic *pas de deux* with Mr. McNally and Mr. Shapiro—until suspended by Mr. Shapiro's disappearance with an empty bottle, leaving Mr. McNally to solo in anticipation of a "Druidy drunk," terminated by Mr. Shapiro's reappearance with a full pint of booze. Another *pas de deux* of payment? Got it whole hog—Mr. Shapiro was arrested for bootlegging several times, paid several fines, but somehow, by bribery and cunning, managed to survive in the enterprise, until he had amassed enough wealth to buy a fine place in Bensonhurst by the time "Prohibition" was repealed. A *Yiddisher kup,* no doubt.

Jake was stubbiest of everyone in the "crowd," though not as slight as the stunted Baer brothers. He had a fine oval face, curly auburn hair, and a tip-tilted, oily nose. No one was as artistic nor as physically adept as he was. He could pick out tunes on the old player piano in the Shapiro living room. He was master of the tango, and even dropped Izzy Winchel's homely sister on her head in her backward terpsichorian flings. A pool shark, the best of the bunch; so exceedingly proficient was he that at those times when he was between jobs, seeking an increased salary, he managed to support himself by betting on his skill at the pool table. Ira had sat in the Fifth Avenue poolroom, a flight up on the corner of 112th Street, and watched Jake play, his oily nose under the green lampshades gleaming. And of course, Jake was an artist. For years he had worked as an apprentice for a firm of commercial artists. For years, Ira heard about his friend's work with an airbrush. Besides that, Jake had enrolled early in the National Academy of Design, and he often brought home samples of his work, admirable in their technical skill, Ira thought, charcoal drawings of plaster casts of classic sculpture—shapely nudes and bearded Greek deities.

The two often walked to the Metropolitan Museum together. Jake would admire the skill and craftsmanship of painters—as a professional; the way some of them rendered armor or other metals, or the composition of a painting. Rarely, or so it seemed to Ira, did the aesthetic quality, artistic depth, "meaning" of a painting ever make an impression on Jake—just once in a while, certain painters, like Robert Eakins, Winslow Homer. It was curious, and Ira more than once told himself so, that what Ira was looking at and admiring was more than the painting per se, was the things he might have encountered in his reading concerning the painter: Leonardo, del Sarto, Rafael, Titian, Rembrandt, Rubens. And yet Jake did admire Rubens, did admire Rembrandt, called Ira's attention to Frans Hals, to Vermeer. It was odd, an artist strangely deficient in intellect, so Ira would think later, then correct himself, try to seek a deeper reason: perhaps an artist deficient in awareness of even rudimentary ideas. Jake confessed that he often sat for long periods of time, sometimes for hours, when he had the leisure, sat for hours, conscious only afterward that not a single thought had entered his mind.

During all those months of his commercial art apprenticeship, and there were a good many, out of the small allowance or allotment from his pay granted him by his stepmother to defray the expense of carfare and lunch, day in, day out, Jake bought his meals at the Automat. His victuals never varied. At the cost of one dime, his luncheon consisted of a small crock of Boston baked beans and a glass of milk.

Said Jake, as Ira shook his head in admiration at the charcoal sketch of a bust of Zeus Jake had brought home from the academy, "You know what we have to do now? Everybody in the class has to draw an original composition."

"What does that mean?"

"From our own imagination. No copy of anything. It has to be what we thought up ourselves."

"Do a pinochle game in the back of Maxie Dain's father's store," Ira suggested facetiously. "Oh, I know, the pool hall."

"Nah, that's not imagination."

"But you're a shark at pool. Look, doesn't that long-distance pool-stick rester make a triangle with the pool stick?"

"Yeah, but he'd say it was like a mechanical drawing. You know what I was thinking? I was thinking of a Bowery bum. He's sitting in a doorway, and he's dreaming about a stein of beer and a pretzel. It's like a cloud over his head. The same as some of the Christian holy picture clouds in the Metropolitan."

There were others of whom a lackadaisical memory retained scraps. Sid Desfor, who lived in the same house Jake did. A gangly, humorous, whimsical youth, and generous too, oldest sibling of three, Sid began an apprenticeship in a photographer's studio immediately after graduating from public school. The photography studio was across the Harlem River, which Sid had to cross on the El train. And he was always seized by an inordinate desire to urinate as soon as the train crossed the river. Sid appreciated Milt Gross, quoted him often, and considerately cut out the humorist's column for Ira to read. His father owned the tailor shop on the other side of the street, and Sid twice made Ira a present of a tobacco pipe found in a man's suit to be altered.

All had spending money on weekends, but Ira rarely—once school began—except for the few coins he could mooch from Tanta Mamie. At Baba's house, pickings became less and less as aunts and uncles married and went to live elsewhere, in Flushing chiefly. It was less a dreary time in actuality, Ira reflected, than it was in recollection. For he knew that he spent many an afternoon in the fall playing association football, "touch football," in Mt. Morris Park, in the playing field on the West Side. He had become an excellent punter, and fairly adept at catching the larger, slower-moving football, so he was always in demand when sides were chosen—quite the opposite of his rating in baseball. Hence there must have been some joy during those months following his admission to DeWitt Clinton High School, some joy in the abandonment of the flight and the chase, the shout and touchdown.

But it was as if one had to compel a reluctant memory to acknowledge happy recollection. On Saturday nights, to the music of the Victrola in Izzy Winchel's living room, the "gang" foregathered there, finding dancing partners with Izzy's older sister and her friends. Ira had no facility as a dancer, and fought off acquiring any. He didn't know why. Petrified by self-consciousness, he also detested the music the others reveled in, the triteness of sound, the embarrassing mawkishness of lyric—without being able to put his dislike into words.

Sunday mornings the group usually found itself in the upstairs poolroom on the corner of 119th Street and Third Avenue, on the same level as the Third Avenue El, which could be blamed for spoiling a shot when a train pounded by. A more dreary, stultifying atmosphere than that of the poolroom on Sunday mornings Ira couldn't recall. Penniless, and hopeless duffer at pocket pool that he was besides, he would sit on a chair against the wall, listen to the crack of pool balls, the patter of players and their epithets, watch his friends strain above the green baize lit up by the low-hanging shaded electric lights, lift cue sticks to slide scoring markers on their wires overhead.

Frowzy, vacuous, dismal. It didn't occur to him then that these companions-by-default were the first American-born generation of Jews, the bridge between the poor East European immigrants who landed here and the American Jews their offspring became. And his distaste of their pursuits and recreations already indicated an indefinite rejection of the typical path the mass had taken. He was aware only of his own unhappiness, of his misfitting, of not belonging, of his disdainful boredom. And yet, despite his moroseness, sometimes, discontent and apathy at others, he often realized that they made allowances for him, because he did go to high school. Even though he was offish and intolerant, lived, sought to live, in a different world, they were generous beyond his deserts. Sid, especially, chipped in to buy him a ticket to the movies, chipped in for the pastrami sandwich in the delicatessen after the show, even paid Ira's half of a pool hour to give him a chance to go through the motions.

No. He hadn't been fair to them, as he wrote in his yellow typescript, when he thought of them in later years, and the injustice of his former attitudes became even more pronounced when he grew old.

One gem stood out in the lusterless setting of his friends' pastimes: a phonograph record. It had come with the Victrola Izzy's parents bought: on one side were "Humoresque" and "Angels' Serenade," on the other the "Prize Song" from *Der Meistersinger,* the latter transcribed for violin, and both sides performed by Mischa Elman. The music on one side Ira found transparent, easy to follow and easy to appreciate. The other perplexed him; it seemed disagreeably impenetrable. Over and over again, while the others played pinochle or open poker on Izzy's kitchen table, Davey Baer whacking a card down with a crack of knuckle on wood, a knack he had learned literally on his ne'er-do-well father's knee, Ira, with a tenacity born of sheer anomie, played and replayed the "Prize Song" . . . until suddenly he understood it! Finally cacophony became deliberately ordered sounds, not just ordinary harmony, but unique sounds and cadences that once comprehended became inevitable, that made a unison of its own. So that's what they meant when he read about Wagner, when they wrote that Wagner was not only a great composer but an innovator. So that's what they meant by great music. After a while the music went through your head. It was a different kind of tune, altogether different at first, but it slowly became familiar, and when it became familiar, it sang—in its own way, and yet it was right.

To be entirely faithful to the narrative, this modern aside, written probably in late '79, ought to be deleted, Ira thought. But it gave an intimate, even touching picture of his life with M, when they were still living in Paradise Acres, a mobile home court in the North Valley of Albuquerque. He had written the fragment soon after he had had his first "total hip replacement"—when the full brunt of rheumatoid arthritis staggered his entire system:

"Loath to write, loath to continue. . . . After M unfastened the depleted hummingbird feeder, and concocted a fresh batch of scarlet-tinted sugar water, and filled the vessel, she went back to the piano. I found pretext for procrastination (while she was practicing in the living room) in hobbling out to the small hanger under the metal awning above my study window, and suspending the feeder therefrom.

"'When are you going to get me a grand piano?' M teased when I reentered the house.

"'You get anything your heart desires. Where will you put it?'

"'In your study.' Her own studio, of about fourteen by fifteen feet floor space, what with Naugahyde couch, armchairs, record player, and coffee table, not to mention the small Steinway piano, had about run out of free area. 'A grand piano would allow my mended hip so much more freedom.'

"'Well, why not?' I agreed, and went back to my room. Once in it and seated before the typewriter I found myself sorting out implications. I looked about my study: a grand piano in here would mean that my cot against the wall would have to go. And this old, scarred desk that I write on, against which the filing cabinet abuts—those would have to go as well. And a small bookcase or two. And the captain's chair I sit on. Now the room could accommodate a modest-sized grand piano. And of course, I too would be gone. The inference seesawed within volition: the longing to depart, the regret at leaving M.

"Well . . . above my study window hangs the ruby-red feeder. And already the first hummingbirds hover devotionally about it, their wings vibrating with a speed that makes them diaphanous. Imbibe, I urge, you feisty-looking clothespins on a toothpick. Go ahead, imbibe. Drink to my prospective memory. And to *memoriam harum rerum.*"

II

Soon after he was admitted to DeWitt Clinton that fall, Ira reapplied for work at Park & Tilford, was rehired, and was assigned to a store on Broadway and 103rd Street. It was within easy subway distance from the high school, also on the West Side. Yet Ira worked there for only a couple of months. The place, the people, were altogether different, and so were his duties. Gone were the free and the old-fashioned, traditional ways of doing things—even though they had taken him so long to learn. No trucks set out from the store to upper reaches of Manhattan and the Bronx. Whether there were any deliveries by truck anymore, Ira never found out. Perhaps all that was centralized in the very large P&T downtown, as his former mentor, Mr. Klein, had once remarked. But there was no Mr. Klein for shipping clerk; in fact, there was no shipping clerk. Instead there was a cellarman, who had charge of everything down in the cellar, which effectively interdicted nibbling, sampling, *noshing,* snitching. He was a hulking, prematurely gray-haired bully, a brute if there ever was one. Yeager by name. It was the first time in his life Ira had ever come in contact with anyone who seemed to relish cruel petty tyranny, callous domineering for its own sake, far worse than Ira's father. Whenever afterward he heard the word "bully," it was Yeager who personified it, Yeager who came to mind. Clearly of German origin, and yet anti-Jewishness seemed to play very little part in his hectoring and bluster, at least very little that was overt or specific, for the other after-school delivery boy, a gentile, younger than Ira, and with a shriveled arm, came in for the same kind of brutal hazing that Ira did. His first day on the job, assigned the task of transferring canned goods from carton to shelf, feeling at home, at ease, doing the things he had learned so well to do, he began whistling.

"Cut out that whistlin'!" came Yeager's threatening bawl. "There ain't no dogs down here."

Ah, the vain retorts sixty-five years too late, to launch at one undoubtedly long since dust: "But I thought there was a dog here," he might have snapped.

And all the consequences that would flow therefrom, all the consequences that could be envisaged. "What d'ye mean by that?"

"You know what I mean."

"What're you, a wise guy?"

"Just as wise as you are."

"Hey, you wanna get the shit kicked outta you?"

"Try it."

Oh, the violent reprisals. And the lawsuits. Or the even more vicious countermeasures, such as Bill Loem of a later volume would have taken at that age (and did). The quart bottle, held in both hands, and brought down treacherously, rashly, and with utmost force on the back of Yeager's head—and the job finished by slashing the throat of the prostrate figure with the jagged shards of the same bottle. It was the kind of deed Bill Loem would have committed.

Alas, Ira reflected, he himself was a murderer by nature: he never forgave . . . . And even thinking not only about the incident now, but his reaction to it, threw light on the attraction Bill held for him, and Bill's hold on him: that he dared to do, and did, what Ira, and how many million others, only daydreamed of doing.

Ira saw the big brute a few days later waylay one of the pretty girl clerks seeking an item in the cellar aisles, seize her, and force her over backward while he planted kisses on her. Her pleading— "Please, Mr. Yeager! Let go! Mr. Yeager!"—went unheeded—as if Yeager were indeed the frightening plaster *golem* he looked like, his long body encased in his white work apron. Ira gaped, cringing in revulsion at the *golem's* rut—like that in the movie. Sneak over to the manager of the store, was all Ira had to do, squeal on the sonofabitch—if he had the nerve. He didn't.

The end of the job came when Ira's schoolboy workmate attempted to tuck a more than usually heavy box of groceries under his arm. To Ira, the episode would shine in retrospect as the only one in his whole boyhood informed with a redeeming element, a genuine show of courage. The box slipped from under the youngster's shriveled arm, and the boy was powerless to prevent the box's downward slide with his withered limb. Contents spilled out—before he managed by dint of knee and good arm to keep his entire burden from tumbling to the cellar floor.

"What the hell's the matter with you?" Yeager barked. "What're you, a cripple?"

"He is a cripple!" Ira blurted out. "He couldn't help it!"

Contrite and silent, the youngster picked up the fallen canned goods.

"Gimme dem," Yeager ordered gruffly. "Dey got dents in 'em." And to Ira: "You takin' care of him? Or what?"

"No."

"Den stay out of it."

Still, Ira could tell that Yeager was taken aback, if only by his altered tone of voice and the way he stalked off. Ira was startled at himself. And when he calmed down and helped his skinny, crippled workmate repack his box and tuck it safely under his arm—without permission from Yeager—Ira felt more than startled: scared. Scared that he had involuntarily been, been for only a moment, what he would have to be from now on, if Yeager was to be what he had shown himself to be just now. He would have to stand his ground, Ira sensed, and he couldn't: the very thought scared him. He had caught a glimpse of Yeager's vulnerability, and Yeager knew it: his bullying was nothing but a sham, a false front. Now Ira was vulnerable. He'd have to cringe and toady to stay on good terms with someone he knew was a fake. And he couldn't. Then what? He'd have to quit.

Saturday evening, after he received his pay envelope, Ira left the store, never to return.

III

Ira could feel changes taking place within him. In February of 1922 he was sixteen. By then, Einstein had become a celebrity, a household word, and a comfort to Jews everywhere. It was said that only twelve people in the entire world could follow his abstruse theories of the universe. A *Yiddisher kup,* Jews bragged. Sir Oliver Lodge, world-famous physicist and spiritualist, may have been miffed at the unceremonious discard of his theory about the role of a universal ether. But Mom gloried in admiration of the supreme Jewish intellect: *"Aza kup!"* she exclaimed in sheer transport. In its own rollicking, inimitable fashion, the Police Glee Club also paid tribute to the great physicist. When they were invited to entertain the students of DeWitt Clinton during their regular assembly on Friday, the cops vocalized with zest:

> *"How high is up?*
> *How low is down?*
> *How fast is slow?*
> *And when do we get the dough?*
> *When it's nighttime in Sicily,*
> *You can't get a drink in Massachusetts.*
> *How high is up?*
> *How low is down? . . . "*

Dr. Paul, the school's principal, sharing the platform with the singers, could hardly have been amused. His stiff posture, his grave face, made all the more dread by a slight stroke that paralyzed his cheek, all indicated he scarcely thought the ditty edifying. But of course the assembled students cheered and clapped in lusty approval.

Oh, there were spiral nebulae in the cosmos, island universes strewn light-years away; whole universes, not mere solar systems, remote Milky Ways. Oh, so much to free one from oneself, or almost, to set one dreaming, entranced by vastness, freed by insignificance, if only, oh, if only he weren't trapped. Why was he trapped? Why did he have to be trapped? Far worse would happen to him than what happened when he lost his briefcase, worse than happened to him over the silver-filigreed fountain pen, if he were caught! Oh, the unspeakable, the abominable act, the limitless punishment it would merit. And yet, what ruse, what provocative coaxing, what consummate opportunism, shifty suborning, did he resort to, stoop to, until the blistery green kitchen walls lilted with consent. Incorrigible, unscrupulous, sardonic, treacherous, turning to advantage solace and tears, comfort and sympathy to ploys for undermining defenses. What use was his never-ending, ever-reiterated, never again? Like steel against flint, remorse struck sparks out of fear to rekindle desire, desire that inflamed.

Oh, yes, the world was changing: a mélange. There was the Teapot Dome scandal, about oil and Mr. Doheny, yes? And Disarmament Conferences, no? And the "Yellow Peril," that the jingo, scare-headline-patriotic *Journal American* warned about, the Hearst newspaper Ira never read, except when Pop brought it home from the restaurant. Oh, there was Henry Ford and his *Dearborn Express,* blaming the Jews for being insidious, grasping, in league against America, spreading Bolshevism, atheism, seeking to infect a wholesome America with their godless virus. . . . Everyone was sure Lenin and Trotsky would soon be overthrown—in another year at most. There were Palmer Raids, chain gangs, vigilantes, Ku Klux Klan in white robes and hoods, and lynch mobs who "strung up" Negroes. And there was William Farnum, the movie actor with the mobile eyebrows, and the lightning draw, and unerring aim, and the effortlessly acrobatic Douglas Fairbanks and melting Mary Pickford and Bull Montana— and wonderful, wonderful Charlie Chaplin.

And there was Normalcy and the High Cost of Living, and Prosperity, of course. Pop worked. Mom hoarded for a Persian lamb coat. Ira's uncles Max and Harry, who had failed to finish school, abandoned their original trades, glove-making and fur-matching, and joined Morris and Sam in the restaurant business: they opened a cafeteria in Jamaica, in Queens, and prospered beyond their fondest hopes.

And for Ira, a new experience, a wholly novel and at last marvelous scholastic experience, far beyond mere gratification, the preening of excelling, or even getting high grades. Ennobling, he would have said, except people would have laughed at him; and yet that was how he felt, raised in his own esteem, elated, vouchsafed at least in one region of mental wholeness. For the first time in his life, he felt he not only comprehended a subject fully, in all its aspects, but comprehended the foundations on which the subject rested. The subject was plane geometry. It became a saving unity for him, a kind of beatitude in his aimless, deeply troubled, dejected, self-distrustful life. Plane geometry endlessly minted new truths out of old, miraculously reared a breathtaking edifice of proofs rooted in a few axioms. It was like annealing dull truisms into lucid truths.

At first, at the very beginning of the spring term, Ira was in a panic: why did you have to prove something so intractably obvious already? How could you demonstrate the manifest? Opposite angles were equal! They just were. By what method, what procedure, did you go about showing the patent was the true? You would have to rummage among, beg assistance from that lowly handful of postulates that he had scarcely deigned to notice at the outset because they were so self-evident. That was how you did it: supplements of equal angles were equal . . . oh, that was it! He soon doted on the subject—often to the neglect of other subjects. A's in blackboard recitations, A's in quizzes, became routine.

And now, my friend, and now, my friend—Ira clamped the palms of his hands between knees—that time approaches, the crisis.

> —*That time of year thou mayst in me behold*
> *When yellow leaves, or none, or few, do hang . . .*

Yes. But not yet.
   —Or let this cup pass from me.
   Yes. But it was later, Ecclesias. It was in the fall, not the spring. It was in the second half of Euclid looks on beauty bare-ass and all that, not the first

half. You know something, Ecclesias, I can show that Jesus himself proved that God didn't exist.

—Pray, don't bother.

It's a fact, though. He said: If it be possible, let this cup pass from me. It didn't pass from him. So it wasn't possible. A valid inference, Ecclesias? If it wasn't possible, then how can God exist, to whom all things are possible? Neat, no?

—No. You're forgetting something. Jesus added a proviso to the effect: nevertheless as Thou willest, not I.

Too bad. Wily of him—of the trio of 'em, what?

Four hummingbirds skirmish squeakily for supremacy over the feeder. Their menacings and tiny swashbucklings seem to consist of pointing their bills like miniature rapiers at one another—while they hover on translucent wings. One of them, apparently the ruling cock, sits on a strand of barbed wire hard by, ready to defend the food supply against all intruders. I am becoming a naturalist. . . . What of Henry Thoreau? The guy never married; why not? Why did he write in *Walden Pond*: "What demon possessed me to behave so well?" Why? What demon possessed *me* to seem to behave so ill?

It was early in the summer of 1922. By the end of the school year, and thanks in part to his excelling in plane geometry, to his pride in being so proficient in something, Ira had begun to feel secure in his new high school. He liked it. There was a swimming pool across the street, a few houses west, where he could indulge his fondness for water sports. And now that he thought of the swimming pool, the recall brought in its train the neighborhood about the school—on 59th Street and Ninth Avenue, a block or two away from the Hudson River, a block or two away from piers and freight yards and other sites in a direction he never explored. The area was considered too tough. Was the neighborhood just north, uptown, from the ill-famed Hell's Kitchen? he wondered. He knew no student who went home that way; perhaps there were none, or if of high school age, since the neighborhood was largely Irish Catholic, what few went on with their education after public school attended parochial school. He didn't think they were ever cautioned against going that way. They simply never did.

Their route—that of the overwhelming majority of them—lay eastward, along 59th Street. They passed by a block of seedy and rundown tenements, in some of which lived black children who loitered on stoops and before doorways. And yet, oddly enough, by contrast, interspersed among the tenements were well-kept buildings of a clinic, a medical school, a hospital.

The next intersection was Ninth Avenue, dominated by the Ninth Avenue El. Under its perpetual shade, like that of an endless canopy, the stores and shops kept incandescents burning in their show windows at all hours of the day. Most of the students walked another block east to Columbus Circle, where the Seventh Avenue and Broadway subway crossed Eighth Avenue at the southwest corner of Central Park. There, cast in bronze, the great Navigator himself, Columbus, stood on his pillar of marble contemplating the noisy, incessant swirling of pedestrian and motor vehicle below. Behind him, at the corner of Central Park, a lady charioteer, also cast in bronze, directed her motionless steeds into traffic. To the east, across the street from the south end of the park, stretched a wall of luxury hotels and apartment houses, where gloved and uniformed doormen assisted passengers of taxis and limousines stopping in front of numerous marquees. Last vistas these were, together with the hurly-burly of people and automobiles on the street, as one descended with a swarm of fellow students from daylight down to the dusky amber of subway visibility.

Fifty-ninth Street was a local-train stop, and Ira usually boarded the first local that came along, whether it went to his destination, which was at Lenox Avenue and 116th Street in Harlem, or to the local stations on Broadway. It didn't matter. Mopey schoolboy.

At 116th Street and Lenox, where Ira left the subway, he still had three long crosstown blocks to walk—from Lenox to Park Avenue—and three short, "regular" city blocks. He made a chart of the different ways he could go home: there were indeed eighteen different ways. Many years later, with the aid of Pascal, he calculated that since there were eighteen different ways to go home, and eighteen different ways to hie him to the subway after leaving the house, there was a total of 324 different ways he could do both. Perhaps, in the three years he attended DeWitt Clinton, zigging and zagging through mean and grubby routes to and fro, he succeeded in filling the full complement of combinations.

The truth, the actuality, buffets the mind: the fourteen years he lived in that slum street in Harlem! The hundreds of times he walked to the subway at Lenox Avenue (for even when he later attended CCNY he sometimes took the Lenox Avenue local downtown to 96th Street, and changed there for the Broadway train uptown). What was he driving at? Those years, those passages, how could one avoid being instilled by a chronic despond: of not belonging, of refusing community, of existing under duress. But the psyche is an extraordinary entity. Without knowing it, it converts the mean and the baneful, the despised, into a symmetric exultation, out of the same components wreaks a clandestine furor.

But I am out of my depth. *Le Bateau Ivre.* . . .

IV

He was still a youth of sixteen in that summer of 1922, the end of his first year at "Clinton," though he was ranked as a sophomore. . . . The ad in the Help Wanted column of the *New York World* looked promising—and without the usual restrictions of "Gentile Only." "Conductors Wanted," the ad read. "Newly Franchised Bus Line. Fifth Avenue–Grand Concourse. No Experience Needed. Training on Job." Ira applied at the address given in the ad. It was the bus company's office-garage at 130th Street and Madison Avenue. There he was interviewed briefly by a corpulent executive in a pink-and-blue-striped silk shirt. Asked how old he was, Ira lied shrewdly: eighteen. And what references could he give? Park & Tilford, ever reliable, ever respectable: the store on Broadway, Ira prevaricated inventively, was rumored about to close, like the first one he had worked in on Lenox Avenue and 126th Street; so he had taken the day off to look around for a new job. The portly, perspiring boss seemed favorably impressed: Ira could have the job, and the company would train him, but—he had to deposit a hundred dollars cash as security.

A hundred dollars! Now Ira understood why bus conductor jobs were still vacant, why they hadn't been grabbed up long before he came along. A hundred dollars!

"You'll be handling our money," the portly man explained, mopping his face, "and we want to make sure you're going to be honest, that's all. You get your hundred bucks back when you quit."

"I can't pay part each week till it's a hundred dollars?" Ira was surprised at his accession of acumen.

"No, that's not the way we work. You can't start here unless you put up your security. You could walk off the job at the end of the day with thirty, forty dollars in your pocket, the whole day's receipts."

"All right, Mr. Hulcomb, I'll see. If I get it, I can still come in tomorrow?"

"Oh, certainly. The job's yours if you put up your security. We'll keep it open for a day. But you can't expect us to hold it for you longer than that."

"No, sir."

That terminated the interview. And at home, the same evening, with Pop there, Ira relayed the substance of the formidable stipulation: "I can get a job that pays twenty-four dollars a week, if I give them a hundred dollars security. The boss said they'd break me in to be a bus conductor, but first I'd have to give them the security." He gave an account of the other relevant circumstances.

"How is it I was a trolley car conductor on the Fourth and Madison Avenue line in the War, and I didn't have to give security?" Pop queried. "What do they need security for?"

"And so much money," Mom added. "*A gantser hunderter.*"

"He says that's so I'll be honest."

"You could have assured him you would be honest for much less," said Mom. "What? One nickel mistake, and you forfeit your hundred dollars? A covey of connivers."

"No. He didn't say mistake, he said honest," Ira contested.

"But a whole hundred dollars! *Gotinyoo!*"

"It's only security."

"And where's the security for your hundred dollars? Do they give you a receipt?" Pop asked.

"I think so."

"Oh, you think so. I wouldn't give him without a receipt."

"No."

"And how soon do they repay?"

"I told you. The boss said the same day you quit. That's what he told me."

"A whole summer, and every week twenty-four dollars," Pop considered receptively.

Deliberations continued for a long time. Nobody could deny that it was a bona fide bus company. Their buses ran along uptown Fifth Avenue for everyone to see. So . . . they wanted a deposit. So . . . Why were bus conductors considered so deceitful and dishonest? Would a coin cling to their palms more than an ordinary person's? *Noo.* The upshot of their deliberations was, after much cautioning and behest, Pop would advance the hundred dollars.

"Don't dare filch a nickel," Mom warned. "You know well what happened to you."

"Yeah."

And Pop, in semi-humorous vein, recalling his own problems as a trolley car conductor, cautioned, "Get diarrhea, and you can bid farewell to the bus line."

"I won't get diarrhea."

"And be discreet with drunkards and ruffians," Mom admonished. "Always a soothing word allays a quarrel."

"Uh! Here she is with drunkards and ruffians." Pop took umbrage. "Because a mad, drunken sailor attacked me without warning in the trolley car years ago? His hands should be lopped off."

"Indeed," Mom placated. "I mean only that he should avoid facing up to a blustering goy. Let him be slaughtered. Call the driver for help. For a nickel it's worth being assaulted?"

"I won't be assaulted."

His hundred dollars for security advanced, Ira was furnished with a visored cap, on which he paid a deposit out of his first week's pay, as well as a numbered badge that attached to the cap. He was "broken in" in a single day by an experienced conductor, a veteran of only a few weeks himself. In the four round trips he made that day he learned the route, more or less, the main intersections of the Bronx, hitherto vague terrain. He learned the route and the ropes, he would aphorize later: the number of tugs on the bell cord that signaled stop, start, and emergency stop.

The buses were double-deckers—like the high-toned ones that ran downtown on Fifth Avenue along Central Park. But the fare was only a nickel, not a dime, and the buses were anything but high-toned. His initial training took place on the second shift, the slackest hours of the day, to enable him to concentrate on learning the street names along the route, the main intersections, and to familiarize himself with manipulating the "clock," the handheld nickel counter, to make change in careful but collected fashion, and to gauge the exact moment when a passenger was safely on or off the bus, and then tug the bell rope without another moment's delay.

He was on his own the following day, a solo conductor completely in charge of the job. He was assigned the same run: from afternoon to final return to depot at midnight. All by himself, reigning on the rear platform, in official capacity, the long afternoon. He gained confidence, congratulated himself on having settled into the job, even though he had had to hurry up front to the driver from time to time to ascertain where they were for the inquiring passenger's benefit.

Near midnight, the bus on the last run—back to depot, where he would be held accountable for the day's receipts—the strain of the new job, the anxiety, the staggering responsibility he felt those first hours, all told on him now: he became drowsy standing up. Streetlights, house lights went by like those of a strange city, withdrawn and aloof. He felt as if the bus had come from nowhere, was going nowhere. A few blocks from the Harlem River, a passenger got on the bus; the last passenger of the night, he dropped his jitney in the clock, and climbed the spiral staircase to the upper deck. The bridge, the swiveling bridge at Madison Avenue over the Harlem, would be approaching soon. Ira's instructions had been to climb upstairs and warn all passengers to be seated, because the superstructure of the bridge was so low, and so close to the upper deck. He climbed up to the upper deck, stood waiting—

"Hey! Hey, you, conductor! Duck!" The alarmed cry came from the lone—and seated—passenger. "Watch it!"

Fortunate for Ira that he reacted in the nick of time. The dark steel superstructure whisked by overhead, only inches away from his visored skull.

"Jesus, fella," said the lone passenger. "Waddaye tryin' to do? Kill yerself?"

Ira learned, slowly as always, but he learned: that with rare exception, all women—and the fatter and more elderly the more prone—alighted from the bus facing the rear. One well-padded matron tumbled backward at a slight forward lurch of the bus. He pulled the bell cord in a trice thrice, and leaped down from the bus to assist her to her feet, apologizing profusely all the while. Jewish, and seeing that he was also, she deprecated the mishap. "It's *gurnisht.* It's nothing with nothing." Pretty young girls daintily descending the spiral staircase, with flouncing dress inverted over high, lovely thighs like lilies, drove him into ecstasies of yearning when he chanced to look up. Transfixed, and all too often he brooded bitterly though transfixed, he would hear his impatient driver yell back at him, "Hey, Ira—a little faster on the bell!" And arriving at the sylvan Kingsbridge terminal, "Chrissake, Ira, what about a li'l more pep. Ye'll have the next bus on my tail."

"Yeah. Okay. I'll try to make it snappy." And all the time he mourned that he no longer could say, was disabled from saying, to the lissome damsel descending, as others his age would have said, "Watch your step, good-lookin'." And being encouraged by an appreciative smile, as he had seen others so encouraged, Lotharios, cheeky and sportive: "What's your phone number, good-lookin'? What about a date?" He no longer had access to that surface world, but was interdicted, like a mosquito larva under water of a ditch sprayed with kerosene. "To whom the goodly earth and air are banned and barred, forbidden fair," he thought, echoing Byron in *The Prisoner of Chillon.* "Okay, I'll try to make it real snappy."

The buses were old, "older'n the hills," declared one of the drivers. Obsolescent buses from a New Orleans bus line, bought by Hulcomb for a song, at the price of junk, so another driver asserted. They rattled and jounced, they growled and smoked. Tony Oreno, a driver with whom Ira was often paired, slightly built, and tending to be queasy, was twice sickened by fumes from the exhaust. He pulled up to the curb, got out, and retched at the side of the bus. Another driver, Colby, reported he had to bear down on his horn while he leaned out of the cab window to shout and wave at the cop directing traffic on Fordham Road not to halt traffic on the Grand Concourse—because the bus wouldn't stop; the brakes were gone! Fortunately, the cop understood the desperate message—and obliged. Colby managed to steer his way to a stop.

Fares were tallied as soon as collected by the handheld "clock," a kind of register of the day's fares, which was furnished each conductor at the beginning of his run. The nickel was thrust into a slot at one end of the clock, which rang a small bell inside as it passed, at the same time increasing the number on the digital counter by one; then the nickel fell into the conductor's palm. Conductors had to have some cash of their own in order to make change; and at the beginning of the tour each one had to declare how much cash he had on his person. At the end of his tour a most peculiar routine awaited him. He was expected to empty his pockets—of every cent of money. Receipts for the day were shown by the number of fares registered on the clock. These were deducted from the pile of cash the conductor heaped on the counter. And all surplus in excess of that claimed by the conductor at the outset—and again, before the accounting was made—was confiscated by the company: on the grounds that the surplus obviously indicated negligence on the conductor's part in ringing up fares; so of course the surplus belonged to the company. Shortages too indicated negligence on his part in collecting fares; so of course he was docked.

With the lesson of his expulsion from Stuyvesant still vibrating in Ira's consciousness, and with Pop's hundred dollars amplifying the fearful reverberations of dishonesty—and with "spotters" on the lookout, about whom Ira had been alerted the very first day he was broken in—he was scrupulous to the point of penalty. His honesty was so far above reproach that it bred small shortages at the end of the day, disparities he had to make good out of his own stock of cash. Less than a week after he had begun work, he was transferred from the second to the first shift, the early-morning shift, which began at six and entailed a brisk walk in the freshness of nascent day from fetid tenement to the corner of 110th Street and Fifth Avenue, downtown terminal of the bus line. Irrelevant detail and treasured memory: the corner of Central Park, tree and grass, rocky outcrop and pond, still, and under canopy of wavering, fragile blue of predawn, humid, scented with verdure. . . .

It was while Ira lolled in the dingy, cigarette-reeking, cigarette-strewn anteroom, along with other conductors waiting their turn to "check in" at the end of their shift, that he was drawn aside by one of the older men, Ira's senior by about forty years, Collingway, sour of visage and hard-bitten. "Listen, kid, lemme tell ye sompt'n. Yer makin' it tough fer the rest of us. Ye know that? Goddamn tough."

"Me?" Ira was startled open-mouthed. "How come?"

"Yer makin' us look bad."

"You? W-what'd I do?"

"Fer Chrissake, git wise to yerself. Yer toinin' in every fare. Didn't nobody tell ye yet? We all take a little rake-off. You ain't. Waddaye think *we* look like?"

"Yeah, but there's spotters."

"Don'tcha know 'em yet? Foley an' that other guy who sneaks in sometimes. You seen him in the back talkin' to Hulcomb—the guy wit' the cauliflower ear. Fitz, they call him."

"Oh, that one? I saw him on the bus. That's Fitz?"

"Oh, you did?" Collingway rubbed in his sarcasm. "You saw him on a bus. You keep up what yer doin', and Hulcomb'll hire a altogether different set o' spotters fer a day, maybe a coupla private dicks from a detective agency. All they'd need is ride the buses one day, an' half of us'd be shit outta luck. Maybe he's got 'em already—because o' you. If he wuzn't so fuckin' tight he sure would."

"But nobody told me!"

"Chrissake, ye didn't think the guy breakin' you in wuz gonna spell it out fer ye?"

"But nobody else told me."

"*I'm* tellin' ye. Yer gonna git in wrong wit' the drivers too. We all buy 'em a little somp'n: a cold drink or a sandwich—ever buy any of 'em a pack o' butts?"

"No. Nobody asked me."

"Aw c'mon! Ye know what'll happen to you?" Collingway jerked his head significantly. "Somebody'll give ye a few good belts in the gut. The way they give it to one prick. He puked up his lunch, an' he quit." Collingway paused, to watch the effect of his words on Ira. "Christ, it's easy. You git a pack o' dem guineas in the mornin', just drop de clock—like dat." He let the clock roll around his index finger and hang there. "Git it?" His hand above the clock was curled into a hollow. "Most of 'em knows: they'll slip you the jit. Or some old fat slob gits on, a Jew-woman maybe. She's safe. Jesus, you ought to be able to tell 'em by now. A nigger gits on."

Still, Ira was afraid. Pop's hundred dollars was at stake. The very thought of getting caught made the terrible memory of the Stuyvesant crisis well up anew, as if just suffered. "Don't dare steal a nickel," Mom had enjoined. But against that now jangled Collingway's sour, parting words: "You'll sure as hell git in dutch wit' everybody. Keep it up an' you'll find out."

No use telling Mom or Pop about it. He knew what they'd say. Should he tell them anyway, and quit? Ask for Pop's hundred dollars back? Or keep on doing the same thing as always: ring up every fare? But his receipts would continue to be more than theirs—every day, every day. He'd get beaten up. He could just envisage one of the drivers punching him in the gut over some pretext: the bell. "I told ye, ye punk! Hurry up on that bell." Bell. Belly; where nobody could see. Pop at least had gotten black eyes. Oh, Jesus. Why hadn't he asked Collingway how much should he try to swipe: a dollar? More?

Dispatched from 110th Street in the early morning, the driver took the bus uptown along Fifth Avenue to the side of Mount Morris Park on 120th Street; there, he steered east a block to Madison Avenue, and then north again to the bridge over the Harlem River, the "turn-bridge," and crossed over into the Bronx. A few blocks more, and the bus rolled into Grand Concourse— It was from then on, culminating in the wild melee on 149th Street, under the gloom of the Jerome Avenue elevated, confused in the lingering gloom before dawn, that hordes and hordes of Italian day laborers stood in wait, stood in droves. Like an invading army before the breach in the wall of a medieval city, they stormed the bus. They charged inside; with shout and outcry, with paper bags exuding garlic in fleeting passage, they swarmed up the spiral staircase, scaled the upper deck, jovial, boisterous, helter-skelter, crammed into every niche and foothold. They plied Ira with coins, jabbed them into the clock or jabbed them into his hand, heedless in their rush to find a seat—or just standing room. Pinned at last to the back rail of the bus, Ira could scarcely move, even less than they could. The day laborers took over, as a single body. They collected fares from delinquents on the steps of the spiral staircase, or from deep inside, where Ira could never hope to penetrate the crowd. They pulled the bell cord—"Let her roll." They chorused directions at the driver—"Hey, walyo, give it the gun. Hey, walyo, step on it!" Irrepressible, garrulous, their Italian intonations impacting on English, in lusty good humor, young and grizzled gray, they hailed with hoot and guffaw fellow laborers stranded on street corners, and waving furiously for the already overloaded bus to stop, gesticulating hugely when it didn't.

At last the growling, burdened, backfiring bus brought them to their destination—the far reaches of the Bronx. It was there, all along the Grand Concourse, that an immense building boom was in progress, there the lofty iron framework of new high-rise apartment houses loomed up near and far. That was the end of the line, and there, chaffering, bawling, with thrashing limb and brandishing redolent paper bag, they discharged, a cascading throng that made the bus rock with their departure—and there, for the first time, Ira was richer by about a dozen pilfered nickels.

He got the hang of it, became adept. Not only was the pack of day laborers in the morning a source of easy pickings, but he came to recognize "safe" passengers, the innocents who boarded the bus during the day: youngsters proffering nickels before they were well on the platform, Jewish mamas, old codgers with canes. He brought the driver refreshments and cigarettes, as the other conductors did, won grudging approval from hard-bitten Collingway, grudging because he didn't think Ira was raking off enough.

"What're ye scared of? You can go a little more. We're all takin' at least two bucks."

Still, Ira felt he had reached his limit. A dollar, a little more than a dollar maybe, was already more than twenty nickels, more than twenty fares, twenty passengers, twenty people on the bus. No. He was scared. And then there was all that anxious calculating he had to do on the last run, before the bus pulled into the office-garage at shift change: when he waited his turn to report to the watchful clerk, the checker at the counter. Ira had to remember how much cash to claim as his own, and had claimed, how many fares the clock registered, how much cash he actually possessed, subtract the difference, maybe claim more or withhold a small amount not to excite suspicion when time came supposedly to disgorge all pockets in front of the checker. Do all this, and be an efficient conductor too, for it was still early afternoon when the first shift ended, and the bus fairly well patronized. A lot of finagling was required to keep records straight amid distractions and fluctuations of receipts during that last hour, and Ira was never good at mental arithmetic, and this was mental arithmetic under stress. It entailed going over and over his perverted accounting, to reassure himself he wasn't about to betray himself. Over and over—while restraining a kid from getting off too soon, or cautioning a *yenta* to hold fast please, or turning away giddy at the sight of lilylike gams floating down the spiral stairs—and being snappy on the bell. He got by. Craftily, he made a practice of erring one way or the other by ten or fifteen cents, showing surprise when he was "over," chagrin when he was "under," like a somewhat slow-witted dub, perplexed by manifest evidence of his clumsy probity.

And then one early morning he was sure everything was over for him. He saw himself fired. He saw Pop's hundred dollars taking wing. Should he blubber? Should he bluff? Clutch at what excuse? *Oy, gevald*, at home, what? Pop would broil him. Pop would roast him. And Mom—!

First run of the morning, and the bus loaded to the rafters with wop laborers, the bus bowling along Grand Concourse. And behind it, a sedan trailing unnoticed. And in it, who but Mr. Hulcomb, chauffeured by one of the clerks. Oh, God, he must have spotted me! Ira panicked. Inured and deft, he had purloined even more than his usual quota—he couldn't remember how much, couldn't give an accounting—but that didn't matter. If the bus was stopped, if a head count was made, he'd be fifteen or more fares under the clock. It would be just today that that barrel-built, grizzly, fierce old dago anarchist with half-foot handlebars each side of his snoot had posted himself next to Ira and collected fares in every direction, officious helpmeet warden, Cerberus growling at the remiss. "C'mon. Giva de kid." And dumped the whole handful into the pocket of Ira's alpaca jacket. Jesus, if Mr. Hulcomb didn't see that, he couldn't see anything! It wouldn't do to ram nickels into the clock now; pinned against the back rail, he'd be seen from the car. And if he tried it when the bus stopped, his two superiors would hear the jitneys jingle in mad succession. They'd know. Ira's goose was cooked!

"Hey, you! Conductor! Hey, Stigman!" Hulcomb was shouting out of the car window.

"Yes, sir," he quavered. If only he could blow away like dust. Just leave everybody else on the platform staring back at the pursuing vehicle, except him, vanished from sight.

"Hey, Stigman, you hear me?"

"Yeah. Wha'?" Torture: maybe third degree in a police station, confession and courtroom, maybe judge in black robe, maybe jail, maybe bail, maybe—

"Tell that driver he's goin' too fast. He's way over the speed limit. Tell him to slow down! Tell him I said so."

"Yes, sir, yes, sir, yes, Mr. Hulcomb. I'll—right away! Hey, lemme through, will you please?" Ira appealed to his passengers. "That's the boss."

"Fuck him." They refused to budge.

"I gotta—" Tony would never hear Ira over the battering of the engine. If he pulled the rope three times, Tony'd stop the bus. No good. "Please, everybody!" Ira pleaded at the top of his voice. "Please! Come on, gents. Please! You up front, tell him to slow down, the driver, please. The boss just told me. Hey, Tony! He'll lose his job!"

"All right," they relented. "Hey, Giovanni, hey, Paul, tella de driver de fuckin' boss is on his tail." And someone with a croaking voice up front relayed, "Hey, *paisan*, we don't wantcha t' git in no trouble. De kid says slow down. Ye got de fuckin' boss on yer tail. . . . Wha? Yeah? Heh, heh, heh. Ye know what he sez?"

"Who?"

"Him. De driver. He says fuck de boss."

"Yeah?"

"He says tell dat fat sonofabitch to drive dis bucket o' bolts widout pukin'."

"Heh! Heh! Heh! Ye hear dat, kid?"

Nevertheless, the bus slowed down to a lumbering speed. The trailing sedan dropped behind, and once out of sight, "Let 'er rip!" arose the clamor within, and once again they bowled along. Never was relief so delirious. Ira had escaped! He could have jigged for joy, hopped anyway, in spite of all the pressure of brawn fixing him against the rear rail. Wow! No, he'd have to cut it out. Even though they knew he finagled. It wasn't worth it, that's all. Scared the hell out of him. Ira had nearly died then. He didn't care what Collingway said. Take the goddamn nickels they shoved into his hand and plug 'em into the clock, that's all. Feed the clock with them, ring 'em up. Buy the driver his soda pop, his butts, his sandwich, out of his own dough. Be better than this. Don't tell anybody what the receipts were, make it lower than it was: by two dollars. Still, by the sidelong look Collingway would sneak at his face when he spoke, he knew Collingway suspected he was lying. Would somebody beat him up? Or what? The third week of August came to an end.

It was one of those peculiar instances, Ira thought, instances of diversion that the main narrative could do well without, and yet that never or rarely failed to intersect real life. So it struck him now pondering that past. For he could recall the summer morning in the street, 119th Street, the shafts of early sunlight slanting from tenement rooftop eave to gutter and sidewalk, shafts fraught with motes. Grubby 119th Street, slummy 119th Street, humid with New York summer, though the day was scarce begun, pristine shafts athwart the tenements, in a street still quiet in the early morning.

And there was Izzy Winchel, thorough scamp and unflinching pathological liar, persuading Ira to ditch the bus conductor's job for a more lucrative, exciting one: a good racket, the one Izzy was plying—

hustling soda at the ball games in the Polo Grounds. Ira shrank at the prospect. Hustling, yelling out the names of soda flavors to those mobs of people, in front of those mobs of spectators, calling attention to himself, eyed by thousands. No, not he.

"You can make all you make on a bus all week in just two days," Izzy coaxed. "On a weekend when the stands're packed for a double-header. They're so excited, they give you a five for a bottle o' near beer, and you give 'em change for a buck. I got away with it lotsa times."

"No. I can't do it. I don't have that nerve."

"How d'ye know ye can't? Once you get in, you'll find out how easy it is. If the customer calls you back: 'Oh, excuse me, I made a mistake.' The whole thing is to get in. And I can get you in. I know Benny Lass—he comes out in front o' the ballpark. He's the guy who picks you out."

There was no getting away from Izzy. He was attached to Ira, for no reason that Ira could fathom—except because he went to high school, and Izzy had flunked out, because Ira was a whiz in plane geometry, and Izzy had tried to cheat his way through the exam, so flagrantly he was caught and automatically flunked—and then had dropped out of school—or perhaps because they were so different temperamentally, Ira shy, Izzy brazen. Ira studious, Izzy a fake. Ira didn't know. Maybe Izzy out of his unmitigated perfidiousness felt he had to protect Ira in his timid innocence.

"Come on. I'll take you there," Izzy urged. "I'll get you in. I'll show you what to do. Getcha father's hundred dollars back. I'm tellin' ye. You better get in now."

"Yeah?"

"You never know what'll happen to it, that's why. And hustlin' soda, you don't need to make no deposits. They'll give you a white jacket and a hat free. I'll bet you'll hustle in the World Series. That's where you'll make a day's pay without even tryin'. And see the game too, don't forget that. Frankie Frisch and Babe Ruth and Gehrig and Ty Cobb and Walter Johnson."

"I'm not so crazy about baseball." Ira warded off Izzy's enthusiasm-laden words with a shrug. "I'm a ham. You know."

"So you'll sell more." Izzy promptly closed the loophole. "You like football, don'tcha? Notre Dame plays in the Polo Grounds. Army. Cornell."

"Yeah?"

"There's prizefights, too. You get in good with Benny Lass, you can hustle at Madison Square Garden. You can see the champeen bouts: Benny Leonard, what a fighter, and Battling Levinsky, maybe Dempsey."

That same evening, "I'm gonna ask for the hundred dollars security back," Ira announced.

"Uh-huh," said Pop. "What is it? Why? You still have three weeks before school, no?"

"Everybody steals there—I mean the conductors," Ira explained virtuously. "I'm afraid. I turn in more money than they do."

"*Noo?*"

"They don't like it. One of 'em told me, a lousy antee-semitt bastard, you keep makin' us look bad, you better look out."

"*Azoy?*" said Mom. "*Zol er gehargert vern.*"

"Ah, what they talk about," Pop scoffed. "You mind your own affairs, nothing will happen. I know these loudmouths."

"For three weeks more pay that he brings home, I can dispense with the risk he runs. If they begin to talk that way, they'll bother him even more. I can do without."

"Izzy Winchel said he can get me a job at the Polo Grounds."

"Meaning what?"

"Polo Grounds, that's where they play baseball."

"Baseball. And what has that to do with you?" Mom asked.

"You sell soda water there," Ira answered testily. "It comes in bottles—don'tcha know? All kinds of flavors."

"Aha, you'll be a peddler."

"It's not a peddler! It's called a hustler."

"Then let it be hustler," said Mom. "*Abi gesint.* Without beatings, God avert, and without stealing."

"Then let it be that way. But get back my hundred dollars," Pop decreed. "Don't fail to get it at once."

"No. As soon as my day off."

It was Thursday. He put in an early appearance at the checker's window. "What're you doin' here today?" The younger and the more easygoing of the two checkers, Lenahan, dark-haired and noncommittal, blew a tight cone of cigarette smoke. The two "backup" conductors in the office in case of emergency listened idly.

"I'm quitting. I came in to get my hundred dollars."

"Your what?"

"My hundred-dollar security. It's my father's."

"What're you quittin' for? You're doin' all right. We like your work." It was the older checker, the thin guy, Hallcain, who shaded his watchful eyes with a green visor.

The question found Ira unprepared. Why hadn't he anticipated it? "I—" Should he mention hustling? The ballpark? They might try to persuade him not to quit.

Behind Mr. Hallcain, Mr. Hulcomb at his desk took note of the proceedings. Together, Ira felt their disapproval, disapproval verging on hostility, bear down on him like a menace. "I'm going to go back to high school," he said, clutching at another excuse.

Mr. Hulcomb arose from his desk, came over to the counter, and took charge. "What'd you say?"

"I'm going back to high school."

"That's a hell of a time to tell us now!" Mr. Hulcomb seemed to stamp his heavy black eyebrows down on his glistening scowl. "Why didn't you tell us that when you came for a job? We'd never have hired you. That wasn't what you told us, was it?"

"No. I didn't know I was goin' to go back. My mother wants me to. I didn't wanna."

Mr. Hulcomb paid no attention to Ira's alibi. His lips swelled with repressed wrath. "You hire Jews, that's what you get. No notice or anything. They'll quit on you cold, every time."

"I can't help it." Ira lowered his head sullenly, stubborn and cowed into sullenness, and in his desperation only hoping that Mr. Hulcomb wouldn't see through his flimsy alibi and remind Ira that the opening of school was still three weeks off. "I got my receipt. You said I could get the money back as soon as I quit. That's why my father lent it to me." He didn't have to look around at the two backup conductors on the bench behind him to feel their absorption, their fixity of attention.

Neither did Mr. Hulcomb. As if by implicit consent, almost as if consternation were like a tiny unseen whirlwind that brought them together, he and the two clerks held a short, tense, muted council, reached a decision quickly. Mr. Hulcomb went back to his desk.

"All right, Stigman. We haven't been to the bank this morning yet. Come back this afternoon—about four o'clock," Hallcain instructed, with reassuring adjustment of his green visor. "We'll have your security money."

Even Ira could figure that out, or thought he could. By four in the afternoon, the whole first shift would have turned over its day's receipts. Then the company would have enough to pay him his hundred dollars. But he didn't want to conjecture; he didn't want to speculate. He was worried enough as it was. All he wanted was Pop's hundred dollars back.

He waited until almost five to give the office a chance to collect the money. When he entered the stinky waiting room, only Hallcain was there, behind the counter, strands of thin blondish hair across the top of his head, separated by visor edge. Would he say, "Come back tomorrow"? That would be the unmistakable signal for Ira's moaning retreat home, his whining to Pop about another fiasco. And then all kinds of wrath, all kinds of invective, all kinds of trouble. . . .

Approaching the counter, Ira displayed his receipt, laid his badge down beside it. To his pent, soaring joy, he watched Hallcain count out a hundred dollars in tens and fives, and with an air both severe and peremptory, push the little stack of bills toward Ira. Fives and tens, they were receipts! What the hell was the difference, as long as they added up to a hundred. Ira picked up the bank notes, uttered a fervent thanks. For once he could march into the kitchen proudly and say, "Okay, Pop, here's your money." And for once he did.

Mom blessed him: *"Zolst gebentsht vern."*

And Pop, as he counted over the bills: "Indeed a novelty. Something went well for a change. That such a thing has come to pass requires invoking a *shekheyooni*. Indeed. That we have survived to witness this day."

"And beside his clothes for the coming year, he bought a fuzball he longed for—for months." Mom rocked for emphasis. "And a swimming suit with a white woollen shirt top. *Noo.*"

"And added a flourishing increment toward your Persian lamb coat," Pop baited in fine fettle—as he arranged the currency by denomination in his black billfold. "And what interest do I gain? Ten weeks, nearly ten weeks of twenty dollars in *your* till. I should gain a small rebate on the weekly allowance you mulct from me."

"Gain proper burial," Mom rejoined, ruffled at once.

V

Almost immediately after Ira quit his job as bus conductor, the very next weekend, he was inducted by Izzy Winchel into the Polo Grounds. He met him on 119th Street, about 9:00 A.M., and they proceeded at a fairly rapid pace to the Third Avenue El on 116th Street. There they took the uptown train, and once across the Harlem River, by some changing of trains on the other side, their new route led to the Polo Grounds. There must have been some junction with the west side of the El in those days that enabled them to travel from Third Avenue to the west Bronx, to Coogan's Bluff, as the sportswriters called it. They climbed down from the El platform to an El-shaded sidewalk that seemed even gloomier than usual because of the high, dark wall that reared up from it, and through which opened the main entrance to the ballpark . . . gloomy and forbidding in the morning, though later in the day, when the ticket booths were opened, and the sun was higher, and the fans queued up, compact and restive, poised to dash for the best seats in the grandstands, most of that initial dourness was dissipated. Posted at the dark entrance, when Izzy and he arrived—to join a small flock of other hopefuls, other candidate hustlers, slouched, reading tabloids, or shifting about—was a single uniformed guard, an elderly man, large of frame, his hair gray, his face weathered and expressionless, and yet with the peculiar gravity of a man biding his time, patiently enduring it.

"That's old Rube Waddell," said Izzy, and his voice still harbored a trace of veneration.

"Who?"

"The watchman. They gave him that job after he was down and out. You heard of Rube Waddell."

"No. Who's he?"

"A pitcher. He was some pitcher, Waddell. Boy, in his time." Izzy's blanched blue eyes shone. Hook-nosed, weak-chinned, barefaced liar, he was unperturbed even when caught in the most blatant prevarication; pitching was his one fane of sincerity.

And such was Izzy's limitless brash, but he made good on his boast. After they waited around a few minutes, out came Benny Lass in the white coat and white visored cap of the ballpark hustler—and was instantly surrounded by claimants to vendor jobs. It was he who chose them—and later, since he was in charge of the cloakroom also, it was he who issued those he had selected white uniforms like his own. Strident, Jewish, though sharp of feature, vituperative, harried, and tyrannical, he chose the regulars first, the "old-timers" who worked in the Polo Grounds every day that a game was scheduled. In return for always being chosen, in return for being regulars, old hands had to report for work at games that it was known in advance would be poorly attended, that "wouldn't draw flies," as well as those with "big gates," games on holidays and weekends, doubleheaders, crucial series.

Izzy, veteran hustler, assured of recognition and admission, simply towed reticent Ira after him. "Hey, Benny, he's a friend o' mine. Give us a break, wi'ye? I'll go good for him."

Benny glanced at Ira, sharp-featured, sharp-eyed behind glasses. And to Izzy, "You, ye prick, you'll go good for him? You goddamn fuckin' chiseler! You'd short-change your own gran'mother, ye muzzler!"

"Aw, give us a break, Benny." Izzy rode the tirade unfazed. "He's from my own block. I know him. He'll work hard. You can see he won't try to get away with nothin'. Come on, Benny, waddaye say?"

His consent sour and obscene, Benny thumbed Ira in, cringing, but elated—and bewildered.

"See? I tol' ye." Izzy led the way.

And the way wound through the shadows under the grandstands, with glimpses of the ballpark, the diamond, vast tiers of seats, seen through the exits that opened at regular intervals from the shadowy route to the bright grass of playing field and pennant-studded sky overhead.

Other hustlers joined them. They hurried along until they came to a large, damp, vaultlike structure, a kind of depot, the main depot, Ira soon learned, a very large multipurpose chamber, in which the first thing that met the senses was the redolence of roasted or roasting peanuts. Bonded to the tang of peanuts were the sight and sound of a motley crew—mostly young people—of prospective hustlers, all seated about a number of very large wicker hampers, much like those in which groceries were packed to be loaded aboard Park & Tilford delivery trucks, hampers loaded to the top with peanuts. Men and boys, perhaps six or seven to a hamper, sat about the rim. They jabbered incessantly, while bagging peanuts.

Ira followed Izzy to one of the more sparsely occupied hampers, ranged himself alongside him, and tried to imitate his manipulations. Several small steel cylinders, measuring scoops, rested on the mound of freshly roasted peanuts. A scoop to a bag was the rule, although some of the hustlers, "for the hell of it," to relieve monotony, added extra peanuts, excessive surplus, to see how many could be gotten into a bag and the bag still be closed. The bags were small and brown; in bagging peanuts, the open end of the bag was folded over: two small "ears" protruded. Like tiny paper prongs, the ears were held between thumb and forefinger, and the bagful of peanuts whirled about to close it. Ira's forefingers soon became raw from the unaccustomed abrasion.

Chatter, chatter, jabber, jabber across the expanse of warm peanuts (with which he soon became sated, discouraged by their seeming inexhaustibility). Talk of ball clubs and their standings in their league, of ballplayers, their batting averages and their idiosyncrasies, their prowess with bat and ball, spitballs, knuckleballs, fastballs, Heinie Groh's bottle bat, the Babe's home runs and Meusel's throwing arm. And when not that, what size they estimated the crowd would be, and who might get a break selling peanuts or ice cream, and who never got a break but was always condemned to selling soda pop—and what flavors sold best. It was an opportunity for Ira to look about, and he did.

The place was lighted mainly by weak light from several high windows, although a few electric lights served as supplements. Against one wall was a low, very long, deep wood-sheathed tank with a metal lining, filled with cracked ice, and piled full of hundreds, perhaps thousands of bottles of soda pop—of every hue, from that of orange to the mahogany of sarsaparilla. At the far end of the tank, steel trays were stacked, soda pop trays, partitioned into small crates, like those Pop had once delivered milk in. Ranged against other walls, all about the room, were other utensils and equipment for preparing and vending food and drink to the fans. There were long, narrow baskets each containing a rectangular, nickel-plated utensil at one end. A sort of rectangular double boiler, they kept hot dogs warm inside, Izzy told him—and in the same breath, indicating the ordinary, simple market baskets thrown together in a rough heap next to the others, "That's for the *shleppers*—after they're finished selling scorecards at the gates. And the Irish mick kids too, Harry M. Stevens's pets, from his church."

"What d'ye mean?"

"Peanuts." Izzy reached for a scoop. "They're a cinch. There's a hundred bags to a basket, a dime a bag. And they don't weigh nothin'. Not like twenty bottles o' soda. Fifteen cents a bottle."

He had already told Ira that hustling soda would be his lot—as it was Izzy's. "Yeah, but what d'ye mean, *shleppers?*"

"They're the real regulars. They come in early in the morning," Izzy explained. "Ye see, there's more than one place where you can load up when you finish selling a tray of soda—I'll show you later. There's both ends of the stands. And upstairs, too. Didn't you see the upper stands? You can't come runnin' back to this place every time when you're empty. We'll walk aroun' afterward. I'll show you where to go. And in the bleachers, too. They stink."

"What d'ye mean?"

"The bleachers, the cheapest seats. You can't make a pretzel there most of the time, but once in a while, all of a sudden they get thirsty from sitting in the sun. So you can sell a few bottles—hey, look, here comes another basket of peanuts!"

A general cry of protest arose. "Hey, I thought we wuz done!"

"Last basket," said one of the two men who had trundled the hamper in on a dolly.

"Last basket, my prick," was the consensus. "Why'n'tcha bring it in before?"

"It just got roasted." Both porters seemed distinctly Jewish, middle-aged, settled men; and the man who spoke, beside his deprecating mien, even had a Yiddish accent. Said the other, "What d'ye want from us?"

"Fuckin' *shleppers,*" said Izzy. "See what I mean?"

"Come on! Come on! Some o' you guys on the empty baskets." Benny Lass's whiplike voice named members of the crew around each basket. "None o' you muzzlers leave till it's finished—if you wanna get your white coats."

"Balls," said those summoned, but got up nevertheless and addressed themselves to the fresh basket.

He hadn't called either Izzy or Ira. "Is that what they do?" he asked.

"They're like trusties, the *shleppers,*" Izzy explained. "They're like porters. They get here early in the morning and start loading up the soda in the different tanks all over the ballpark. Then later they cover 'em with ice on top. *Shleppers,* you know what I mean? Sometimes on doubleheaders, or World Series, even we gotta help *shlepp.* But those bastards, they get scorecards afterward. You know scorecards? With all the ballplayers' names in them? They sell themselves. A nickel apiece, and they get hundreds of 'em right next to the gate where the fans come in. Then they get peanuts to hustle, somet'n easy. Or ice cream cones. Those little trays over there near the door. They ain't breakin' their ass for nothin', don't worry."

Ira was beginning to understand: little trays near the door. "Ice cream cones in those?"

"Yeah. Fifteen cents a throw. Same as soda. Wait'll you see Moe." Izzy grinned.

"What d'you mean?"

"With his ice cream. Sometimes he gets peanuts after scorecards, but when he gets ice cream, he's—you'll see him. He's short; he's got a hooked nose an' big blue eyes." Izzy chuckled. "Everybody knows him."

"You talkin' about Moe?" the hustler bagging peanuts on Ira's left asked. He was swarthy, short but supple. "That sonofabitch, he'd eat the linin' out of a cunt. Did you ever see him down at the beach? That's always where he goes when there's no game."

"Yeah?"

"He never goes in swimmin'. Lays around the beach. Jesus, he can see a pussy through a bathin' suit."

"That's Moe, all right," Izzy confirmed. He turned to Ira. "He was a *shlepper,* and a cake of ice fell on his foot. So he gets all the breaks." And to the other hustler, "Ain't he the cats with ice cream, Steve?"

"I don't know why the hell Walsh gives it to him. He brings half of it back melted." Steve swung a bag of peanuts closed. "Jesus." He glowered dangerously. "I thought we'd be outta here by now. Play a few innings o' handball."

"They must be expectin' a big crowd," Izzy surmised.

With as many hustlers as possible crowded about the hampers, the peanuts were bagged at last. They were free to leave. It was now about 11:30 A.M. They streamed out of the big utility room. "Here's where you come back an' get your checks." Izzy indicated the large zinc-covered counter, with drawers under it, and a heavy drawbridge like a portcullis in front. The place had been at Ira's back while he bagged peanuts. It was adjacent to the main passage through which they'd entered.

"Get checks?" Ira asked.

"Later. When he calls you. You stand in front there." And as they came out from the cavernous utility room into the gloom under the stands, "I'll show you later. Right now you gotta get your white coat an' hat. Or you can't get in again. Get the idea?"

Ira followed Izzy to the cloakroom—presided over by Benny Lass. All of the hustlers crowded in front of the cloakroom counter, and with imprecation and reviling, Benny hurled their uniforms at the boys. Ira's hat was too small.

"I'll change it for you," Izzy volunteered. "He needs about a seven and a quarter, Benny." Izzy proffered the hat.

"Why the hell didn't he ask for it? What the hell is he? Dumb? What the fuck kinda hustler you gonna be?" Benny demanded. "Can'tcha open yer mout'?"

"I didn't know."

"Next time you'll wait till the last one." Benny threw the larger-size white hat at Ira.

What had he been saying to his wife, darling woman? No, she wasn't at the washing machine, which was installed just outside his study door. He thought she was at the washing machine, because the appliance whirled merrily about, and he thought she was there. Women didn't have to wait in attendance on washing machines any longer, thanks to technology. The machines were computerized; after they were set spinning, they went through cycles on their own, rinsed on their own, drained, stopped on their own.

What had he been saying to her? But he was digressing. Then digress within the digression. Was he afraid he wouldn't return to the main theme? Oh, the past was there, not like an inert lump, to be sure, malleable still, but only within limits. After he had said what he had said to her, she murmured to herself at the washing machine, almost to herself, "I can't stand it when you get depressed. When you get depressed, I get depressed. I want you to be happy." Ah, beloved wife . . . so interwoven within him, as he within her. What would they do without each other? She was steady enough to survive losing him; what would he do in the other event?

But he chose to ignore the question, admittedly more difficult, and thought instead of their lunch of tea and toast, peanut butter, apple butter. Ira had said to her, "I wrote a piece about my experiences as a plumber's helper in Freshman Composition, second half of my freshman year. The instructor thought it merited printing in *The Lavender,* the CCNY literary magazine."

"How old were your teachers?" M asked.

"One, Dickson, I think may have still been in his twenties, late. He gave me a D in the course. And Kieley was middle-aged, fifty or so.

"But in the second semester of Freshman Composition, which I took in sophomore year, everything turned around. We were instructed to write descriptions for our weekly theme papers, and my grades were suddenly quite good. Mr. Kieley—I think his specialty was Edgar Allan Poe, and maybe he too was partial to the bottle—would get up and say, 'Once again the star of the class has given us a fine specimen of a description.' It was mine. Now why the hell didn't they encourage this guy? At nineteen, think of it, how close I was to all this: the bus conductor, the ballpark soda hustler. A hundred other things I could have dug up for long themes, or maybe salable sketches, given the encouragement, the incentive."

"Teachers work pretty hard," said M. "They may not have had energy enough left to spend on you."

"No, I don't think that was the case. When CCNY gave me the Townsend Harris medal for notable achievement—and what a sinker of a bronze medal it was!—I told them that I hoped they didn't let other guys flounder around at a loss the way I did. At that age you're usually not autonomously activated, not confident; that's true only of the mature writer. At that age, unless the guy is a prodigy, he needs assignments, a definite theme, a project."

"We were taught one thing at Chicago," said M. "How to write acceptable exposition. How to get our thoughts in connected form, cut out waste in a paragraph."

"I would have been out on my ear," said Ira. "I never learned how to do it."

Ha! At his desk again, he threw his head back, vocalized his breath. He couldn't say why he did so: compound of regret, wordless expletive imbued with all the days and years gone by, expletive inveighing against time alone, the abstract past. . . .

Self-conscious at first in his white raiment, Ira trailed Izzy out of the ballpark. They had a couple of hours to themselves, during which most of them ate their noonday meal. A few blocks away was the restaurant where many of the hustlers had dinner. It was a restaurant combined with a saloon, but one that served nothing more potent than "near beer," a brew whose alcoholic content did not exceed one half percent. There were white tablecloths, waiters, a large dining room with mirrors, buffalo horns adorning the walls—and a large reproduction of *Custer's Last Stand*. Depicted in it, the last, doomed remnant of blue-coated U.S. Army regulars vainly held off hordes of torso-naked, buckskin-fringed Indian braves. Frenzied with victory, they wielded tomahawks against the few survivors, or ripped the gory and all too realistic scalps from the heads of fallen foes. Custer himself stood proud and erect, aiming pistol, brandishing sword. Never did scalped heads look so meaty.

Ira ordered—frugally as usual—a roast beef sandwich and a glass of near beer. That consumed, and a nickel tip left, he accompanied Izzy back to the ballpark, or rather to its immediate environs across the street. The sun at its height shone down on a bare tract of ground, a large parking lot. Empty at present, as it would be for the next hour—by which time they would have to report back—the area lent itself to a "handball" game. Only too aware of his hamminess, Ira stayed out, but Izzy played, and so did the swarthy workmate around the peanut hamper, Steve, who was not, as Ira learned from Izzy, from Puerto Rico, but from the Philippines. He had been a lightweight boxer, was a dependable and aggressive hustler, and this season had been advanced to selling peanuts. He belted a ball, fielded a ball, with the same pugnacity he did everything else, bagging peanuts, tossing a bag to a fan in the middle of a row—and as redoubtable in concentration, catching the dime thrown to him afterward. Ira found himself wondering what a lone, or seemingly lone, Filipino did in New York. He couldn't imagine, but knew better than to ask.

On the same ground where the hustlers now played, several dwellings, "railroad flats," had evidently stood before, and had been razed to the ground, the rubble cleared away to make room for a parking lot. The only house still left standing, the one overlooking the parking lot, was a five-flight "dumbbell" tenement. Bereft of its former neighbors, it presented an expanse of rough, mortar-slopped brick wall, almost shaggy in appearance, and without a single window in it, except for those in the recess where the airshaft had been. In the windows of the recess on every floor sat Negro men, women, and children quietly watching the activities below.

Though Ira accorded little meaning to the sight, social meaning, and did not even consciously try to remember it, it would remain in his mind always, preserved by contrast or innate pathos—or simply by inherent design.

The rough, mortar-spattered wall from which the bricks of an abutting wall had obviously been torn away left a grayish-red, crude expanse. And opening on El and street and ballpark, a row of windows occupied by black faces, one above the other, framed in a vertical succession to the ledge atop the roof. Below them, on the bare dirt of the parking lot, Harry Stevens's hustlers in their white uniforms played ball.

Across the way, under the El, fans were already lining up in front of the ticket booths. Gates would be opened in an hour or so—which behooved the players to end their game, and to go in for their assignments. He soon found out that meant the hustlers had to assemble in front of the window where both assignments and "checks" were issued. Once again, he followed Izzy to the big wooden portcullis, already lowered, behind which with pencil in hand and pad in front of him on the counter sat Walsh. He was in charge, an Irishman, in his early thirties, and with a crimped bridge of nose that spoke of a prizefighting past. Beside him, his assistant, Phil, sallow, Jewish, chain-smoker, who continually hawked up yellow-green phlegm and spat it on the floor. On the other side of the counter, in the dusk under the grandstands, the white-coated hustlers waited, a half-moon bunch, for the wares that Walsh and Phil would assign them to peddle for the day. Together with the assignment of wares they were tossed a menu card, on which was printed in bold letters the item the hustler sold, and its price; this was worn above the visor, affixed to the white cap. At the same time a numbered badge and a small stack of "checks" were issued, ten of them, square aluminum tabs, each indented on the edge and stamped "$1," all held tightly together by a rubber band.

Preference was given those who were to vend popular or favorite items. First to be chosen were the peanut vendors, many of them young Irish kids; then the ice cream vendors, the hot dog vendors. Last to be chosen, and composing the majority, were the soda pop

hustlers, lowest on the scale of hustling. Even here, though, preference was shown to the more aggressive veterans by calling out their
names first, which entitled them to fill up their trays at the depots before those called after them, which gave them an edge in selling. Izzy
was called about midway among those assigned soda, but he stayed
with Ira until the very end, when only two or three novices were left,
in order to vouch for his friend. Ira was now equipped, except in
temerity, to sally forth into the world of baseball fans, proclaiming his
shibboleth, as inculcated by Izzy: "Gitcha cold drinks here!"

A quarter hour still remained before the gates were opened.
Empty of fans, the green grandstand seats stretched about on both
sides, and from box seats next to the playing field to the high tiers in
the back. They had their choice of seats, and Izzy and Ira joined the
scattering of white coats at the side of the safety net up front watching the Giants finish their batting practice. McGraw was with them—
who could fail to recognize that bloated figure that filled his uniform
as if pumped into it? "Atta boy, Kelly," some of the kids among the
scattered hustlers cheered the Giants' first baseman. "C'mon, high-
pockets, slam one right over the fence!" Others picked up the cry. It
was pleasant sitting there: warm and yet in shade, and so near the
players in their white pin-striped suits one could see every move. Ira
had watched a big league team, certainly, never been so close to big
league ballplayers, seen their grace and dazzling fielding, their unerring throw—from catcher to second, from third to first. "Yay!" he
tentatively joined Izzy in cheering.

A sudden rigor seemed to fall on the field; the figures on the diamond became motionless. His coarse, mean face hardened into a
scowl, McGraw turned away from the players, strode toward the railing before the box seats, his wrath seeming to swell with every step.
"Who the hell's askin' you fer yer two cents? If you Jews don't shut
up, I'll have you thrown outta the park. Shut your goddamn trap!"

He turned his back on them, strode toward the players before
the net. Ira would never forget the expression on the face of the
young pitcher warming up next to the rail. It was beyond finding
words for: a mixture of youthful embarrassment, boyish apology—
within the enforced respectful mien. Ira and Izzy sat there another
second or two, stunned by the outburst, and then all of them got up

and went elsewhere. In the bewilderment of his own silent rancor at the affront—that the manager of the world-famous Giants would talk like an ignorant slum-bred mug, a 119th Street hard guy—unbelievable, vicious—Ira couldn't help wonder what the Irish kids thought, what the Irish kids felt, called Jews for the first time in their lives. He tried to imagine the kind of double rejection that may have gone on in their minds. Or the moment of indignant identity the epithet may have enforced. One thing was sure: he knew he would never root for the Giants as long as he lived.

So began his first day with his steel tray loaded with twenty bottles of soda pop, according to directions given by Izzy—orange in the ascendancy, lemon, grape, cream soda, root beer, sarsaparilla, carefully picked out among the jumble of bottles under and between chunks of ice. And those favored hustlers privileged to load up first were already back again for a second load before he was out with his initial one. He paid the checker at the door with three $1 checks, walked hesitantly out through the dugout: from the muted obscurity under the grandstands into the vast crescendo of daylight flooding the thronging, clamoring stands. Multitudes in tier upon tier of seats converged on him in cynosure, he thought, a weight of gape and gaze through which he could muster only the feeblest of feeble "Gitcha cold drinks," a cry that was swept away by concentrated inattention, like a fart, as they said, in a windstorm. Not a soul paid him the least heed.

"C'mon!" Izzy hurried past with an empty tray. "Don't be scared. Hustle! Hustle! Git a col' drink here!" He paused long enough to demonstrate, raising face and voice boldly at the crowd. "Ice-cold drink here! Hey, go ahead, there's one!" he prompted Ira. "Git him before that muzzler on top comes down. Run up the steps."

Ira hurried upward. "Wha' flavor you want?" He could scarcely raise his voice above a peep.

"Got any ginger ale?"

"No. Root beer, orangeade, cream soda—"

"All right. Give us the cream."

So he made his first sale, snapped off the bottle top, asked the fans to pass the bottle, which they did, and the quarter the other way, and the dime change in return—which awoke a surge of thirst in the immediate neighborhood of the transaction, so that he sold another three bottles then and there.

Encouraged, emboldened, as much by the sale as by the realization that he was universally ignored, he increased the volume of his cry—to which nobody paid any more attention than before—until once again, out of the illimitable haphazard of the crowd, "Hey, you got an orange?"

"Yes, sir, yes, sir." He served up an orange drink.

Despite the increased volume of his appeal, other hustlers—Ira could see—had some kind of magic in their cry, a compelling urgency. Fans bought soda in rows he had just passed half a minute before. He was flaccid, he lacked something, goddamn it, what? There was Greeny (they said he was going to college), tall, spindly-lean, a dynamo, he never seemed to tire, to get discouraged, or slacken; he had sold four trays already, and Ira hadn't quite got rid of two. Half the bottles in Ira's first tray had become warm before game time, and he had gone back to the depot, got credit for them with metal checks of smaller denomination, and reloaded with a new and dewy supply—which increased his self-confidence to the point where he felt justified in bellowing his wares. Dispensing a lukewarm drink embarrassed him, intimidated him. A fan might call him to account. Other hustlers, like Izzy, brazened it out, didn't give a damn. They got their dough and scrammed out of sight. He didn't have the nerve, the barefaced, the public, dishonesty.

It was a question of nerve, Ira told himself, his failure of nerve, not his scrupulousness, not his honesty, that slowed him down. His scanty aggressiveness too, he had to admit, was a primary factor in his mediocrity as a hustler. He replenished his tray with cold, fresh bottles of soda, instead of driving doggedly on with tepid ones as the others did. He was a plain, mopey, good-natured slob. And he was indolent; he loitered. He climbed up to the top of the stands, where the near beer bar and hot dog counters were, looked down over the slope of tiers solid with fans, and beyond them to the infield, the outfield, the base lines, the greensward, and lingered, watched, listened, enjoyed, daydreamed. All the things he shouldn't be doing.

But he couldn't help it: all that restlessness and tumult: the way Frankie Frisch's cap flipped off his head when he dove headlong into first base to beat out the throw from infield. The way the umpire called a strike, as if he intended to overawe everyone within hearing. The way a Texas Leaguer, so they called it, dropped right in the middle of everybody. No wonder your soda grew lukewarm. . . .

Ira scratched the back of his head meditatively. He had come to a divergence within himself, a kind of fork in the road of narrative. All he needed now to do to close off the account of his novitiate at the Polo Grounds was to state merely the predictable—and the actual.

When time came, almost at the end of the ball game—when not even the most determined soda hustler could hope for another sale—when time came for everyone to check in, to cast up accounts, Ira had sold thirty-six dollars' worth of soda, which entitled him to three dollars and sixty cents, ten percent of proceeds. That was his take for the day. Izzy, on the other hand, had sold over fifty-five dollars' worth, and Greeny almost seventy dollars' worth, which indicated what persistence and resolve could accomplish, or the differential between a good hustler and a poor one (only a single soda hustler sold less than Ira, a kid who must have watched most of the ball game). But Ira was a neophyte, after all.

"You didn't do too bad," Izzy encouraged. "You didn't know all the ropes. You didn't know where all the places to fill up were. There's places on the upper stands, too. Did you know that? You went up there, didn't you?"

"Yeah. You could fall out of 'em, they're so steep."

"You sometimes can get a good break up there," Izzy assured.

Ira had made three bucks and sixty cents for his first day's work. But there was something else. His—and his fellow hustlers'—work still wasn't done. Not till all the grandstands were cleared of soda pop bottles. After the game was over and the fans departed, by now in the late middling of afternoon, a pair of hustlers were assigned a block of seats, each hustler given a basket. And his chore? To collect all the bottles left under the seats. Only then was it permissible for him to leave the Polo Grounds—if he wanted to be rehired the next day.

It seemed to Ira that he had reached a fitting place to finish the section, a logical and satisfying place. Later, he could resume again his documenting of the tyro's further experience and development as a hustler. That was one option; the other was Freudian. For Ira the choice was a simple one: the Freudian, his forte, in preference to the social.

VI

Ira stood on the runway behind the top tier of the grandstands, surveying the multifarious movement below, spying Izzy hustling way over at the left wing, Greeny charging up the stairs on thin, long legs, and that ugly, stunted, raw-nosed Jew, Moe, who was always given the sinecure job—ice cream or peanuts to hustle. He started to ask why. Why so many Jews in the place? Ira pondered. What kind of symbiosis existed between them and the Irishman, Harry M. Stevens, whose baronial reign held sway as franchised caterer at the ballpark, stadium, and racetrack? Clearly because Harry M. Stevens had long since learned none were so enterprising as Jews, none so immune to the temptation to slacken efforts in behalf of watching, of enjoying the game?

Business before pleasure, that was it. *Gelt, gelt,* money, that was it. The more commission they earned, the more Stevens grossed. Of minor importance to them who had just scored, who stole a base. And yet, though true in general, there was always the exception. There was Eppie, short for Epstein, as old as Ira's grandfather, and still speaking with heavy, thick Yiddish drawl, a Litvak, Eppie, sauntering along with a half-basket of peanuts, taking it easy. He was a privileged character in the Stevens establishment; he came and went when he pleased, responsible to no one but to Harry M. Stevens himself. Rumor had it he had been with Stevens when the latter owned only a modest stand outside the Polo Grounds, in the way back when, long before the War, in the heyday of Christy Mathewson and Honus Wagner, when Walter Johnson could throw a fastball that crossed the plate no bigger than a pea, when ballplayers sneaked over the fence to get a beer.

Eppie was a Giant fan, a staunch, unswerving Giant fan. It was hard to believe: an old immigrant Jew, yet a Giant fan (especially after Ira had heard McGraw's uncouth, insulting bawling at the hustlers that morning!). It was like Zaida being a Giant fan. Who could imagine it? Looking up from *davening* the *Mishnah* or *minchah*, or whatever the prayers were called, to ask the latest standings of the ball clubs. Ira expected that kind of enthusiasm in the younger generation of Jews, his generation. He took their partisanship for one or another of the baseball clubs for granted; he hardly thought about it. But with someone as old as Eppie, who was about Zaida's age, it came as a kind of shock, the realization that the cleavage had begun long ago, the branching away from Orthodoxy. It made the cleavage dramatic to have someone Jewish as old as Eppie a baseball fan; it dramatized that there was a cleavage, and it had long been going on, not something hit-or-miss, as he felt about his own muzzy shrugging off of being Jewish. He had even thought he was one of the first ones—oh, no, it had been going on always.

His eye caught Moe, limping, big-nosed, down at the very lowest aisle. It was more than a mere aisle; it was the passageway between the box seats at the edge of the ball field and the first row of seats of the grandstand. His scorecard stint finished ("Scah-cod!"). At each gate, the *shleppers*, Benny Lass and Moe among them, had bawled in monotone at the incoming flood of fans, "Getcha scah-cod. Can't tell the players without a scah-cod." Moe had elected ice cream for his second item to vend. He seemed to cry his wares within a narrow range of seats, as if he were on a tether, limping a given distance to the right, then after a space, a pause, returning and limping to the left, his gaze lifted under his white visored hat. His mouth forming the words "ice cream," inaudible through the mingled noise of intervening voices jeering, cheering, rooting, he stood transfixed at the center of his tether—for a single moment—and tore himself away, and traveled a long distance.

In direct sunlight too, he oscillated, the sun's rays glaring on his tray of vanilla ice cream. What was wrong with the guy? What was the jibe they had made about him around the peanut hamper? Ira had forgotten to ask Izzy afterward. Moe was his name; that much Ira remembered. Curious, and guilty at having loitered so long, Ira walked down the steps, dutifully hawking his wares; and reaching the bottom, turned toward the section of grandstand Moe had been frequenting. Why? He hadn't sold anything. Still wondering why, Ira reached the end of Moe's seeming tour, and retraced his steps. Moe had kept looking up. So did Ira—and suddenly felt: a vertigo: a stunning inner gasp without a sound. The woman, not young, in her forties, not pretty, buxom—was she sitting deliberately with her thighs spread? Cunt, the word came unbidden to Ira's lips. Big red cunt in a black muff that at the moment of spying engulfed him with desire, plummeted him in a sudden, swooning spasm. Like Moe, he couldn't tear himself away, but did, had to. Secret that was stolen, evil, stealthy, yes, that—he went on, his head bowed, shaken by a kind of wildness, grimness: realization there at the foot of the packed grandstand. Look what he was. Look, where it was leading him, where it was dragging him, like the way he got started, that same feeling all mixed in it, not stealing silver pens, but right in his inside, like his will, like the thing he wanted. That way: lurk, waylay, oh, Jesus. Why did he have to hear about Moe, see him do that? Why always that goddamn accident he was always in the way of, like he was set for it to happen? Jesus, that was exciting, that was exciting.

Moe approached, limping on crippled foot, his big Jewish nose prominent—and his eyes, as though he were suffering, suffering, his eyes seemed like red-rimmed, great, sick circles of crimson around terrible sadness. The vanilla gobs of unsold ice cream cones in his tray were all part melted, had begun to sink below the rim of the cone. That's all he sold ice cream for; that's all he lived for. Jew, Jesus, homely crippled Yid. But you're worse than him—

"Hey, fella! You got a cold grape soda?" Reality, hearty American reality, boomed out from three rows up.

"Grape? Yeah. Huh? Grape soda?"

VII

He welcomed the electronic routine of the computer, recording date and time and the code for the eighty-column print on the monitor. Ecclesias, his friend, both his friend and life-support system, helped bring him back from the past—that would be the simplest way to say it—bring him back from that complex confusion, loss, anxiety, frustration of those years before M, and even after, those years, long years of grievous depression and literary desuetude in Maine. These were the interminable years of immobilization. He hadn't felt that way in a long time, not for months, but once again, as so often in the past, a conjunction of circumstances had brought it on. And he had dreamed too, dreamed most of the night, it seemed, apprehensive of what he would do next morning, how to start the next day's work, sorting plans, proposals, introductions. No, he had weighed returning to beginnings: prefacing the beginning of his work in progress with a foreword. But no, that would never do; that was like a reformed drug addict—or even cigarette smoker—saying to himself, "Now that I've given up the drug, the weed, just to show how free I am of it indeed, I'll tantalize it, toy with it, flout it by trial." Anybody, even a fool, would know that wouldn't work.

He had considered prefacing the day's work by saying as much. Or, discarding preface, eschewing names and exordium, and beginning *in media res*, proclaiming: no, James Joyce, the bastard is like a literary black hole. You aren't meant to go on writing after that, after you've come in contact with him. You can't escape him, once you've entered his stupendous gravitational field; you're lost, caught in the vortex of the event horizon where time piles soon to stop. And that's what *he* tried to do, that Pied Piper of Dublin, make time stop, erect so colossal a roadblock against change, there could be nowhere left to go, nothing left to do, except stand before his works, his image, to worship him as icon—such was the monstrous immensity of the man's ego. And he had just that kind of submissive votary in his avid exegete Stuart Gilbert: every fault of his fetish became a hallowed attribute, every weakness, every dodge, every cop-out, a stroke of genius. . . .

Ira had in the previous month set himself the task of reading Stuart Gilbert's explication of Joyce's *Ulysses;* and that had been its effect—to throw him under the sway of the sorcerer again, him whom he had so explosively, so violently repudiated, repudiated to the pitch of irrationality. Repudiation had begun seething in him ever since Moira P, professor of Irish studies at UNM, had nominated Ira as the guest of honor at the Joyce festival to be held in Albuquerque. It was in celebration of Bloomsday that the festival was held, and it was on Bloomsday that Ira, the erstwhile Joycean disciple, had reached the point of rupture with his great master. It was exactly on Bloomsday that James Joyce's Jewish Junior had blown his top. He would! What a time to kick over the apple cart. But he had to. Like all revolutionary, drastic rectifications, whether of soul or of society—or of tecton—his readjustment had gone to extremes, gone to excess, before he regained any sort of equilibrium. He had gone off the deep end. He felt embarrassed by it, but it couldn't be helped, or rather, couldn't be recalled.

And why the rupture? That was the important thing, far more important than the form it took, its immoderation. Why the rupture? Because of the clearly felt, the profoundly felt, need to bring to an end the self-imposed exile within himself, come to grips with the new reality of belonging, of identifying and reuniting with his people, Israel. The vanities, the insanities, of Joyce, for so they seemed to Ira, despite all the extraordinary artifice, the prodigious virtuosity, the verbal interlacing—or what to call it?—circuitry, intricate upon intricate, interconnected inlay, unbelievable in its cunning as the network on a ceramic chip, all served to conceal the fact that the human element, the interchange, the unavoidable confrontation between man and man, man and woman, especially with regard to the latter as intellectual equals, bringing into play respect for their minds as well as amorousness for the sexual roles, without both of which true tenderness could not be felt, nor delineated—was never addressed in *Ulysses.*

One and all, men and women, to him whose false superiority consisted of his supreme virtuosity of the word, as if that alone ordained him high priest of beauty and truth—and that alone was enough to relieve him of any responsibility to his fellow humans and to his folk—to their aspirations, their centuries of suffering and their struggle. His virtuosity obviated all kinship. Oh, there were a hundred indictments he could hurl at Joyce; and reading Stuart Gilbert's salaaming adulation, ground-kissing obeisances, incited a hundred more. On every page: commencing with the scarce nominal Jew that the great Guru foisted on the reader, a Jew without memory, without wry anxiety, exilic insecurity, not merely oblivious of his heritage, but virtually devoid! Of the Kishinev pogrom the year before, nothing, of Dreyfus, nothing, nothing to say to Dlugacz, or whatever his name was, the Hungarian butcher, no sally about the pork kidney: was it kosher? No inference, no connection between a newspaper offering plots in Palestine and the possibility of a Jewish community in Dublin. No recall of Friday candles, no recall of *matzahs*. Jeez, what a Jew, even one converted while still a juvenile—no *cheder,* no *davening,* no Yom Kippur, no Purim or *hamantashen,* no *brukhe,* no Hebrew, no Yiddish, or naught but a negligible trace. And despite the lack, daring to depict the Jew's "stream of consciousness," the inner flow of a Jew's psyche, an Irish quasi-Marrano of the year 1904. What unspeakable gall that took, gall and insufferable egotism! Gall and ignorance! And Madame Tweedy, out of a "Spanish"-Jewish mother. Had Joyce even looked at Sephardism, Ladino, the Inquisition—let alone, for all his highly touted erudition, Yiddish, Hebrew, or Chaldee, as the truly erudite Milton termed Aramaic? Didn't Mama remember anything either to tell her half-Sephardic daughter about? Not a brass candlestick, not a *dreidel,* a *challah* on Friday night, the agony of 1492, the expulsion? No. As long as Mama's name was Lunita, satellite of her Gaia-Tellus daughter, *shoyn genug, wunderbar!* Torquemada, the *quemadero,* the *auto da fé,* what was that? Consider, Master Jew-Joyce, the effect of the altercation with the Citizen (when Bloom was actually at his Jewiest—and note: *when presented from the outside,* the outside!), wouldn't that have devastated you the rest of the day, hung over you like the ancient pall of exilic woe? And here was the difference, aye, the crucial difference, between your Irish Catholic self, qua-Jew, and the genuine article. Bloom would have gone home to his wife, even if she was cuckolding him, if he loved her, or she him, even a little, for the comfort she might give him (she was "part" Jewish, you know), for all that he suffered, outcast among the gentiles, a Falasha, alien, even though she had descended from a *converso?* Granted that Molly were totally a *shiksa,* she would have consoled him; she would have understood something by now of the Jewish condition—not to the extent that Ira's beloved gentile M understood, but after these many years, something, something, of the Jewish plight. Instead of turning to her, Bloom did what Joyce himself would have done, treated a wife like an appurtenance, slack-Irish, never thought about the thing again—by the master artificer of allusion, of interspersal, of intertexture, juggling color and orgon, art and rhetoric and logo. Instead, the Yid is farcicalized (as Pound observed, calling Joyce anti-Semitic, the very cream of the jest, coming from Pound). Instead, the earth shakes as Bloom flees via hansom cab, the seismic shocks registered at grade 5, at the observatory. All of a sudden, gratuitous *goyish* flapdoodle of Elija Bloom ascending to heaven at an angle of forty-five degrees, like a shot off a shovel. Who said that? Joyce himself. Why? Yes, why this intrusion, this irrelevant commentary on his own story, and by the most self-conscious, superb literary craftsman of his time? And the most notably "tolerant" of Jews in an age rife with intolerance? Yes, why? First and foremost: failure of courage, the courage of sensibility, without which, as Eliot said in different words, there could be no great art; cowardice in the contemplation of violence, even if the man himself might be physically afraid, no matter. And all this rationalized by his championing of so-called Aristotelian stasis, when what he actually meant was fear of contemplating violence, violence at every stage the usher of change, of development, of maturation, of casting off the old, of growth into the new—resisting all this, until finally, he wove himself a chrysalis, a verbal shroud called *Finnegans Wake.* Cowardice, that disguised its shrinking under Olympian buffoonery: at the very moment of truth, twisting the knife in the Jew in his quandary, in his millennial Diaspora, with gratuitous burlesque temblor, burlesque Ascension in chariot of fire, all this in the name in fidelity to gigantism, to Cyclops, Polyphemus. Bah! Pound saw through it, cagey, crusty Pound, in spite of all his batty political economy and his loony anti-Semitic "usura," a man. A man worthy of respect—and sympathy too—so Ira felt—for the stupefying torment and remorse the realization his own monumental misguidance inflicted on him. One glimpse—

had Joyce permitted himself that, had he summoned up the courage to take one glimpse into the harried Jewish soul, pariah and scapegoat of Europe— and the author's whole Homeric house of cards would have tumbled to the ground. Nay, more than that: he would have begun to grow up, develop, change, he would have begun to win the state of mind of a modern man. He would have liberated himself from the self-imposed constriction of myth, freed himself from his Procrustean spoof, and sued for reunion with his folk. It wasn't the nightmare of history from which he was trying to awake; it was the daylight of the present he fought not to awake to.

Well, he had said his say, thrown off the spell of the arch-necromancer. He had to have his say, however chaotic, or he would never have been able to proceed, sucked in by that dread black star. No. He would not continue perusing Gilbert's book on *Ulysses,* Ira decided. By no means. You could not fool with old habits, old addictions, old vices; precisely because they were old, were deeply ingrained, they were never, never dead, never entirely banished. Part of one always, they waited, in suspended animation, like a dormant virus. No. Dear acolyte Mr. Gilbert was going back on the shelf, banished there for good, as far as Ira was concerned. Bloom had become a Zionist, Stephen ambushed Albion's Black and Tan. Nor could Ira help, grinning to himself, taking note, one last time, of the large number of Jews who figuratively, and literally, clasped Joyce to their bosoms, because he was among the very, very few of that generation of literary men not openly anti-Jew. Joyce didn't portray Bloom as a grasping, avaricious, unscrupulous Fagin or a contemporary Shylock, or as Hemingway's Cohen presuming to Western culture, Western grace in default of Western virility, or as Eliot's Sir Alfred Monde, Sir Ferdinand Klein, Bleistein, or the Jew in the window in "Gerontion." One of Ira's Jewish friends, a Jewishist and Hebrewist of note, even pointed to the delicacy the great writer showed to Jewish sensibilities by having Bloom attribute his wife's infidelities, not to her Jewish blood, but to her "hot Spanish blood." But to hell with Joyce and his holy writ. And with genuflecting Stu Gilbert to boot. It was with M that he, Ira, had found the way to adulthood. With M, the adult, sensitive and sensible, admirably intelligent, courageous, artistically creative, wife of his bosom, mother of his kids, he was safe, his soul growing in his pride in and admiration of his beloved spouse, which awoke finally to identity with his people, Israel.

*   *   *

He was free again, free to return to his narrative, employing Joyce's method, many of Joyce's devices, though freed of his impediments. True. But why, Ira couldn't help wondering the other night, when he could feel the Joycean incubus settle on him. As if encumbered by the fabled Old Man of the Sea, held in his relentless clutches, all this when half asleep, he had worried the night through, talked in his stuporous state, imagined he was taping his somnolent discourse—why, why had he dreamt of Ida, Ida Link, his last living aunt, aunt by marriage, the deceased Uncle Moe's widow, dreamt that she was feeding him a sandwich made of a full pound of butter between two slices of bread? He had nibbled at it, trying to accommodate filler to its jacket, its filly, he had thought.

At the same time his aunt was telling him about Moe, and not a word could Ira understand. Which meant what? And so vivid. Then she showed him Moe's workbench, a strange contraption with a work surface of thick gray glass, translucent windows, as once of old, bathroom doors were fitted with. Did that recall his cousin Stella and her bath in Tanta Mamie's house, and of the high jinks of the Rabelaisian fanfrelucky yet to be told? It was a weird contraption that Ida kept turning round and round until it was flush with the wallpapered wall. Why? Years ago, when she owned a store in Flushing purveying ladies' "foundations" (Ida was large of girth herself— just right for Moe), after her husband's death, she had asked Ira if he would lend her, waive, whatever the legal term was, the one thousand dollars Moe had bequeathed his nephew Ira. He did—when, as M sagely and discreetly remarked, "Your own family was in need. I wore torn petticoats and slips for months." M darling. But what? What did his consuming of that inordinately pinguid sandwich mean? That the long-delayed legacy would soon be restored? That would be oneiromancy, not Freudianism. But then how convenient if the "debt" were restored, not that he didn't wish Ida all the ripeness of old age mortality was vouchsafed, ripeness and over-ripeness as well.

And perhaps—last aside—all this convergence of the peripheral was intended to forestall that dread, that rending of the soul, soon now and soon. . . .

VIII

Ira became in time a regular hustler, after a fashion, a lackadaisical one, but conversant with most of the tricks of the trade, if lacking the cheek to foist them on his customers. He was accepted, for some reason or other, by Benny Lass in the morning at the shape-up outside the ballpark. Rarely did Ira earn more than five dollars for his day's work, at a time when Izzy earned nine or ten, and the indefatigable Greeny twelve or more. Oh, once in a while, he was favored with a windfall. When? Probably it was during the World Series, or during those "crucial" games at season's end that would determine who won the pennant. Probably it was then, when Harry M. Stevens needed all the hands he could muster—not in the hustling department, there he had a plethora of hands, but in the fiscal, the managerial cadres, the overseers, the checkers. In these departments he was understaffed, he was woefully shorthanded.

And there, behind the counter, henna-haired and balcony-bosomed, smoking a cigarette in a silver cigarette holder, presided Mrs. Harry M. Stevens, Jr., lacking only a lorgnette to complete her stylish demeanor, as she moved toward the till with leisurely noblesse. She had a large tally sheet in front of her, and in it she kept a record of all the "checks," the notched metal counters that each hustler bought from her. Business was extremely brisk, feverish in fact. Her strongly built husband, red-haired too, tended to other duties: overseeing the emptying of cases of soda in the cooling tank, in which by now much of the ice had melted into ice water. He also stood guard at the door, and collected the metal checks from the vendors on their way out of the depot, after loading up their trays inside. Even their redheaded, rotund, well-nurtured son seemed to be making himself useful in an agreeable way: topping ice cream cones with balls of vanilla ice cream. And Harry M. Stevens, the renowned proprietor himself, white-haired, doughty, and baronial, stood in the dugout that connected depot to grandstands, smoking a cigar and waving on his assiduous vassals to ever greater achievement: "Go on, get it! It's out there!" he urged. And to Ira: "Come on, boy! Get a move on!"—imperiously uttered, as might a monarch, easily irked and short of temper, spurring his subjects forward into the fray (and yet, as Ira sensed, the mogul had a saving touch of compassion in him, a touch of Irish sentiment). . . .

So, there stood his daughter-in-law, waiting behind the zinc-covered counter, svelte and stately Mrs. Harry M. Stevens, Jr. Her movements were a bit fastidious, or a bit disparaging, as befitted the heiress of a catering empire, to which she was just now lending a helping hand, graciously easing the heavy burden on her father-in-law in his need. Usually Phil, experienced and loyal Jewish hench-man, tended to that job, the job of presiding over the main depot, but Phil was sick, suffering from severe bronchitis. Ira stepped up to the counter.

He had already noticed, he had long ago become uncomfortably aware, that he either shed some kind of perverse emanation or was invested with a peculiar propensity that had the effect of mussing up the smooth flow of clerical work, of generating all kinds of hitches in mechanical routines, tics in established procedures, aberrations in formalities. Perhaps it was because he himself was so often just not present in mind, sufficiently absentminded that like an induction coil he induced a corresponding or reciprocal absence of attention within the mind of his counterpart in the transaction, frequently his counterpart on the other side of the counter.

He placed two one-dollar bills on the zinc-lined surface before Mrs. Harry M. Stevens, Jr., and asked for a two-dollar roll of nickels. He was running short of small change. And the lady, with decorous but businesslike bearing, accepted the two one-dollar bills and laid on the counter a paper-wrapped roll of coins. The exchange com-pleted, her long cigarette holder in hand, she stored the paper money in the drawer and turned away. But not before Ira, his hand curling around the roll of coins, knew he had struck it rich, struck a treasure. His heart leaped up with guilty rapture. He pocketed the roll instantly—and scooted out of the place. He lost himself at once in the grandstands, climbed up to the top, then up the ramp to the upper stands. There, as luck would have it, or because he stood there dazzled, he sold in a sudden jiffy of demand a half-dozen bottles of soda. And now justified in replenishing his near-empty tray, he went into the auxiliary depot in the back of the upper stand and refilled with freshly iced bottles, and also managed to get a little extra small change beside. He came out of the depot carrying twenty bottles of soda pop as if they weighed nothing, as if he were walking on air, levitated by the soda pop itself. What bliss! She had given him a *roll of quarters* instead of a roll of nickels, a roll of quarters worth ten dollars, instead of a roll of nickels worth two dollars. Boy, would that make a day's pay, boyoboy! Eight bucks ahead without scarcely lifting a finger! She would certainly never remember him, never remember the incident when time came for her to "check in," to cast up accounts. She would be—no, she wouldn't be—the *till* would be eight bucks short. In her wry dismay with herself, would she redress the discrepancy with a trifling eight bucks from her own ample purse? Or would the Stevens dynasty joke about the incident at cocktails before dinner that evening?

He had bought himself a small pipe a short while ago, small enough to fit easily into his pants pocket without bulging out too much, and he filled the bowl with tobacco from the pouch to which he had transferred the Prince Albert tobacco from the can this morning before leaving the house. He struck a match, applied the light, and puffed away exultantly. The lucky break was worth giving *himself* a break. The afternoon was cool, already autumn.

From where he stood, at the very top of the uppermost stand, at the very back of the last tier of seats, cloud and sky and Bronx rooftop, smudge of smoke, and blue neck of water in the distance. Below him, just below the grandstand roof, back of the mob of fans, he puffed on his miniature pipe a minute, and then—why not give himself a real break? He had already garnered a day's pay and more. He deserved more than a minute's relaxation. Why not enjoy part of an inning, watch a batter or two at the plate?

Way over at the farthest end of the grandstand wing, behind the steel pillars holding up the roof of the grandstand, was a ragged parcel of empty seats—he knew why they were empty. Not only were they at the farthest remove from the diamond below—sitting there, you could hardly see the home plate, hardly see the game any better than if you sat in one of the high tenement windows where black faces crowded together—not only because of the distance, but because the pillars supporting the roof partly blocked the view. Only during the World Series were fans driven to sit in them, only a belated few.

He would loaf for only a minute, Ira promised himself, take a few puffs. Just long enough to savor at its fullest the exultation of the wonderful break that had befallen him: ten bucks' worth of quarters instead of two bucks' worth of nickels. No matter how far behind Izzy or Greeny or any other soda hustler he was, he was still bound to finish ahead at the end of the day. With an eight-buck break like that!

He felt the roll in his pocket. How could the grand lady have missed telling the difference? The weight alone, even if your fingers didn't recognize the heftier round, the sleek, packed, solid, geometric cylinder of ten bucks' worth of quarters in comparison to the unprepossessing, light roll of nickels. Well, she didn't, that was all; she wasn't used to it. Rich—and who did that look like up at bat? Ira craned forward to see around a column. There. He could just barely descry the batter. Who was he? What player? He pushed his eyeglasses closer to his eyes, squinted, studied the batter knocking the dirt from his spikes with the end of his bat—

"Would yo' mind movin' over a seat?"

Odd, how nearby words could come through the great swell and roar of rooting fans watching the batter outrace a bobbled bunt. Odd too, he knew right away the voice was a woman's voice, and before he looked up, he recognized the voice of that of a Negro woman, and a young one. But he didn't know how pretty she was, until he raised his eyes and saw her: light-molasses brown, maple syrup he used to help pack in the hampers for Mr. Klein when he worked in Park & Tilford.

"Oh. Oh, yeah." Ira stood up. "I'm not supposed to be sittin' here anyway. I'm supposed to be hustlin'. I didn't know this was your seat."

"Yo' jest sit there if yo' want to. I'll slide by you." She did. Back of her knees rubbing his knees. Her sky-blue attendant's uniform was sliding over past him. He knew there were toilets in the upper ends of the wing. They had always been empty, except once or twice, he had noticed, during packed stands, attended by a heavy colored woman. This attendant was pretty, regular-featured, her speech smooth Southern, friendly. His heart began to hammer. Jesus. A scramble of goofy impulses commandeered his mind. He couldn't talk, only sidelong, tried looking dumb to see who was looking his way, their way. The game had reached a tense pass. And pass indeed: the pitcher was deliberately throwing wide to the next batter. Try to double-play next guy. The crowd booed the manager's strategem. Jesus, if any other hustler came up, and saw him sitting next to a—this high-yeller, comely colored girl—he'd better get up. Two more puffs. . . .

"That pipe sho' smell good. What they call that tobacco?"

"Yeah? What they call it is Prince Albert."

"Smell good." She pulled out a cigarette. "Yo' make much sellin' soda?" She held him there by speech alone, her tinkly musical dialect. "I see a lot o' yo' all sellin'. You sellin' all the time. I see money comin' in all the time."

"Yeah?" Well, it wasn't his fault she sat down beside him. So what? He prepared his excuse: he had just sat down for a second. "Well, maybe it looks like money comin' in. But all we get is ten percent of all we sell," he informed her, scarcely looking at her. "Ten cents on every dollar."

"Oh." She raised light brown eyes to the sign on his hat. "How much that make you make fo' the day?"

"I'm not a good hustler."

She laughed, high and lilting.

He hadn't meant to be funny. "Not as good as some of 'em, I mean. Like today," he explained, "I only sold maybe forty-five dollars' worth. Some of 'em sell twice—" He stopped because she brushed against him, moved her hand sleekly in her uniform pocket, rummaging—

"You want a light?" he asked.

"Mmm. I got matches. I know."

"Here's my pipe." He proffered the ember in the bowl. "Or do you want a regular light?"

"Mm-mm. No, that smell good."

She inclined her head, almost straight her hair, unkinked. Puffing her cigarette alight in his pipe bowl, she inflamed him as well. His breath became short, curtailed, inadequate to the demands of his thumping heart. "Wha—what do you make in there?" Rigid, Ira could barely indicate the ladies' rest room at very end, the uppermost walkway.

"I gets fi' dollars a day an' tips. An' ain't very many tips. Man tol' me in the office I'd make twice as much in tips. And I ain't made over a dollar. First time I tried it, but I ain't doin' it again. They tell you anything." She laughed.

"Maybe down in the lower stands they do better." Ira looked straight ahead.

"I don't know. I jest know I need the money. Look what my little dog did to me this mo'nin'. Scratch my bes' stockin' befo' I go to work."

"What d'you mean?"

"Look at the run in it." She showed the calf of her leg, round, muscular, honey-colored skin visible under the shirred run.

Blood pounded, rammed against skull. The packed grandstands below fluttered and swam on the thump of his own pulse. They all could hear it, couldn't they? The rush of blood hammering, hear it all the way to the pinch hitter out there, him with two bats swinging as he walked to the batter's box, the home-plate umpire who came into view to brush the dust off home plate, yes, the batboy trotting by, couldn't they hear? He bent down, dropped his hand below the handle of the tray of soda—touched the bare caramel-hued skin. "Run," he said, his tongue just moving of its own accord—but never had he felt so starkly certain before, so animal-certain. Why? What was he suddenly? Because she was colored? He didn't know. "Ballpark's the right place for a run." His jumbled thoughts found words.

"They goes together, you mean. Tha's right." She suddenly laughed her high, fluted laugh. Would anyone look their way? But no one did. Pinch hitter in the batter's box, and the crowd roaring in wild hope. "You cute," she said.

"You too." And now there was nothing more to say, nothing that didn't go beyond saying, beyond barrier of spoken small talk into commitment. "You live around here?"

Her shapely hand, fingernails above the same rosy flesh as his, floated to her temple, smoothed the long waves of barely tinted coppery hair. "I live in Harlem."

"Where? I do too."

"You do? Where you live?"

"On East 119th Street."

"East 119th Street? I live on West 137th. West of Lenox."

"Listen," Ira heard himself saying, heard a frightened automaton within him speaking with temerity, "you want me to come to where you live?"

"Oh, yo' just foolin'. Yo' jest like the rest of 'em."

"No, I'm not." She had put him to the test, put him on his mettle before he knew it.

"How I know you ain't?"

Bewildered boldness answered, "I got a lucky break today. I'll show you. Look." He drew the green roll of quarters out of his pocket, let her peek. "Look at that."

"What dem?"

"Quarters. Ten dollars' worth." He opened his curled hand wider.

"Mm-mm! They nice." She looked from the roll of coins to him. "Yo' comin' with them?"

"I hope so. Comin' with them." The roll of coins was already like a hard-on as he stared at her. Just like a dusky shade on pink skin, hers. And she must have known it suited her too: round pink disks covering her earlobes, a hint of pink under her attendant's uniform, cloudy pink against taffy. "You ain't talkin' about all o' ten dollars, are you?" he said, adopting dialect. To a mingled, myriad-throated cry below, the pinch hitter swung and missed, hopped to regain his balance. "I gotta go. How much you charge?"

She laughed, with faintest hint of embarrassment; and after a moment of hesitation, "Three dollah."

"I got that right here. That's only twelve of 'em. So where do I go?"

"Oh, you jest foolin'."

"I tell ye I got the dough." He pocketed the roll of quarters, searched under him, gripped the handle of his tray. "It's just that I've never been to a—you know."

"Well, I ain't regular. I don' walk the streets."

"All right. So where?"

"You goin' remember?"

"I'll remember. I'll write it down as soon as I get upstairs."

"Pearl Canby," she said. "Two thirty-seven West a Hundred Thirty-seven. West o' Lenox. Room eighteen. You remember all that?"

He repeated the number. "At night?"

"Uh-huh. Like after nine or ten. That make sure I'm home."

"Am I right?" Ira repeated the directions.

"Room eighteen," she corrected. "Ground flo'. My little dog bark when he hea' you, but don' pay him no mind. He jest bark."

A long fly ball— "All right." Ira stood up, stepped into the aisle, repressed his cry of wares as he climbed to the walk at the top behind the last tier. The ball went sailing to Bob Meusel of the phenomenal throwing arm—not a hit, but a good sacrifice fly. Would the runner at third make a try for the plate, or hold? Ira didn't dare look. Her name and address preempted all else. Pearl Canby. Two three seven one three seven, he kept repeating to himself; until he got his stub of pencil out: to jot in haste on the back of the menu on his soda placard, standing on a cement runway behind the last tier, with the dense roar of the crowd in front of him. Would he go? Nah. Yeah. She was right. And three whole dollars yet! Wait a minute. He reached into his pants pocket, felt his warm pipe. No, it wasn't burning. But ah! That slippery roll, slippery, stiff roll. Gee, so that was what the lucky break was for: Mrs. Stevens should know. Three dollars: twelve quarters made three dollars. Ten dollars was forty quarters. He was flush, Jesus, he was flush. Was he game enough? Jeez, she was cute: peach color nearly.

There was McGraw, right at home plate, arms akimbo, the tunbellied bastard Shakespeare called Falstaff arguing with the ump. Guess what? Meusel's throw from outfield must have beaten the runner to the plate. And look at that crowd of black faces in the top-floor window of the mortar-lumpy wall above the parking lot outside the ballpark: gleamy teeth and brown skin and gleamy eyeballs. All excited, gleefully meshed together. Jesus, to be one of them. Just for that compactness, that oneness. . . .

I can't do anything with it, Ecclesias.

—No? Why not?

You know very well why not: the stile I have set in my way.

—Something not there is scarcely a stile. Or do you mean style?

Oh, no. The blockade, stockade. The taboo. The unspoken. The unspeakable. Do you have any advice? ... Do you?

—Only that the unspoken and unspeakable must become spoken and speakable, and the taboo broken and ignored. This has been taking place over the months and years.

I realized that.

IX

It wasn't the silly two dollars and twenty-five cents he had paid her, before dropping his pants, paying for a condom retail, re-tail. The whole thing had turned out to be like a slash through his existence, not delirious, not something stunning—oh, no, not even entitled to the word "sordid"; just untidy, sleazy, at best a cross between feverishness and something damn near somnambulism.

After the Friday-night supper, the traditional Friday-night supper, the same, ever the same. Pop was as usual in a relaxed mood, hastily sniffing *challah* in order to relieve the sting of a dab of the freshly ground horseradish he had just eaten with the *gefilte* fish. And the flavorless boiled chicken. Oh, hell, the same: *Fraytik af der nakht is dokh yeder yid a maylekh*, went the ditty: every Jew was a king on Friday night. He was some Jew, he was, he, not Pop: a circumcised Prince of Wales.

He had delayed, wavered, couldn't make up his mind ... observed the way the melted wax slipped down the two candles, until the wax itself provided a warm spillway over the lips of the golden brass candlesticks: formed pearly stalactites. And Pearl was her name too.

Pearly, pearly, seminal goo,
I got a hard-on for you.

How painful were the associations that you couldn't avoid, that intruded unbidden into your consciousness, like waiting for the other shoe to drop. The channel in the mind had been dug, and there was no refilling it. How could you undig the dug, the ditch? And there went the associations unreeling again.

He sat there long after the last petal of candlelight guttered out, couldn't get himself to break the spell of even a vitiated *Shabbes*. To go—oh, if he went now, right now, he could make it: make it easily to the 135th Street station. Stride over to Lenox Avenue, and take the Lenox Avenue subway. Two stations. Nine o'clock and west of Lenox. But the worst of it was, as so often happened to him, to the seemingly easy arrangements he made, she no longer appeared in the upper stand as attendant in the ladies' room. He never saw her in the ballpark again, as he hoped to, in his uncertain, ever temporizing frame of mind. He hoped to be reencouraged, coaxed, urged on. But she wasn't there. She wasn't even there the rest of that same afternoon, in a sense: so that he could speak to her again, sit down negligently in the same spot he had sat before. No. A portly black man, light in color as she was, and attired obviously well, in a tan suit and a panama hat, despite the advent of fall, easy, well-fitting, tailored suit yes, sat there all the rest of the afternoon, in intimate, relaxed conversation. Ira felt a twinge of jealousy. And after that, the next afternoon, only one of those fat black women occupied her place, and again, two or three times before the World Series ended.

One Hundred Thirty-fifth Street. Crosstown trolley there also, Ira knew, like 125th Street, like Jewish 116th Street: promenade street, window-shopping street; maybe now becoming the dividing line between white and black. He recalled Farley's more than mere annoyance whenever he mentioned "they" were moving downtown. "They" threatened his family's home. The safe old brownstone, on 129th and Madison Avenue, and the undertaking parlor there were sure to be engulfed by the spreading sea of color. Nearest he'd ever seen Farley look so hostile, so baffled, as if his father's business worries had filtered down into the son's consciousness, undermined the son's security. . . . And Park & Tilford too, on 126th and Lenox Avenue, gone, the decorous, fancy grocery store, gone, never to return. He hadn't been in that section of town in months, years, not since the time he used to hunt up different libraries in hope of discovering new brands, new series, of fairy books: in the years of myth and innocence—before the Great War. No, not innocence, ignorance. How could you be innocent on 119th Street? Pearl. Mulatto. Octoroon. Pretty, milk-chocolate mellow, smooth high yellow, that skin under the stocking run: three dollars the price, the cost, and he had the money, even had a few of the same quarters left. "You're just foolin'," she had laughed, laughed seriously; she wouldn't believe him. Well? She was right. He really didn't have to go. Ah, the hell with it. Three bucks, and way up there in black Harlem. Beside, he'd never laid a woman, a real full-grown woman with big tits. Maybe if he did, he'd, maybe if he did, he'd—so what was the difference? That nobody else did it? Did what he did; that it was bad, double bad, double, triple, quadruple bad? Horrible bad. Unspeaka-babble bad. Abomination bad. He was fated to do it. That was what the river said, when he stood on the flat diving rock. Now the comely, café-au-lay-he-oh, la-ay he-e oh waited on 137th Street. A light, hardly almond. Compare that to . . . his pig-men-tation. Yeah.

The dishes done, Mom and Pop divided the Yiddish newspaper between them. They read. They read what? All of that immense world of 1922, all that was happening in *Yiddishkeit*, in *goyishkeit*, in the United States here with President Harding, with his Cal Koylitch for vice-president, and there in Russia with Lenin and Trotsky, and the hundred thousand other events he paid no attention to: the killing of scabs in the coal mine strike in Illinois. And about Sacco and Vanzetti, the poor Italians, accused of murdering that paymaster in South Braintree, Mass., just because they were wops, anarchists, in jail. And how more and more all over Europe the Jews were being persecuted. Open up his Spanish book, or better, his chemistry book in which he was floundering so, with its moles and molals and molar solutions and normal solutions, and gram molecular weights. Even his English book: try to work out a secret code—that was the assignment over the weekend—a cryptogram, like the one in Poe's "Gold Bug"—but he stunk at that. Or in lieu of that, he was given the choice of writing a book review, and he stunk at that too: underlying ideas, character, local color, suspense, anh! He could get it out of the way, though, if he did it now—not plane geometry, no. He saved that for the last: that was *tsimmes,* his dessert, but get the others out of the way. . . .

Pearl. Her face seemed to grow lighter all the time: Pearly gates, not bad. He could still make it, even now, without hurrying. . . . You got nerve? Phantasmagoria, said Poe. What a word. Phantasmagloria *in excelsis deo* on the church's high obtuse-angled lintel. Trouble was Pop had switched the last few Sundays with those Catholic police and firemen and who knew what other communion breakfasts and fraternities and Rotary Club and from Tammany Hall in Coney Island to "extra jops" at evening banquets for Elks and Shriners and Odd Fellows. So Pop was home when Mom went out shopping for the week. What lousy luck. Ira had hoped maybe after school, but Jesus, no luck. Hoped for a chance to flip up the little goddamn brass nipple that loosed the tongue in the lock. He thought of the goddamnedest things: but boy, that was exultation, wow! When he snapped the lock in the door. But Jesus, no chance; it hadn't happened. Saturdays were no good; there was always the Harlem Five-and-Dime, where she worked all day. And tomorrow a college football game for him to hustle at. Even so, there would be time. . . . So on Sunday, no belly lox from Park Avenue, no fresh bagels, no news from Baba, Zaida, Mamie, the aunts, the uncles, and who was pregnant, to listen to afterward, could make up for the lost chance, even though he felt worry-free afterward, and thankful not to be gripped in the cruel clutch of doubt, instead of feeling wicked. Still, what the hell was wicked? . . .

So it would be a long walk—no, no, a short ride, a ride; so beat it over to Lenox Avenue.

Mom looked up when Ira got to his feet, but Pop only glanced sideways past the curved sheet of newspaper.

"I'm just going to go out," Ira said. "Maybe I'll go across the street to the candy store."

"You need to stay with those gamblers?" Pop queried, frowning. "You'll grow into a gambler."

"I won't grow into a gambler."

"No? Keep on going there, and you'll see."

Mom intervened, "Believe me, if you would go visit Zaida and Baba, you'd perform a *mitzva*. They haven't seen you in I don't know when."

"What do they want me for?"

"Go. Only yesterday Baba said to me, 'When your sonny-lad has no money, he comes to visit us. Now that he works and earns a few dollars, he has no need of us.' You know, my son," Mom summed up, "you're a little like your father."

"Aha!" Pop's head snapped back. "Immediately she hales in his father."

"It's not true? When you need somebody, you pet and stroke him, no?"

"Leah, it's a Friday night. Spare me your recitals, your complaints."

Ira raised his voice impatiently. "I've been here in the same house already since I came home from school. I want to go out."

"Then go out. But why do you have to go into that candy store with its gambling den in the rear to play cards?" Pop demanded sharply. "And lose money to those sharpers? You think I can't tell from your long nose when you lose money?"

"All right, then I'll go somewhere else. I'll walk." Ira shifted tactics.

"Don't you want a coat? Nights are growing keen," Mom suggested.

"Well." He stood motionless a second or two, thoughts almost crackling audibly in his ears with the swiftness of projected eventualities. "No—okay. I'll put on that little sweater under my jacket. So I'll walk," he directed a faint jibe at Pop.

"Don't roam about too long. You're a toiler these days. You have to go to work tomorrow."

"Yeh."

"He toils through thick and thin," Pop scouted. "Once a week, through fast and loose. Wait, just wait," he prolonged dire prophesy, "he'll have a wife and child on his hands someday. He'll learn what it is to toil; he'll learn the affliction of running from place to place in search of livelihood. Shall I wait in Local Number One to be called? Shall I run to Waiters Local Two?"

"And why do you think I strive?" Mom asked—and answered herself. "Only to keep him from becoming that kind of menial toiler."

"Af mayne playtses."

There he went again: on his shoulders.

"Why does one have children? To whom will you turn in old age?" Mom contended.

"Hah! As long as I can serve a customer, as long as I can go on the dining-room floor, I need no one to help me. In old age. He'll help me? The Messiah will come," Pop chortled unpleasantly. "When that day comes that I have to turn to him for aid, may God help me indeed. You think I'm like your father?"

"Now he brings in my father," Mom retorted. "What have you got against my father?"

"Nothing. To find a more pious Jew you would have to search every cranny in America. But has he done a day's work since he came to this golden land? Has he ever done a day's work, even in Galitzia?"

"Well, with him," Mom condoned, "his study of holiness provides us, his wife and many daughters, with the right to enter paradise."

"And you believe it?"

"No. But then, God forgive me, I'm half a *goya.*"

Pop smiled sardonically, jerked his chin up. "Half a *goya.* But the other half is a Jew, no? Then which half recognizes the pious old fraud for the shirker he is?"

Disgruntled, silent, Ira lined his jacket with his lightweight gray sweater. The way they argued made him almost lose interest in his venture. Almost. But boy, now if ever. Those pink earrings. Pearl in pink earrings. Three bucks from a ten-dollar roll of free quarters. How it went together, one innuendo—was that the word?—nuance, nuance, no. Suggestion. Risky risqué. . . Don't stand there blowing, flattening afflatus between the edge of teeth and lip. Go find her.

But when he got there, entered the muted, still, stuffy hallway, knocked at the door in the rear of the "basement" floor, Pearl's number, the black girl who answered his knock, the black girl who opened the door was—was scrawny and homely and black-coffee brown.

"Pearl?" he asked, gaping in uncertainty. "I'm sorry. Isn't there a Pearl here?"

"You mean the girl who live hea' befo'?"

"I don't know. Yeah, I guess so. She told me she did."

"She found her a man. They said she gone live with him, ef that's the one yo' mean."

"Pearl?"

"I didn't pay no mind to her name." Asperity gleamed from her dark brown features. "Come on in. You don' want to stan' outchea. You lookin' fo' a girl?"

"Yeah, but I—"

"Yo' get what you come fo'. Come on in." She opened the door wider. "I'm Theodora."

"Theodora?" he repeated stupidly, stock-still.

"That's what I said. This is my place."

Her scrawny body, as she turned to indicate her lodgings, appeared to be negligently, yet acceptably clothed: a white, open-throated blouse over a flat torso, a maroon skirt above bare, dark feet in sky-blue, fur-trimmed house slippers. Sinewy, undernourished, or just skinny? In her twenties still. He wouldn't know her tomorrow; he wouldn't know her in an hour, that swart visage, skin barely sheathing tendons. . . .

"Ain't you comin' in?"

"I musta made a mistake. I was lookin' for Pearl."

"You lookin' fo' somebody that ain't heah. But I'm heah. Come on in, honey, I take care o' you. Come in." She stepped over the threshold, encircled his waist with thin arm. "Yo' jes' a mite shy, ain't you?" She ushered him in. "No need to be. I know yo' kind. I like yo' kind, honey. Yo' ain't the kind that like to slam a woman in bed. See ef I don't treat you right." She shut the door. "Yo' didn't make no mistake, honey. That girl an' her dog went off with the service agency man."

"The who?"

"The man who hire her. He cullud too. But that don' matter. You can get a little lovin' rightcha, honey." Deftly, she undid the single catch in front of her maroon skirt, held it to one side before dropping it on a sofa. As if she had stepped out from between portieres in a single step, she stood with lean legs forked from a jet-black muff—under a white blouse: "You got it, honey. The nearer the bone, the sweeter the meat."

"Yeah, but I—" Shaken, Ira stared, wavered, stared, assailed by a last sortie of caution. "So all right. So how much you charge?"

"All depend on what kind o' fun you wants to pay fo'." She could make her black muff squirm.

"Just plain."

"I gets two dollars an' twenty-fi' cents." Her attitude indicated payment in advance. "An' twenty-fi' cent mo' fo' a bag."

He hesitated just briefly, but he paid her, a single greenback and the balance in quarters—and an extra quarter for a condom.

So that was it, that was it. He knew all along that was the way it was done, but he'd never done it. She showed him. In the depth of her dark, skinny, upraised thighs, legs doubled to receive him, forked like a mahogany-human oarlock. And could she wriggle it! She rowed him home. He rode her, but she rowed him. Scull, skull, her workaday, dark face opposite his, until . . . his oncoming orgasm transformed the face he stared at into something desirable, something beautiful, her body his to lift in his embrace, and despite fleeting awareness of the false endearments on her full lips, his to will they were genuine. He pumped furiously, reached culmination . . . and it was all over.

In the minute or two afterward, buttoning up his fly, even through eagerness to get out, came inklings of his surroundings: how stuffy her room was, not a window open, and the weather wasn't so cool yet. And all kinds of hangings around the walls too, *shmattas*, Mom would have said; was that to muffle the sound? Who put the *shma* in *shmattas*, oh, boy. Like a séance place. When had he ever been to a fortune-teller place? He never had. Seen it in a movie, maybe, a vaudeville skit, a mystery. Everything in deep shadow as if starved for light. Was every one of the rooms like that, the whole house a cathouse? She was friendly afterward, kind, cheerful, yes sympathetic, giggled watching him wriggle into his jacket. Sensation, that was it, that's what he bought. Blew his nuts into her. Oh, nothing as excited as he had been in the Polo Grounds that moment when he felt the skin on Pearl's leg through the run in her stocking. Oh, no.

And Jesus, nothing like Pearl's long-waved copper-tinted wealth of tresses. Instead, on Theodora's twat and head, when he clumsily caressed them: fine-drawn wires, a wiry poll, a wiry bush. His palms would remember their surprise of contact long afterward. What would Pearl's wavy coppery locks have been like? Well, it couldn't be helped. But still, he couldn't resist the impulse afterward—what a strange thing: he had kissed her on the brow, her round, shiny, mahogany brow. How she had giggled. He was silly. Sure. But he felt that way: kindly disposed. Why? Because she was considerate, she understood he was a novice, or what? Because he felt guilty? But he didn't. He felt foolish. No transgression (he was well versed in that). No, just fornication in the dim light of that tiny little rose table lamp, her thin shadow thighs up, and yes, penumbra about umbra pussy, not the weak contrast as when there was only fuzz, but total eclipse. Well, so that was it: going to a whore. A businesslike screw, orgasm, cost you, with the condom, two and a half bucks.

And it was over so fast. Jesus, he just pumped a few times, and it was over; he just, and it was—but it was (and his eyes fixed anew in astonishment, a turbid astonishment at his ignorance—and the simplicity of the discovery). Oh, he had plans now as soon as—oh, it was a little squishy, but it would make it easy, once he tried, wheedled, and she succumbed. You heard the noise she made, wooo, wooo, wooo, as she did only that one time, woooah! Wooooah! Wooo-a-a-ah! Now he'd tell her, the right way. That's what you have to do. But now you'd have to, now that she got monthlies, now you'd have to . . . yeah. Oh, Jesus, if he ever, Jesus, if he ever. Nah! But that was it. Jesus, you dope. You saw dogs—yeah, but that wasn't the way it started— Jesus, you gotta try it. Soon as—tell her you found out it's altogether different. Then maybe anytime. Don't have to beg. Oh, gee. Anytime when any chance.

He quickened his pace, as if the opportunity were already present. Dark 119th Street, ahead of him, walking at a good clip toward the Cut, the dark trestle, the way she was on the bed—he smirked at himself—her twat licorice embedded in dusky chocolate.

He crossed Park Avenue, stepped up on the curb, before Yussel's house, as they called the massive five-flight pile of grimy brick on the corner right next to the trestle, the home of Yussel, the landlord.

Now wait a minute. What was it? In the winter, when he wasn't hustling, and he was broke, and couldn't buy a condom. . . So he'd have to be careful. That was it. Just be real careful. Wait till he told her. Oh, he'd be careful. Yeah, yeah. But better keep up hustling even in the winter: the prizefights in Madison Square Garden, the wrestling matches, when they featured Zbysko. How much were they? You couldn't say rubbers, scum bags, to a druggist. You had to say safeties, you had to say condoms—what was the name on that little tin he saw her take one out of? Name over the crested helmet? Trojans. Trojans. That was it. But why Trojans? They lost the war, didn't they?

X

"Absolute, absolute, 'solute," Mr. Fay, Ira's teacher in American history, would say when stressing a point. The Louisiana Purchase, Gadsden Compromise, Tippecanoe and Tyler too, about Henry Clay or the great Indian chief Tecumseh, about General Grant at Cold Harbor. Or old Thomas Jefferson lying on his deathbed at Monticello, where he could watch the American flag undulate on its staff, old Thomas Jefferson already haunted by premonitions of the impending disaster inherent in black slavery—Mr. Fay, with his gray mustache, so dignified, tall, spare, an American, conducting the class in American history.

"Hello, Mr. Fay," grinning, embarrassed in his hustler's white jacket and cap with the frankfurter menu card on it, while with both hands he held extended in front of him the handle of the long hot dog basket and rolls, Ira hailed his history teacher at the Princeton-Columbia football game. What a change took place in Mr. Fay when Ira greeted him. No longer encountering one of his students qua student, no longer juxtaposed by classroom polarity, but instead a football fan, there with his son, Ira guessed, a loyal supporter of his college football team at an Ivy League game, the teacher—and his student, a hot dog vendor. "How are you, Mr. Fay?"

"Is that you, Stigman? Why, yes, yes, it is! Business going briskly, eh?"

"Oh, so-so, Mr. Fay."

"Good weather for it, I should think."

"Yes, sir." Cordiality and laughter.

It was now November, the first week of November, and fall's thin, sharp edge—oh, one could feel it even in cities, even in New York streets—thin, honed edge shaving away the last of balmy Indian summer, slitting the last ties that bound one season to the next. That was the way autumn freed itself, Ira daydreamed, hiking home from the everlasting 116th Street and Lenox Avenue subway station. "Autumn" was a nicer word than "fall"—he glanced up at the windows of gray old P.S. 103. How long ago, how far away 6B, gee, when he was a kid. With the—oh, look at them, paper pumpkins in the window, and witches wearing cone hats riding broomsticks. And turkey gobblers in the taller windows, and more paper pumpkins with triangles for eyes and nose. Halloween over, and Thanksgiving coming in. Once, when he wore kneepants, he and the other kids on 119th Street had socked one another with flour-filled—or ash-filled—long black stockings on Halloween. *Goyish* holiday Halloween was, but not Thanksgiving. No more. It could be Jewish, could be anyone's holiday. "Tenksgeeve"; even Mom had learned to say it.

He was thinking, no what was he thinking? Autumn, with his razor-edged cutlass between his teeth, bandanna over his head boarding the good ship *Summer:* what kind of ship? Sloop or galleon, frigate, schooner, pinnace, boy, the names that ships once had; they were so beautiful. *Brigantine. Caravel. Argosy,* Antonio called his in *The Merchant of Venice* . . . from the Greek Argonauts. . . .

Ira had continued to hustle, and not solely on Saturday football games, but on other occasions.

There was Madison Square Garden: the prizefights! "Lade-e-z and gentlemen." Joe Humphreys, the announcer, in the middle of the ring, took off his straw kelly, and with it damped down the rowdy crowd. Stentorian (oh, he knew that word): "In this corner, wearing purple trunks, the worthy contender for the welterweight crown, Cyclone Mulligan, at one hundred and forty-three pounds and a *hawf!*" Oh, how that low-browed throng of spectators loved that *hawf;* nearly everyone echoed it, Joe Humphreys's fancy, high-toned, Bostonian Brahmin *hawf*. Hawking soda pop at the Garden, between rounds, then ducking down out of the fans' way, squatting on the steps; they'd lynch you if you didn't. But he was absolutely riveted by the spectacle anyway, watching Benny Leonard with his black hair slicked down, and never mussed, slipping a right hook, dodging a left. What muscles, how they glided under the skin, bunched and rippled. And then again, peddling "red hots" at football games: given a hot dog basket and hawking: "Get your red hots here!" And they weren't any more red hot in their double containers, after a short while in the chilly grandstands, than—than your nose.

But if he bought a hot dog himself, at a football game, just as soon as he came out of the depot, it was still hot, and he could get three rolls with it. The checkers didn't count rolls, only franks; so it made a meal: three rolls squashed around one hot dog, little bit of meat, mustard, plenty of free sauerkraut, and gobble—lurking in an out-of-the-way dugout—while he watched Kaw of Cornell make those wonderful broken-field runs. Or the Four Horsemen, they were called, Notre Dame's backfield playing against West Point: the cadets in gray uniforms, like those worn in the War of 1812. West Point, that faded dream, and those beautiful girls, *shiksas*, and gentile people with the colorful pennants, all jumping up and down cheering in those puffed-up, cozy raccoon coats. But Ira knew too much; that was the trouble. He knew too much that was sad, that was wrong, blighting knowledge, yes.

Still Ira made a few bucks, at the same time that he went to high school, earned a few dollars once a week anyway, and maybe a weeknight at Madison Square Garden too, skimped on his homework assignment, unless it was a Friday, skipped downtown, and waited for Benny Lass at the main entrance. . . .

He was a junior, and not too good in any subject, save one. And in that he got A, A, A, every quiz, every test, every recitation: it was the second half of plane geometry, the concluding semester of a sophomore course, but he was retarded because he had lost a term when he was expelled from Stuyvesant. But, ah, for once Ira felt in command, for once he sensed the unity of the subject he studied, the coherence of every part of it: oh, gee, he hated to have the subject end.

So there he was, Ira at the beginning of November 1922, the latter part of his sixteenth year, and technically a junior at DeWitt Clinton, though not quite, Ira sauntering through 119th Street homeward toward the gray trestle on Park Avenue. And with not a worry in the world, not an overt worry in the world. With a canker in the soul, yes, but then he kept that under control by buying a little tin of two condoms now and then, because most of the time Sundays had become his again. Pop had shifted from evening banquets to regular breakfast communion "extras" in Rockaway Beach. He earned a little less than he did at the evening banquets in Coney Island. But he hated the stairs in the Coney Island banquet hall. The Rockaway dining room had no stairs between it and the kitchen. That was worth a dollar, a dollar and a half less. So Sunday mornings, in the fall and winter, Ira could lie abed, usually awake, lurking, wait till Mom took her black oilcloth shopping bag, and went shopping for the week among the pushcarts under the Cut.

"Minnie. Okay?"

She said all kinds of dirty words at first; where did she learn them? After he showed her how different it was, "Fuck me, fuck me good!" He wished she wouldn't, though he liked it. He wished she wouldn't, because it incited him, spurred him on too much. He wished she wouldn't, though he grinned about it afterward: so *prust*, as they would say in Yiddish, so coarse: "Fuck me, fuck me good." It made him come before he wanted to, though he knew he ought to come fast to be safe, but not so fast as her dirty words made him, that and her crying out, "Ah, ah, oooh wah, ooowah!" Still, it made him feel proud too, and even prouder when she almost whooped with rapture, "Oooh, you're a good fucker. Oooh, don't get off yet!" But he had to, right away quick, as soon as it was over, quick and into his own bed, or start dressing. And he hardly had to coax anymore. She was ready as soon as he snapped the lock; a minute after Mom left, he pressed the little brass of the lock down: tink-tunk. Everything with celerity, everything coordinated. Nearly. She slid out of her folding cot, and into Mom and Pop's double bed beside it; while he dug for the little tin of Trojans in his pants pocket, little aluminum pod at two for a quarter. And then she watched him, strict and serious, her face on the fat pillow, her hazel eyes, myopic and close together—

THE FAMILY OF IRA STIGMAN

Ira's Mother's Family Tree

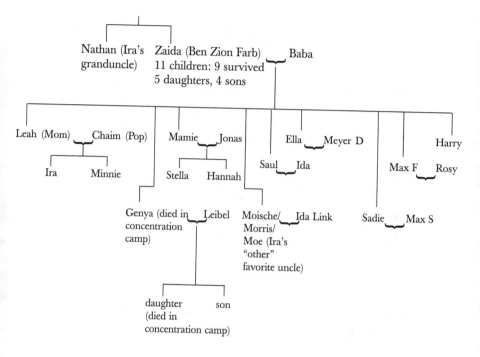

Ira's Father's Family Tree

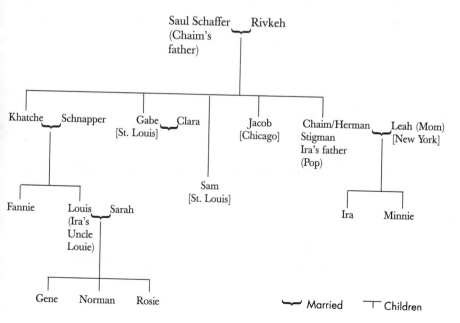

like Pop's—watched him roll a condom on his hard-on, readying her pussy while he hurried toward her, opening her flower to him when he reached the bed. What dirty words she greeted him with: "Fuck me like a hoor. No, no kisses. I don't want no kisses. Just fuck me good."

"All right. All right."

"That rubber all right? I don't want that white stuff in me—"

"No, no. I just bought 'em. Okay. A-a-h."

"O-oh. They're like the ones before?"

"Yeah. Real Trojans. Yeah. Come on."

"O-oh. So you can give me a dollar, too."

"All right. Later. Later."

Afterward she might even haggle with him for more than a dollar. "You worked in Madison Square Garden last night. I want a new sash on me; I want to get a wide sash with a bow."

"How much d'you think I made yesterday? Two dollars and a half! You made some money yourself working in the five and ten Saturday."

"Mama doesn't give me anything. Everything is for you. For you and for her Persian lamb coat—I don't count."

"Aw, come on." He had to get things settled fast, because you never knew when Mom would be back. If you argued too long, and delayed until after Mom returned, he'd have to sneak the money to Minnie anyway, but she would look sulky, cheated. And that was bad. Hearing them disputing once, Mom had looked puzzled. "All right, all right. I'll give you the dollar and a half. Only don't make a fuss. Jesus!"

—Oh, horror, horror.

That's right, Ecclesias. That's why I turned to you. As a buffer against my demon, my *dybbuk*, my nemesis—haven't I changed? *O me, Angnel, come ti muti!*

—Your pseudo-recondite self.

But I *have* changed, haven't I? Still, for all that, I could sit back this very moment, and raise my eyes to the window, the curtained window above the word processor, above imaginary you, Ecclesias, and wish myself fervently never to have been.

—And well you might. But what good does your fervent wishing do? Evidently something blocks the act itself. What is it?

I have an illusion I owe something to the species, as a specimen.

—Your offering may be of value. There's no telling. In any case, since you've chosen this mode of oblation, chosen to live, to scrive, then there's no undoing the done. There's only the outwearing it, the outwearying it, the attenuating of remorse, and guilt. That's all you can do, as far as you personally are concerned. And of course, there's always room for enhanced comprehension. How deep can one delve into platitude? As to your wish never to have been, that will soon be granted, if that's any comfort.

It isn't; it isn't the same thing at all.

—There's no expunging of the been, of the past, if that's what you mean. How can you expunge that which has ceased to be? Carry on, as the British say. What else is left? At worst—what is it at worst? Senescent erotic fantasy. At best, you've breached a mighty barrier within yourself, and done so, witting or unwitting, for the benefit of others. If in your own lifetime you've achieved an accession of reality—to give it a name, and a clumsy one—a long-belated transformation of view that conforms more closely with the actual, that's all the consolation available to you at this stage of the game.

Was grinsest du mir, heilige Schädel? said Goethe, said Faust (said Ira?) to the skull on the table.

—Did Faust say that? But I still don't know why you're quoting Goethe.

Yes, contented was he, and why not, when everything was under control. It was like a sneaky mini-family, a tabooed one, and discovered by him, by cunning exploitation of accident, to seal off a little enclave within, utterly unspeakable, vicious, yes, near brutally wicked, oh, wicked was too insipid, all the evil consummate, rolled up, concentrate, essence, wild, and made him feel so depraved that anything went, anything he could think of, rending all the enclosures: Mephisto wrapped in a bedsheet in front of a mirror, the pier glass mirror, in a moment of playfulness: "Look at that, Minnie. I'm a Roman in a Roman toga, sticking out with a rubber Trojan."

And she giggled, but only enough not to delay proceedings. "Don't fool around. Hurry up."

Wasn't he lucky though?

Even at this late hour, and yours truly a man near eighty; for these things are like to one who has sniffed the coocoo, and never lost the beatitude; that was the worst of it, the ambivalence of sin, if you call it that, of depravity, the amphi-balance of it, the Escher fugue, the optical illusion, the Jekyll-Hyde slide, the *fleur du mal.*

Lucky, supremely lucky, the luck of having Pop a waiter, on a Sunday morning again, and long gone to Rockaway Beach to wait on table on a breakfast "benket." Well, it got so actually it wasn't limited to Sunday mornings. Hell, no. At sixteen going on seventeen, and lusty, and Minnie at fourteen plus, and now in Julia Richmond High School. And she was dating boys, and going out a bit, and to dances, and someone must have broken her cherry already, and he was the one reaping the full benefit, because there was never any blood, though she would never let him inside before. Maybe the guy had hurt her. "No, just between. I don't want that white stuff in me."

And then she finally surrendered, after he told her about Theodora, and how it was done, how it had to be done, for her to get the real thrill he got out of it, not her way, and how it was safe, it was safe, too.

She knew about it. "So you got one o' those?" she asked.

"Yeah." His head began to reel.

She knew. She knew. "So is it a good one?" White-and-pink cheeks had she, somewhat a severe face, cold, unresponsive, even for a fourteen-year-old kid, translucent hazel eyes. She wrinkled her nose skeptically under wavy red bangs. "Is it brand-new? It's clean?"

"Brand-new," he protested, and more vehemently, "What d'you think? I'll use a secondhand one? I'll show it to you. Look."

And almost as if against her will, but consumed with need, want, heat, his pitiless aphrodisiac wheedling, she stood up, from homework table, green-oilcloth-covered—she made for the closed bedroom door, closed, now that the other rooms were cold, and only the kitchen gas-heated. "So come on."

What delirium, surprise and dividend, even though she was so peremptory, serious; yet the green-painted blistery kitchen walls did a jig, a veritable jig—still, *she* didn't notice anything, he everything: the walls dimpled, the walls jigged, they rippled to and fro as the little brass nipple loosed the tongue-plunk of the lock, close sesame, magic-charm plunk that freed the walls from being walls, changed them to shimmering, rich green drapes. Freed them and him and everybody, liberated, when you were really going to do it to her, sink it inside your sister, really into Minnie. She was letting him into her. What luck he'd bought the little tin, after—after Theodora. Yip silently with joy. Yip, yip, yahoo. Look at those walls doing a Highland fling in ecstasy, a lilt in kilts. Yippee.

Delirious he, so prosaic she, as if begrudging a needed item, a staple of oestrus. But what the hell, begrudging or not, his, his to have, to have, to fuck her on edge of bed, his bed, first bedroom, on his bed athwart, just two feet away hardly from airshaft window, and the cold no longer felt. Don't lose a second before Mom came home. For a minute into Minnie, sink it in her, sin it in her. Quick, go. O-o-oh, look at her: carmine between lifted thighs. Quick! Roll it on, pale sheath over fiery shaft.

"Okay?" Ira asked when they came back out of the bedroom into the kitchen. He'd been super-lucky: the second time this week. The first time was in Mom and Pop's bed Sunday—that was good. He had used his last condom, but was it ever good! She made so much noise he was nearly afraid. So early in the morning. And on Sunday. All the neighbors home. Jesus, if they ever guessed he was doing it to his own sister. He fucks his sister, the micks would say. Hey. How about us gittin' a piece of her ass, too? He knew them.

"Okay?" Ira repeated when Minnie didn't answer—though he suspected it wasn't.

"Oh, don't ask me. It was all right." She sounded none too ravished, as she followed him into the kitchen. "Sometimes you get bigger at the end," she complained. She yanked at her stocking.

"I had to hurry," he conciliated. Actually, he felt sheepish, because the surprising opportunity had caught him unprepared. It had overaroused his ardor with wild, evil greed of transgression, the dire joy of perpetration. The flood of the heinous had been too much for him to withstand. He had barely synchronized with her. "You wanna try again?" he offered belatedly. "I can wash the rubber again."

"No, I don't wanna." She cut off further allusion sharply. "Don't wash it again. Don't do me no favors—" She halted abruptly. "What d'you mean, again? Wasn't it a new one? You said it was brand-new."

"Oh, sure, sure," he lied vehemently. He had washed it once.

"Then I don't wanna talk about it."

"Yeah? So okay. Okay," he snapped at her. Hell with her. Main concern was to get back to the kitchen table speedily. Roll back the tongue of the lock fast. Compose everything back to normal. Get to the toilet with the squishy condom. . . . He opened the toilet door, exited from the kitchen, dropped the rubber in round miniwhirlpool, flushed it down in noisy maelstrom, out of sight of the dingy white enamel.

And back in the kitchen again, he sat down to his textbooks, features engrossed, maybe even hostile, as he often was, when she asked him a question in English, and he shook her off or derided her. Easy to be surly this time, complemented by her glowering. Gave authenticity to what they were ostensibly engrossed in doing: studying high school homework, ignoring each other. So it wasn't so good. So she didn't plead, Fuck me, fuck me good. So she didn't animal-yearn, O-o-wah, o-owah. He had laid her. Got his. Settle down now. Safe.

"Is it all right?" she asked, guarded, darkly.

"What?"

"When you went in the toilet."

"Oh, sure," he blustered, then contemptuously, "Jesus! What d'ye think?"

"Aw, you stink," she said.

"Oh, yeah? Just because of this once." She was belittling his prowess. He could tell she meant he had gotten more out of it than she had. "I told you I was in a hurry."

"No more! That's all. If it's such a hurry."

"But Sunday in the morning was—"

"Not even Sunday. No more."

"All right, no more," he agreed cynically. He could get around that one—next time.

"*Briderl.* You stink, if you wanna know."

"Aw, go to hell. Waddaye want? So once I got too excited." And then it suddenly occurred to him that he might have cause for concern. "Oh, Jesus!"

"Whatsa matter?"

He stood up. Had he pulled that chain long enough? Swirled the damned thing down? Really down for good, not just out of sight? He stepped hastily toward the bathroom door.

"I hear Mom," said Minnie.

Flop down again, or else Mom might think—might think he was dodging. Flop down to chair, bend over book.

And in came Mom, bringing fresh, cold air with her, as if in the container of her coat, breathless from the climb, her short, heavy self toting handbag; and at once, down on the table with it—and right for the bathroom!

Oh, Jesus Christ, oh, Jesus Christ. If he didn't, if he didn't! Minnie was right: never again, never again! Go to Theo, Theodora, Theotorah, Theowhorah. Anything. He still knew the way. Go to anybody, take a chance, get a dose, anything—Ira shut his eyes, waited. No. No. The toilet flushed and gurgled. No. No. It was all right. Got away with it. Of course. What the hell was he so scared about?

Mom came back into the kitchen. "*Noo, kinderlekh.* You must be hungry by now. No? When Mamie goes to buy a corset, she's a worse *kushenirke* than even I am. What am I? I'm a lady by comparison. If she didn't torture that shopkeeper on 116th Street to prostration with 'Ah, it's so dear; you make too much money on it, it's outrageous, it's exorbitant. What is it? Is it made of gold? It's only a corset. From cloth, from bone.' She has a nerve of brass."

"Oh, is that where you were?" Minnie asked. "I wondered. So did she buy it?"

"Indeed. Finally. *'Ai, vey, vey,'* the shopkeeper said. *'Frau,* you should wear it in good health. To earn what I have just earned cost me a parcel of health.' 'One has to look well about you before loosening purse strings,' she said. 'Heh, heh, heh,' he laughed. A clever Jew he was. 'Look well about you. That's a shred of comfort. About you indeed. May you rejoice in the wearing of it about you too.' Then I hurried home as fast as I could. A little coffee and milk and a bulkie?"

XI

Oh, Ecclesias, would that I had been spared the need to mention these painful events. Could they have believed that no sister ever existed? No. The story cannot continue without this admission. And I damn near don't give a hoot about the literary quality, friend Ecclesias.

—You don't? It seems to me you're overlooking something much more important than that, important as that is. You've showed your hand.

Yes, the tale's run away with me. Spell it howsoe'er you like.

—Once again, levity is out of place. You're in most formidable difficulties.

Yes. I might as well confess to what has been all along a kind of spirit beneath the deep: Ira's incestuous relations with his sister, Minnie.

—Confess it? It's obvious. Has been that quite awhile. But now that you've introduced her as a character, what will you do with your planned treatment of the thing later on, the revelation, the frightful disclosure you held in reserve?

I don't know. Perhaps I wish to curtail what comes later on. Leave off much nearer than that. Truncate. I could, you know.

—Yes. Or you could begin again: introduce the omitted character—

No. None of that. For one thing, it's not reasonable for me to expect to live that long—or better said, to be able to draw on the necessary vitality to accomplish what you propose. I'm in mid-seventy-nine. I'll ignore her again.

—That's scarcely tenable.

Who makes the rules? It's either that or collapse. He lives in two worlds, your client-friend Ira, the overt and covert, the inner and outer, the abysmal and the surface. Why not? Joyce divided himself into a flimsy Jew and an Irish super-intellectual. The one rarely stopped dwelling on his short arm, the other rarely stooped to dwell on it. He seemed immune to the prurient interest, but nevertheless, "before the play were played," he frequented a whorehouse. From whence the sudden infusion of sensuality? Does anything better illustrate the artificiality of Joyce's device, the cleaving in two of the person who was essentially one? And that individual was none other than Joyce himself. But however daring his innovations were, *that* innovation, that admission, he lacked the nerve to make. And therein lies what may be called the fatal flaw in the *Ulysses.* The guy masturbating at the sight of a seminaked limp leg, the guy shoving a carrot up his ass, the voyeur peeking up the statue's hind end, the guy pseudo-suffering at the thought of his own cuckolding, but in all probability wishing he were there to behold the act, the guy polluting the liver, was Joyce himself. I'm not going to prolong my insights any further, beyond saying I think they're apt and they're honest. I'm no super-verbalist, super-designer of irrelevancies, super-scholastic. I'm just striving to restore one individual to himself. I'm not proclaiming that I go into the stithy or the smithy of the human soul for the thousandth time—and then recoiling at the threshold, as soon as he smelled the smother and stench of seared hooves, After you, M'sieu Bloom-Dedalus. . . But why—I should refrain from asking, but can't quit— did that sister of Jimmy's who became a nun refuse to say a word about her renowned brother? "Answer me that, my Trinity scholard, out of your sanscreed into our herian." Beginning with the Pontiff Ellman, what all those erudite Jewish worshipers of the Master wouldn't give to learn the answer to that one.

XII

Smugly he walked east on 119th Street toward Park Avenue, the recollected little spat of the other day summoning smirk to his lips. Oh, everything was under control nicely. He had even bought a fresh tin of brand-new ones that would obviate all caviling incurred by her suspicion of his parsimonious reuse. Trouble was he might have to wheedle again: wheedle, wheedle, little Yeedel. What a tempest's in your needle? Hey, not bad: need, needle. Rotten bastard, Ira thought, you, you had to wake that bestial taloned talent in you. Perfidious, yeah, that would spread his predatory rut about her like a seine from which she couldn't escape. And you know, the funny thing, pal, she said, "I love you so much, and you're so lousy." She loved him so much, and hee! Hee! He was so lousy. That's why when it was right, just right, like the time before, once, then the dirty words suddenly stopped, and she, "Oooh, oooh, my dear brother, my dear brother!" It was, you know, the word flicked into his mind again: it was a snug enclave. Ha, ha, ha, ho, ho, ho. Robert Louis Stevenson, and his little shadow: he had a little enclave that went in and out with him. Little enclave in the family.

Was it his fault? He stole the silver fountain pen, yes, that was his fault, but this just happened, didn't it? No one could blame him. He stole the silver fountain pen after this happened, didn't he? Yes, yes. So? They swiped his briefcase, they swiped his fountain pens. Till next Sunday morning . . . Go over to Mt. Morris Park, he thought, and get into a game of association football.

That was what he would do, he resolved: forget about the same thing, same thing, same thing. Skip upstairs, lay down briefcase. Hurry up, while it was still light. Dunk a bulkie in sweet café au lay-hee, and off to Mt. Morris Park. . . .

The approaching figure planted itself squarely in front of Ira. Spongy purple old overcoat, though it wasn't cold, and face purplish, as if it were cold. Who? Challenging and hard-bitten, the other addressed Ira, "You're a lucky sonofabitch!"

"Oh! It's you, Collingway." Ira recognized his accoster as his fellow conductor of this past summer. But he looked so lean, hunched over with vindictiveness, different from the guy who had mingled semi-feigned asperity with advice when the two worked together on the Grand Concourse bus line.

"What's yer name again?" the other asked.

"Stigman. Ira. You remember. You know what? I didn't recognize you at first. You looked all—" Ira drew in his shoulders, as if shrunken.

"No? I reco'nized you all right. You're the Jew-kid I had to tell to draw off a couple o' bucks every day, so's you wouldn't make the rest of us look bad."

The brunt of rancor in his voice, the flinty spite uttered sideways by the purple-writhing lips, made Ira cringe. Guilty, superstitious almost, guilty of enjoying good fortune, of being bestowed with a superior, enviable lot: *keyn ayin-horeh*, he could just hear Pop, or Mom too, say in Yiddish. Avert the evil eye! To be free of work, as he was, free of worry too, going to high school, while the other had to stand on the platform of a jouncing, beat-up bus—and soon to be winter—collecting fares, fretting over slow, decrepit passengers, and maybe like himself when he worked there, that awful time the boss's car trailed and he thought he was caught, sure, always anxious for fear some spotter might nab him—no wonder the guy eyed him up and down so full of hate.

"Talk about luck," Collingway continued. "Jesus, you got it by de shitload. You'll never have to worry about nutt'n wit' de kind o' breaks you git."

"You mean this?" Ira raised his briefcase apologetically. "You mean I'm goin' to high school?"

"Shit, no! Jesus Christ!" Collingway rasped, wagged his head in utter disgust. "Jesus H. Christ! Don't ye read the fuckin' papers?"

"Yeah, once in a while." Ira hesitated, perplexed.

"Once in a while?" The other's countenance sprouted veritable quills of contempt. "What the fuck do ye read dere? De funnies? You see any buses runnin' on Fift' Avenue lately?"

"No . . . gee, that's right. I didn't. So what happened? What did you do? You lose your job?"

Collingway could only vent his despair with a soughing sound. And finally, "Well, I'll be a sonofabitch. I had to buy my way into dat fuckin' job. What the hell chance have I got as old as I am? I had to buy my way in. An' this punk—" he addressed an imaginary third party.

"So what happened?" Ira pleaded.

"Lose my job! Shit, that was nothin'. That goddamn bunch o' crooks went bankrupt. Every goddamn one of us conductors lost his hundred bucks."

"Your security!"

"Yeah, yeah, yeah, our security! Not a fuckin' one of us got his hundred bucks back again!"

Ira whistled.

"Only you, you lucky sonofabitch, you quit in time."

"I didn't know it. I had to go back to school."

The other shook his head in sheer bitterness. "Yeah, you can laugh, you lucky bastard."

"I'm not laughing. I'm sorry," Ira protested. Lucky Jew bastard would be next. Ira could hear it coming. Boy, would he like to remind the louse how much he stole from the bus company himself; maybe if he and the rest hadn't stolen so much he'd still have a job. But he wasn't going to get into an argument with that *farbisener hint,* as Mom would have called him. Angry dog, he looked like a wolf.

"Yeah. You're sorry. In a pig's ass you're sorry."

"I am. I gotta go." With an arbitrary wave of the hand, Ira parted abruptly, before Collingway could say anything in opposition. "I'll see you."

Frig you. Ira felt resentment mount after he had distanced himself from the other by a few steps. Good for you, you bastard: you made someone else steal, a kid, who was scared to, scared because he had learned his lesson, made him steal, so the company wouldn't notice your own gypping. To hell with you. Bet he made over a hundred dollars long ago. Way before the company went broke. So he had to buy his way into the job? So he was too old, he said. That didn't mean Ira owed him the hundred dollars. That's how he made Ira feel.

By the time he reached the stoop, the ironic absurdity of it all brought a grin to Ira's face. These guys gypping the bus company, and then the bus company gypped them. But this guy, he deserved it. Just because somebody else got away, he blamed them. . . . Gee, that was lucky, though . . . for a change. Maybe he was being lucky. That ten-dollar roll of quarters. Hey, and Pearl—but that turned lucky too: homely Theodora showed him how to put it in where it belonged. And he got Minnie to let him in, put it in that way. Don't get to be like Pop: superstitious. His luck had changed *before* he went to Theodora. He got the ten-dollar roll from Mrs. Stevens first. Had nothing to do with talking to Pearl, with screwing Theodora. He got his hundred dollars security back *before* everything else, before he was even a hustler. So maybe he was just plain getting a little lucky for a change. Twice in one week. He might even be lucky right now. He had a new tin in his pocket. He'd tell her, Look, this time I'm not so excited.

Complacency with self changed to eagerness as he climbed up the stone stairs of the stoop.

After an unrewarding glance through the scrolled apertures of the dented brass letter box, he entered the long dreary hall, mounted the battered steps to the landing, weakly lighted by the window there that opened on the clutter of washpoles and fences of the neighboring backyard. Then up to the "first floor," as the first flight was called, through the ever-crepuscular hallway—with its green dumbwaiter door nailed shut—to the kitchen door under clear afternoon transom light, with a few flecks of paint still adhering to the glass.

He opened the door into the kitchen. All seemed tranquil and customary in form and movement—reassuring: bobbed, steel-gray-haired Mom at the sink in black-figured fire-engine-red housedress, her puffy feet in faded felt mules. She was paring onions over the black sink. In the large wooden bowl on the washtub cover, freshly peeled onions imbued the atmosphere of the kitchen with their pungency.

"Ah, my precious Iraleh." Mom bunched together light brown onion skin. "I wanted to go to the window to watch you come home."

And his inane "Yeh? Here I am, Mom."

"So I'll work a minute longer. What's new?"

"I'll tell you right away. I'll get my football shoes outta the bedroom."

He passed Mom disposing of the onion skin in the metal garbage pail behind the silly little pink curtain that hung from the sink, masking cleaning implements and roach powder behind it. It was not the pink of the curtains that brought Pearl's earrings to mind, at first, but the light tan onion skin, not only tan, translucent, smooth and lambent. Would he ever forget her? So beautiful. What would it have been like? Well, the prosperous man in the panama hat had her. Make shift, they said. So . . . there was still Minnie. He got his football shoes from their shadowy cardboard carton at the end of the bed, tied the laces together in order to sling the shoes over his shoulder. He heard the kitchen door open, Minnie's voice, Mom's exchanging greetings. So she had just come home from school, too. He returned to the lighted kitchen.

Her bulging leather book satchel already on the table, she was slipping out of her blue overcoat when he came in. In white middie blouse with blue ribbon about collar, she bent her bobbed, wavy red hair to open the satchel. Her brow was furrowed for some reason, fretting over annoyance of some kind, her greeting was sour. "Hello. Where you going?"

"Going for a little football."

"Where? In Mt. Morris Park?"

"Yeah. Whatsa matter? You look—" He left the rest unsaid.

"Oh." She allowed a long dissatisfied pause. "That Latin. You're lucky you don't have to take it."

"I couldn't anyway. I could only take Spanish."

"Wish I never took it. But at Hunter College, if you're gonna teach . . ."

"I wonder why?"

"Why what? Why do you think? It's so hard. And *you* can't help."

"No. I didn't mean that. Why do you have to take it?"

"I told you. If you're gonna teach."

"Oh."

"And you're such a big helper."

"Well, I didn't take it."

She folded her coat, brushed by him on the way to the bedroom closet. Boy. He watched her leave the kitchen. Boy. He'd better go, catch the last of the daylight, but couldn't: something unusually stiff about her. He hesitated.

"My poor daughter," said Mom. "*S'iz azoy shver.*"

"Yeah."

"A little light coffee and a bulkie?"

"No. I better run. It gets dark so fast." Still, he lingered. Something, something . . . uneven . . . worrisome . . . what?

Returning, Minnie was careful to circle about him, sat down on a chair. "I gotta begin studying right away." She pulled her Latin text out of the satchel on the table. "We're gonna get a test tomorrow on all the conjugations of the four kinds of verbs. Four kinds yet."

"Yeah? You look like you're really gonna study," he probed.

"What d'you think?" She opened her textbook. "My teacher is Miss Robin. An old maid, and is she a *meshigener*? You never know what she'll ask you. She says she'll give you a test on all the verbs. So you study all the verbs. Instead she'll give you a whole page to translate. Everybody thinks she's crazy."

"A little light coffee with a bulkie, my daughter?" Mom suggested. "You look as if your little heart needed cheering up."

"Oh, I'm—no—oh, all right. A real light coffee."

"And a little something to dunk in it?"

"You got any of that *rugeleh* left?"

"Indeed. Good. Good. It's going to go stale."

"I like it that way. Just right for dunkin'." She began poring over the open page.

Ira studied her for a minute. Was she really peeved, and over what? Offish. The Latin test, and his inability to help. Fortunate. Yes, fortunately he didn't take Latin, so he always had an excuse for not helping her—but it was a double-edged excuse—his mind complacently impinged pros on cons—because he couldn't exact a promise of opportune recompense for helping her, as he had done at times in other subjects in the past. . . . But he was getting the real thing now, so was she; so it didn't matter so much. Still, he wished he had studied Latin, as she was doing now, because he might have got a few more dividends that way. What the hell: he was forever correcting things in retrospect. And yet such little things made such a big difference. That lousy junior high he attended, and that fag Mr. Lennard's half-assed teaching of Spanish. If he'd gone to DeWitt Clinton from the beginning, he probably would have taken Latin. For someone taking a "general course" to prepare for college, Latin would have been right. And there she was struggling with it. Boy. To have taken a look at her textbook, even now, and said—right in front of Mom—with that faint ulterior slur, You need some help? And when she said yes, how innocently he could have rejoined, with tutorial-level voice: Okay. But don't forget. You owe me a favor. What delicious dirty double-meaning. *Amo, amas, amat,* he had heard her repeat in the beginning. He should have tried to catch up with her. And then—he could have softened her up, mollified her with a little help—what a cinch, right? Yeah, right now, siphoned off her annoyance with him—why? What for? Oh, of course: because of that last time, what else? Just on account of his coming too fast?

He hitched his football shoes over his shoulder. Boy, they were dandies, with a hard toe for getting off a good punt, and cleats that clawed the ground for abrupt stops and shifts. He stretched his hand out to turn the doorknob, then remembered—just as Mom was opening the kitchen window to get the milk bottle out of the window box cooler. Maybe spending an extra minute regaling her might cheer her up. And at the same time, he'd gain Mom's congratulation for his cleverness and his good *mazel* by relating briefly the encounter with the ex–fellow conductor cheated by the bus company of his hundred dollars.

"*Azoy?*" Mom paused with hand on the bedroom doorknob, smiling as he sharpened the point of the anecdote: that this guy was the worst *goniff* in the place. "One moment. Mineleh, I'll get the milk."

Mom laughed when he finished his account. But Minnie never lifted her head. Boy, she was still sore. Or was it more than he thought? Something significant? Mom lingered while Ira lingered, and Ira lingered because Minnie's frown was threatening and impenetrable.

"So why don'tcha go?" Minnie invited disagreeably.

"Whatsa matter with you?" Ira answered in kind.

"*Kinderlekh,*" Mom admonished. "What for? Akh. At once you begin to feud." She laughed in spite of herself. "I'll fetch a bit of health, Mineleh." She blinked in the direction of the chopped onions in the wooden bowl on the washtub. "I'll clear my eyes by leaning out of the window and watching my shining son leave." She made for the bedroom and, trailing her inveterate sigh, shut the door behind her.

Must be some reason Minnie glowered so. Ira waited, waited for the most favorable interval: between the sound of Mom's heavy tread and the estimated time for her to reach the front-room window.

"Whatsa matter?" Blunt inquiry was safe. He heard the front-room window open.

"Shut up. Nothing."

"I gotta go. What? Just because that once?"

Sidelong, her eyeglass-darkened girlish features scowled in contempt, her girlish voice fraught with resentment. "No. Who cares about that? I didn't get my period yet. I'm three days late."

Let the ceiling fall, the house cave in on him, for him that would be no fearful dread—compared to this, to which all he could say—dazedly—was: "You didn't?"

"No."

"You sure?"

"Of course I'm sure. Whatta you mean I'm sure?"

"Jesus." In stunned silence he stood; the whole world plunged to smithereens about him. "I gotta go. Mom's by the window."

"So go ahead. You wanted to know. I told you. Maybe I shouldn't." Suddenly she didn't sound mean at all, no, but surprisingly, almost solicitously, deeply troubled. "Go ahead. It's nothing."

"Gee, I hope not. You been late like that before?"

"Oh, yeah. It's nothing, I told you."

"Three days?"

"Go ahead. Mom'll be wondering why she doesn't see you."

"All right. Jesus." He went out into the hall. With dragging step to the landing, with spiritless tread down the stairs, his football shoes an unwelcome burden over his shoulder. Out of the house doorway, down stone stoop, he forced an unwilling countenance into dissembling. Hard as hell to writhe adamant visage from its grim set, as if pressing against opposing steel springs, forcing recalcitrant wedges to prop up fear-stricken features into a blithe mask that looked up from the sidewalk, looked up at Mom's fleshy, fond face looking down, saying in Yiddish, "Have a good run. Only don't forget supper. The sire will be home."

"Yeah, I know. It gets dark anyway, Mom—before." He raised his voice, but could scarcely lift his eyes to her projecting face more than once. "I'll be home, Mom. Don't worry. All right?"

"*Oy, s'iz git kalt.*" The window overhead slid with slight thud to its sill.

Oh, Jesus. On the sidewalk, and in the street, the kids, a few pedestrians, and across the street, just then climbing the stoop of one of the twin red-brick tenements where Davey Baer and his family still lived, was Mrs. McIntyre, *dos tseyndl,* Mom dubbed her, in charity, not derision, the little fang, because Mrs. McIntyre had only one front tooth; so prominent when she smiled. And she loved Mom, as so many of the neighborhood *goyish* women did, despite her faltering English. Mrs. McIntyre literally beamed, brightened, with pleasure when she talked with Mom, as if talking to Mom were a joy, an honor. But oh, Mom, what your son's got himself into. Or did you, Mom? A noble woman, Zaida called her. So don't blame her. Only yourself. Boyoboy. He drove himself to stride with enforced alacrity toward the everlasting trestle on Park Avenue.

Everlasting trestle. Everlasting shadow under it . . . often agreeable, relished in hot weather, not now. Into shadow under overarching steel; and out of shadow into abating light of afternoon . . . crossing to the west curb, hoofing toward Madison Avenue, each step more dispirited. Right here, in midblock, Collingway had accosted him. Yeah, lucky bastard, yeah. The goy gave him a *git-oyg,* Pop would have said: the evil eye. *Keyn ayin-horeh,* Ira should have said to himself: avert the evil eye. Been superstitious like Pop. *Mazel.* Jesus Christ, how lucky he thought he was. Boy, he would rather have lost that hundred bucks . . . a hundred times over, if he had it to lose, than be in this fix. A hundred, hundred, hundred times over. Ten thousand, ten thousand, ten thousand times over. So Pop would have torn him into little bits, when he came home without the security.

But what was that to this? Three days late, she said. Three days! She said it was nothing. So don't worry—if she said it was nothing, so it was nothing. Jesus, he shouldn't have washed that condom. Washed it and reused it. Been a cheapskate, like Pop. Oh, no, Jesus, no. And it looked all right afterward, dried, turned inside out, rolled up, looked as good as that first time, when she said it was so wonderful. Maybe it split. Maybe that's why he felt something different when he came. Oh, Jesus, warmer, delightful, moister all of a sudden. Maybe that was why he came so soon. A dillar, a dollar, a ten-o'clock scholar . . .

Why had he met Pearl, gone to Theodora? His luck. All right, don't be like Pop. Luck. Brains. Why didn't he keep on going to Theodora? He knew the address, how to get there, and how much. And it was safe. And no trouble, nothing happened. He just said goodbye, walked back to the subway. Two stations downtown and good old 116th Street. And he could have bought his own condoms next time, instead of hers: the extra quarter could have bought two. So he knew the ropes now; why didn't he go? Because he was a cheapskate, like Pop. Why did he have to hump his sister? Because he got started doing it. Then why didn't he do it the way he used to do it before? Sandwiched it, the way it tickled her, the way that wouldn't let him go in. He never worried when he used to do it that way. Oh, shut up, shut up, shut up. Oh, if it ever—

He reached Madison Avenue, turned toward 120th and the corner of Mt. Morris Park. Oh, Jesus. He didn't want to play football. Association, or any kind. You gotta. Forget it. You gotta forget, you gotta forget, you gotta forget this morning, you gotta forget, you gotta forget today. Taps. No, no, dummy, that wasn't taps; that was reveille. March on. March on. Sing the *Marseillaise*.

Ahead of him in the brown, bare playground in the park he could see and hear the cry and chase of a touch football game. Boy, to be like them. Shut up. Grab a bench and get your cleats on. It's nothing, she said.

"Hey, fellas. How about a game?" he called as soon as he passed through the 120th Street entrance.

"Hey, Irey, c'mon. You're on our side. Hey, Ginsburg, here's somebody else. You can play now."

Ira had become too closely identified with his narrative, and not merely with that, but with the impasse he had reached by this re-creation of his sister into the narrative. He worried that he could only examine his own mind, however deranged, and not hers. How did she feel? How had this depravity affected her? He felt he was incapable of such comprehension. He had no answers, none at all. He thought perhaps he saw a glimmer of a solution by reverting to the role which he had adopted for himself at the beginning of the novel: that of amanuensis—no, rather that of editor of his own first draft.

Yet, the present suddenly erupted into frightful events, frightful atrocities wrought by lunatic fanatics. The so-called black box lay at the bottom of the sea that might explain the circumstances of the explosion that sent three hundred and more human beings, passengers in the Air India jumbo jet, together with the aircraft, to their destruction. The Sikhs were thought to be the perpetrators. . . . Dragging on into a second week, the Shiite Moslems in Beirut held some forty Americans hostage, and demanded that Israel redeem them by the release of seven hundred Shiite prisoners (and some of the hostages had Jewish-sounding names, according to the dispatches). . . . A horrendous plot by Irish terrorists to blow up summer and seaside resorts had been foiled. . . . In Japan, a bomb had exploded in the luggage destined to be loaded aboard another Air India plane, and several baggage handlers were killed. What else? Where else? Everywhere else. Planes in flight returned to the airports of departure because of false rumors that explosives were aboard. In all the media, talk of safeguards to be taken, actions to be avoided, reaction, and overreaction.

And to add mordancy to it all, one of his and M's friends showed up unannounced, for the nth time, despite the fact that Ira and M had asked the ineffable jackanapes to phone before he called in person. Would he? By no means. He was not to be dictated to. Ira had retired to his study, after slamming the door. Worst of it was, that locked in as he was, M had thought his ire extended to her, because he had refused to answer her knock, thinking it to be the insufferable boor he was excluding, and what with the noisy evaporative cooler churning away in his study, Ira hadn't heard her voice.

His poor lamb, become upset, by him! But honestly, could anyone imagine such boundless boorishness that would deliberately refuse to telephone before calling, even though repeatedly asked! And to barge in just as Ira wrote the last lines trying to portray, trying to recapture, the fearful panic he had gotten into at Minnie's disclosure, the onset of those disastrous depredations the predator was to wreak on himself!

Result of this all was, he had been unable to fall asleep that night—not until he took a Valium. He had sat up two or three hours, then he became worried that if he sat up any longer, he might have another attack of "adrenaline failure," the shock of adrenaline insufficiency that he had suffered a few months ago. It had necessitated his being taken by ambulance to the hospital, and spending a couple of days there. To obviate that, he took the tranquilizer.

And he awoke the next morning—a wreck. Well. But it had been while he was lying sleepless beside M, fast asleep, that something like an illumination blossomed within him, something like a whisper of grace, a dispensation that would enable him to go on through this slough of his past. It was to turn for respite to M's love for him—that's what he lived for; that was the meaning and mainstay of his life. At last, yes, that such as he, intolerable egoist, had learned that more important than his writing (whether it would eventually be deemed significant or not) was the showing, the activity, of his love for her. All else was subordinate. The miracle was that he should conceivably have reached that stage. He couldn't sleep, no, but the epiphany consoled insomnia. Jane Eyre, Lizzy Bennet of Austen's *Pride and Prejudice,* which he had almost finished reading, hovered over the sleeping figure beside him, his wife. She was as good, as gentle, as well-bred, faithful, loving, wise as they, and courageous and competent and gifted beyond them.

And he a Jew, apology of a Jew, apology of a man, redeemed by her. What was that other notion floating about, muddled as usual? That as Hitler had destroyed the core of Orthodox Jewry, its vital, fertile nucleus proliferating in Eastern Europe, then what was left of Orthodoxy outside Israel, except for the fossilized kinkies, flaunting their earlocks and fur *shtramls?* Only the diluted remnant of rabbinical Jewry here in America. By assimilation, by intermarriage, by deliberately reduced fecundity, the remnant would painlessly disappear, except for the professional practitioners, the rabbis, watching their flocks dwindle. As in a vision, he saw the far-flung Diasporas wither, the boundaries of each, even that of the Soviet Union, surviving despite policies of attrition, nevertheless in the end contracting like a stagnant pool. Only in Israel could Judaism thrive, only in its own land survive and evolve.

XIII

The hours and days, whole days! went by, an ache, a woe, the hours stretching Ira on the rack of days, howling in silence in ever-growing anguish. Back home from school in the afternoon, in the earlier and still earlier darkening afternoon of the kitchen, the ebbing of daylight, the obscurity of the room became a sinister setting for the single window on the backyard, became the repository of his anguish: the washline pole opposite the window, the spiked footholds in the rising gray mist, the washlines on their pulleys drawn in different directions—the little house next to them, only two stories high, where Leo Dugonicz had once lived, and before him the Italian barber and his family. And across the fenced yard, Yussel's gloomy, massy, six-story, cold-water fortress on the corner. Every scrap of deprivation and poverty became a bit of congealed, of concealed anguish. To all his agonized inquiries, no, no, and again, no, was all the answer he received. She hadn't got her period. No. Nights he could put himself asleep only by summoning up behind his eyelids the facade of the Metropolitan Museum, to which even from his ninth year, he had hiked . . . hiked, hiked alone, and with Jake Shapiro, all the way from grubby 119th Street and Park Avenue to the corner of Central Park, the pond and rowboats on it and across the pond the granite outcrop rising to a summit of shrubs and trees. All familiar. And then the walk, the long, lovely excursion along Fifth Avenue until the corner of the Museum building. Could he remember the steps, the broad steps leading up to the great wings of the stone facade on either side? How many steps? And the doors? And the famous names above the doors, and the tubular brass turnstiles inside the wide marble anteroom, and the guards in blue uniforms on duty? That was easy to summon up. And the lofty, lavish, palatial interior, all around majestic and light. But what was the first thing you saw after you were inside? The first thing that met your wandering gaze was the tapestries, the Gobelin tapestries on the high matched marble walls, with all kinds of Biblical scenes, was that it? Turbaned rulers and martyrs, armored soldiers with spears and ladies in costumes of long ago. Remember? That statue of Good and Evil, big as could be, that stood beside the marble stairs: he was standing on her, you thought, at first; but it was he standing on him. Both the same; so it looked like a fight, a wrestling match, evil overthrown and on the ground, always evil overthrown and on the ground, except Ira. So now he'd have to pay for it, as he did for the lost briefcase, as he did for the swiped silver fountain pen—but Ira didn't for that roll of quarters he copped, and he didn't with scrawny Theodora in that stuffy room showing him how he could go in for two dollars and a quarter. How did he know he wasn't paying for going to Theodora now? She showing him how, and he's paying for it now. Didn't she giggle when he started to do it the wrong way? He said, nearly ashamed, "That's the way I started with my"—and stopped himself in time—"my first one."

Go up the marble stairs then, Ira dreamed—ah, the way those marble stairs whisper under your shoe soles, s-s-s-sh. And the wide pale marble balustrades slide beneath your palms. Wonder, is that alabaster, what they call? Oh, Jesus, it wasn't even so good that time; it wasn't even so good. Shut up. What's the first thing you see? That new Hercules, Herakles, they call him, over the marble railing on the first flight, with one foot against the boulder pulling back the bow? He might see that first. But if he didn't, then on top of the stairs is that Madonna in blue with the little Jesus. That's Mary. *Goyish.* Ira looked away at first, but then read the name on the fancy gold frame: Raphael. Oh, Raphael, Ira knew him. Then . . . Then . . . Then . . . There's that deep deep, first deep breath . . .

During waking hours at home, plane geometry sustained him, majestic plane geometry, assuaging plane geometry, the only entire, pure world, only entire, pure world that offered him unquestioning sanctuary, benign, set before him a problem or a proposition, shared with him his rapture that the solution should be so inevitable, so wondrously spare and immaculate—and so ingenious, even dazzling sometimes. Who would have dreamed that the angle between two tangents or two secants drawn from a point outside the circle would equal half the difference of the intercepted arcs? How could it be? Why should it be? And yet it was. Such a beautiful world whose parts all fit together. Even if a proof stumped you, as long as you knew there was one, you could prove it finally, because for once you knew how a world, a system, went together. He exulted because he excelled in class, at recitations, at the blackboard. His grades in plane geometry were perfect—to the detriment of his other schoolwork, which he did perfunctorily, just to do it. No other subjects had the force to hold at bay the horrible fate, the horrible demon every hour closer to exacting its toll. His fear penetrated everything else, slipped through English or Spanish or history, as if the print were pores, a filter, a grille. She still didn't get her period. She still didn't get it.

Days. He couldn't tell when, how late, how long after, maybe three after she first told him, there came a day when he knew he had reached his limit, the limit of his endurance. When she said no, he knew. He had entered the screaming phase, not a phase, a nightmare universe; he had entered the realm of the unendurable. When she said no, the modes of the world no longer held sway, the behavior, the accepted strands of common sense, the sensible aspect of things, their causes and acts no longer dictated, no longer ruled or applied, became flaccid. When she said no, he felt as if certain ligaments had given way within him, mind-ligaments, as if in a certain place within his brain they parted, like fibers, fraying under the strain. They would never come back, reverse to their original soundness, never wholly mend. He could feel their sickening twisting irrevocably writhing out of place. Or wilting? So what should he do? Kill her. If he killed her, that would be an end. Kill her. How? Choke. Hit. Stab. A big rock. Push her out of the window. Maybe best. But kill. That was the word, the name of the loathsome shape spawned out of the terrible, irreparable rending within him. He was a murderer. He could murder. He could plan: how, when to kill; but kill. She was killing him, kill her. . . . But wait, wait: one more assignment. Wait. No, it wouldn't help, it couldn't prevail over his anguish. But wait, wait. He'd do only the problems he pleased, the starred ones; the hell with the assignment, do only the starred ones, ill-starred, do just those, the hard ones—

Balefulness impeded the hand that reached for the textbook, *Wentworth's Plane Geometry;* ferocity strove with him as he drew the book toward him. They were the winners, the starred examples. What was the problem in that thin shrieking madness, what was given? Given. Given. The figure in the text, always so friendly, so laden with sly challenge within its wily frame; the figure lay dead. Mom stood with broad back toward him at the sink. Lethe. Last bliss. Straight lines intersecting on nepenthe.

He heard Minnie come in from the bedroom. He looked up, not in hope, in last despairing corroboration of despair. But no, something was different about her demeanor. Altogether. Unmistakable. An emanation, a ripple of promise, contrary to the expected negation. She smiled at him, and nodded. He gaped for confirmation: aimed his unremitting stare at her, mimed in silent entreaty behind Mom's back. All right?

And received nods, several, unmistakable, emphatic. She made for the bathroom.

Glory. Oh! Oh! Oh! Beatitude! But he couldn't rest. He had to know: certainly, positively, explicitly, absolutely. She *had* to tell him. Tell him, tell him. He waited for her to come out of the bathroom. What could he say or ask? Something that was neutral, something that Mom never could possibly suspect. What? "Okay? Your homework?"

"Everything's okay," she replied shortly.

And still not satisfied, he glanced at Mom, and dared, his eyes intransigent, sounding Minnie's face, her features, his own lips like grapnels importunate to engage her in reconfirmation formed noiseless words, "Got your period?"

Impatiently and with vehement nod, "Yes!"

Oh, boy, oh, boy, oh, boy! Every nerve in him sang hallelujah! He couldn't stay in the house. He had to get out, get out and prance, tear through the streets, hug himself and rejoice, yell crazy anthems without meaning. Jesus Christ, what a break! He stood up, fairly sprang toward the bedroom, announcing, "I'm going down." He grabbed his jacket from the bedroom coat tree.

"Where are you going?" What could Mom guess?

"Down. Around the block. No place."

"And the coat. It's cold—soon as it's dark."

"Nah. I'll be right back."

"You want to do me a favor, since you're coming back soon?"

"Sure. Sure." Ira was all heartiness, all willingness. "I'll buy a kosher elephant. What d'you want?"

"Go, ninny." She smiled. "I'll give you the money. He knows me, the dairy storekeeper around the corner. If he has cracked eggs, no matter how many he has, let it be a dozen. Tell him I was in his store this morning, and he didn't have them."

"Okay. Cracked eggs, a dutsin, a dutsin, a wild, woolly mutsin. Hutsin, clyutsin, shmutsin, abutsin." He shifted weight from foot to foot in impromptu jig. "Let's go, Mom. It's nearly a half dutsin o'clocko—*makh shnel!*"

"What's got into you? The boy is mad," Mom said with tentative amusement.

He cocked an eye, postured zanily. "I just made a wonderful discovery. *Wunderbar.*"

"He's crazy," Minnie censured with unfeigned disapproval.

"*Nar.*" Mom tendered him a quarter. "Don't forget. He knows me, Mrs. Stigman, tell him: the lady from 119th Street, he always saves the cracked eggs for—*oy, gevald, bist takeh meshigeh!*"

In one motion, Ira snatched the quarter from her hand and threw open the kitchen door. "Adee-ee—you." An instant later he was out in the hall.

Though he strode, strode as rapidly as he could through the darkening street, in spirit, he leaped, he capered—no wonder they said "high spirits." "Ta-ra, ta-ra"—he broke his silence from time to time with low outcry. But he wished he could bellow, trumpet, blare out his relief. No, never again, not e'er again, no ne'er again. He'd throw the goddamn condoms away. Blow 'em up into big balloons till they burst. Pretty bubbles in the air. No, sir, he wouldn't throw them away either. He'd go to Theodora again. He knew the way. The price. Yes, yes, yes. Or somebody else. Maybe better-looking. Oh yeah, yeah, forgot. You goddamn liar. Oh, boy, oh, boy, was he ever made of—iridescence was the word: efflorescence, concupiscence. Hah, ha, ha. Effervescence. Boyoboy! What other essences were there? He was it, he was all of 'em. Gossamer. Downy little flames overlapped into plumed vanes beating in splendor. Gee whiz, the way the words spouted up inside you! Was it gossamer from Coleridge? Jeez, it was a Life-in-Death before, though, wasn't it? Jeez, only two people knew about it, he and Minnie. Not like some guy laid some bimbo, all a-blabber: hey, you ought to see that broad I laid last night, and maybe he was a lotta bull. And maybe he wasn't. But for him, Ira, silence. Silence. There was no brag, no parading, nothing but shame. Genie in a vase. Pandora's box. His sister's box! Can you imagine bragging about that? Jesus, it almost made him shut his eyes in the enormous twinge the very thought caused him. Hey, fellers, I thought I knocked up my sister! Was I scared. Boyoboy. Holy Jesus Christ, of all the things he had ever heard those guys say: pratt and blow and lap and go down on it, back scuttle, and every other goddamn thing he once believed was just make-believe, but even if it was true, nobody ever said I laid my sister. Yeah, the Italian kids said, aw, yer mudder's ass, yer sister's cunt—but what was that compared to: my sister's cunt?

Subsiding slowly to the level of self, he turned at Madison toward the park. Sure, they were still playing football in the very last light of dusk. He could see and hear them when he got there. But he didn't need football, didn't feel like it; last thing he felt like was to get off a punt. No shoes, anyway. But no urge to, he meant. Gee. He'd walk around the park once; that would calm him down still further. Walk by all the places he knew, past the Eye and Ear Hospital, around the corner of 124th Street, where he used to leave the park behind on his way to P.S. 124 further uptown on Madison Avenue. Or to Farley's house, also on Madison. God, he couldn't even tell *him;* he couldn't tell Farley, his best friend once, Ira couldn't tell anybody.

And then west alongside the park, and past the gray library so many, many times ago. And then the brownstones on the same street where he had delivered groceries for P&T. And then around Mt. Morris Park West where the small apartment houses stood that he liked to walk up to, with his box of groceries under his arm, while Shea guarded the Model T. Which one was that house, he wondered, which one? Where you went in the back, and there was a service elevator you could operate yourself with a cable—like a real elevator man: you remember what a trick it was to get the elevator platform just even with the apartment house floor? Jiggle up an inch—too far. And down again—o-o-ps. What fun. What bigger fun, if he wasn't already doing bad, doing bad, yes, kid-word: doing bad with Minnie when she had only a small round white ass, like a penny balloon. Penny balloon, but it was big as a cloud in his mind, already casting an encompassing shadow. Still, it was only that, only a shadow then, not this scare, murder, murder, kill her.

Stop!

120th Street. Walking east. The nearer to Madison Avenue, the grubbier 120th became. Yes, but they had hot water, they had steam heat just the same—two people could take two bathtubs full. No wonder. To the car tracks on Madison Avenue, and the corner of Mt. Morris Park, and the beginning again. Getting too dark for football. The players had quit. Twilight-empty, quiet, the playground. So back to 119th Street. And drab, darkling way home. Elation had completely worn off. Something remained now, as if exposed: not just the self, the familiar self, as his had been, before, as he had been before. No. He could have killed her, he, Ira Stigman, the coward, he could have killed his sister; that's how torn he was inside. And he felt that way still: the separation, the twist. A sorrow had dislodged something in him. He had worried too far: like prying apart something that wouldn't come together again, wouldn't come together right, had left a weakness, a chronic vulnerability to unhappiness. Nah, it would go away. It was like any other tear or rip or something like that within the self. It would heal; he'd get over it. No, he wouldn't, that was the trouble. No, even that cheese knife with which he had cut himself left a white scar on his thumb. This one was dark. Odd, how you could feel your worry twist, wrench, and wouldn't let go. What was it like? Clockworks did that, when he opened the Big Ben that had stopped running. A toothed wheel caught each second, each time further, further. Something broke. Or snapped. Or . . .

"*Noo,*" said Mom, "the cracked eggs?" when he entered the kitchen.

"All right, I'll go right now!" He retreated hastily.

"Never mind. Give me the quarter back. I'll go there myself tomorrow. You have a head like my wooden chopping bowl."

"That's right," Minnie seconded. "He's got a head like a tack, my darling brother."

XIV

In the spring term of his junior year, beginning in the winter of 1923, there moved into the six-story pile of an apartment house above Biolov's drugstore on the corner of 119th Street and Park Avenue (exactly opposite Yussel's drab fortress) one Bob S and his divorced mother. Bob and Ira soon recognized each other as fellow students at DeWitt Clinton. Bob was a senior, scheduled to graduate a year ahead of Ira. Jewish, purposeful, self-confident, above average height, with black straight hair parted precisely in the middle, he wore "shell-rimmed" glasses on the bridge of a pointed nose, reminiscent of his soda-hustler boss Benny Lass, and, of course, of Harold Lloyd. Bob was unusually quick mentally, acute; he ranked high academically, was involved in high school politics, a member of the debating team, and of Arista too, the high school honor society. Bob's goal, preset and undeviating, all but preenacted, was to become a lawyer. That too found Ira less than enthusiastic: he had worked in a law office once, and once was enough.

But the two did live in the same street, if only for a short while. They did take the same train after school—and before school. They became acquainted, willy-nilly, on Ira's part, for lack of a more companionable friend, one not so interested in school elections for student offices, in the school newspaper, not so pat about his future. But in the course of acquaintance, Ira learned something else about his new friend, something that interested him, intrigued him, in fact: Bob was on the DeWitt Clinton rifle team.

Ira loved rifles. He had never had anything to do with a real firearm, only that Daisy BB gun of years ago, which he had trusted, so hopefully and so childishly, would eliminate the rats down in the airshaft, and had proved such a debacle when put to the test. Naturally, Ira told Bob about the air rifle, entertained Bob with accounts of his disappointments and mini-fiascos connected with the air rifle. And perhaps Ira may have mentioned the few times he had splurged a quarter in the penny arcade on East 125th Street, where in addition to other diversions, such as life-size fortune-telling Gypsy puppets and electric-shock handlebars, there was also a shooting gallery, where you got ten .22 Shorts for your two bits, a wild extravagance, and could plink away at either stationary bull's-eyes that rang when struck or gliding iron-clad ducks that obediently bowled over when plunked. Yes, Ira very much liked rifles.

It wasn't very long before Bob invited Ira into the "cage." It occupied a corner of the gym, and a cage it quite literally was: a small space completely enclosed with very heavy fencing wire. Its gate was of the same material and could only be opened with a key, which only team members possessed. Inside the cage, a .22 target rifle, of regulation weight and size, hung suspended from a sensitive metal arm or spar. The actual target was on the other side of the gym floor, about twenty-five yards away, but aligned with it inside the cage was a tiny target the size of a calling card in front of the needlelike pointer. When the trigger was pulled, the pointer impacted on the card, leaving a pinprick in the miniature target ring corresponding to the spot the actual bullet would have struck the real target twenty-five yards distant across the gym.

Bob fired four or five "shots" by way of demonstration, and exhibited the group of pinholes in the little card. He suggested that Ira try his hand at the contrivance too. He did. Although Ira knew that his training, if it could be called that, consisted mainly of endeavoring to exterminate rats down in the airshaft with a Daisy air rifle, still, the experience had taught him something, if only intuitively: to hold his breath while aiming, to aim by holding the knife-edge front sight under the target and within the center of the V of the rear sight. And following his own previous practice, Ira aimed and fired. He scored a bull's-eye, a pinprick in the ten-ring. But could he have still been thinking of Minnie, before the reassuring discovery, before the disclosure that had saved his life? And then the next four shots were grouped close by.

Bob was elated. To have discovered a promising rookie in such unpromising circumstances, a lackadaisical, myopic denizen of a cold-water flat on slummy 119th Street—that was abundant cause for congratulation! Moreover, Bob, who was team manager, was due to graduate from DeWitt Clinton this summer, as was the team captain, and another two seasoned veterans of the team. It was imperative that adequate replacements be found as soon as possible. Bob kept the miniature target card to show to the team captain. On the strength of Ira's performance with the mock .22, he was invited to show what he could do with a real firearm, one that fired live ammunition. He accompanied the team to the downtown armory in whose tunneled basement the firing range was located. No faculty adviser accompanied them. The team seemed to be completely on its own—as if part of a confraternity of others on the firing range: men in plain clothes, men in army uniforms, in police uniforms, men who fired revolvers and automatic pistols in nearby shooting ranges.

Ira was given a half-dozen .22 Long Rifle cartridges to fire—at the regulation target, with a ten-ring the size of a dime, and at the regulation distance, twenty-five yards—and he fired two rounds prone, two kneeling, and two offhand. His score was sufficiently impressive so that he was inducted as a permanent alternate member of the team, a substitute.

Weekly practice sessions followed in the basement of the armory. His scores fluctuated from commendable to mediocre. . . .

His scores did, did they? Ira drifted off in tangential reverie. Didn't your performance depend more and more on where you stood, in what quarter of mood and moon you stood, in comparative repose or frantic agitation, after fitful sleep or sound one? He shrugged at himself: who the hell could correlate the one with the other? Only that there were the two planes the adolescent was living on: the wholesome overt, the abysmal hidden. What terrible torsion—or distortion—the two wrought between them, alternately, a charged field or an inert one: between plates of a condenser, between leaves of a Leyden jar—Leyden, yes, *leydn* in Yiddish meant suffering.

Ira suffered after the taboo—in spite of all, frenzied with wild accessions of desire because of the taboo, infusing him with vile ecstasy. It affected even Minnie, despite her previous disavowals; her demurrals gave way, moaned into surrenders. He suborned her, subverted her.

Ah, better than in Pop and Mom's bed on a Sunday morning were those rare, swift, hurried minutes of unexpected afternoon furor, when they were alone together. Those green, blistery kitchen walls visibly swayed with frantic evil, triggered by her passion's fierce onslaught—"So all right, come on." Oh, that trailing at her heels to the bedroom, rolling on two condoms to assure her, a quarter's worth at once! Ecstasy of the iniquitous. Double condom coupling, yeah, to slow him down, be safe, sure, but pump that "o-oh, my darling brother" out of her. . . .

Double-sheathed, but he was safe. He was safe, and she was safe. Still he worried, couldn't help it—even if she was only a day late, couldn't help it. Balance the wild ecstasy with wild panic: immediately the rift within him widened. Common sense was impotent against it. Fuckin' your own sister, fuckin' your own sister—he couldn't say it to himself any other way. Boy, if she got a big belly, boy, if she got a big belly, a bouncing baby boy, if she got a big belly. Some joke! And again and again, he would think: try to reflect, conjure away his cage, like the rifle cage down in the gym, yeah, cage and rifle: he saw the connection: why, that slum kid on the high school rifle team, by himself, unperverted—had it only been by himself as he was supposed to be, might have been, would have been nothing but another example of the happy success story that America stood for. Here he was, ex-immigrant Jewish kid mingling with regular and mostly non-Jewish Americans: Bonnar with his bewitching Southern accent, and of course Billy Green wrinkling his nub of a nose, immune to becoming rattled, incapable of losing his temper. He was the son of an engineer. Corey Valens was the son of a judge. What well-bred, gentile, tolerant teammates they were: friends, decent, yes, normal, level-headed—that was the word—well . . . actually it was the fact that they were normal that made his awareness of the hideous torque within him, his deviation, all the more unbearable. . . .

Supposing none of this, no return to high school after that first disaster, the expulsion from Stuyvesant, just menial, ordinary non-skilled or semiskilled work, being part of the mass, then what? Probably that would have forestalled the other. Or if not, and yet only too likely, given the amorphous lump he was—become the sloven loafer—what then? Outcast, sooner or later, depraved, since he had the propensity. Perhaps dragging Minnie with him, having knocked her up. Awful to think about—made the saliva, full to brimming the well of his mouth, too unpalatable to swallow. . . .

The team's first match since Ira's joining them was against the rifle team of Morris High in the Bronx. And who but the best marksman of the team, Granshaw himself, a senior, rocky, aggressive, relentless-eyed Granshaw, was unable to attend. As permanent alternate, Ira was called on to take the other's place. It was an afternoon when he felt easy, and he had reason to, his mind free of anxiety, a Friday afternoon when he felt free, felt all but negligent, with a weekend beginning. He fired the required number of rounds in the compulsory positions. And the result? The DeWitt Clinton High School newspaper ran a banner headline on its front page next week:

ROOKIE RIFLEMAN RACKS UP SENSATIONAL SCORE!

And below the headline, the subheadline:

IRA STIGMAN SCORES HIGHEST IN TEAM.

And in the text below, the first paragraph began:

Leading the DeWitt Clinton marksmen to a crushing defeat over Morris High in their invitational match Friday, rookie rifleman Ira Stigman fired a 188 out of a possible 210. The steady-nerved rookie had no difficulty finding the ten-ring again and again. And so little did the strain of his first competition faze him, he was heard to chuckle frequently when reloading. . . .

Never was he able to equal that score again. In fact, in the interscholastic rifle match, in which all the high schools of greater New York participated the following year, when he was already a veteran marksman, had his marksmanship been no better than average, even mediocre, let alone the "sensational" shooting of his debut the previous spring, the team would have won gold or silver medals. But his performance was wretched, poorer than that of the rookie just recently recruited and regarded as a tyro.

In his previously written first-person account, he most certainly had spared the reader the details of this episode with his sister and the rifle team, Ira reflected. And just as well. It was always easier to talk about Farley, about footraces. But no exorcism could be achieved talking of the 100-yard dash.

Following the near-orgy he had enforced on her the Thursday before, with the luxury of privacy till almost midnight, when Pop and Mom, with Zaida, Baba, and most of the tribe, attended the benefit play for the Galitzianer Verein, she wept, for other reasons than safety or dissatisfaction: "You're gonna ruin me for somebody else," she sobbed.

And his cynical, exultant, feral jibe: "Aw, c'mon, we don't even kiss. All we do is what you say, 'Fuck me, fuck me good,'" and then he snickered at her.

"Aw, shut up, you louse."

He had had no condom the second time, exited in time, he thought. But he scarcely needed specific cause for the gnawing to begin, no longer belatedness to incite worry. The plies of self—or so they felt—once parted, as they had, near the close of that demented fear of a year ago, were ever disposed to become so again, and he obsessively undone with them. Even if he thought he was safe, ought to be safe, had no reason to think otherwise (hell, for Chrissake, you're all right. You're crazy), the plies of self unraveled, and whatever courage, carefreedom, was woven in them dispelled. Supposing he no longer—supposing he didn't live at home, moved away, out of range of this, this recurring opportunity, away, away, would the fear (fear of what? Worry, just call it worry, peculiar invading sadness, despond, despond) haunt him anyway? No, it wouldn't, would it? How could it? It always had to be some reason, *that* reason. Trigger, like that of the target rifle. Springe: what a beautiful old word, not a spring, but a snare. Had to be that, like the pedal of a steel trap. The crushing weight on top of a figure 4 that baited the rabbit. How many ways were there to say it? Or was fear built into it by now? Built into him, built into the act? Try somebody else. Find out. Does Theodora live in the same place? If not, so somebody else. Find out. Ask. Nah. Who else?

The rest of the team had done so well at the match that even with his execrably poor shooting, they won the bronze medal; but only after it was disclosed that a member of the other team mistakenly awarded the bronze medal was disqualified on account of his failure to meet minimum scholastic standards. Christ, the three leading teams were so closely bunched, anything approaching the first score of his novitiate would have won them the gold. And even as far as their receiving the bronze they were too late. By the time the dis-qualification was discovered, the medals had been bestowed on oth-ers, never to be retrieved, as if strewn to the wind.

Ira found himself trying to coalesce into epigram the fatuity of a never-received bronze medal for his abysmal marksmanship. But as so often hap-pened to him, his attempt ended not with an epigram, but with a rank double entendre.

What a title, he mused as he typed, what a title that would make—with the tacit reservation that it could always be deleted: *The First Murderer in "Macbeth."* What a title, Ecclesias, wouldn't you say? And alter the quo-tation slightly in the epigraph:

> *I am one, my liege,*
> *whom the vile blows and buffets of the world*
> *have so incensed that I care not what*
> *I say to spite the world.*

And there again, we're back with Baudelaire, he reflected: saying in-stead of doing.

Still, there would abide with him—owing to his membership on the rifle team—many precious sequences, American sequences, he would term them. They were even more American than with Farley, because free of the implicit Irish Catholicism restricting Farley's outlook, and of which one was always aware, freer because traditionally and actually freer, neutrally Protestant, unclouded by bias. Billy Green, the only regular member of the team not to graduate the following year, became the new team captain—and Ira, by default, the new manager.

A more disarming, modest, clear-headed, even-tempered youth than Billy Ira had never met. "Boyish" was the word that might best describe him: boyish in the best sense, in the American sense: self-reliant, sportsmanlike, outdoors-oriented, adventurous and yet supremely sane. He was about Ira's height, which was then considered slightly above average, muscular, compact, with seemingly endless endurance and stamina, endless patience, courage, and good humor, Yankee fair of countenance, brown-eyed, with trait of crinkling his small nose upward, indicative of a whole range of tolerant negations, from belittling difficulties, to skepticism, to disapproval. One of two children of a widowed father, a hydraulic engineer by profession, and away from home a good deal of the time, Billy lived with his older sister in a well-kept apartment on the Upper West Side of Manhattan. Except for a cleaning woman who came in once a week to take care of the general housekeeping, Billy was mostly on his own, made his bed, got his own breakfast, helped his sister prepare supper, and helped with the dishes and the tidying-up afterward: all the chores that Mom did, and that suddenly became extraordinary when Ira pictured himself doing them.

Billy's self-reliance seemed to Ira the very epitome of the polar opposite of himself with his increasing feeling of a corrupting infection, a vulnerability he had inflicted on himself, as if all of him were haunted in the sad traces of his Jewishness, while Billy was so free, wholesome, airy as the outdoors, so cheerfully mettlesome. And living with his sister—there was the greatest contrast! All right, she was older, yes, but living with his sister, alone, night after night in separate beds. And Ira knew nothing ever happened between them. He just knew. Oh, God, to be alone with Minnie night after night—alone with Minnie! The very thought made him giddy, whirled by alternating impulses of shame and desire.

Billy owned golf clubs, a football, tennis rackets, ice skates, and hockey sticks. And he owned his own canoe! Canoe, paddles, camping gear of every kind, campfire cookware, and sleeping bags. And it was all housed in a boat club of which he was a member. Boat club and dock were on the banks of the Hudson only a few blocks away from where he lived. Would Ira like to go canoeing?

"Would I? Boy!"

They launched the little craft together, and with Ira in the bow, a tyro with a paddle, they paddled out into the Hudson. Even when Ira weakened against the tide, Billy manfully, with a determined grin, manifesting no dismay, uttering no complaint, no reproof, but as if what he did was a welcome test, brought the canoe back to the dock. Later, after Ira had learned to manage a paddle more adeptly, the two canoed all the way across the wide Hudson, so alone, so close to the green expanse of flowing water. They went camping overnight on the opposite bank. Vivid in memory still, those precious vignettes: the New Jersey constable interrogating the two friends in the morning as they sat about the small campfire preparing breakfast. And with Billy so self-possessed, so candid and natural in rejoinder, what middle-aging American would not have recalled his own boyhood at the sight of two half-grown youths in the morning, seated amid the river-worn boulders next to the softly lapping waters of the Hudson, and then gone off smiling?

As Ira's skill improved, the two indulged in harebrained stunts. Following closely the tubby paddle-wheeler, the broad-beamed, brick-red St. George's ferry, just after it left its slip on the Manhattan side, they rode the churning white crests in the wake of the ferry, plunged down into the tumultuous troughs, paddling for their lives and shouting with glee, within an ace of being swamped, while passengers in the stern stared in wonderment or reproof at the madcap, juvenile folly. If only he could have been reborn! Late and soon, many were the times the wish clashed against the dismal actuality. If only, if only he could have been reborn. On the majestic Hudson, paddling in the dark, alone on that great breadth of water, or on shore, in nighttime silence, snug in sleeping bag, under the steep gloom of the Palisades: if only that one thing—why did it have to happen to him? Why? Because he made it happen.

On the New Jersey bank during the Easter vacation, when they camped out several nights, Ira greedily devoured for the first time, along with the fried bacon and beans for supper, slabs of bread sopped in bacon grease. Who would believe he could digest it? He could and did. Around a driftwood fire, after a day of canoeing, anyone could digest anything. And in the morning, unforgettable April morning during the Easter vacation, they dared each other to dash into the water from the shore. Ira had never experienced the like. He doubted whether he ever would again, would ever try the stunt again. When he came wading back to shore, after that headlong fling into the frigid water, he couldn't speak; he could just barely breathe. His scrotum had shrunken flat, his testicles had burrowed out of sight within him. The very breeze that only short seconds ago had seemed so cool now laved his skin like a balmy zephyr of midsummer. If only he could have been reborn! Walking through the uptown shopping street near Billy's home, after the canoe was stowed away in the boathouse, Ira sampled, for the first time in his life, freshly made potato chips that Billy bought. What a heavenly flavor and crunch: potatoes transmogrified! Billy laughed at his friend's ecstasy. And striding along Broadway from Billy's apartment house to the subway station, their target rifles in their canvas cases slung over their shoulders, they explained to the tolerant Irish cop who stopped them that they were captain and manager of the DeWitt Clinton High School rifle team. . . .

Oh, America, America! There was no going on beyond the outcry of remembered affection, because history would not bear out its promise, as it seemed to the youthful understanding: only if he were different. Nor could he have entered on an equal footing into that expansive, affirmative, vibrant society—even if he were sound in temperament, instead of being already badly warped. Still, he had had a glimpse, thanks to his membership on the rifle team, thanks to Billy Green, of that dynamic form and ferment that was America, and of the joy due youth, of the sportiveness due youth, a glimpse of the means that made for joyous wholesomeness. Beyond him now, poignantly appreciated, but beyond him, the pristine play, to one already ineffaceably scarred, mutilated by mutilations incessantly craved. Still, in the flush of novelty, under the spell of campfire, the outdoors, pulsing with infectious self-reliance, independence, hardiness, the chill night winds and freedom in his blood, he would come home at last, full of vigor and boldness, to a surprised Mom and Pop and Minnie. And while washing the weekend's scarce-washed sweat and dust from face and hands, announce: "This is going to make a new man of me!"

Oh, America! Mingling for a brief interval the free and lusty air of nature with the Jewish atmosphere of the cold-water flat on 119th Street in East Harlem.

The whole thing is nuttier than a fruit cake, Ecclesias; to an old man, sex is nuttier than a fruit cake.

—Why tell me? It didn't evolve to suit your criteria of rationality. It evolved out of other and deeper needs, needs of survival, not reasons. Remorseless needs.

—Yes, of course.

The monotony of the procreative cycle is hypnotic. So it affects me. The very consideration of everything having to do with sex makes me drowsy. And most of all, the perpetual compulsion of it.

—You wouldn't be here otherwise, if the compulsion were any less.

Ah, yes, do tell. I am one, my liege, whom the vile blows and buffets of the world— I wonder what M is doing? She is so quiet; she must be writing music. I have made a tentative resolution that I would note down her very, very slight foibles, her predilections and customs. She likes to buy new clothes, *shmattas*. The poor girl was so deprived as a child in that indigent, earnest Baptist clergyman's household she was reared in, though not so indigent as her calculating mother pretended, that she finds new clothes irresistible. And later, as wife of an impractical and impecunious husband, and mother of two boys, a schoolteacher in Maine earning a rural schoolteacher's salary, how long she had to wear patched and rent slips and petticoats. So now she loves to buy a gay new blouse. Important to me too, Ecclesias, is her practice of gathering up the few gray strands of hair that may have strayed in front of her fine brow, and train them, as it were, annex them to the main fold of coiffure with a bobby pin. Interesting, isn't it? I didn't know that.

—Very interesting.

It's a fact, just the same.

XV

On the very first day of classes after the summer vacation of 1923, it had so happened that the person who was scheduled to be Ira's regular teacher in Elocution 7, a course for seniors, was Miss Pickens. She was absent that day. Her ocean liner had been delayed by storms, so rumor ran, on her return trip from Europe. Her older brother, the august, gray-maned, thespian Dr. Pickens, head of the elocution department, made shift to substitute for his absent sister by combining her class with his in one and the same room. As a result, the classroom was jammed; and only by making every seat do double duty, accommodate two students instead of one, could the crowd be contained. Even so, there was a shortage of sitting room; some few had to improvise a seat out of a textbook on a radiator.

It chanced—ah, it chanced—that the one whose seat Ira had hastily and randomly chosen to share was occupied by a well-groomed, well-dressed young man, his straight black hair silky and parted to one side, his tweed jacket heathery and rich, trousers spotless and creased, his cordovans dull brown, richly tooled. A gentile, Ira supposed, as he edged into his half of the seat. The other's fine, well-fitting raiment, well-bred manner, regularity of feature, dappled, lambent skin, his untroubled lineaments, all bespoke the gentile. He was not only a gentile, but affluent too. Ira thought of that silver fountain pen he had purloined long ago, so it seemed. That kid's parents must have been affluent too, but probably Jewish. How different gentile affluence was—even in youth: poised, polished, mature; if the other weren't beside him in a high school classroom, Ira would have taken him for a worldly young man, one who had outgrown high school, a collegian at least. . . .

During the prolonged confusion caused by latecomers finding seats, or rather, half-seats and parts of radiators and windowsills, Ira struck up a conversation with his neighbor. Ira remarked, with his usual unerring ingratiation where gentiles were concerned, that the seats were admirably fitted for half-assed people. And with that droll observation, the two were off on a course of repartee whose twists and turns Ira no longer remembered, except that he was intent on entertaining his seatmate: and his chief resource was his lowbrow witticisms, lowbrow and snide. He succeeded in his aim; he was very amusing to his partner, and his partner was liberal in appreciation. It seemed only minutes, and they were beguiled with each other.

Attendance was taken by Dr. Pickens—somehow. The combined classes were called in a businesslike way to order, and dutifully the new acquaintances nipped off further sallies. But not for long: the momentum of mutual entertainment was too great to arrest. Ira began whispering again, and induced a reply. They were too engrossed in each other's inimitable wit to take more than fleeting notice of the frowns of annoyance Dr. Pickens directed their way, until—just as Ira was ventriloquizing in sidemouthed whimsy, "It's gonna be slim pickin's either way, ye know—"

"That big galoot in the third row, fifth seat, stand up!" Dr. Pickens thundered, glaring at both.

Ira would always recollect with admiration his seat partner's courage at that critical moment. While Ira shrank back in fear before the blast of pedagogical censure, his classmate gamely stood up.

"Not you!" Leonine and histrionic, Dr. Pickens boomed in devastating tones, "That big galoot beside you. Stand up!"

Larry, for that was his name, sat down. And Ira stood up. He already quaked in fear at the penalties he might have to pay for his misbehavior: gross disrespect before so august and commanding a figure as Dr. Pickens, head of the department of elocution, gross disrespect within the assembled view of two combined classes as witness.

"What is your name?"

Faintly Ira answered, "Ira Stigman."

"What do you mean by talking when the class has been called to order, talking when I'm addressing the class? Are you a senior?"

"Yes, sir."

"A senior, and not have the common decency of behaving your-self in a difficult situation like this! A senior and not have the cour-tesy owing a teacher of DeWitt Clinton High School! What do you mean, you big galoot? You're not fit to be a senior! You're not fit to be in this class!"

"I'm sorry," Ira mumbled.

"Get out! Get out of here at once! Out of this room! Out!" Dr. Pickens blared. And shaking a finger fraught with menace, "Report to me after class. And don't fail to."

"No, sir." Hangdog, in a swirl of fear, Ira made his way through the crowded aisle of shod feet and briefcases to the door. Even as he closed it behind him, he glimpsed a fellow classmate already slipping from his perch on a radiator to occupy the vacancy Ira had left. Down the stairs he went into the study hall, to wait for the end of the period, and who knew what punishment to be meted out, what sen-tence. Trepidations such as he hadn't felt since the Stuyvesant ordeal came flooding back. He hadn't stolen anything, but he was guilty of grave affront to a head of a department, and a most haughty one at that. There was no limit to the amends he would be required to make. The cleavage of nameless dread began its remorseless move-ment, impervious to the exhortations of common sense. Already he summoned up in imagination the lean, crease-jowled, draconian Mr. Dotey, the dean. Already Ira heard Mr. Dotey's pronouncement, that worst of all penalties—no, not quite; Ira knew the worst—to bring one of his parents to school: Mom or Pop. To have to go through that again!

He had taken a seat close to the assembly-hall doors, and sat swaying the minutes away, while he chafed, cold damp fingers to-gether—all too soon the fateful gong rang for the change of classes. Plowing among fellow students, he made his way up the three flights of stairs to the room from which he had been expelled.

Larry, Ira's new acquaintance, had left, but apprehension obliter-ated everything from his mind except to obtain pardon for his mis-deed. "You asked me, sir, to report back to you, Dr. Pickens. I'm sorry."

"That's all very well." Leonine Dr. Pickens gathered up atten-dance books and papers. "I still intend to bring your insulting, your gross misconduct to Mr. Dotey's attention."

"Please, Dr. Pickens. Please. I—it was just that one time," Ira begged. "Please! You can ask any teacher if I ever did that before."

"I don't intend to do anything of the kind. It was as disgraceful an exhibition of bad manners as anything I've experienced in my years of teaching. Utterly. And I can think of only one thing proper for that kind of behavior, one that may cure you from ever repeating it again. And that is a visit to Mr. Dotey's office. And that's where we're going."

Ira's eyes began to fill with tears. He would have reached out, if he dared, and seized Dr. Pickens's hand. "One chance, Dr. Pickens. I'm just asking for one chance."

"Can you give me a single good reason, young man, why I should grant you one?"

"Yes, sir."

"Yes, sir, what? That you have a good reason? I don't believe it."

"We were doubled up in the seats, and I couldn't help it."

"That's the *very* reason"—Dr. Pickens's finger described an uncompromising arc from himself to Ira—"the very reason why it was your obligation to show greater self-control. Better manners were clearly called for in this kind of emergency situation, and did you show them, a senior? You displayed the very opposite."

"I know."

"Then you have nothing to say for yourself."

Ira was at wit's end. Tears began to trickle from his eyes. He would have to gamble. He would have to tell the truth, trust that it was as compelling to Dr. Pickens as it was to him. "I felt like I found a friend. He was rich and he wasn't Jewish, and he liked me."

Dr. Pickens drew back, as if (Ira's fervent hope) glimpsing or confronting something grave, unique, beyond discourse. His close-set gray eyes searched the face in front of him with a relentlessness that intensified his leonine aspect. A second passed in silence, two, and then he cleared his throat forcefully. "I think you're telling the truth."

"I am, Dr. Pickens. I am. That's why it happened."

"Well, don't you ever let it happen again in my classroom."

"No, sir! I won't!"

Dr. Pickens deliberated another moment, retributionally, without serious intent. "Very well. You may leave." His gesture of dismissal seemed peculiarly remote from the white-maned, florid, age-pocked features Ira saw blurred through tears. "You may leave." Dr. Pickens twiddled two fingers in impatient dismissal.

"Thanks, Dr. Pickens! Thanks!" His heart on wings within him, smearing his wet cheeks, Ira raced to his next class.

And now having had my cup of tea, Ecclesias, I am alone in my mobile home study. The evaporative cooler throbs at my back, while outside the west window, all but one sunflower droops in heavy-headed ripeness. I tell myself it is time to pick up the thread of narrative where I left off, forget the Kurdish rebellion and Sadat and Begin, forget the copperheads and the assassins, and behold: at this very moment, a roadrunner, neck outstretched and tail rising and falling like a feathery bascule, pauses, scans, speeds over the parched, buff adobe dirt, and disappears behind the newly heeled-in trees in the nurseryman's strip of land on the other side of the fence. *Io digo seguitando.*

With the return of Miss Pickens by the next session of Elocution 7, the two combined classes were separated into their original sections, and, of course, each section met in its own classroom. Ira was in Miss Pickens's class, and his congenial seat companion, fortunately or unfortunately, was in the class conducted by her brother. Still, the new acquaintanceship continued to grow: by hasty encounters in the hall between periods, on the stairway, and the once-a-week coinciding of lunch periods in the lunchroom on the sunny top floor of the high school. The new acquaintanceship grew until it struck a kind of balance against Ira's other friendships and interests.

It was on an afternoon in early October, a clear, bright afternoon, as befitted October, that Ira and Larry Gordon met by chance on the steps before the school. Ordinarily, Ira might have spent the hour or two after school in the "den," an enclosed coign or utility closet under the staircase that led from the main floor down to the assembly hall, the assigned gathering place of rifle team members. It was the place where the team discussed prospective rifle matches, where letters of invitation were written to other high school rifle teams, where guns were cleaned, all amid shoptalk and banter. Billy was absent from school that day, and though Ira had a key to the den, he had a hunch that maybe . . . if he went directly home, well, one could never tell. Usually his hunches, his ever-present, ever-hopeful hunches, proved empty, but then, once in a while, once in a long while, they materialized: that time Mom had to wait so late in the afternoon in the Harlem Eye and Ear Clinic seeking relief for the terrible noises in her ears; and that time she stayed with Ella in her 116th Street and Fifth Avenue apartment when Ella had a baby, and—hell, oh, you never could tell. But there was Larry descending the steps before the school at exactly the same time as Ira came out the door amid a noisy swarm of fellow students.

He and Larry greeted each other warmly, and fell into step, walking east with the jabbering throng of schoolmates.

"I don't think you really told me where you live," Larry said.

"It's a dump. It's really crummy."

"That's what you said before. You said something about living in a tough neighborhood."

"I'll say." Ira took refuge behind one of Farley's quips, "Where I come from they're so tough they play tiddlywinks with manhole covers."

Which brought a gratifying chuckle from Larry, but without deviation of purpose, "But where? Harlem, that much I know."

"Yeah, Harlem is right. Slummy old Harlem. 108 East 119th Street."

"Where's that?"

"Did you ever ride on the New York Central? The overpass?" Ira gestured.

"The New York Central Railroad? I used to go with my father, and my mother too sometimes, when my grandfather and grandmother were alive. They were the original Hungarians. My grandfather came from Buda Pesht. He owned a small department store. In New Haven—you know where Yale is?"

"No. Is that where it is?"

"You know, Yale is a Hebrew word: *ya* standing for *Jahveh*, and *El*, the lord."

"Yeah?" Ira glanced upward, narrowly, at the taller Larry, in step beside him. How did he know that? He was gentile. Knew more than Ira did. Well, because of Yale. Of course.

"My father thought of selling his dry-goods business, and taking over, but my three sisters, my brother Irving, were all against leaving New York. My mother, too. And the dry-goods business in Yorkville—you know, it's a German neighborhood, and both of my parents speak German well. So Grandpa Taddy's store was sold. Just as well. New Haven isn't as exciting as it once was. We used to go there on Christmas. Everyone was off from school. Wilma and Sophie were both going to Hunter Normal then."

"Oh, yeah?"

"I didn't mean to get off the subject." Larry smiled down at Ira, spread the fingers of his large hand.

"Oh, that's all right."

"What's the New York Central got to do with where you live?"

"Just about everything. If you'd looked out of the window when the train passed 119th Street, three houses, you'd've seen where we live."

"Which way?"

"Oh. East."

"Is that so? You know, my brother Irving just set up a ladies'-housedress-manufacturing plant on East 119th Street."

"Yeah? Where?"

"In a loft east of Third Avenue."

"Is that so? On 119th?"

"Ladies' housedresses are all the rage today. Finished goods. He has about a hundred operators there."

"Huh!" Ira exclaimed. "A hundred. Well, just walk a block west from your brother's place. Now you know where I live."

"That *is* a coincidence."

"I'll say. And you, where do you live?"

"I live on 161st and Sommers in the Bronx. It's a very quiet neighborhood, nice but not too showy, just across the Harlem River. We own our own house."

"Oh, you live in a private house?"

"No. It's a small apartment house. One family to a floor. We live a flight up."

"Yeah, we do too." Ira grinned.

"How do you go home?"

"Me? I have to take the Broadway subway and switch to Lenox at 96th. You take the Bronx Park train?"

"No. I take the Ninth Avenue El."

"No foolin'. The Ninth Avenue El?"

"Yes. It lets me off a few blocks from where I live."

"Oh. But it's in the Bronx?"

"Yes. The near Bronx."

Walking with Larry in public was different, Ira realized, from encountering him those few times in hall and lunchroom. Exchanges in school were mostly confined to school, had the school environment to buttress them. Here in the street, Ira felt a certain awkwardness of new acquaintance. Also, personal appearance mattered more. It was not only that Ira was conscious of the contrast between Larry's "rich" clothes and his own rumpled, seedy ones; but that Larry's appearance, Larry's bearing, drew the attention of passersby, women especially, young and (to Ira) middle-aged, to which Larry seemed to pay no attention, as something he took for granted. He wore no eyeglasses; he was at least three inches taller than Ira. Not only were his features extraordinarily regular, and his skin the fresh, dappled smoothness of cherished rearing, but his whole body was finely proportioned, again "regular"—except for his thick eyebrows, like wings above his soft, brown eyes, and arms, longer than average, even disproportionate, and his hands: they were exceptionally large. Taken together with the regularity of bodily proportion and feature, Ira was suddenly reminded of the cast of Michelangelo's *David* in the Metropolitan Museum: the frowning eyebrows, the big expressive hands, one in front, one reaching over his shoulder for the sling. "Are you still on the rifle team?" Larry asked.

"Yeah."

"Really like it?"

"Yeah, sure. You don't go in for any sports?"

"I'm in *The Pirates of Penzance*. In the chorus. I don't know if you can call it sports."

"Oh, yeah, yeah, you told me. You sing."

"Are you going to see it?"

"Nah, it's gonna cost a dollar. It's at night."

"It's very good. It really has a good cast. And I don't say that because I'm in it."

"I know. I saw a piece of it in the assembly. I liked it."

"That was our preview. For publicity. We sang 'A paradox, a paradox, a most ingenious paradox.'"

"That's right. It was funny."

Larry laughed, a deprecating, introductory laugh before something amusing: "When the stage director isn't listening, some of us in the chorus sing, 'A pair o' socks, a pair o' socks, a most ingenious pair o' socks.'"

Ira grinned—self-consciously. How little attention Larry paid to the crowd of students moving with them, some of whom turned to smile in appreciation of his freely delivered snatch of song.

Musical, his voice, and flawless the way he held a tune. "'I am the captain of the *Pinafore*, and a right good captain too.'"

They were nearing Ninth Avenue, the dark El structure's shadow charring the avenue below. And like so many beacons in the bustling gloom beneath the El, the United Cigar store's electric lights were already blazing around the margins of the show window.

"Do you smoke?" Larry asked.

"I had a little pipe—I liked it—but I left it in my white jacket when I was hustlin' soda."

"Hustling soda? Oh, yes, you did tell me," Larry added quickly. "Selling it."

"Yeah. So now I smoke—" He was about to say *yenems*, other people's, but that was Yiddish; Larry wouldn't understand. So Ira grimaced, shrugged negligently instead.

"I like a pipe too," said Larry. "I've got a calabash I bought in

Bermuda. And a Dunhill. But they're too bulky to take into class. And you have to carry a tobacco pouch too. You smoke cigarettes, don't you?"

"Oh, sure, sure."

"Let's stop in here. I'll get a pack of Camels, okay? I like Camels. Do you?"

"Yeah. I don't like Luckies—"

"Not a cough in a carload."

"Yeah. They're raw as hell. Maybe after you get used to 'em. My grandfather smokes Melachrinos. Not even half a Melachrino at a time. They're mild, but boy, do they cost. You know what he does?"

They had almost reached the corner. "Puts a toothpick in the end of his cigarette?" Larry was beguiled.

"Oh, no. He puts 'em in a paper cigarette holder and takes maybe three and a half puffs. Then he dinches it."

"Dinches it? I never heard that one. Clinches it?"

"All right, clinches it."

They paused at the corner. "You're Jewish, aren't you?" Larry asked.

Well, it had come, the ineluctable question. In a way he had invited it, Ira thought, but it had to come sooner or later; it always did. So, if this was as far as—what?—their friendship would go, they could always joke with each other once in a while in school. "Yeah, I'm Jewish," Ira stated, as appeasingly as he could.

"I just wanted to make sure. I am too."

There could be no more generous spoofing on the part of a gentile. It was charitable in the extreme, a humorous unguent alleviating the chronic sore spot.

"Oh, yeah?" Ira prolonged his drawl—making sure his disbelief registered.

"I am!" Wings of Larry's dense eyebrows converged. "What did you think I was?"

"Aw, you're kidding!"

"I'm not!"

They had stopped—because Ira had—on the very curb of the street corner, stopped and stood there, toes on the granite curb, while the crowd flowed past them into the deep shadow and across the avenue through openings in trolley and auto traffic. Strange pause. It was like something inside the self, not merely bodily arrest. The guy wasn't kidding; he couldn't be kidding. That would be taking things too far, and they never could have gotten this far, if he were that kind of a guy. There were *goyim*, sure, the straight-faced practical jokers; but hell, he had learned to tell those a mile off. And there were others like Billy, who never showed the slightest sign of even being conscious of Ira's Jewishness. This called for reexamination, for keenest scrutiny. Yes, there he was, still, Larry, regular Arrow Collar countenance, well, almost, under gray felt hat, in fine navy-blue wool topcoat over matching tweed jacket, and wearing a blue knit tie. In good taste everything, you just felt it, even if you didn't know what good taste was, refinement, oh, what the hell, had to be gentile, with that kind of luster—but no. Or maybe not: the lips were a little too thick, rolled out: Jewish softness there, Jewish sympathy. No, Larry couldn't possibly pretend to being so earnest. He must mean it—

Reorientation felt almost physical, as if accepted landmarks were reinterpreted by a sudden jolt. "Boy, I never been so fooled before in my life. Honest."

"Let's get across the street," Larry nudged. "What did you think I was?"

"A *goy*. What else? You—you're Bar Mitzva and everything?"

"Of course. I used to teach Sunday school, too."

"Sunday school!" Ira echoed incredulously. "Sunday school is for—" He was glad the El train passing above rattled over his near display of ignorance.

"At Temple Beth El on Fifth Avenue. I just loved teaching Old Testament stories. They mean a lot to me still."

"They do? Old Testament stories? You mean from the Jewish religion? Right? From the Bible? In English?"

"Oh, certainly in English. Oh, a few of us knew some Hebrew. But very few. The stories I taught were in English. They were the same stories I loved hearing myself when I went to Sunday school. You must know them: about Saul and David and Absalom. Samson."

"I know *about* 'em. I learned them from reading English too—I mean not from reading Hebrew."

"Really? I thought of you as being a lot more Jewish than I was."

"But we didn't learn it that way. I mean in the *cheder*—you know what a *cheder* is?"

"Oh, yes, I've heard about it. My brother-in-law Sam told me about it. He's a lawyer. And he knows quite a bit of Hebrew. And some Yiddish words too. That's where you were taught religion, wasn't it?"

"If you wanna call it that. This one was on the East Side. Jewish East Side. Mostly. I learned in Harlem, too. But we learned to say prayers, you know what I mean? To *daven*. You know what I mean?"

"That means to pray, doesn't it?"

"To pray in the *shul*, in the synagogue. You shake when you're doing it." Ira mimed as a way out of engagement with the subject any further.

But Larry was still interested. He smiled tentatively. "I lost out on a lot of that kind of learning."

"Lost out? Say, it's not like that temple on Fifth Avenue. I know that one. It's beautiful. These are little dumps like huts in the backyard."

Larry shook his head. "I didn't know they were that bad."

"Hell, I hate 'em."

"Really? And you didn't find the Biblical subjects inspiring?"

"Nah. Maybe I might have—if I learned them the way you did. But I didn't get any Biblical subjects."

"There's so much inspiring about the Bible. I mean, it relates to so much in the American tradition, the English tradition, I should say. But the American tradition is much more meaningful. Do you know that King Saul and Custer have a lot in common?"

"Huh! General Custer?"

"I'm writing a poem about both men. A Jewish king and gentile general—"

"A poem? You're writing a *poem*?"

"A long poem. A connected series, half narrative, half sort of lyric."

But Ira continued standing stock-still, frowning and incredulous. "A poem? You're still in high school."

"That doesn't matter. People younger than I am have written great poems. And no one's ever done this before. It's very exciting:

man opposing fate. There's a universality about it, whether it's Saul
on Mt. Gilboa, or Custer at Little Bighorn."

Larry led the way into an aromatic, brilliantly lit cigar store. With
what a worldly flair he ordered a package of Camels from the
promptly obliging gray-mustached clerk, even as he continued to address Ira—"Of course, I can't speak Yiddish," he said with complete
self-composure, as Ira felt himself curdle slightly with self-consciousness—and effortlessly returned the clerk's thanks while picking up
his purchase and the change. "I can speak a little Hungarian. Mostly
because of Mary, our maid. My folks use a Hungarian word or two
with her. I've picked up a few words." He led the way back out into
the open air. "And sometimes on the school holidays when we visited
my grandparents in New Haven. They were both born here, but my
great-grandparents on both sides came here from Hungary."

"Yeah? You got any of 'em left? A grandfather or somebody?"

"No, I was the baby of the family. You?"

"I still got a grandfather and grandmother."

"You have? Were they born here?"

"Hell, no. I wasn't even born here!"

"You weren't?"

"I was born in Galitzia. In Austro-Hungary. There once used to
be an Austro-Hungary."

"Of course. I know. Before the Great War."

"So we're some kind of *landslayt,* nearly."

"I know that word. *Landsleute.* It's the same in German. That's
what I'm taking."

"Yeah? It's Yiddish too."

"Is it? I know a few words of Yiddish. *Tsuris.* I've heard Sam say
that. Troubles. *Keyn ayin-horeh.* He says that when somebody praises
my niece. Actually, I think I know more Hungarian words than I
know Yiddish—I spent so much time with my Uncle Leon in
Bermuda. He'd say something in Hungarian once in a while."

Silently, resentful of his own bewilderment at the peculiar dis-
placement going on within him, he watched Larry's big capable
hands tear a square of foil from the top of the yellow package of
Camels, tap the package expertly until several cigarettes extruded.

He did everything with such superb assurance—and facility. "Cigarette?" He proffered the pack.

"Yeah. But you're goin' upstairs, to the El, aren't you?"

"Oh, we can *shmooze* down here awhile. I hope you're not in any hurry. Are you?"

Shmooze. It was as though Larry were dedicated to authenticating his Jewishness, placing a seal on it. "Well . . ." Ira hesitated, took a cigarette. "No, I'm not in a hurry." Probably Mom was home anyway. The thought, the evil prompting, flared up in his mind: tell her about Larry next chance, the handsome acquaintance. Stir her up that way. Yeah. What the hell. Larry wrote poems, he could tell her. A poet. Jewish, you'd never know—but something sobering, suddenly sobering, perplexing, preempted: what kind of Jewish? What kind of world?

They found a niche of refuge under the slant of the El stairs. Wonderful, the way Larry could hold a lit match in the cup of his large, white hand. "Then how did you learn prayers at the *cheder*, as you call it? Didn't you translate out of the Hebrew?"

"Oh, no, I told you. The old guy with the whiskers slapped you around when you didn't make the right sounds. *Komets-alef 'o'; komets-beys, 'bo'; komets-giml, 'go.'* You ducked as soon as you saw his pointer drop from his hand to the page."

As though the scene were animate before his eyes, Larry listened with lips parted in pleasure. "Is that so?"

"Oh, sure. We learned Hebrew in a little shack in the backyard, or a cellar store. Till I was eight and a half. I got pretty good at it, too. The *melamed,* you know, the teacher, told my mother when I was about seven that I could have had a real future. But then we moved to Harlem."

"I practically grew up in Bermuda. My older brother and sisters lived in Yorkville a short while. I spent only a short time there, and now we're in the near Bronx." Larry inhaled. "I told you I'm the baby of the family."

"Oh, now I see. You mean you got older brothers and sisters." Ira raised his arm in gesticulation. "That's why."

"Haven't I? Two are married and have children." And speaking through cigarette smoke, "Then I have an older sister, Irma.

She's the next older. She lives with us. She's a private secretary. My older brother, you know about him. He's in the ladies'-housedress-manufacturing business. He's going to be married soon—to his secretary."

"So he lives with you too?"

"Oh, yes. My brother Irving. He was in the army. Wilma and Sophie both taught school. They're both married now and have children. I have the sweetest, loveliest niece." Larry's face brightened with genuine pleasure. "I get so much sheer delight out of the way she talks and moves. Do you know she's already writing an opera?"

"Oh. A what?" And then Ira, startled, added, "An opera? How old is she?"

"She's four. Listen." He began singing, " 'Some people like banana splits and other things. But I like my chocolate soda!' Isn't that a wonderful aria?"

"Yeah." Ira felt a presentiment of embarrassment—and with nothing to say, except an amenable, "Four years. That's all? I got a cousin who's nearly fourteen years old. Stella. My Aunt Mamie's kid. She wouldn't know an aria from a—" A new prompting coalesced into consciousness. "—a hole in the wall. Yeah." He puffed on his cigarette.

"Is your family very close?"

"What d'you mean?"

"Close-knit. I mean, do they have strong family ties? Are they affectionate with one another, with you? Do you have any affection for them?"

"Oh, no. Jesus!"

Larry studied Ira in his vehemence. "Is that so?" He shook his head. "You're so different. In a lot of ways, it seems. We're a very close-knit family. I don't know why. Maybe it's the Hungarian influence. Anyway, we are. Both my brothers-in-law are like members of the family. My sister Wilma is married to a lawyer, I told you: Sam, Sam Elinger. Incidentally, he went to CCNY for his B.A. You were talking about going there."

"Yeah. That's right."

"And my oldest sister, Sophie, is married to a dentist, Victor."

"Yeah? Gee." Something warned Ira not to say what he was about to; it had such a Jewish mercenary overtone. But the momentum of the remark prevailed despite misgiving. "Your sisters are well-married?"

Larry looked a little pained, for the first time almost disapproving. "I wouldn't say they were well-married. They're happily married."

"Oh. I guess that's what I meant." Ira felt chastised, confirmed in his misgiving. You don't say "well-married," he instructed himself, like *zey hobn gemakht a gitn shiddekh.* It wasn't proper. Happily married. Yeah? Who was happily married in Baba's family?

"What about *your* folks?" Larry asked.

Ira's lips moved without sound: well. He suddenly felt glum. He had told Billy that Pop was a waiter; that was nothing to Billy. It would probably be nothing to Larry either: just another curiosity about Ira that Larry found so quaint, why so fetching, like Ira's stock of gags, picked up in a hundred places. Or what? And all this taking place within the mind while thousands of people, vehicles, were making new configurations in tumultuous passing, and overhead too, rattle of the rolling coffins, the El trains.

Within the mind and within an instant, so it seemed: when an instant kindled, it never went out, was never extinguished, it lasted fiery forever, receding. How was that? Even that stylish young dame, yes, hoity-toity, slinky dame, in her purple cloche, staring at Larry as she passed, had lasted forever, had lasted ever since then.

Ira looked up from the cigarette, glowing within gray ash at one end, yellowing in a ring where he put it to his mouth at the other. "I'll tell you," he said, then grinned—that grin that Mr. O'Reilly had warned him against, when? Then, when it first began with Minnie—ah, that must be the crazy, hidden bridge between him and Larry, the bond of strangeness or something, that had even got him into trouble with Dr. Pickens. His goofy, no, his clandestine, worry-haunted ways made him different, more different all the time, possessed him with an utter uniqueness, spasmodic in new situations, uncouth often as well, an ultra, ultra something which only a Mr. Sullivan, crippled, deformed Mr. Sullivan, could see through: "thatsh right, made a boob o'yourshelf—"

"My father is a *lokshn-treger,*" Ira said—deliberately in Yiddish, the very thing he sensed would intrigue Larry; but why? Why did he surmise so often the rightness of the results he could produce in another, when he sought to, without knowing why they were effective—with Farley, with Billy Green, even Eddy Ferry, the janitor's kid, long ago in early boyhood? And now Larry. Something *goyish* he had adapted himself to (he had thought Larry was a *goy*), or something *goyish* he preferred, he was becoming.

"A what?" Larry's laugh was bright and forthcoming. "He's a what? A what *treger?*"

"He's a *lokshn-treger,* a noodle porter."

"Noodles. Oh, yes."

"My father's a waiter."

"Oh." And again Larry laughed, his features all eagerness. "Is that what you call him—I mean, a waiter?"

As Ira had guessed, in nothing so wily as this. He had completely deflected Larry from fact to word, from word to mirth. "*Lokshn-treger,*" Ira repeated. "It's Yiddish."

"Is that Yiddish? I know that word, *tragen!* It's German for 'carry.'" He was delighted at the discovery. "Is that how you say *Nudeln? Lokshn?*"

"Yeah. A *loksh* is any kind of gawky sap. I made that up outta Yiddish. Where are you in German?"

"This is my third year. My parents speak some too. You know—because my grandparents did. When Hungary was part of Austro-Hungary. *Lokshn-treger.* Noodle porter." He savored the sound, highly entertained. "Why don't we take the El train together," he urged. "We can talk while we ride uptown."

"It's about a league outta me way," Ira declined with antic solecism. "Listen, I got only a few puffs left on my butt, so that means the curfew tolls the knell of parting day, and I gotta go."

Not even his heavy-handed humor could dispel the disappointment settling about Larry's soft brown eyes. He let a billow of smoke all but escape from his open lips, then withdrew it again on the inhale. "I'll tell you what: this Friday let's take the El together. All right? We won't have to worry about preparing for class the next day."

"Okay."

"Front of the school. Friday. Right?"

"Right."

"I'll see you before then."

"Right. Abyssinia."

"What? Oh, I get it. Abyssinia."

They parted, Larry dropping the cigarette as he mounted the El steps, Ira his in the gutter on the way east to the subway. If that wasn't strange, strange, and flattering too, even if Larry wasn't a gentile. Wonderful, wasn't it? He was a gentile, and suddenly Jewish. Like magic. Something Ira had seen change that way just by being stared at for a time: an optical illusion. But Larry couldn't change back again, could he? Was that why Jews were circumcised? What an idea. Lucky he hadn't known Larry was Jewish when he pleaded with Dr. Pickens that first day. He might not have got off. And suppose Dr. Pickens knew? Boy, talk about things doubling back on themselves. Like Jessica, Shylock's daughter: pretended to be a boy, masqueraded as a boy. But she *was* a boy! In Shakespeare's time, said the English teacher, boys played women's parts; Portia's too, so there you were, being yourself, but not supposed to be yourself. . . .

Ira made his way east on noisy, restless 59th Street. . . . And what would he tell Billy about Friday? Just say nothing. Not show up. Billy would wait awhile in the gun room. . . . Still, wasn't that funny, though, the way Larry laughed at *lokshn-treger,* noodle porter . . . as if he enjoyed hearing things out of that lousy world that Ira lived in. Only some of it, yes. But Billy wasn't interested in any of it. He really was a gentile; that was the difference; Larry wasn't. Could you be a gentile in part? Half-assed Jewish, bringing some of his own selected rotten world to Larry . . .

Boy, the guy was rich. His clothes, tweed jacket. That sheen on his skin, brought up delicate. He was the baby of the family, he said: that was why. . . .

Sky, open space of Columbus Circle hove into view. . . . Bermuda,

Larry said he had spent so much time in Bermuda. Was that why he talked that way? About calabash pipes and Dunhill pipes, cost a fortune. And what was that Ethical Culture School where he said he went for a while? He had drama and ballet there. Not just dancing, two-step, fox-trot, shimmy. Ballet, gee. Where the hell was that jitney for the subway?

Life is real, life is earnest, Ecclesias. No? You never can be diverted, can you?

—Occasionally. You certainly managed to evade that snare. If I knew anything about the game, I'd say gambit, but that's only another cliché.

You're right. Any will do.

—Fairly adroit. You were virtually on the gaff, to vary the metaphor once again, but managed to escape. Having told you something about his immediate relatives, he asked you about yours. Which was only natural—

Oh, I expected to regale him with tales about my immigrant Zaida and Baba and uncles and aunts. And tales of the East Side.

—He asked you whether you had any brothers and sisters. That's more to the point.

So he did. You see the fix I'm in?

—Then what will you do later?

What I did then. Yes, I have a younger sister. Let it fade.

—When will you admit her to the realm of a legitimate character, acting, active, asserting herself, an individual?

I don't know, I don't know if I'll ever be able to write about her in all the emotional dimensions she deserves. But I have to do something. I'll have to: sometime opportune, in passing mention . . . a flake of this terrible, unspeakable inter . . . inter . . . interlude. Ssss. Interplay, flay, slay, clay, lay. Curiously enough, though she was omitted altogether in my first draft, I arbitrarily, mind you, introduced her (and I shall come to it) with very little apology, as I remember, or ceremony, simply because to continue without her became unfeasible. So, you have your answer, Ecclesias, at least in part.

XVI

Came Friday, Ira simply absented himself from the gun room. Why waste time in lame excuses? He joined the millrace of schoolmates, out of the open front-door sluices, down the stairs. Larry was already waiting on the sidewalk corner.

Once more together out of school jurisdiction, where they were allowed to smoke a block away from the building. And now with a solid kernel of intimacy formed—formed and inviting augmentation—they crossed Tenth Avenue amid droves of schoolmates, and sauntered the more slowly to enjoy each other's company through motley, clamorous 59th Street. Did Ira ever read modern verse? Larry asked.

"Wha'?"

"Modern poetry?"

Ira felt at a loss, puzzled. When did poetry become modern? Where was the dividing line? What the hell did he mean by that, anyway? When Ira had read *The Idylls of the King*, which was a pain in the ass, that wasn't modern. He really thought—no, actually, he didn't think about it, but if he were pressed for an answer, he would, well, come close to saying: how could anyone write a poem that was studied in high school, if he wasn't already dead? Tennyson was dead. So was Leigh Hunt with his Abou Ben Adhem. Coleridge was dead, Coleridge of the wonderful "Ancient Mariner." Shelley was as dead as the Ozymandius he wrote about. Keats with his "La Belle Dame Sans Merci" had died of T.B. Byron—everybody knew he kicked the bucket at Missolonghi. And *The Lay of the Last Minstrel*—ha, ha, ha—the Last Minstrel's lay—Walter Scott was pushing up the daisies. They were all dead. Longfellow with his spreading chestnut tree, FitzGerald with Omar's book of verses underneath the bough—poets you liked, or didn't like, if you studied them in school, they were dead as doornails. Q.E.D. What the hell was modern verse?

"Edna St. Vincent Millay," Larry prompted unasked. "Vachel Lindsey, Sandburg, Teasdale, Aiken, Robert Frost."

Jesus, he didn't want to appear too dumb; still, Ira had to admit he didn't know any of the names. He didn't know whether to adopt a contrite or bumptious stance. "I never heard of 'em," he confessed.

"No?" Larry wasn't in the least condescending. "I've got a copy of Untermeyer's *Anthology of Modern Verse*. It's a good introduction to modern poetry. Very good."

"Yeah? Where'd you get it?"

"My sister Sophie gave it to me for a birthday present."

That wasn't exactly what Ira had intended to find out by his question, but—

"I could lend it to you," said Larry. "I'd love to lend it to you, if you're interested."

"I guess so." People bought, gave, owned books; was he so stupid not to know it? Or betray not knowing it? "I'm used to going to the library," he explained. "That's why I asked."

"I don't know whether public libraries have the Untermeyer collection or not. But one thing I'm sure of, you'd enjoy it."

"Yeah?"

"'Fat black bucks in a wine-barrel room,'" Larry recited. "That's Vachel Lindsay: 'Barrel-house kings, with feet unstable, sagged and reeled and pounded on the table, pounded on the table, beat an empty barrel with the handle of a broom'—I'm not sure of just the way it goes—'Boomlay, boomlay, boomlay, *Boom!*'"

"Chee!" Ira was spellbound. It was like an incantation. "That's modern? That's how modern poetry goes?"

"Isn't it wonderful? The rhythm: 'Then I saw the Congo, creeping through the black, cutting through the jungle with a golden track—'"

"Wow!"

"I thought you'd like it."

He felt the familiar, the commonplace, become puzzling. The street opened up toward him, throbbing, as if he were at the flaring end of a great horn, overwhelmed by an unexpected confusing crescendo. Buildings seemed to skew about. Wearisome perspectives shed their gadding and humdrum crusts. What did it mean? It was something like the way Larry transformed from gentile to Jew; only this went the other way. What did this mean, Larry reciting modern poetry? How could he be so coequal, so at home in all this; as if it were an everyday going-on, as if he were part of it, used to it? Modern poetry. Here and now. All around.

"'I saw God! Do you doubt it?' You'll like this one by James Stephens," Larry overflowed. "He calls it 'What Tomas Said in a Pub.' You know what a pub is. It's English: a bar, a saloon."

"Yeah?"

"'Do you dare to doubt it? I saw the Almighty Man! His hand was resting on a mountain! And He looked upon the World, and all about it—'"

Black youngsters in tattered garb, like stamens surrounding a gangly adolescent girl on the stoop of a tenement along the route to the subway on 59th Street, giggled at the spectacle of Larry's large white hand in wide, unrestrained sweep in keeping with his recitation.

And Ira, dazed by a new kind of, new kind of what? A new kind of meaning, of being, of feeling, almost like coming out of a labyrinthian basement into daylight. That was it: it was today! "It's like that?"

"Yes." Larry smiled with pleasure. "Did it take you by surprise?"

"I'll say. You mean all these writers—these poets—they're alive? I know it sounds foolish. But that isn't just what I mean. I mean—" He was silent, a long perplexed interval. And then in nearly painful revelation, "It's going on. That's what I mean. Right now."

"That's right. I know what you mean," said Larry. "People are still writing poetry. It didn't end with Longfellow. Or with William Cullen Bryant. 'Thanatopsis.' Or *Idylls of the King*. That's the trouble with the way English is taught in our high school. Any public high school, nowadays."

"Oh, yeah? Then how?"

"Well, compared to the English ones I attended. Compared to the Ethical Culture School I went to for a few months here. You're a good example of what's missing in our English courses. I don't mean to be funny. There's no sense of the contemporary in any course I've taken in DeWitt Clinton. That's the problem with teachers like Dr. Pickens. Know what I mean? There's a clean break between what's gone before and now. You get the idea? I'm not trying to be superior. Or highbrow. But it's going on. Just what you said. The only time I had that sense of timeliness here was at Ethical Culture. They made sure you got a sense of relevance with everyday life. Know what I mean? Maybe we'll get a chance at something like it in the last term of our senior year. You know you have a choice of your preference? Mine's going to be modern drama. What about you? What's yours?"

"I don't know. I never thought about it. But you act like you're living right with 'em. I think that's what I mean." Ira scratched an itch in a wrinkle on his brow, then a more imperious one in the convolute of his ear.

Ira felt suddenly under strain. It was like an avalanche of newness, all this modern poetry. Larry wrote poems. Larry understood, was initiated, belonged. He . . . actually wrote something that was his own, about . . . about . . . experiences, no, about what he felt, no, not that either. They had the shape of what he felt. He did it by himself, for his own . . . not, one couldn't say, for his own good . . . he did it for—no, not for a contest. Hey, Jesus, you could scratch all over, it was so unsettling, even a mere glimpse of that kind of purpose, just for the sake of doing, finding the shape that fit, that kind of a game.

Ira found himself wishing he hadn't agreed to ride the Ninth Avenue El with Larry. So new an outlook would take a lot of time—and examining and dwelling on—a lot of ruminating to get used to—if you wanted to get used to it, to learn something about it, how it was done, what changed you.

Maybe he ought to disabuse Larry now, Ira thought. Sure, it was flattering to be with Larry; he imparted a sense of the rich and the glamorous. But Ira didn't want to go on. That was it. He recognized in himself something unwillingly complementary, something receptive, nay, susceptible, to this—this strange new shedding of exteriors of everything, shedding of fixed panoramas, of used perceptions you could call it. But that was just what he had done with his own interior, torn away, not on purpose, but by mistake, torn away from the regular, the customary, the wonted, yeah. And now if he did the same with the external world, that contemporaneous world that Larry was exhibiting, Ira didn't know what would happen; if he allowed himself to be exposed to that disquieting new process, that new relation to the outside world, one that changed the outside world. God, he could feel he was too susceptible, too beguiled by new departures in the perceived; given to forsaking the rote, gee, he'd have nothing left, be nobody. At least now, yeah, he was a crumb, all right? Humping his own sister, Minnie. But he was on the rifle team; he could go out with Billy in a canoe, paddle across the Hudson, accommodate to Billy's world, hang on to Billy's world, feel a little—a little bit better. American wholesomeness. Oh, hell, he couldn't say.

They paused at the foot of the El stairs. Ira hoped Larry might loosen their previous agreement to ride on the Ninth Avenue El together, render it tentative, say something like "Are you coming up?"

Larry didn't. Instead, he said as they neared the El steps, "Let's not smoke. I got an idea."

"Yeah?"

"You're taking the El anyway. Let's not stop. Let's not stop riding together till 125th Street. Why don't you come home and have supper with us."

"Me?" Ira was startled into brusque bodily withdrawal.

"Yes. And take the Untermeyer anthology home with you afterward."

"Yeah, but look at me! I didn't even shave this morning."

"You're all right. You look fine. I'll lend you my new Gillette, if that's all that's worrying you. It wouldn't matter anyhow. We don't stand on ceremony. We don't dress for dinner and that sort of thing." He smiled winningly.

"Oh, no. Oh, Jesus!"

"Here we go again. Why not?" This time his brown eyes were merry instead of disappointed. "My mother would love to have me bring home a guest. I never do. She'd be delighted. She keeps complaining that I don't have any friends. And I don't. I didn't in Bermuda either. I simply haven't found anybody interesting."

"Yeah, me!"

The heavy irony in Ira's voice seemed to startle Larry. "What's wrong with that? I mean, why not you? I can choose my friends."

"Well, I like—" Ira let gesture indicate his meaning. "But I—"

"But what? You don't have an inferiority complex, do you? Or something like that?"

"Yeah, I think I do."

"Oh, come on."

"I do," Ira insisted. "I know it in myself."

"Why should you have an inferiority complex? I don't see why. What did you do to get it?" Larry was unconvinced, but diverted.

"What did I do? You remember Hamlet: about filling up the porches of your ear? I could clutter 'em up. But I ain't a-gonna," he clowned verbally. "Nah, it isn't that." Ira decided to change tack. "It's Friday. *Gefilte*-fish-and-chicken-soup night. I didn't tell Mom." It was a deliberate subterfuge. Mom had long ago been alerted that on Fridays he might go off with Billy: not to be alarmed about her son's absence on *Shabbes bay nakht.*

They reached the stairs, and as they climbed up to the platform, Larry said, "I know it's short notice. Here, I've got two nickels. No, that's all right"—he declined Ira's proffered coin, and followed him through the turnstile. "Is your family religious?"

"Religious?" Ira shrugged. "No. My mother only lights candles on Friday. You know, she holds her hands in front of her face and prays."

"Yes?"

"You never saw it?"

"No."

"No? Maybe I ought to invite you to our house so you could. I would, if we didn't live in such a dump."

"You needn't feel so apologetic about it," Larry appealed. "It doesn't matter. Really. As a matter of fact, I'd be glad to go to your home. I have so little experience—contact—with any kind of Jewish Orthodoxy. I don't want to brag—I can have all kinds of Jewish friends, liberal, rich—oh, my. I mean, the wealth of their families makes mine look—very modest in comparison."

"Yeah?"

Larry's thick eyebrows neared each other in sign of distaste. "But talk about bores! I can almost predict what they're going to talk about. Dances. Dates. Cars. Fraternities. Beside, they fawn, and I hate that."

"Yeah?" Ira snickered. "You know, that's funny. I never invited anybody to my house—I mean, the way you just did. In all my life, I can't remember once. Maybe it's their accents, I don't know." From being odd, it became something to wonder about as he strolled next to Larry over the gray, weathered planks along the airy platform. "We don't—we don't do things that way."

"No?"

"A relative maybe. Once in a blue moon. *Your* family—I mean, they're all Jewish?"

"Yes, but we're all agnostics."

"Oh."

"It's like saying we don't know."

"Yeah. I know what it means." With each step he took along the platform, the spear of light advanced on the tracks below: agnostic. "You know, when I was fourteen, I told my mother and father I didn't believe in God. My father called me an *apikoros*, an Epicurean. That Greek name actually came into the Yiddish. Can you imagine? *Apikoros*."

"Is that so?" Again Larry seemed eager to learn. "*Apikoros*. I wish I knew a little more Yiddish. I told you, only my brother-in-law, Sam, can speak a few words of Yiddish. He's the lawyer. *Mitzva*. There, I remembered another one. Sam knows some of the prayers in Hebrew—he's the one I told you went to CCNY."

"Still, you teach Sunday school, you said. In that temple on Fifth Avenue. But you don't know any Hebrew?"

"It isn't necessary."

"No?"

"I love the stories, as I told you. They stimulate me. Just the other day I couldn't help daydreaming about Absalom escaping. Would his father, King David, finally forgive him? Or would he be an exile all his life? You know what I mean?"

"I see. . . . You think about others, other things, don't you?"

"What do you mean?"

"You don't think about yourself. What you would do?"

"I express what I would do through them. Is that what you mean?"

"I think so."

Larry stopped in stride. "You know, I don't think I quite followed you that time: not thinking about myself."

They turned to retrace their steps. "I can't think about anything but myself," Ira admitted. "Half the time I hardly hear anybody else. Honest. That makes me so dumb." Perhaps that would put a brake on Larry's cultivation of literary matters way over Ira's head; it might curb the friendship as well.

His remarks seemed to have the opposite effect. "I don't believe you don't listen. No. I think you listen all the time, I think you don't listen to things that don't interest you. I wish I could do that. It's really a kind of polite waste of time. I get enough of that."

"Yeah?"

"Too much. And most of it doesn't matter. I don't know whether you listen or not. What makes you interesting is that you never parrot anybody. Everything comes out of your own experience." His large hands delivered his meaning with an expressive trajectory. "Everything comes from the inside."

Ira's facetious "Yeah? Where else?" brought a smile to Larry's face. "No, I wish I could. I can't. You can get away from yourself: Absalom, King Saul, Custer. Not me."

"Then seriously, I think you ought to try to write. I'm sure you'd come up with something pretty good. Have you never tried to write?"

"Me? Compositions in English. What d'you mean? I'm gonna be a bugologist," Ira said.

"Well, I don't see that should keep you from trying to write. I wish you'd come over to our place and let me read you two or three of my poems. Or you read them yourself. You'd get the idea of expressing—of giving form to your feelings. I can't explain it—just by example: of what I do. I'd love to hear your comments too."

"Hey. How would I know what to say?"

"Simply whether you liked the piece or not."

"That's all?"

"Just as you did a few minutes ago."

"All I said was 'wow.'"

"That's enough," Larry glowed with good humor. "'Wow' is good enough." He canted his face to show his affectionate appreciation. "Beside, I don't consider myself on the same level as the poets I quoted from the anthology. They're mature poets, most of them. I'm at the beginning stage, but I still think I have something to say."

Something to say? Ira could only wonder—and keep silent.

"I've got another idea," said Larry. "Next Friday night. Have supper with us, and stay overnight."

"Wha'?"

"I'm putting in a bid right now for next Friday night."

"Not overnight. Say. Even if there's no rifle match—"

"Can't you arrange it? You said you wrote the invitations."

"Yeah, but I work at the football games Saturday. Till Thanksgiving. This one's going to be at Yankee Stadium."

"The new stadium? You can practically walk there!" Larry urged triumphantly. "It's so close by, you can see it from the end of our street. You can shower before bedtime. We've got two baths. I'll lend you a set of pajamas. We'll have breakfast together."

"Two baths . . ."

"All right? Let's make it definite."

"No."

"No? But this time you can tell your mother in advance where you'll be. You'll be in safe hands. I know how mothers can be."

"No. I'll come Friday night for supper, but that's all. That's enough."

"You're not going to inconvenience anybody. You'll be perfectly welcome. My parents have been hearing me talk about you for some time. So they won't be surprised. I've got an extra couch in my room. You'll be comfortable. And we're all completely informal, you know. My parents. Irma may be there, my older sister. My brother Irving— and of course, Mary, our maid—"

"I'll come for supper," Ira said stubbornly, aware he was being stubborn. "Nothing else, no. That'll be enough."

"Enough?" Larry was amused at Ira's strenuous reluctance. "You sure?"

"I'm sure. I'm sure."

The platform began to quiver before the approach of a train.

"Okay." Not the least vexed, Larry leaned forward to view the square-nosed wooden train noisily devouring the track as it approached the platform. "Honestly," he said, raising his voice, "why don't you want to stay overnight? I've got a big full-sized bed. You can have that if you prefer. I'll sleep on the couch."

"No. I said no."

"Are you just plain shy?"

"No. I wet my bed," Ira replied gruffly. "It's called *pisher* in Yiddish. I'm a *pisher.*"

Larry burst into a spontaneous, hearty laugh. "That's a new one I've just learned. *Pisher.*"

"Yeah?"

"And now I just remembered another word Sam uses sometimes: *minyan* for a group of ten. . . . Oh, *megillah*, yes! *Megillah*, that's another. *Megillah. Pisher* and *minyan*."

"Boy, you're gonna build up a vocabulary."

They waited for the train to come rattling to a stop. The blue-uniformed guard, with gloved hands on lever handles, dull bars connecting with the gates shiny with leather buffing where grabbed, clanked open the low steel gates to the train. . . .

XVII

Dissatisfied, Ira let his arms hang down beside him, fingers of arthritic hands painfully opposing his flexing. Even as he typed, he was aware of minuscule notions darting about in his mind—and vanishing as if sifting through the same neurons that engendered them. And some were probably important, but what the hell, every prose writer experienced that. Some are coming, some are wenting, said dear old fuddy-duddy Longfellow, do not try to snatch 'em all. No. But there was much more to it than mere volatile fancies, conceits. Ah, there went one! As if he had to throw a body block at the idea to stop it before it dodged by him. He had to get back to himself. That was the important thing. Like Antaeus, the giant, to his own Mother Earth. Too inflated a metaphor maybe, but it conveyed the central thought, the nub, the imperative. He had to get back to himself. It was a primal necessity. This matter of juggling the devastating business of his incestuous "relations" with Minnie, never originally intended to be revealed, in the first place, and now a determining, nay, *the* determining force in Ira's thoughts and behavior. Like that of a dark binary star on a visible one, it had altered the entire universe. His task now was to juggle, to wield a preponderant, unintended element that he had introduced into the rendering of his portrayal of why his central character opted for the future he did, why he stumbled upon a literary career, brief though it may have been; he would have to incorporate that new element in the total design—somehow.

In his first draft, he had made it seem—yes, damn it!—as if Ira were choosing one of two kinds of America open to him: Billy's kind of America, the open-air, the active, the adventurous, the gregarious, and Larry's kind, well-to-do, cultivated, settled, conservative, clannish. But hell, the dominant conflict at this stage wasn't that at all. . . . And even if it were, he was incapable of convincingly portraying such intellectual distinctions, nor of the deliberations these would require of his central character in the making of his choice for the future. No. He was drawn blindly toward what offered the greatest possibility of the satisfaction of need, of appeasement of the remorseless inner disquiet, perhaps provide an avenue for its release, even partial. Larry seemed to offer that.

So Ira was left with (as he had said before) a canvas he had to paint over, whose original showed through, or something of the sort; he had to overwrite an untidy palimpsest. Only if his central character was relatively free, free from the continual and often unbearable spiritual warp, a veritable gnarling of the psyche, could he, the author, even hope to continue to pursue his original intention of representing Ira as choosing between Billy's and Larry's America. Though there may have been a grain of truth in the way Ira was initially affected by Larry's appearance on the scene, it was nothing decisive, only a grain. Ira was already under a ruinous cloud, with Faust's skull all atwitter at the table. Choices were dictated by other things than sensible considerations, choices were dictated by—the unspeakable, the unspeakable, and by preoccupations with schemes, ruses, connivings, that would succeed in gaining the unspeakable. How to win Minnie's surrender; nothing he craved for more. Better, more obsessively sought after, for being a sin, an abomination! Boy, that fierce furor, with her alternately foul and tender outcries of the essence of wickedness. Always in his mind. Always in mind. He wouldn't miss it, exchange it, for anything else in the world.

Now with this new element fouling up the act, foully deflecting it anyway, what say you, Ecclesias, guardian? I'm in a quandary, am I not? What?

—I'm listening.

I need guidance.

—You're too reckless to be guided, too unruly, headstrong, injudicious.

Yes? Then favor me with a single word of advice. A precaution. Anything. I'm not going to revise five or six hundred pages. Just a word then. Please. Anything I can do?

—Salvage.

Salvage?

—Yes.

Salvage what? The results are bound to be a mess.

—You managed to accomplish that in person; then why not in fiction? Now wait a minute.

Next Friday evening at Larry's home. Jesus, try to eat right when you sit down at their table. It's gonna be high-toned. Don't *chompkeh,* Ira admonished himself, the way Pop always rebuked you for doing. Don't gobble, gulp, smack your lips, suck your teeth. Should he say to Larry before they went to his house, "Look, I'm a *fresser.* Do you know what that is?" Larry had already seen how Ira ate in the lunchroom. Still, he wanted him to come to his house for supper—no, for dinner. So he'd put on his best suit, his best secondhand suit that Mom had bought after she tore another buck off the price. What a *geshrey,* their haggling. Oh, Jesus H. Put it on, put it on—make a joke out of it. Tell him. Not at the table, but before. Mom holding the ass of the pants up to the light, ridiculing the dealer (in Yiddish, it didn't sound so bad). Shameless trickster, you call these weazened threads cloth? Go. Cheat. Two dollars and a quarter. Not a penny more. While Ira squirmed into a corkscrew. All that . . . and try your best when you're in Larry's house. Say "Yes, ma'am" to his mother. Say "sir?" to his father when you don't understand, Ira drilled manners into his head. You know: on your best behavior they call it. But that's next week. Call Billy tonight. Skip Polo Grounds football tomorrow. Go canoodling (as Billy and he called canoeing) Saturday, but don't camp overnight. Right? Right. That gives you Sunday morning. Sunday morning, when Mom goes off with the shopping bag. Can't miss that. A diller, a dollar, a shopping-bag scholar. His sister says, "Don't come too soon." Ha. Ha.

His plans went agley that very weekend, the day following his ride on the El with Larry. He telephoned Billy early in the morning. They met at the boathouse. In brisk, breezy, fine weather, they canoodled

across to the rocky New Jersey side. Soon after, they built a small
campfire, and toasted cheese sandwiches in a frying pan—cheddar
cheese and package bread Billy had brought. Ira had never tasted
cheese so tangy until he met Billy, and he had asked Mom to buy it.
Cheddar cheese, he told her, remember, it's called cheddar, cheddar,
like—but he couldn't remember anything Yiddish that rhymed with
it—unless you mispronounced *cheder.* Anyway she couldn't buy it in
the stores on Park Avenue. It wasn't kosher. That was last Sunday,
when Minnie had her period. So what the hell good was anything?
Anyway, they kicked around a football, which Billy had tossed into
the canoe when they set out, after they cleaned up the frying pan and
coffeepot.

And then what the hell had gotten into Ira? That was the question. First manifestation of the flaw, first definite, tangible manifestation of his emerging neurosis. Billy had gotten off a poor punt. It
went astray, way out of bounds, almost to the water's edge. And Ira
had suddenly let loose a string of goddamns and fucks. "Why the
fuck can't you kick it so I can catch it?" A barrage of profanity and ob-
scenity—at Billy, his pal, Billy, so often his benefactor, as now, whose
canoe it was, whose provisions, whose air mattresses to flop on, whose
football. "Why the fuck can't you kick the ball straight?"

Billy, even at the distance between them, turned visibly pale, his
jaw suddenly clenched. He could have fought, Ira felt, if it had come
to that, but he said nothing. They could have come to blows, such
was the impact of his insult. Easier for Billy to fight him than to say
anything, but he said nothing. And here they were, the two alone beside the Hudson on the Jersey side.

The fit of wrath left Ira—in minutes. Billy threw a forward pass
instead of kicking the ball in return. Fury like a gust, a squall, struck
and went on. Ira apologized. He apologized several times, "I didn't
mean it. I don't know what the hell hit me. Okay, Billy?" Ira pleaded.

He showed a cheerful face; good sport, determined, but unable
to wrinkle his nose. Equable, he let the past go by. He comported
himself as naturally as always, with free swing of arm, torso, attention
to the thing in hand, the football. But despite Ira's humorous urging—"Go on, kick it, Billy. I don't care if it lands in the water, I'll get
it"—Billy continued to throw passes. And Ira knew the damage had

been done, irreparably done, forever and forever. He had lost his best friend's friendship; he had lost Billy's respect.

He had exposed to Billy's view the loathsome pit within himself, exposed the hideous disfigurement under the mask, become a different person in Billy's eyes. And no way to undo ... expunge the new perception, reverse the shock he had inflicted, no way ever. The damage had been done. ...

They regained equilibrium with regard to each other, but it was an altered equilibrium, subdued and correct. They paddled back after a while across the Hudson to the boathouse. They moved quietly. They lifted the canoe back to its rack among the others, stowed gear away in the locker, walked together as far as Billy's street, and parted, awkwardly.

So his little plans went awry. And sooner than he expected, and in a way he never foresaw, he lopped off that option; he lopped off his ties to that kind of America. A severance had taken place on the New Jersey shore ... on their favorite camping site, where the pebbles and stones were fewest, between the river and the Palisades. And on such a bright, brisk November day! A Saturday that should have been so carefree and happy, that should have left a carefree and happy memory, became instead an ugly turning point in friendship, irreversible and dismal. "Why the fuck can't you kick that football straight?" A spewing up of the vile turbulence within himself, disclosing beyond mistaking to a tolerant, unsuspecting Billy Green. ...

XVIII

The ride to Larry's home the following Friday after school Ira would always say was windier than windy Troy. The trainman who opened the El train gates at the station not objecting, the two chose to ride with him on the rear platform of the El, the roar platform, Ira had quipped, their fedoras jammed down on their heads, topcoats buttoned up to the collar against the gale that mounted from one sta-

tion to the next. They shouted snatches of information about themselves, about anything of interest. What delightful family reunions
the Gordon clan had almost every weekend. They were *gemütlich*,
that was a German word, "cozy, I think," Larry translated. "There's
really no word in English that gives you quite the full meaning of it.
Homey. Agreeable."

Information, in shouted remark, together with much humorous
comment about his family, passed from Larry to Ira during the trip,
that first trip to the Bronx. Larry evidently loved his family. He loved
them—all of them. Jesus, how could that be? No, no, Ira could feel
himself almost physically raise up barriers to ward off dwelling on the
contrast between the two. Now *there* was something intriguing. How
much new he could learn.

Larry was a better friend to have, to cultivate, especially now
that Ira felt he had broken his precious link with Billy. With Larry
there could be still a way . . . to a world elsewhere. He *was* dreaming.
He had smashed something in himself: a romantic something. He
couldn't be romantic, he who gave his sister a dollar in the slept-in-
smelling bed. And when she asked, "Is that rubber thing all right?"
he said, "Sure, what d'ye think?" Romantic? For him the unexpected
lucky break in the afternoon, after school, that was romantic, boy,
when the green, blistery walls trembled as if they were stammering
with joy, his joy at Minnie's quick, curt "All right, so, c'mon." That
was romantic. He'd never get over it, never get over it. It towered
above him, hulked over Larry's romantic image, barred the way forever, oh, forever. When the class read Tennyson's *Idylls of the King*,
look how different, Ira told himself, look how different. The teacher
told the class that the huge, black-armored knight that blocked Sir
Gawain's path was death, and not to be feared, because only a child
was inside (even if it was nutty to think that a kid could sustain such
huge bulk of armor, but . . .): that was Tennyson's meaning, yeah,
and the class accepted it. But for Ira what did the parable summon
up? Himself and Minnie, himself when he was twelve, and she was
only ten—child she, with a smooth little round ass. And after it happened, the bad, the bad, the bad took over. Now he was death, the
child in black armor; he was death, the one who killed the romantic.

Pulling on his discolored leather gloves more firmly, the

crabbed-looking Irish trainman came out of the car, straddled the space between cars, and grasped the burnished steel lever handles on each side of him, while he waited for the train to come to a stop.

"You're going to major in bio, aren't you?" Larry asked.

"Huh?"

"I mean in college."

"Oh, yeah. Bio. Bugology."

The gates snapped open. *Tête-à-tête,* in the brief quiet of station pause, the two stood against the gate opposite the one the few passengers left by or came in. Only at certain express stops, when the local opened gates on the opposite side, did Larry and Ira have to shift sides on the platform. Larry knew when.

"Biology, boy, I love that stuff," Ira added. "I've been getting A's in everything."

"It doesn't pay very well. That's the only trouble with it."

"What do you mean?"

"You said you might teach."

"Oh, yeah, high school. I wanna teach bio."

The gates snapped shut.

"That's what I mean," Larry said. The trainman pulled the bell cord overhead. "Schoolteachers don't earn very much." The train began moving.

"They don't?" Ira felt unaccountably disconcerted, as if something mundane had intervened where he least expected it, roiled up glamour, smudged Larry's romantic luster. And what about those poems Larry wrote, and was taking him home to show him? Like the modern poems that he had recited, poems that liberated one from stale perspectives, made free and vibrant the grimy streets and filled them with promise. Money? Earning? All that freedom was suddenly hedged, that shimmering romantic freedom Larry seemed to possess a minute ago constrained. Something was amiss, something didn't fit. "I don't know what high school teachers get paid," Ira said, disturbed by his own display of vacancy.

"You don't?"

"No."

"That's the first thing you ought to find out. I could ask my sister Sophie—or Wilma—what a high school starting salary is. Of course, they both taught in the elementary school, and they didn't have to support a family. You might."

"Me?"

"I don't mean at the start, at the beginning of your teaching career. But sooner or later. You don't intend to be a bachelor, do you?"

"I don't know. I mean—well, I never thought." Support a family? Boy.

"I'm sure the starting salary is a little more in high school than elementary school, but it can't be too much more."

"No." Ira suddenly understood. It was practicality, practicality that tethered the entrancing world of Larry's modernity, that hobbled its visionary freedom. Practicality that trammeled the romantic. Jesus, what a dope. He didn't understand anything. "That's why I was telling you about taking the Cornell scholarship exam." Ira tried to exonerate his improvidence, gain purchase on defined, on accepted, attitudes. "Maybe I could be a zoologist, a real zoologist in a lab or something. But . . ." He reverted to refuge in levity. "I'm a *melamed*, that's all."

"A what?" Larry invited, alert to apprehend.

"A *melamed*," Ira raised his voice against the train clatter and rush of wind. "That's the guy who teaches you to read Hebrew. My father calls me that."

"What do you mean? It's a joke?" Larry laughed a little helplessly. "A *melamed*? Do I say it right? Doesn't he want you to be one? Or does he?"

"Oh, well. He doesn't really care. I mean—" Ira tossed a shrug. "It was my mother who wanted me to go to college. And I figured teaching school is about the best thing I can do. Listen, you know what a *shlemiel* is?"

"Oh, I've heard that expression. It's funny. Sam uses it too. It means not very—what?—capable, bright."

"Well, I'm a *shlemiel*. That's what my father means."

"Just because you prefer teaching as a career?" Larry awaited a reply, and receiving only a vague, mute, indeterminate gesture, he went on: "I like teaching. Honestly I do. I told you I love teaching in Sunday school. But not as a profession. It's absolutely the lowest-paid one of all. It's really a pity, but—"

"Yeah, but you gotta remember," Ira interjected. "With us, in my family, except for my father, Pop, but with Mom, in the rest of my family, and where we live, it's got a lotta respect. You know what I mean? My son is a high school teacher. *Ousgeshtudiert.* You know what *ousgeshtudiert* means?"

"*Ausgestudiert* is German. It means learned, scholarly."

"All right. And besides, for me, by teaching high school, I'd make a lot more money than I ever made—even though I don't know how much, how much high school teachers get paid." Ira grinned sheepishly. "I know it's more. And long vacations too. It's easy too. It's just as if I'm keeping on going to school. So instead of being one of the pupils, I'm a *melamed.*" Ira watched the black railroad ties slur together, separate a moment, slur together—almost emblematic of what he was trying to say. "You know what my principal, Mr. O'Reilly, used to tell us? Those marbles he didn't lose, the other kids stole from him. That's why he became a schoolteacher. That's me."

"It's not as easy as it sounds," said Larry. "I've heard my sisters talk about it. All kinds of record-keeping and preparations for lessons. And sometimes very annoying disciplinary problems. I prefer dentistry."

"What?"

"I'm going into dentistry. I talked it over with Victor, my brother-in-law. I think I'm—"

"You said dentistry? You mean you wanna be a dentist?"

"Yes. That's what I said."

"You?"

The train was slowing down again. Ira felt oddly as if it were himself slowing down, all kinds of fancies, flighty illusions, slowing down, all that new marvelous promise, pristine look of things, hope of a world elsewhere . . . somewhere . . . maybe . . . all the more yearned for because . . . because—aw, he was screwy. Larry didn't have to get out of the trap he was in, the vise, yes, vice, between the jaw of delirious craving and the gnawing jaw of guilt. Ira gazed hopelessly downward to the street passing diagonally below the mixed din of the train. Maybe you could be romantic and a dentist if you were normal, he mused. He watched the seedy little storefronts down below slide by.

Seedy little storefronts had already become incandescent in the shadow of the El, in the premature twilight of the El, their wares becoming more distinct as the train slowed down before a station. Cross streets opened up more leisurely too, presented their grubby vistas a little longer, before the drab, monotonous brick walls, inset with fire escape and window glass, engulfed them again. In the succession of bleary tenement facades, a worn old man, a blowsy housewife, a child, looked out from behind closed windows. How random they appeared, like those flat chesspieces in the slits of flat chess cards. Random, forlorn, keeping lackluster vigil for some kind of fulfillment that Ira was certain would never be realized.

Pity stirred him, pity for them, pity for self, a peculiarly generalized pity; and as the train entered the station, Ira wondered whether Larry noticed the same things he did, and felt the same way. But no, Larry was talking about how much he liked to use his hands, that he had good hands for dentistry—he splayed out his strong white fingers. In a strange, confused way, Ira became conscious of a sense of superiority, about those same things Larry had introduced him to only—only when? A few weeks ago? The modern, the disclosure of the mood of the contemporary, his time, its latencies, the way the street, the buildings, yes, the imago—cast off its stultifying shell. Odd. He had never thought about that before; who cared about that before? Not when he was part of Billy's world, the outdoors, the gun club world. But that goddamn football, that freak explosion of temper, yeah, freak, and not so freak. As if it were the cost of his new kind of liberty, somber liberty. He was freer than Larry, that was it: nothing to reckon with, nothing to hold him back, family, warmth, what did he call it? *Gemütlichkeit.* Comfort. Ease. Dental office. Fees. It rhymed. Hell, he—the child in black armor—had broken barriers Larry never dreamed of . . . had committed, Jesus, horrendous, transpontine acts—nutty name, nutty acts—and paid for them in toll of dread.

Once more the trainman stepped out of the car door, took his post at the gate handles. You could almost smell the urine in the toilets when the train came to a halt.

"So don't you have any friends?" Ira asked. "You know, I mean, how come you don't have friends like yourself?"

"I think I told you."

"Oh, yeah, there I go, not listening again. No, I remember."

"Yes. Some of them—my age—they're a lot richer than I am—I mean my family—but they're climbers, and I hate climbers."

"Yeah? I thought you had to be poorer to be a climber."

"Oh, no. That's not always the case. They're just vulgar, that's all. They have no class, you know what I mean? Nearly everyone I know my age—it's clear, it's obvious: they try so hard to ingratiate themselves. They're Jewish, but pretentious and tasteless—and so-o middle class." Larry drooped in comic despair. "So conventional, so material. Ah! I can't tolerate them, the way they equate everything to money. Dollars and sex!" He suddenly straightened up for emphasis. "And that's no joke, either. They've got cars too, big allowances. Murray, for example—he's a freshman at Columbia—wants me to go everywhere with him. But God! You'd go crazy listening to him about his fraternity, tuxedos and proms, the heiresses he's dated, and how much rent their folks pay for their apartments on Central Park West. The pull they have at City Hall. His father's investments. His father's Packard limousine. A chauffeur too. And yes, the law degree Murray expects is going to make him an independent millionaire by the time he's thirty. Who cares about that? The guy is still vulgar."

"Yeah?" Ira only half understood. Middle class, what did that mean? Those rich people? More than just that, they had hot water, steam heat, like almost everybody who lived west of Park Avenue in Harlem, real-allrightniks as Jews said. And they had cars, too. Chauffeurs. No, there was something more than that. He had read the term before in some book, but only now did the term come to life. They were more like the people he delivered fancy groceries to, or steamer baskets, when he worked for Park & Tilford, people who lived on Riverside Drive or West End, whose dumbwaiter ropes he pulled. But why was Larry so disparaging about them? What was wrong with being in the middle class? Didn't everybody on 119th Street, everybody Jewish, try to climb up—yeah, "climber," that was the word Larry used—climb out of the dumps they lived in, the cold-water flats like his? Success, yeah, all his relatives strove for that. Was that what he himself disliked about them, without knowing why? Them, his relatives, Pop too. His Jewish interim friends on the street, who shot pool, patronized the delicatessen after the movies, ate pastrami sandwiches and drank celery tonic. Middle class. That was their ambition: success. Boy. And Billy's father, the engineer? Wasn't he middle class? So what about Farley's father, the undertaker? Ira uttered a short helpless laugh as the train moved on again. "Jesus, there's so much I don't know."

Larry looked at him inquiringly.

"I mean, you said middle class. Everyone wants to be in the middle class. Everybody I know wants to be in the middle class. My mother wants to be in the middle class."

"That's the trouble."

"Why?"

"That's exactly what I'm trying to escape. Middle-class standards. Middle-class values. That's why I write, I think, why I've been writing, trying to write poems, ever since I attended Ethical Culture. Even before I began going to high school."

"But you're going to be a dentist."

"There's nothing wrong with assuring myself of leisure, you know what I mean? Of decent surroundings. But I don't have to think the way the middle class does. And I don't think the way they do. I know it. I don't value the things they value. I have other values, to me much more important, values most of them don't have the vaguest ideas about. Poetry. Art. Theater."

"You're way over my head." Ira grinned, sighed without knowing why. "Yeah."

"Wait till you meet my family, you'll understand."

"But you love them? Don't they know you're writing poems that are sort of against what they—they believe in?"

"Not against that exactly. Just free of it. Of course, I don't think they always understand. And when they do, well, that's just a youthful phase, as far as they're concerned. They can't think of lyrics beyond the kind they would hear in *Rose Marie* or *Indian Love Call* or some other musical comedy hit on Broadway. Maybe not my sisters so much. My brother and my parents are terribly conventional."

Conventional. There was another inert term suddenly come to life, emerging from the abstract, and becoming troublesome. He wasn't used to that kind of thinking: categories, that was it. The classes that people belonged to. And people who were conventional.

In Billy's America nobody worried about that. He never once heard Billy mention anything like that around a campfire, or while they toted guns to a rifle match. Too intangible. Billy never said anything about society. "Hell, I know!" Ira burst out. "I know what you mean. 'Class,' you were saying. I don't mean middle-class. Not classy. Class. I get the idea."

"Now you know what I mean by social climbers now."

"Yeah. When you talked about society, I just thought of a party I barged into the first day I worked for Park & Tilford. I had a steamer basket to deliver—a real expensive one—and I went to the wrong door. Upstairs instead of downstairs. I'm always pulling boners like that. Talk about high class." Ira grinned, scratched. "It wasn't the champagne I could see the butler serving, and the maids—you know, the dough. I came away thinking what they were was more than money. Class."

Larry regarded him with his soft gaze, his brown eyes appreciative; then he shook his head. "You've got some wonderful stories."

"Yeah?"

"You make everything so graphic, it's really fascinating."

That was enough. Ira scrolled the pages down. No, the El ride, the journey, couldn't contain any more, anyway ought not to. Maybe interesting stuff, but a plethora. Then what? Delete? All that followed? What a shame. He sat, quietly, soberly, with hands cradled in lap, pondering. How rescue it, where interlard or append it? The monitor indicated that the RAM was already sixty percent of capacity, and he was jittery about going any higher. Exceeding sixty percent by too much, he had had difficulties once or twice in retrieving the document, at least from a floppy disk, though it was true he had a hard disk to fall back on. But actually his worries were groundless. Fiona, his secretary, expert in these matters, could be depended on to rescue him. Ah, yes.

Had he taken his second diuretic tablet, his furosimide, as its generic name went? Had he? When he took his luncheon cup of tea? No, he hadn't. He had forgotten to. Still, he had been sitting here a long time, and he had to urinate. Well, there was the urinal hanging in his three-wheel walker. He could use that. Not take any chances of mishap during the trek to the bathroom in his bedroom. Better save right now, and get up and answer the call of nature forthwith. No chance of embarrassment either, right now, using the urinal. Diane, his housekeeper, was away; she had gone to pick up her daughter at school. So, except for himself, the place was vacant.

Old bore, they would think—he had broken his resolution not to intrude on his reedited manuscript, not to intervene with extraneous or current reflections into his already revised text. But he was eighty-six years of age now, and could brush off previous resolutions, if he chose. Even so, his doing so now gave him a sense of guilt, of sinfulness in breaking his own pledge made to himself. Maybe he ought to delete this intervention too, this bit of Nestorian garrulity. But the fact was it was more than that, more than an instance of the garrulity of senescence. The seemingly rambling passage played a key role. Unless he deleted the material that followed, and he was obviously loath to, his sense of rightness required this interlude. In short, his present intrusion, in this, the month of May, in the year 1992, into a text considered final two years ago was necessary, if he would include what followed, and he would. The *balance,* figuratively and literally, of the long dialogue already recorded aboard the ride on the El needed respite, needed relief. He hoped his aside had provided it. Anyway—he adjured himself—only in extreme cases, such as this, a dilemma between inclusion or deletion of work already accepted, would he permit himself another such infringement, another such flouting of a solemn contract he had made with himself. Well, have fun, Stigman, he heard mind speak to itself. Have fun.

XIX

Upon arriving at the El station where they got off, it seemed as if they were in the country, at the foot of a hillside, so low-lying the station was, by a brown cliffside via a short platform hewn out of the hill. All sedate it seemed, the cliffside above the station, above the tracks. He would never see it so again: that such an undreamed-of rural enclave would never be a station on the route of the old, beat-up Ninth Avenue El. He would never see it that way again—an El station at the foot of a brown cliff.

They got to Larry's home, one flight up in a neat and tidy hallway, stairs all quietly carpeted. The apartment was sedate and commodious. There were introductions to parents, and to sister Irma; brother Irving was not present. Ira awkwardly expressed formal admiration of their home, followed by his warm and sincere joy at beholding Larry's own room, Larry's own study, large enough for a full-sized bed, and a couch, an ample desk—and with a typewriter on it! Scatter rugs, a handsome five-drawer chest, a walk-in closet. All Larry's own. And the design on the papered wall that he himself had chosen when he was "a lot younger": of an old-fashioned choo-choo train chuffing by a river, through an old-fashioned village, with nostalgic farmhouses, barn, and steeple.

The living room was furnished with an inviting oak recliner; and—novel to Ira—the slant of the recliner's back depended on the position of an iron rod in a kind of wooden ratchet in the rear. Sharing the floor space, or rather carpet space, were a large sofa of dark green cloth and two fat, opulent easy chairs of dark leather. Under them a lively, florid Turkish rug, rich with intertwining vines, spread from mopboard to mopboard. Electric sconces on the walls lit up reproductions of paintings that reminded Ira of the Corots, the gentle landscapes he had seen as a boy in the Metropolitan with Jake Shapiro. There was an arresting reproduction of a Maxfield Parrish landscape. *Dickie Bird* was its title; in it were depicted a cluster of round castles rising up to different heights, stiff and attentive, forming a bastion to a naked maid on a swing reaching its apogee. High in a sapphire sky, smooth and mellow as the dusk in paradise, the naked damsel swings, tits like macaroons. Boy . . .

And supper: lamb chops, with divine never-tasted-before creamed spinach, served by Mary, the homely Hungarian maid. But who would believe that spinach could be so transmogrified? Ira lauded the dish with the most extravagant superlatives he could summon. Later he so inspired Mom, in the course of her interrogation concerning the kind of home the Gordons lived in, the food, the furnishings, the personae, that she undertook to prepare the same thing according to her son's rapturous description of it. Nah! It didn't taste like that at all! Ira growled, rude as ever. Poor Mom. She tried.

Ira could not get out of his mind Maxfield Parrish's *Dickie Bird* in the living room, where the two youths sat afterward listening to records played on the phonograph duly cranked up by Larry. The dainty, the fair, the nude maiden with the pretty tits, shaped like a teacher's bell on a desktop, disported on a swing, and all about her, turrets arose, high and low, yearning upward into ethereal, blue heaven. Beautiful. But see how dirty your mind is, Ira chastised: Dick for Dickie, and the turrets were hard-ons all around. Nobody else saw them, only he, crude and coarse: *tukhis afn tish*—the vulgar saying in Yiddish, ass on the table. Jewish immigrants who left their wives behind, like Pop, and screwed a twenty-five-cent *nafke* standing up, must have demanded *tukhis afn tish* before they paid. Only this time it was damsel's ass on a swing. Not a sling, but a swing. Why did you have to think of it? Why? Why? Because he had bartered a stolen fountain pen once for Minnie's "charms," as she lay athwart his bed in the dingy little bedroom. That was why? One of those afternoons when the green walls tingled, and he nipped the little brass nipple of the lock upward—oh, hell. What a serene and homogenized sky the maiden swung into. Boy, supposing he was on the swing with her, and she was sitting straddle as they swung. "Boy, it's cerulean," Ira praised reticently, as he gazed.

"It's what?" Larry asked.

"It's cerulean. Don't I say it right?"

"Oh, yes. Cerulean. That's just the right word." Approval distended Larry's handsome countenance into smiling beguilement. "Better than my lapis lazuli. I got that word from Browning. Where did you get yours?"

"You mean you expect me to know?"

Later that evening, after Larry had loaned him the Untermeyer anthology, the two youths left Larry's home to walk to the subway line, a much longer walk than to the El, but in the end, after change and reversal at 96th Street, a ride that would bring Ira nearer home. A new book under his arm, a new kind of book to read, a new friend.

Impressions of Larry's parents: his father spoke without an accent; only flaw in his English, perhaps deliberate, he said um-possible for im-possible. Not taciturn, but spoke little, grave in appearance, though now and then his face would light up with pleasure at something Larry said. He was clearly his father's favorite, the son of his advancing years. In his sixties, Ira guessed, a man above average height, not lean, not overweight either, flat-fronted, Mr. Gordon was dark in complexion, had a full, gray mustache, and wore his thick, speckled gray hair in close-cropped, military style. Probably when younger, he looked more like his daughter, Irma, Larry's next-older sister, than like Larry.

Jews were like chameleons, Ira had begun to notice. Live in Hungary a couple of generations, and they commenced assuming Hungarian features—the way Baba looked Slavic, with blue eyes and snub nose, descendant of Jews who lived among the *goyim* in Galitzia. So did Mamie: Slavic. But not Mom, with her dark hair and broad nose. And not Moe either with his broad nose. Still, Moe was fair-skinned, blue-eyed, and blond. Well, exceptions and mixes, and some, like himself, ran true to the ancestral, patriarchal stock, the map of Jerusalem on his pan.

Larry's mother was pretty, actually pretty. Mother of five children, she seemed much younger than her husband. She was a brunette, with a puffy cloud of hair untouched by any glint of gray. Her features were fresh, scarcely marked by a wrinkle—and regular (almost gentile)—another surprising characteristic Ira thought he discerned among many Hungarians, classically proportioned features, a finely delineated nose, like Larry's, far too regular to be Jewish, with a smooth skin and brown eyes radiating cheerfulness. And yet she wasn't a true Hungarian; she was Jewish. And besides, Hungarians were supposed to have descended from Attila's feral oriental Huns. All very puzzling. Anyway, Mrs. Gordon was most cordial, solicitous, loquacious, and hospitable.

And there was Irma, resembling her father, and even Larry to some extent, but lacking the well-nigh classic symmetry of his countenance. Like her father, darker in hue than Larry, her lips prominent in their swelling roundness, so much so that she had developed

the noticeable trait of rolling her lips inward to thin them. It seemed
nothing short of a preoccupation.

So much for Ira's first impressions of some of Larry's folks. But what had
happened to *him* in the past twenty-four hours since he had written this
passage to cause a new listlessness? It was a change in plans. He had intended to advert again in passing, as he had to Larry's folks, advert to the
Untermeyer anthology—and then append the journal entry that he had
been unable to append the day before. This time he, or rather old Ecclesias, would certainly have RAM enough to contain the journal entry still
waiting without. There ought to be RAM enough, even if he included here
something he had omitted, namely, reflections on the young Ira's de-
plorable table manners, his eating habits, his jerky, ravenous, noisy,
chomp-chomp, despite efforts to deport himself with restraint, with a little
decorum. It seemed to Ira, even after these sixty years, he could still see
Larry's gentle gaze resting on him, tentatively, sympathetically. He had
planned to include all that and still have room or rather RAM for the journal entry. But in the twenty-four hours that had passed, the projected col-
lage had waned in interest. The urge to interrupt his yarn had passed.

XX

Once again events sped up, piled up in the course of the last few
months of Ira's senior year at DeWitt Clinton, in the spring of 1924.
There was home life, with its permutations and combinations, grim,
pent-up pending and rending, and vicious release. There was the
gun club, mix of routine, boredom, and playful pastime. And there
were classes, and the subjects elected: solid geometry, under the tute-
lage of Dr. McLarin, for Ira a delight. Then there was the second half
of his biology course, his proficiency and avidity making him ever
more certain that biology or some aspect of it would be the field of
his vocation. Even the second half of his chemistry course at last

emerged from preliminary confusion. His work in English was mediocre as ever. And, alas, the last half of third-year Spanish dragged along well into his senior year.

He and Larry enrolled in the same Elocution 8 class (though they now knew better than to sit in proximity), a class under the auspices of Mr. Staip. As far as stature was concerned, Mr. Staip was a gnome of a man, probably less than five feet tall; and yet he was capable of reducing his students, most of them standing head and shoulders above him, to mere gnomes themselves, subservient and docile. If ever there was a martinet of speech, it was Mr. Staip. He shrank his students to stammering puppets by the sheer fastidiousness of his pronunciation. No consonant or vowel but received its due when he uttered it, crisply, distinctly, and he expected, nay, he exacted the same from his quailing students. And very few could measure up to his demands.

That spring, as baseball got underway, Ira still hustled soda: at the Polo Grounds, at the new Yankee Stadium, occasionally at a prizefight in Madison Square Garden. Larry's curiosity had been aroused by Ira's accounts of his work there. And assured by Ira that he could obtain permission for him to put in a stint as a soda hustler, if only for the novelty of the experience, he met Ira one morning at the main gate of Yankee Stadium—not far from Larry's home. Ira vouched for his friend before the ever-irascible Benny Lass, as two years before Izzy Winchel had vouched for him. After a cursory glance, Larry was admitted.

To Ira's chagrin, it shortly became evident that for Larry the reality of work at the ballpark corresponded little to Ira's entertaining descriptions of it. By the time the first inning was over, Larry had expressed his indignation to Ira at what a disgusting ratio obtained between commission and sales price, between remuneration and the amount of hard work entailed in earning it. Their paths crossed several times during the course of the afternoon, and each time, Larry's offended demeanor, his asides, bordering on humorous reproach, left little doubt he felt imposed on, deceived. By the time the day's work was over, he was thoroughly outraged by the meanness and surliness of personnel and fellow hustlers, the rudeness of fans. Once again, as at that moment on the El a year ago, Ira felt a peculiar superiority within the terms of Larry's own, proper realm, realm of sensibility, because he sensed that somehow, compensating for the drudgery, the labor, the brusqueness, the affront, the rough and tumble of the workaday world yielded valuable aspects of the commonplace, though why he valued them he didn't know. They became his, perhaps uniquely his, recognizable signatures of his surroundings, almost a kind of currency, limited in exchange, but highly prized by people like Larry. Well . . . he didn't know. He knew that certain kinds of perceptions affected him, and not Larry—something he could scarcely put into words: that Larry was irked by the piddling pay for so much hard work, and also because his charm and poise and good breeding were ignored in the hurly-burly of excitement and competition. He should have borne all that as Ira did, with a certain wry tolerance, in exchange for access to the raw and the turbulent, to all that was going on, a chance to see and feel the crude power of the mass, and not allow sensitivity and wounded vanity, even considerations of fairness, to get in the way. What if Billy had been in Larry's place? How differently Billy would have reacted: wrinkled up his short nose, like the good sport he was. And grinned.

Billy was a good sport, and Larry wasn't. Billy gave little heed to monetary factors; Larry did. Larry wanted to write poetry, short stories, but not at the price of his comfort, not at the price of not being a dentist—so Ira felt—not at the risk of too great exposure to the unceremonious, certainly not at the expense of participation in it. And yet, such was Larry's attraction, the charm of his comfortable, Jewish, cultivated life, that Ira found it impossible to resist its appeal. And Larry was so generous: he loved to share, to guide; he took pleasure in initiating Ira into whole domains of which he knew almost nothing, the names only: ballet, the stage, modern sculpture, opera, architecture, orchestral music. Larry loved to lead, and Ira was only too ready to follow.

Billy noticed the new attachment (he and Larry had long since met, each a sort of curiosity to the other); and even though Ira felt changed in Billy's eyes since his uncontrolled outburst on the New Jersey shore, they still shared common interests: the rifle team, canoeing, camping, and golf. Even so, Billy continued to take Ira to the golf course in Van Cortlandt Park, paid the admission fees, and supplied the clubs (as the winter before, ice skates for ice hockey). "Still trying for Cornell?" Billy asked with stoic tactfulness.

"Oh, sure." But actually Ira had begun to doubt. He had applied for the requisite permission to take the examination, and he intended to take it, but would he go if he placed? Larry had applied to NYU, to the college's new branch or extension opposite Washington Square Park. In two years he could complete his "predental," as it was called, his academic prerequisites in the humanities, before going on to dental school. Tuition was charged at NYU, but not at CCNY, a city college, and except for texts and incidentals, free. Ira had applied there as a matter of course, because of his circumstances, his indigence, and as his only hedge against his likely failing to place in the Cornell scholarship examinations. But truth was he already felt himself drifting away from his original goal, drifting or drawn away, just as he had done from his strong affinity for Farley. And though he might adjure himself that he mustn't allow the same thing to happen again, that he ought to keep his sights fixed on Cornell, keep steadily in mind his goal of a career in biology, and prepare himself as best he could for the coming examination, he kept repeating Mom's bracing maxim *Der viller iz mer vi der kenner*, "He who aspires excels him who knows." Still, despite everything, not so much an involuntary veering away from target was taking place as a wavering of resolve to fix his aim on it. A quibbling within himself whether doing so was worthwhile began to take place without the respite of common sense.

XXI

June 1924. His last June at DeWitt Clinton, the last month of the last term he would be a student there. Soon the finals, soon the "Regents," the New York State uniform examinations, soon the Cornell scholarship exams. In Elocution 8, which Ira shared with Larry, all members of the class were expected to deliver an address satisfactory to Mr. Staip in order to pass the course. The address was to be about some outstanding personage, was to employ the aid of only minimal notes, and was to be not less than five minutes in length. Ira chose to speak on the English poet William Ernest Henley. Ira would never forget that he began by contrasting Poe and Henley, the one dying in a cellar after a drunken debauch, the other undauntedly fighting off tuberculosis all his life. He concluded his speech with a recitation of the ringing "Invictus." And when he finished declaiming the last lines,

> "I am the master of my fate;
> I am the captain of my soul,"

to his utter astonishment, he saw the audience in front of him break into spontaneous applause—joined in by, of all people, Mr. Staip himself. The next minute he accorded a startled and all but incredulous Ira the unheard-of privilege of being excused from class for the balance of the period! Suffused with delight, his head whirling at his unprecedented triumph, Ira made his way down into the study hall . . . there to mull over the ways of fate that had plunged him down here in disgrace and consternation from Elocution 7 in September, and now in breathless honor from Elocution 8 in June.

When next he met Larry, he seemed reserved, so scanty his praise as to seem no more than circumspect acknowledgment. Ira wasn't sure what he expected after his oratorical achievement: something warm, bantering, humorously derogatory—something akin to the way Billy would have behaved: "Hey, what a fluke. Hey, who coached you in that?" Billy would have said. But this perfunctory mention, as if it were niggling recognition, was it envy? Had he taken Larry by surprise? Moved into the vanguard of subject matter where he didn't belong, subject matter akin to the literary? Had he troubled Larry by show of unsuspected gifts—those in which Larry regarded himself as superior?

For whatever reason—it was probably that Larry felt reservations about Ira's choice of personage, his choice of poet or poem—Ira felt hurt, hurt and resentful. Nah, what was he thinking about: attaching himself to Larry? Thinking of alternate ways of majoring in biology: at CCNY. Ridiculous; he was making the same mistake as he had made before, of letting blind feeling rule him. If he won a scholarship, Cornell was the place to go, to Cornell, the college Billy was applying to. Larry's grudging acknowledgment was timely warning that *he*, Ira, ought to consider his best interests as objectively as he could.

"Hey, what did you do last weekend?" Ira asked Billy when he saw him next in school.

"Went canoodling. It was great."

"Alone? Stay overnight?"

"Yeah, I went alone, but days are so long now, you can paddle for hours. You can go across the Hudson and back before dark—if you want to. I didn't. I just sat under the Palisades afterward—talked to other fellows with canoes. Say, a couple of them brought a whole grocery store over: hot dogs and rolls. Apple pie. Blueberry pie. Cheese."

"Wow! You build a fire?"

"A small one, and we swapped stories about camping. One of 'em got lost in the woods for three days. But he had about every Boy Scout badge there is, so it didn't bother him. Say, you know it was still light until nine o'clock?"

"Is that when you came back?"

Billy grinned. "No, quite a few stars were out." His face took on as beatific a look as would ever appear there. "I stayed out till nearly eleven."

"Yeah? You got anybody goin' with you Friday?"

"No."

"All right we go canoodling together? Just Friday. I wanna hustle at the ballgame Saturday. You know—I gotta make a few bucks Saturday—and Sunday, too. I don't have to get up early, but I've gotta be there."

"What about your friend? On Friday. Larry. Aren't you seeing him?"

"No, not this time."

Bright breezy afternoon awaited them as they stepped out of the kiosk of the Broadway subway station at 160th. Sun and wind, agreeable atmosphere pervading a normal scene, the stationary pedestrian and vehicle, and the pace of those in motion. If only he hadn't said what he had said to Billy that terrible minute, minute of flaring insanity, as if Pop's nature had taken hold of him. No, he couldn't unsay it, couldn't undo it, even though he thought he knew why: Van de Graaff crackling bolt, generated by his guilt, but nothing so spectacular: just uncontrollable short circuit across his hairline cleavage. He knew why. Then leave, leave, of course, leave it, separate himself from the source, from home, from Minnie, an inescapable vortex in which he was caught. Yeah. Two bucks for Sunday. Two bucks she demanded! She really had him over a barrel.

But there was Billy's America signaling him: in a multitude of white-capped semaphores breaking out in mid-channel of the Hudson. Forget everything, try to push it all behind, get away, get clear. Ira goaded himself into quickened pace as the two descended from Broadway's terrace to the boathouse on the riverbank. Common sense, at last; it was only common sense to accept America's offer. He could never be Billy, but he could model himself after him, *remodel* himself into something like him. And he had the chance to. If he rejected Larry's "values," as he repeatedly called them, he had access to Billy's model of life. In fact, he had no other so definite.

Whitecaps on the river, lapping the bright air, like so many tongues, clean and white. Start anew, start afresh. A wordless but visible choir, all saying the same thing. Start anew, start afresh. Break away from what held him. A Jewish Dick Whittington hearkening to watery Bow Bells on the river. Almost the same. Remember when you stood on the diving rock? Ira reminded himself of those desperate moments. The river promised you then. Boy. A circumcised Dick Whittington—Dick. Will you cut it out? Yeah, cut it out. I mean it. Get up before breakfast Sunday morning, before Mom leaves. Beat it out of the house.

Once in the boathouse, they went to the rack where the canoe was stored, took hold of each end of the small craft, carried it out, and gently set it down on its keel on the wind-rocked little wharf. Then Billy led the way back into the boathouse to the locker where paddles and cushions were stowed. Here the two could leave their neckties, felt hats, briefcases, while they paddled to the other shore. Maybe he'd spend half the night, munch on Billy's box of crackers and jar of peanut butter, maybe mooch off other guys with a camp-fire. Who knew? With Billy, they'd meet some really nice guys—

"Even if you didn't place," Billy said, fishing in his pocket for the locker key, "heck, I bet you could work your way through Cornell. My dad worked *his* way through." He continued to dig into his pockets. "He did all kinds of things around the college, maintenance work on the grounds, mowing lawns, repairing campus walks. Oh, gosh. He even spent a term being a busboy in the college cafeteria. Your dad's a waiter." Billy grinned. "That ought to come easy. Where the heck is that key? I had it this morning."

"Did you have it at school?"

"Yes. I had it in the gun room. I know I had it."

With mounting determination, mounting gravity, and then with vexation such as Ira had never seen Billy display before, he went through everything he owned; he ransacked pockets, wallet, his briefcase; probed pants cuffs; riffled through the pages of his text-books. The key was nowhere to be found. "Heck, I had it this morn-ing," he kept repeating.

"Maybe you locked it in the gun room?" Ira suggested. "I mean, you left it there?"

"No, I had it afterward. I had it upstairs in the cafeteria, when I paid for lunch."

Billy was certain he had had the key after they left school. Per-haps he had lost it getting carfare out of his pocket on the subway sta-tion. Worst of all, he didn't have a spare at home; it was the only key he had. In the end, they had to give up their planned outing. They picked up the canoe from the small dock. Ira felt something fune-real, like a pallbearer, as with hoisted canoe they marched in step up the cleated gangway to the boathouse. Once inside, they returned it to the brackets the little craft had rested on, left it there as on a perch.

Disconsolately they retrieved street clothes and other belong-ings, strewn on the upturned keels of neighboring canoes. "Well, lucky we didn't lose the key afterward," Ira offered in consolation as he slipped on his tie. "We still got our stuff."

"Yeah." Billy shouldered into his jacket, restrained his frustration with crimped cheeks. "My dad's got a hacksaw in his tool chest. It's too good a padlock, though. That's the trouble."

"What d'you mean?"

They picked up their briefcases, stopped before the locker, where Billy hefted the brass base of the padlock. "This U-part that goes through the hasp is hardened steel. I don't know whether even a bolt-cutter would go through it."

"A bold-cutter?" Ira queried.

"No. A bolt-cutter," Billy said impatiently. "Has a compound leverage, long handles."

"Oh."

"It's all right for a regular steel bolt, but not that. You can read it on this U-part. It says 'hardened.'"

"Say, I got an idea, Billy. Maybe I can borrow a little hydrochloric acid from the lab. You know, bring a small bottle from the house, and snitch a little in chem lab. Maybe we could dissolve it."

"You think so?"

"It interacts with iron, any metal, I think. You want to try it?"

"That darn key! I wouldn't care if I lost anything else."

"I've got lab on Tuesday. I'll sneak out a bottleful." Ira depicted volume with encircled fingers. "We'll go to your house first, and you get a glass. Not too big. Just big enough for the lock to fit in. We'll let the lock soak in it."

Tuesday afternoon, they repeated their trip to the boathouse. Ira emptied the hydrochloric acid into the tumbler Billy had provided, and raised it until the padlock was submerged. Instead of the furious interaction that Ira looked for, that he had seen take place between hydrochloric acid and metal chips or filings, a few bubbles formed reluctantly on brass and iron. Interaction was taking place, but at a rate beyond feasibility, certainly beyond the ability of either one to stand holding up the glass tumbler for the lock to drown in and dissolve. After a few minutes, Ira admitted defeat. "I guess my idea won't work."

"I'll get someone to open it." Billy's optimism had returned. "It's all right. I talked to my dad, and he told me the easiest way to get the darn lock open was to get a locksmith."

"Yeah?"

"That key isn't anything special." Billy mitigated Ira's chagrin. "Dad thinks his garageman would help him out with his acetylene torch, if he asked him. That might be easier than anything else."

Billy succeeded somehow in getting the locker open, whether by means of locksmith or acetylene torch. In the gun room, perhaps for the last time together, Ira congratulated him, congratulated Billy, as Ira would recall later, with a peculiarly impersonal, an accommodating approval, like that of a friendly spectator. And after they ran the last cleaning patches through the bores of the rifles, and were oiling the rope to pull through the firearms for storage over the summer, for the new team, as if observing the end of something they had both held dear, and emboldened by imminent freedom from high school, they dared light up a single cigarette in their gun-club den under the stairs in the assembly hall. Giggling at each other in the camaraderie of mischief, they passed the butt from one to the other, inhaled a few puffs, exhaled down into a corner of the windowless niche, and trusted the stagnant air to retain the odor.

XXII

Graduation exercises approached in late spring just as the pavement began to buckle with the onslaught of New York summer heat.

"*Noo*, you'll take me?" Mom asked eagerly. "Maybe your father will come along too, my paragon."

"I'm not going," Ira responded.

Her short throat flushed, skin crimson and scaled. "Again? A plague on you! Why not?"

"I'm working at Madison Square Garden that night. There's a big prizefight on. I can make some money."

"I'll give you the few *shmulyaris* you'll earn that night." Mom denigrated both the sound and value of the dollar. "Let it be my gift for your graduation. Why are you so intent on earning a few dollars that very night? Since when have you become my breadwinner?"

"I'm not your breadwinner. I just want to make a few bucks."

"How much? Tell me. I'll present them to you now. What will your earnings amount to?"

"I don't know."

"*Noo?* How much do you want?"

He tossed his head violently. "I don't wanna go, that's all."

"Only to thwart me. Is that the reason?" She nodded bitterly. "To make a small sacrifice on this one occasion, he refuses. A small sacrifice, a crumb of consolation for these years he's made his mother suffer, the tears she's cried for him. No. I'm condemned to disappointment. *Ai, vey, vey!*" Mom heaved a deep sigh. "Be sacrificed yourself for the woe you cause me."

"It's just a bunch of speeches!" Ira burst out. "It's nothing. Everybody marches in, then marches out."

"Then why don't you let Mom enjoy the speeches and the marching in and out?" Minnie interjected.

"Who asked you to butt in? Take her to *your* high school graduation."

"Positively, I'll take her. What d'you think, I'm like you? That I'm ashamed of my parents from spending all my time around *goyim?*"

"Aw, shut up."

"I've never attended a graduation," Mom declared, pleading. "Even once to see it. Ira, precious, once more, think about it. Relent. For your mother's sake."

"Oh, you are a louse." Minnie glared at her brother.

Enjoying his manifest complacency, Pop adopted the deliberate tone of the seasoned arbiter. "An upstanding youth, Joey Schwartz next door, who has been working for Biolov's ever since Ira threw up the job—years now, no?—had he been offered such an opportunity as this lout had, the opportunity to attend high school—and to be fostered, to be nurtured until graduation—four whole years—would he not have kneeled before his parents, kissed their hands in gratitude? Would his mother have needed to grovel before him, imploring him to take her to his high school to attend his graduation? What? He would have danced before her on the way. I am willing to wager had it concerned an upstanding youth in this case, a subway train would not have been good enough to convey his parents there, to this Davit Clinton High School. A taxicab, no less. As if it were his nuptials he were attending. A taxicab there"—Pop circled bunched fingers—"a taxicab home. Who knows. He would have skimped and hoarded his earnings to provide his parents with a supper at Ratner's to spare her the preparing of a meal that day—to dine in style—ah, what is there to say? Even a Moe, a Moisheh, *a gruber ying*, sent by your good father, Ben Zion, the pious Jew, to work like a *goy* in the forests above the Dniester River, no? It's a wonder he didn't get a hernia."

"Moe is a *mensh*. He's so stout," Mom retorted pointedly. "*A gruber ying* he's not."

"Then he's not. But every summer, and how many times in the winter, has he taken the oldsters to spend two weeks or a month in a *glatt* kosher summer hotel? Since he came back from the war, how many?"

"*Gey mir in der erd*. A great deal you care, except to relish my torment." She turned from Pop to assail Ira. "You're not ashamed? Base youth. Four years ago, four whole years ago, you told me the same thing. Deprived me of a bit of joy with the same pretext: speeches and marching, speeches and marching, nothing more. How do you know? Were you ever there?"

"I know. I don't have to be there."

"As long as you could go the next day, and get your diploma."

"Louse! Mom oughta throw you outta here." Minnie flared up at her brother. "She ought to throw you out on your ear. Out of the house."

"Hah!" Pop gloated in agreement. "What have I said all along?"

"Aw, take her to your own graduation."

"I need you to tell me? To my graduation she'll go." Minnie was close to tears. "But you, you, you're the one that means everything to her. You're a disgrace, that's what you are. Take Mom to your graduation."

"Oh, shut up."

Her eyes dark with sorrow, Mom rocked from side to side. "He shrinks from his Yiddish mother, that's the whole trouble, that's my curse. You're a Jew yourself, no? And there won't be other Jewish parents present? I'll find some niche, some crevice. I'll hide. No one will notice me, and you need not either. You don't know me. You don't have to present me to your friends. Just let me witness. Minnie will lead me there, and home again. As long as I've seen my son graduate from high school."

Alas, my mother. She breaks my heart sixty years too late, Ecclesias.
—Indeed? Pity all mothers of such sons. The whelp treats its dam better than you did yours, my friend. But you're too late. The grave is a barrier to all amends, all redress.
By that same token, their neglect on my part makes no difference now, does it, Ecclesias?
—Desist. You mar your fable.

"I don't wanna go."
"*Ai, vey, vey!* What do I ask for? A crown? An ovation? No, only this paltry few hours out of all of twelve years to rejoice in. I nurtured him, I suffered for him—him! And yet I may not watch him given distinction, watch him given a high school diploma as other women watch their sons? *Gevald!* Heart of stone." Desolate, she regarded him in tearless sorrow.
"I don't wanna go!" Ira shouted. "I already told you once!"
"Go to hell!" Minnie wept with wrath and frustration. "Please, Mama, don't aggravate yourself with that stupid bum. He—all he thinks about is himself, himself. Selfish, rotten stinker! *Hint*, that's all I can call you. Dirty mutt. You should drop dead."
"*Megst takeh geyn in der erd,*" Pop added his cutting amen.
Mom kept nodding bitterly, kept nodding, like a Norn or a Parca foreseeing endless woe: "Descend into the pit. The Almighty will repay you for this. And the Almighty pity me for damning my own son." She slapped her mouth several times. "*Oy, gevald.* I intercede, *Gotinyoo!* Pay no heed to my implorings."
"He's listening," said Pop. "Believe me."
"*Geh mir oukh in der erd,*" Mom retorted.
"Uh. She's made her prayer." Pop folded his Yiddish newspaper.

"Why is he that way? Why don't you ask? Why is your son not like other Jewish children, upright, sensible—"

"I am well acquainted by now with your reasons," Mom interrupted. "Further store of your wisdom spare me."

"She doesn't inquire why her *kaddish'l* Ira is the way he is." Pop gnawed away on the bone of contention. "There are countless sons and countless mothers. And millions upon millions of sons strive to please their parents. They carry their parents on their fingertips. Their mothers and fathers on their fingertips. *Azoy?*" He illustrated, with upturned hands like sconces.

Mom's face hardened with readiness of scornful reply. "You told me that already. Chaim, go torture the cat instead of me."

"Such a mother, such a son."

"And fathers like you should rot."

"Aha! Utter a true word, and she flares."

"You see what you do? It's all your fault," Minnie upbraided Ira. "A brother like you should go to hell. *Shemevdik,*" she mocked in Yinglish, contracting in mimic cowering. "A neighbor comes to the door, right away he's got his head down. Or he runs to the other room. That's what the trouble is, Mom. He's a stupid *shemevdik*. A high school graduate already, and he still runs away from somebody who knocks at the door."

"*Ai, a veytik iz mir,*" Mom lamented. "*Noo,* leave him alone finally: an oaf."

"You got such a fancy friend," Minnie taunted. "*He's* going to the graduation. He's a *mensh*. Why doesn't he teach you to be a *mensh?*"

"Who asked you to bring Larry into it? Nobody. So shut up."

If he ever got around to it, Ira thought, he'd like to ascertain who were the pugilists who fought in the featured final bout on the night of his graduation exercises. He would append the information in a footnote. Whether it was Harry Greb or Gene Tunney . . . perhaps both . . . or neither. Well, let some scholar, if interested, dig up the data. About one thing he could rest assured—nay, two things: that the earnings, his pretext for depriving Mom of the pleasure of beholding him on the platform with fellow graduates in rented gown and mortarboard, could not have exceeded five dollars, and probably not more than three dollars. And that the inimitable Joe Humphrey was there, was there standing in the middle of the ring, and by dint of straw kelly and stentorian voice, quelling the boisterous fight crowd, while he announced the names and weights of the contenders, delighting the lowbrowed fans with his high-toned Bostonian "hawf-pound."

XXIII

Ira lost track of Billy completely that summer of 1924. He never called Billy again on the phone, nor made any effort to get in touch with him; nor did he ever hear from Billy again, by letter or picture postcard. (Ira remembered vaguely something Billy had said about expecting that his father would get him a job on the survey crew of a new dam in Pennsylvania.) Perhaps he was already in Pennsylvania or somewhere, but their friendship was over with the end of high school, of their participation in the gun club, of their carefree hours of outdoor sports and "roughing it," and with the irreparable breach Ira had caused by his egregious outburst—but more than anything else by his burgeoning attachment to Larry. When Ira looked back, the element of chance seemed to play a great role in his life. Still, it was inevitable that sooner or later he would have found someone with whom he could communicate, communicate those many new stirrings within him, fuzzy aspirations and wobbly ponderings. But then again, who could tell?

Larry stayed home that summer, giving his older brother Irving a hand in the ladies'-housedress-manufacturing plant that he operated. On one or two occasions, Ira walked with Larry to the factory, only blocks from Ira's apartment. It occupied the entire floor of a typical loft building, and everywhere women worked at sewing machines, perhaps a hundred in all, sat and sewed ladies' housedresses. It reminded Ira of the time, years ago, when he was still a young boy on the East Side, and would sometimes ride with Pop on the milk wagon: times when he would climb up the stairs to a factory loft with an extra tray of pints of milk to be distributed among the scores of women working at their sewing machines, under sweatshop conditions for all he knew. But they were jolly, and of course, they were immigrant, mostly Jewish, and they chaffered with Pop, and made much of Ira, and there was a sound of laughter. But now, these women were clearly not Jewish, Italian most of them, assuredly still immigrant, with a scattering of other nationalities, fair-haired Poles and dark-skinned Puerto Ricans. No one laughed, or smiled. A confused conjecture whirred in Ira's mind that the faces lifted from the sewing machines toward the two youthful newcomers, himself and Larry, were fraught with animus, because they were presumably better off—both of them, which wasn't indeed true. He couldn't avoid feeling intensely self-conscious because of mistaken identity—and because he and Larry were Jewish: rich Jews, a category in which he was included, exploiting the poor wage slaves. More than anything else, though, he was aware that on the countenances of some of the younger women when they looked at Larry, a cruel hunger seemed suddenly to possess their features, an almost vengeful desire which he never dreamed that women felt or would reveal; only men would harbor such resentment, he thought.

The summer had begun for Ira with the accustomed routine of the ballpark. But that lasted no more than a week or ten days. Izzy Winchel, the very one who had persuaded Ira to hustle soda pop at the ball games, was now instrumental in dissuading him from doing more of the same. Izzy's older brother, Hymie, after a short apprenticeship, served with his father, an independent plumber with headquarters in a little, sleazy store on grubby Park Avenue. Now married and with a son, he had to sally forth as a journeyman plumber, come what may: he had to break in as a nonunion plumber, as Izzy said, get a job with a building contractor putting up those new two-story frame houses, hundreds of which were going up in the further reaches of the Bronx. All brand-new housing, Izzy assured Ira. No dirty jobs, no cleaning clogged flush toilets or slimy sink drains, no running "snakes" through gunked-up soil pipe or wrestling with rust-frozen fittings. None of that shitty work. No, sir. Everything was brand-new and real clean.

"Yeah?" Ira asked, vaguely forewarned.

"Hymie wants you for a helper. It's twenty-five a week."

"Why me? You're his brother."

"I don't like that kind o' work. The same kind o' work all day. You know what I mean? I like hustlin' at the ballpark. I like all that excitement. Seein' what I can make. You ain't like that. You're different. You just ain't a hustler." Izzy's shallow blue eyes rested on Ira fondly. "Hymie wants you."

Ira wavered. Izzy was too right about him: he could never lose himself in hectic pace and single-minded fervor of competition. He never ceased to feel ashamed foisting a lukewarm soda pop on a fan as if it were a cold one. He was always at the bottom of the list of hustlers checking in earnings at the end of the day. But for more than any of these reasons—and without the initiative as usual—he was beginning to wish for other kinds of work, because he was becoming increasingly loath to be seen in the garb of a soda hustler, a peddler of soda pop, recognized by former teachers and classmates, he who soon expected to enter college. The change in work proposed to him by cunning Izzy found little resistance in Ira.

"You don't have to know nothin' to be a helper." Hooked proboscis, sandy hair in his service, Izzy stoked Ira with inducement. "Hymie'll show you everything. What d'ye have to know? Cut pipe or a nipple, thread it, use a scale. How did I learn? I learned from my father. C'mon over to the shop. I'll teach you in half an hour, how you set up the dies in a stock to thread the end of a pipe. I'll show you the fittings, what they're called, what they're for. Let's go."

"Go where?"

"The shop. Hymie talked himself into a job for Monday," Izzy said. "Tomorrow. He's gotta have a helper."

"Oh, Jesus." Ira followed Izzy along to the shop.

And thus it was he became a plumber's helper. The job wasn't easy—as Izzy would have him believe—but at eighteen, the intrinsic joy of one's own muscular resilience relieved novel toil of much of its laboriousness. In time he became a novice plumber's helper, a barely acceptable one.

He saw a great deal of Larry, sometimes after work, though most often on weekends. Larry was admiring of Ira's new vocation; his parents were amused—but approving too: of the indigent Jewish boy taking any kind of arduous toil in order to win a college education. So they were more than tolerant of the growing friendship between Larry and himself: by his seeming perseverance, his willingness to submit to any kind of toil to better himself, Ira set their son a good example. Respectful, bearing the proper attitude toward them, and always appearing clean-shaven and as decently dressed as he could, Ira was welcome in their home. He began to feel more at ease, his friendship with Larry and Larry's with him becoming something indispensable for both, growing into a deep need for each other's companionship.

After Ira had a Sunday dinner at Larry's, the two lolled on the green sofa in the living room. Later, taking turns winding up the Victrola, they played selections from Rimsky-Korsakov's *Scheherazade*. Was anything more musically fearful than those rending counterclashes of the shipwreck of Sinbad's vessel? Twice they played each side of excerpts from Schubert's *Unfinished Symphony*, which Ira loved inordinately. And then the two walked out together into the quiet evening air to a small park nearby, and sat down on one of the benches.

Larry adverted to Bermuda, to the several trips he had made there, even as a small child, to stay with his photographer uncle.

"Did you always travel with your mother when you visited your uncle in Bermuda?" Ira asked.

"Not the last time. I traveled alone. That was last summer."

"I remember now, you told me." Again Ira noted the air of reverie that settled on Larry's handsome features in the dim light, the outline of some profound recollection.

"You'd be surprised how many schoolteachers spend their summer vacation in Bermuda. American schoolteachers go there by the thousands."

"You don't mean like Miss Pickens, who took a slow boat." Ira grinned.

"Oh, no. She went to Europe. I mean *young* schoolteachers." Larry's voice continued fraught with the imminence of disclosure.

"Oh, yeah? I didn't know that." Already romance infused the night air, a mysterious kind of momentous confession. Hermetic, arcane, Ira could feel it enclosing them irresistibly within the scant lamplight, within the vacant park. "Young is how old?"

"Just out of normal school. That's only two years of college in most parts of the country."

"Yeah? That's all?"

"You'll keep what I tell you between you and me?"

"Listen, Larry, for you to tell me, it's like a—I don't know what to say. It's like I took a pledge to keep my mouth shut. You know what I mean?"

"That's why I trust you."

Summer night in the small, intimate, empty park. Sunday evening, setting its seal on things ended, a seal of pristine, lovely reminiscence. His face set with seriousness, Larry began his account of his shipboard encounter with a young, beautiful schoolteacher. She hailed from Maryland. She had turned twenty-one, he eighteen. It was his initiation into sex, an initiation so beautiful, commencing on the deck of the ship, sailing under starlight, on a night in which wave crests glistened under a waning moon, and soft sea breezes caressed cheeks and stroking hands, so beautiful, it seemed to Ira, that it was as if Larry had been with a fairy princess. His friend, here talking quietly beside him on the park bench, had spent the whole night in the cabin of a beautiful, mature woman, making love to her in a ship far out at sea, making love to her in a vessel gliding through dark, boundless ocean. Glamorous even the listening was, laden with all the magic of romance, romance beyond anything Ira deemed happened in the real world.

He was transported by the sheer loveliness of what he heard, and yet, enchanted though he was, he listened without envy. Such things were not for him; he was barred, however much he might long for them, barred by himself from such raptures: sea and ship and tender caress. The closest he had ever come was to trail a thin, spinsterish schoolteacher from P.S. 103 to CCNY when he was still a boy in grade school. The best he could do now was . . . sordid . . . in a dingy bedroom, opposite the mortar-spattered brick wall of the airshaft . . . like the wall surrounding those blacks as they watched the ball game at the Polo Grounds from the top-floor windows of their tenements, or those five minutes laying homely, scrawny Theodora in her stuffy, ill-lit room draped with *shmattas,* robbed of even the moment of possessing a comely woman like Pearl. Well . . .

When he and Larry finally parted, after having walked the distance to the subway station, Ira went down the steps to the platform enfolded in a glorious cloud of loveliness. At least he had been allowed to participate in it, allowed to know what it was in the reality of a friend's experience, to know what one should seek, even if the seeker felt himself flawed irreparably. Could one dare to strive afterward for that rare, transcendent bliss, even if already marred by the squalid? And yet he knew that was what he wanted to win, hopeless as his yearning was, Larry's world, full of love and refinement and gentle surrender.

XXIV

In mid-July a letter waited for Ira when he came back from work as Hymie's plumber's helper, and two evenings later, another. Mr. Sullivan's rebuke had come true after all. Both contained notices of greatest import. The first letter was from Cornell University congratulating him on having placed twenty-third among the first twenty-five in the city-wide competitive examination for a scholarship to Cornell. He was therefore entitled to free tuition for a period of four years at the university. Added was the school's request for an early reply. The letter also contained assurances that part-time work was available at the university, and that preference would be given to needy scholarship students. He could doubtless earn enough to pay for dormitory room and meals. . . .

Ecclesias, Ecclesias, the missed, the spurned opportunities, and the missed, the spurned decent life I might have had.

—Yes, the heart wants everything, both ends and the middle. How would you have met M, I ask you for the millionth time? How would you have written a notable novel?

The novel I can dispense with, Ecclesias. With M I can't. It's not only what would I have done without M that concerns me, but as much—and more—what would she have done without me. And this is no self-flattery. For her tender, her concealed, her reticent girlishness, her artist's sensibility, her nobility, her truly unique and yet wholly unsnobbish requirements for companionship, all that contrasted with an innate sadness born of the recognition of the hypocrisy and pretense of her middle-class rearing. And at the same time, her matchless self-restraint, her diligence, sense of propriety, all taken together, would have closed her in upon herself. This recognition would have congealed the passionate, sensitive girl within her, and kept her from flowering. So I feel, knowing her a little, Ecclesias, that someone truly worthy, not myself but M, was freed to grow and win a belated maturity, and through her, I too. For she would have survived without me, unhappily perhaps, but survived; I without her not at all. Through her I was vouchsafed not only a measure of growth, but of life itself.

—So now you're reconciled to the course of events?

No. Not reconciled. Resigned perhaps, not reconciled. I want all my blunders undone, my lamentable choices annulled, a different itinerary through life, that would have bestowed Cornell, and M—

—*Go, and catch a falling star, get with child a mandrake root.* I trust you know the next line or two.

Alas, I do know Mr. Donne. But why couldn't I have been a zoologist and have had M for a wife?

—You had M for a wife. The case is closed.

Indeed. Closed and enclosed—what mutinous turbulence suddenly springs up against the enclosure, within the bosom, Ecclesias, a futile rebellion.

The second letter was from CCNY. The letter endorsed Ira's application to enroll as a candidate for a bachelor's degree in science. He was given instructions where and when to appear at the college in order to register for courses.

So now the choice was his; options had been presented to him, destiny set in motion toward the future. For once in his life, everything had worked out to his advantage. Because his last math course had been in solid geometry, a course in which he excelled, he was sure he had done outstandingly in math. He had breezed through geometry. Biology, his other science choice, he had just finished at DeWitt Clinton with an A. He was a shark in biology. Chemistry had begun to fall dramatically in place in the second semester; comprehension of fundamental principles had come on with a rush; so he felt quite sanguine about his doing well in that. And even all the trouble he had had getting through Spanish in high school, so that it had taken him four years in high school to complete three years of the course, now turned out to be boon. Spanish was still fresh in his mind, even if he wasn't proficient. Competitors who had completed their three-year courses on time, had completed them a year ago, would have had to cram for the test. He hadn't had to. Taking everything into consideration, he was plain lucky.

Ira realized that his choice of CCNY or Cornell had been in actuality a conflict going on within the young man over which kind of America he would elect, which kind would prevail. He had endeavored to embody the conflict, imbue it with fictional plausibility, by recounting an imaginary correspondence with Billy, conveying the good news; and Billy's delighted proposal that they get together and make plans for attendance at Cornell, that they room together.

Of course, none of this ever occurred—but he had gone further, much further, in his envisaging. He had gone so far, internalized his thoughts so deeply, that it had taken on the reality of fact, of an actual occurrence in the past. So much did it vie with fact in the arena of memory that more than once he had to remind himself that it was all figment.

It was real, though not actual. It never happened, only in fancy. But the choice, though it was indubitably a choice between which of two Americas he would throw in his lot with, was made within himself, with no need for externalized tension, for suspense, for specific denouement. Probably the way he posed the question, or the alternatives, was all wrong. There were no two kinds of America open to him. There were potentially two careers available to him at the given time. And had he not chosen, not entirely at random, to share the seat in Elocution 7 with the handsome, apparently gentile youth already occupying it, his career would surely have been different. The terrible fear, the brunt of ruthless savagery, that seemed to wring the very axons of the brain forever out of place, twist them to a murderous madness that only the clarity and calm rationality of plane geometry held in check long enough for reprieve, might very well have been immured within the disciplines of the zoologist. A life could have been led, could have been reared on a localized fault in the mind (something of the sort, however figuratively expressed). But there was a prior determinant to this, the crucial determinant, or really the crucial accident. But hell, once you began that kind of unraveling, it would never end. If there was any single "first cause" he could point to as the one most responsible for the permanent impairment of his personality, for its ever-present floating anxiety, his anxiety neurosis (in today's terms), it was his family's leaving the Orthodox ministate of the East Side.

In the midst of that summer, full of Ira's debatings and speculations about his future, Farley suddenly appeared out of the past, not in person, but spectacularly in the sports pages of the press. He had become part of the Olympic track team that the United States was to field in France. He had graduated from high school the same year as Ira, and the sports pages of the New York newspapers were full of the schoolboy wonder who had been chosen to represent the United States in the 100-meter dash. He was slated to run against the redoubtable Harold Abrahams of Great Britain, who had trained for months, trained assiduously for the event, and was favored to win. Life could sometimes be inextricably tangled together. Ira had first watched Farley run against Le Vine, who, Ira felt sure, was Jewish, and whom, after the first, his novice, trials, Farley consistently defeated. Now in the greatest test of Farley's career as a sprinter, he would be running against another Jewish athlete.

The whole thing bristled with peculiar ironies only to be disclosed later. Abrahams (who was later made a central figure in a documentary film) had dedicated himself to track events in order to attain status with the British upper class, and he presumably did attain it to some extent as a result of his track exploits, and especially his victory in the 100-meter dash. He had won the Olympic gold. Abrahams might have come off second-best had not the head coach in charge of the United States Olympic team decided that Farley was too young to be pitted against so seasoned and world-famous a runner as Abrahams, and instead of Farley competing in the 100-meter for which he had trained and in which he planned to compete, he was replaced by another runner, one of college age, who ran against Abrahams, and lost . . .

Fifteen years were to pass. Ira was already married to M, and M pregnant for the first time, when Ira and Farley met again shortly before Ira left New York for good in 1939. They met one evening, after Ira had been called to do substitute teaching in an English class in a night high school, Haaren High School, which now occupied the same building as DeWitt Clinton. Farley held a permanent clerical position there. Both were overjoyed at this chance encounter, and agreed to meet after the night school session was over. They did. Farley, who had a companion with him, led the way to a nearby bar. They drank beer, and endeavored to recapture a little of the past. Farley had grown corpulent, his jowls heavy, so often the fate of the athlete who abandons training. Still his light hands were bony and delicate as ever, his blue eyes shone as boyishly as they once did, and his high-pitched voice had that same cheery, juvenile ring as it had when he and Ira attended junior high and listened to recordings of the great tenor John McCormack, at Farley's home.

Something Ira said, probably imprudently, because it revealed the depth of his Marxist orientation, prompted badgering rejoinders on the part of Farley and his friend, no less antagonistic for all their flippancy. By quizzical jibe and insinuation they intimated—Ira sensed—a partiality for Father Coughlin's pro-Nazi, stereotyped, infamous anti-Semitism. How far apart Farley and he had traveled, Ira realized with a start, not only politically, but in sympathy, hopelessly sundered in as many ways as once held them bound, and by a myriad of new biases.

He maneuvered the conversation to neutral ground again: the 1924 Olympics. Why hadn't Farley run the 100-meter dash, the one track event of his unquestioned preeminence throughout high school? It was then Ira learned the circumstances that determined Farley's elimination from competition against the renowned Abrahams—and why Farley was assigned instead to run in the 400-meter relay. Too much was at stake to entrust the U.S. colors in the 100-meter dash to so youthful a runner as Farley. The 400-meter relay, on the other hand, important though it was in medals won, meant less in terms of prestige to the United States than the 100-meter dash. Despite the prolonged, impassioned pleadings of Farley's personal coach that he be given a chance—and that he could win—the head coach of track events, abetted by the U.S. Olympic committee of overseers, vetoed the proposition. They were ready to gamble on Farley as anchorman in the 400-meter relay, but to match a high school kid against the fleetest sprinter in all of Europe was altogether too risky.

"They knew better, though, the next day," said Farley, his blue eyes growing luminous with pain and indignation. "Especially the head coach." Because, irony of ironies, the anchorman of the British team received the baton ahead of Farley, and the anchorman of the British team was none other than Abrahams. The day before, he had won the 100-meter dash. The next day the high school kid overtook and outstripped him. "I knew I could beat him," said Farley. And remembering the unassuming, straightforward adolescent who had been his chum in the past, Ira believed him. He too was persuaded Farley could have beaten Abrahams, just as years ago he was persuaded that Farley could beat Le Vine, based on Farley's declaration "I know I can beat him." The great opportunity was lost, and cruelly forever. When Ira consulted the *World Almanac* for reference concerning the 1924 Olympics in Paris, there was no record in it of the anchormen in the 400-meter relay, nor of the runners who composed the team. They were individually anonymous. It was a team effort. The entry stated simply that the U.S. team took the gold.

The 1924 Olympics were to be the culmination of Farley's career as a sprinter. Against all expectation that in college and with greater physical maturity, his running ability would reach new heights, the contrary took place: he sank into mediocrity—and obscurity—never placing better than third, and in the end, not even that. He had peaked at the age of nineteen, and by his twenties had "burned out," as the expression went.

Burned out. Ira shifted eyes away from the monitor. Whatever the expression actually signified, psychologically, physiologically, he knew what it meant, just as everyone else did. He knew what it meant as far as his own forte was concerned. As novelist he too had plummeted into oblivion.

—Was that the intent of this lengthy digression? An excursion into homily?

To be sure. That I and an appreciable number of my talented literary contemporaries would experience the anguish of "burning out" seems to me singular enough. But that the same thing would happen to a youthful runner before he reached his majority is astonishing, is it not? Burned out. He had one chance, Ecclesias, and only one chance; it was all he would ever have.

—Unlike you, his growing old in wisdom would do his legs no good.

Any more than it did mine. I'm curious to know whether he's still alive. I'm more than curious. I think when I next get to New York, if I do, I shall look up the telephone number of the Hewin Funeral Parlor, assuming it's still extant.

—Do that. As a matter of fact, all you need do is pick up the phone, and ask Directory Assistance for the telephone number of the Hewin Funeral Parlor in New York.

Yes. Though I doubt I shall.

Ira gave a copy of his only novel to Farley's mother, soon after it was printed, sometime in 1935. Farley was in Boston then (he had attended Boston University, a Catholic school, Ira believed). His brisk, brown-mustached father had died, and the funeral parlor, still in the same location, which was rapidly becoming black demographically, had passed into the hands of Farley's older brother, Billy. His mother sat in the empty funeral parlor upstairs, sat in a rocking chair, on the sandy rug, still the same quiet-spoken nunlike woman, wearing the same gold-framed eyeglasses, the heavy down quite gray on her upper lip. Resigned. She accepted the book in the absent Farley's name. And Ira dreaded to think of the shock that her perusal of the book would give her.

—Why don't you call him?

Well . . . By brooks too broad for leaping the rose-lipped girls are laid.
. . . Shall I delete?

—You ought to.

Ira sat many weeks later in the front room of the flat in Harlem, on a summer's day, a Sunday in early August, and spread in front of him a sheet of lined paper on the glass-topped table. It was one of the elegant and newly acquired pieces of living-room furniture, bought at an unheard-of price from Mom's affluent cousin Brancheh, because that kind of furniture had already gone out of style. He could only make token resistance against a foregone conclusion: the letter he was about to write to Cornell declining the scholarship. He read once again the request for an early reply, once again the reminder that part-time work was available at the university toward earning dormitory fees and meals. Pop—Ira tried to shift responsibility—had reneged, with typical hemming and hawing, on his first, impulsive, generous offer, an offer made in the flush of pride at his son's outstanding achievement, one that took Pop completely by surprise, even as his ensuing magnanimity took Ira completely by surprise. Pop had initially volunteered to provide his son with a new wardrobe, offered to pay the railroad fare to Ithaca, to defray expenses for Ira's first six months at Cornell. . . . But now he wasn't sure he could afford the added expense that would accrue from Ira's living away from home. There was an expression in Yiddish that summed up that kind of hemming and hawing, that combined the two verbs into a single one: into a kind of evasive snuffle connoting far more than did the English words, singly or both together: *Er funfet shoyn.* Pop *funfeted.*

Ira read the rough draft of his letter over again, meditated, picked up his fountain pen. His heart heavy with renunciation, he gripped the pen with fingers deeply ingrained with plumbing grime, and made corrections in the rough draft. He refined his craven reply. For craven it was, formulated by a mind that knew itself craven, craven and puerile, devoid of self-reliance and initiative. He regretted very much, he wrote, but he had to decline Cornell's generous offer of a four-year scholarship. Parasitic, fresh from this very Sunday morning's skulking, nasty lechery gratified on Minnie, he would rather stay home, stay tied to Mom's apron strings, apron strings that afforded far more latitude than she ever dreamed of, far more leeway for sordid gratifications. He would rather stay home. Why part with all that? And give up his snug and complacent dependence on Larry, on affluent Larry, on charming Larry? Give up his friendship? Nah. Nevertheless, for all the cowardice and pusillanimity inherent in his abnegation of the scholarship, still, stirring within him he seemed to sense (was it an illusion?) an intimation of some kind of undefined foreknowledge, an inkling of a direction in which he *had* to go, and the direction in which he had to go was the direction of his present choice. Within the murky slough of his self-indulgence, he seemed to discern that if he had any hope of escaping from his abject slavery to his contemptible personality into some kind of freedom or self-respect, then he had to cling to Larry, which meant that he stay home and attend CCNY.

He declined the scholarship, couched his fateful renunciation in words written on another sheet of blue-lined paper, words shaped by a thick-nibbed fountain pen. He left the house with the two-cent stamp affixed to the sealed letter, and mailed it in the wide-mouthed slot of the cast-iron letter box on the corner lamppost opposite Biolov's drugstore. The counterweighted lip uttered a cast-iron snicker as the letter box engulfed the white envelope.

PART THREE

CCNY

I

How beautiful, how glorious, the first hour or two spent in the environs of CCNY was! An academic cornucopia it seemed, so bountiful and promising from the outside he was convinced that he had made the right choice after all. The early-autumn afternoon on campus that day in 1924 was nothing short of entrancing. While he waited his turn to register for courses, he tramped over the dry, fallen leaves on Convent Avenue in upper Manhattan, trampling on the multitudes of crackling leaves to the east of the college in the shadow of the white and gray Gothic buildings, benign Gothic buildings sedately housing promise of wisdom and higher learning that would yet raise him above himself into a confraternity of serene and meditative peers. Trampling on the leaves of Convent Avenue, he felt an onset of euphoria, a veritable beatitude at the thought of the great transformations that would be wrought within him inside those white and gray Gothic walls. Change, change, the shedding of his abominable self, that was what he wanted most. Surely that would begin as soon as he registered: perhaps a new, an elevating, a desirable future would commence right here. At last.

He looked about to preserve within him, he hoped, this treasured moment: behind him spread the bare ground of the college playing field, behind him the pale tan parapets of the great Lewisohn

Stadium. Before him were the black steel pikes of the barrier separating the heights on which the college and he stood from the declivity of the small park just below, with its green benches and gray outcrops of rock, its boulders and trees and brown leaves drifting down on the slope and the walks beneath. And the city opened up before him, as if at his feet, all below and beyond him, three boroughs in view at once, Manhattan, the Bronx, and Brooklyn, in their different directions, their rooftops at all levels, chimneys, smokestacks, and spires. Overhead, tenuous smoke streaked the dome of heaven. Everything seemed propitious, seemed an omen of great future consummations. He was still going to major in biology. He might still become a scientist of renown, yes, in time separate himself from the object of his shamefulness, find a normal course for his libido, redeem himself. In an hour or two he would take the first steps toward realizing the felicitous opportunities circulating within those cloistered sanctuaries of study housed in gray and white stone rearing up into the pure azure above them.

After a while, he was joined by another candidate for enrollment, a graduate of a Bronx high school. The other was Ira's age, Jewish, almost as a matter of course, and obviously of more affluent background than Ira's. An amiable youth, already cultivating a wisp of a mustache, he whiled away the time as he paced beside Ira over the crackling leaves, whistling and singing the latest hit tunes, none of which Ira had the least knowledge of, nor cared to have, but it occupied the time of waiting. Welcome as the youth and his friendly disposition were, his tastes and ambitions, as he expressed them, gave Ira the first hint that the halls of learning within those Gothic walls were not entirely as he had imagined. His new acquaintance spoke about joining a "frat" as soon as he could, and said he was only going to CCNY to get the bachelor's degree, which was a prerequisite for entry into law school. Idealism and fancy were absent; practicalities alone predominated. His goal was the familiar one of financial success. *Makh gelt*, the attainment of a lucrative career via the stepping-stone of CCNY. The fellow must be an exception, Ira thought.

And tolerantly, he listened to the other cheerily singing as they strolled together over the russet leaves:

"Looky, looky, looky, here comes cookie . . ."

and:

"When my sweetie walks down the street,
all the birdies, they go tweet, tweet, tweet . . ."

and:

"Do-o wacka, do-o wacka, do-o wacka do . . ."

Ira felt his own euphoria wilt: wilt with his new acquaintance's optimism, wilt with the chill of late afternoon pervading the air. Time came for Ira's group to take its place in the registration hall.

And now the realities of college, of the stultifying mechanics of registration for classes at CCNY, revealed themselves in all their unlovely aspects. In one fell swoop they dashed to pieces Ira's lofty imaginings, dispelled them in a single minute, the very first minute after his turn came to enroll. He was expected to devise a program of courses, a program of courses that would remain valid for the duration of his wait on line before the particular desk at which the registrar—or one of his student assistants—sat. Time and again, and time and again, a quirk of fate would eliminate from his program a course he had chosen—he would see it erased from the blackboard, often with only one or two students ahead of him before the registrar's desk. Thus his entire program, compiled so laboriously, would be reduced to penciled inanity, and he would have to go back to his seat in the big auditorium, and start afresh. . . .

Dilatory, inefficient, slow, and agonizingly uncertain, he would devise another program, only to watch it succumb to the same attrition as its predecessor. Hours passed. Hours! Program after provisional program went by the board, indeed, went by the blackboard. Weary and dejected, Ira cursed his luck, his fate, his ineptitude, his dawdling. And as for Biology 1, the key course in his future career? It had been snapped up long ago by more proficient high school graduates—those with better average grades who were given first choice—snapped up by gifted freshmen, and by diligent sophomores who registered before the freshmen. It seemed as if the majority of lowerclassmen were intent on fulfilling requirements for entrance into medical or dental schools. Biology 1 had disappeared from the blackboard long before Ira was even admitted to the many-tiered lecture hall where students moiled over their programs. Biology 1 was a *nekhtiger tog,* as Mom would have said: it was as irretrievable as a bygone day. Oh, why hadn't he elected to go to Cornell? The iron maw of the letter box fleered at him again, snapping up with straight lips the white envelope containing his letter of refusal, an impassive predator devouring his fate. . . .

Devil take the hindmost was the rule here, and the hindmost were dubs like Ira, laggard and inefficient, pathetic dawdlers. It was past nine o'clock at night, long after the majority of candidates had happily departed, their programs accepted, when Ira succeeded in patching together a program of courses that remained viable all the way to the desk. Viable if undesirable: French 1. Trigonometry, called a conditional course, a course he should have taken in high school, but didn't because of a year wasted attending the newly instituted commercial high school at P.S. 24. Philosophy 1, though he was scarcely more ready than a child to grapple with its concepts and abstractions. Descriptive geometry, which sounded easy, and proved not to be, projections and mechanical drawing, beyond his aptitude, his manual skill. Military Science 1, a compulsory course that he learned would be a sort of calisthenics called the manual of arms performed with a Springfield rifle, in conjunction with a smattering of military tactics. Mili Sci was always open. Phys Ed 1. Even English Composition 1, humblest, and long the most accessible, of courses, had been closed out.

Such was his program the first half of his freshman term. It was a curtailed, a partial, a woefully insufficient program. It lacked the necessary number of credits of work, satisfactorily performed, meaning with a grade C or better, required to pass the first semester at CCNY. He would perforce become a "conditional" student next term, one who trailed behind the class in credits, and had to make them up somehow to be in good standing, to keep abreast of his class, one who ran the risk of being dropped from the college rolls. At the moment, Ira scarcely cared any longer. Flagging, famished, and thoroughly disgruntled by his ordeal, trudging on foot up the hill to the Amsterdam Avenue trolley car, and on foot again from 125th to 119th Street along Park Avenue on the sidewalk parallel to the Cut overhead, he made his way home.

Up the stone stoop, up a flight of dingy tenement stairs, and into the green-walled kitchen at last. The hands on the Big Ben alarm clock on top of the green-painted icebox pointed at ten minutes to ten.

"Oh, here he is, Ma." Minnie looked up from her Latin text.

"Yeah. Here I am." Ira shut the door behind him.

"*Noo,* where have you been?" Mom scolded. "Your father and I have begun to worry."

"Yeah?"

Pop raised his dog-brown eyes from the Yiddish newspaper. "And with good reason."

"Jesus Christ." Ira doffed his jacket, hung it on the back of a chair, went to the sink. "What a goddamn college." He turned on the faucet, soaping hands under cold water. "No wonder they call it Shitty College."

"It's not a shitty college. It's a wonderful college. The smartest Jewish boys go there," Minnie countered spiritedly. "Just because it's free? Mom, tell him how they wouldn't let the Jews go to college in Europe—"

"Ah, nuts. I know all about it. We're not in Europe. You know the Latin words for keeping Jews out of college? You're studying Latin."

"I don't know what they called it. Did you get into college or not?"

"*Numerus clausus.*"

"Did you get in or not?"

"Yeah, I got in." He ogled her with veiled animus.

"Papa, ask him." Minnie rejected his innuendo, jerked her head sharply toward Pop. "Papa, you ask him. Did he get into City College or not?"

"Aw, what d'ye think?"

"Aha! Rueful." Under strain of apprehension, Pop's tone of voice rasped abrasively. "What's amiss?" His weak chin tilted up in short premonitory hitches. "*Noo, noo.* Report. What fresh botch did you commit?"

"Nothing. For Chrissake, I was there till now, making out a program. Every goddamn thing I wanted was closed. No biology, no English, no chemistry, nothing I wanted."

"But they let you into the college?" Mom asked in quick dismay.

"Oh, yeah. I just told you so. I said I'm in. I'm a CCNY freshman, they call it."

"Then what?"

"It's that goddamn programming. The classes. The schedule. How the hell do you say it in Yiddish?"

"He means *vi m'geyt un ven m'geyt tsu hern di professors.*" Her mutable countenance darkening with earnestness, Minnie translated for Mom's benefit, gesticulating all the while. "Like where to go at what time, *tsu velkhe klyasses.*"

"I understand," said Mom.

"Everyone is smarter and faster than I am." Ira wiped his hands on the sink towel, flopped into his chair, and let his arms hang down. "Boyoboy, am I tired. I'm disgusted. Jesus."

"My poor brother." Minnie immediately tempered her acerbity, her pale features quick to wreathe in compassion. "And nobody there to help you? Nobody there to ask? They don't come over when they see you're taking so long, you're having so much trouble? They don't ask what's the matter?"

"Yeah. In a pig's eye."

"Everyone has to do for himself?" Mom inquired. "*Noo, az m'vayst nisht?*"

"Oh, they tell you what to do." Ira shrugged vehemently. "But there's so many fast guys there. Jesus. Real whizzes."

Minnie clucked in sympathy. "*Farshtest,* Mama?"

"*Ikh farshtey, ikh farshtey.*"

Boy, if only Pop and Mom would vanish right now, Jesus, he'd like to stick it into her, sitting slack with concern, lips loose and commiserative, and in the blue satiny dress with the round neck and short sleeves that showed—how white her skin. Boy, he could use a quick lay. Wooh. He could feel an incipient hard-on recruiting under his fly. Oh, hell, not a Chinaman's chance. Ask Mom for something to eat—

"*Noo,* if you're a sluggard," said Pop, "naturally you'll be there half the night. Give yourself a shove. A youth who won a Cornell scholarship can't do as well as the others?"

"Yeah." Ira seized the opportunity to parry and thrust. "I won a Cornell scholarship, all right. But what good did it do me? I wish I'd never thought about the damned place, never even applied. Then I wouldn't have known what I was missing. Anh!"

"O-o-h, you could've gone to Cornell." Grimacing, Minnie pined for his sake. "A nice university way up in the country. They would have helped you. Not like here. You know how New York is."

Boy, was she ripe for a lay. Boy, could he use it.

"*Noo,* it was his choice," said Pop. "The way you make your bed—"

"Yeah, now I gotta eat it." Ira shunted Pop astray.

"Spare me your wit." Pop raised a hand. "You've got to sleep in it, you mean. You could have gone to Cornell, as Minnie just said. They bade you come. What more do you want? You won the scholarship. Then go."

"And what would I have to live on? Room and board. Where?"

"I offered to help you the first few months."

"Yeah, and backed out."

"I'll spit in your face. You blame your sloth on me? Shit-ass. What do you want? To be taken by the hand and guided there by your mother? I told you, if you go, I'll help. If you wanted to go, you would have gone. Don't tell me it's my fault. Your bones are strong and full-grown. Stronger than mine. They offered you work, a chance to make a few dollars, no? Who was to stop you from going? Nobody. Your own laziness."

"Papa, please," Minnie intervened. "He's tired. All day waiting. You see what time he came home. It's nearly time to go to bed."

Desire hissed within him. Oh, Jesus, just the right thing. Time to go to bed. He could project his lust with such vividness, he barely restrained himself from shaking his head.

"I'm tired too," said Pop. "All day waiting at table. And not only one day. All day long and every day, on the restaurant floor. From what does he eat, from what does he go to college? Even to this one, to CCNY?"

"What quarrel do you have with the youth? I pay for it. It's my quarter a day pays his carfare and lunch," Mom interjected.

"And where do you get that?"

"From your skimpy, stinking allowance. From depriving myself. Who keeps house? Who shops? Who haggles to save a penny with the hucksters? You try it. See if you can do as well."

"Uh! Here we go again."

"Please, Papa. I know how hard you have to work," Minnie interceded. "You're an experienced waiter. You're used to it."

"Used to it, the devil. I'm used to it because I must. Must has no remedy, *farshtest*? Comes in a customer five minutes before closing time, and sits down. You have to serve him. You must. Your feet ache, but you must. You need his ten-cent tip as I need a carbuncle on the nape of my neck. But—"

"*Noo*, isn't that enough?" Mom persisted staunchly in her son's behalf. "He's spent with all that striving to get into the college. Let him be now. He's really in college."

"That's right. Please, Papa," Minnie concurred. Ardent in her appeal, she hooked a finger into the neckline of her dress, brought it away from her bosom to mitigate its warmth.

Watching her, Ira's knees closed like calipers. He luxuriated, gazing off into the distance, gave himself over to futile reverie. "Oh, Jesus."

"Here he is forthwith with his Jesus," Pop chided. "Hover over him. Coddle him. Look at that sullen countenance."

"But to college he's going."

"Yes. And you see how it suits him, how contented he is with it."

"Well, if he didn't choose to leave home and go away to college, if he wanted to stay at home, could I drive him out? And if he's as abashed as you are—yes, uneasy as you are among the *goyim*," Mom overrode her husband's objection before he could utter it, "what cure for it is there? He hasn't the *chutzpa*, that's all. He should have been a Litvak accustomed to stand up to Russky insults, not a Galitzianer in one of Franz Joseph's drowsy hamlets, as your brother-in-law Louie says, then he would have had the temerity to venture, to leave home and go to this Cornell." And to Ira, his eyeglasses removed, rubbing his eyes wearily: "Listen to me, child. All beginnings are that way. Difficult, discouraging at the outset."

"Not for everybody."

"For you then. It takes you longer to become used to things. But as long as you're in college, you'll see: the way that began so rough will become smooth. Heed me. As long as you're in college, and becoming an educated man, slowly you'll learn to deal with your troubles, slowly they'll begin to wane."

"Yeah," skeptically.

"That's right. Mom's right," Minnie soothed.

"I wish you could show me your guarantee."

"This hardship is nothing." Mom filled in Minnie's silence with comforting words. "Believe me, you'll look back to this time with laughter."

"Yeah, I got a great future behind me, like the comedian says." He rocked around in his chair toward Minnie, and then back to Mom. "Meantime I'm damn hungry."

"I have potted veal," Mom said eagerly. "A flavor like paradise. And boiled kasha with the gravy."

"I don't like kasha."

"Even starving with hunger?"

"No," he reinforced his churlishness.

"Then without kasha." Mom bustled about with bread knife and platter.

"You don't know what's good," Minnie reproached.

"No, I don't. Tell me sometime."

"Only *this* he doesn't know?" Pop observed. "Only that kasha is good? Does he know good from bad?"

"Believe me, you sin to refuse such delectable kasha." Mom set a plate before him. "Someday you'll mourn, you'll yearn for such delectable kasha."

"Swell. Till that time I'll do without."

"Fortunately, I was prepared," said Mom. "As if I didn't know your ways. my son. I baked a potato *kugel* too."

"Ah, that's better." Ira grabbed a slice of her rough rye bread and chomped while he waited for the rest of his supper.

So he had muffed it again. He bolted down a half-masticated lump of bread. Been deflected irrevocably, just as he had been before: by silly intimations, by irrelevances, by insubstantial, damnfool, dopy irrelevances, by sloth, by following the line of least resistance.

And by—you goddamn fool: by cozy, fierce expectancy, by cozy, coozy, quick coozy on a Sunday morning. Ever anybody have such a goddamn Sunday-morning crib? A crib was a place you humped a harlot in, wasn't it? Or the same word, "crib," helped you pass an exam. Assisted you—hey, ass sistered you. Right? Hey, pretty clever. Crib was a dreary little bedroom, his little bedroom, or Mom and Pop's, next to the airshaft on the first floor, a dreary little crypt, as Mom called it, that became a hedge against pulling off. What do you think of that? Just snap the brass nipple of the lock, after Mom went, and the little crib hurtled into lurid prospects; its gloom dazzled you with arcs of guilt. The cramped crib suddenly shimmered with delirium of connivance, with nimbus of abomination. Oh, boy, what exquisite alarm lurked in the commonplace, alchemic ecstasy that he had discovered by accident: like another Archimedes in a big tin bathtub. Eureka in a bathtub. Yeah, but you know, it was like that alloyed crown and its different buoyancy from the genuine. This time it was buoyancy and girlancy. And what a paralyzing Eureka when he came. Yow! Never to be the same afterward. . . .

Eureka, yeah, the whole damn thing opened up a world nobody ever dared enter; nobody ever dared *admit* he entered. He had come across references to it in the faintest, weakest, most indirect way, hushed, prim and prudish—Jesus Christ, anyone less attuned than he was would never have pricked up his ears at the signal, pricked up was right. And he had read it, gone to the library and taken home Byron's collected poems, Byron, who had imprisoned a willing Ira years ago in the same cell as *The Prisoner of Chillon*. Hell, Byron's was nothing like it: remote, grandiose, and ambiguous, all those supernatural choruses, all those wild chasms; who could keep track of them, or remember them later? Nah. Byron never got any further than just beginning to tell what Manfred did; Manny just brooded in proud solitude in a mysterious, lonely tower, over the enormity of his transgression. Hey, Manny, here's what it's like in a cold-water flat in East Harlem.

Still, you had to give the guy credit for even—yes, even whispering. . . . "Gee, that looks good, Mom." Ira salivated at the sight of the veal in its *shmaltzy* brown gravy that Mom ladled out of the pot onto the chipped white plate before him: "*Potateh kugel* too yet. Yay, team!"

"Eat slowly," Mom cautioned.

"It tastes good?" Minnie beamed.

"I'll say. That's what I want when I graduate."

"You hear, Mom?" Minnie commended.

"*Takeh.* We should all survive until that blessed day."

Pop's newspaper rustled. From behind it came the single curt reproach: "*Chompkeh.*"

"This time forgive him," Mom arbitrated. "The youth hasn't eaten since morning."

"Okay, Pop, I'll try to quit *chompkin'.* But boy, does it taste good. Hard to keep your mouth shut with a load of that *kugel* in gravy." Hunger's first pangs satisfied, Ira suppressed defiance. He darted a brief, veiled glance at Minnie again; she lowered her hazel eyes as if in prayer to her Latin text. So he had muffed, muffed in his choice of colleges. But how did he know? What did Solon say to Croesus? Look to the end, my fine-feathered friend. Same here. I'm the guy who put the muff in muffed. Come Sunday. He'd tell that to Minnie. No, he'd better tell her about looking to the end. Ha. Come Sunday morning. Come is right. And then he'd scoot off to Larry's for the afternoon. So? A few compensations. What else? Jesus, his mind was mushy rotten. If he let his fancy range—boyoboy, going to college, with a head full of—merde, ah. All he could think of was the white-wing dago street cleaner pushing his fiber brush ahead of him next to the granite curb. . . . Tired.

Tired, that was the trouble. Chalked characters on a blackboard at registration still glimmered in kitchen light. Fuck 'em all, we eat, he gobbled, remembered his pledge to Pop, gobbled behind closed lips. Fuck 'em all, we eat—that's what he had heard them say in the street. And his inner ear, perceiving the rhyme, incorporated it:

> *Fuck 'em all, we eat. I wanna repeat.*
> *An' if you screw your sister for a treat, what more d'ye neet?*
> *What more d'ye neet?*
> *A B.S. degree from CCNY, of course, indeet.*
> *Oink, oink. Neat.*

God, he was becoming brutish, iron-clad brutish, wanton, and yet ever more sensitized, caught in and aware of the net of his own endless associations. Would he, could he, ever escape? What did a herring think of when he saw the reticules of the seine closing in around him? What? And his seine was like steel mail—

My poor M. Ira paused, turned expiating eyes away from the monitor. My poor, darling lambikin wife. What you took to yourself, what you gave yourself to. Only the incorruptible—was he borrowing from St. Augustine?—only the incorruptible could have possessed such invincible grace as she did, to have remained as knowing and as unsullied as she had remained all these years of living with him, of abiding him. He stifled a sigh. Boyoboy.

II

Classes began a day or two later. Ira was soon floundering in trigonometry, over his head in a subject that was a precondition for matriculation for a science degree. The pace was simply too fast for him. Ability to keep abreast of the class in a subject that he should have studied and passed in high school was taken for granted for one who was majoring in science. And he was already failing, dismally. In French he fared better—at the beginning—in part perhaps because of his gift for mimicry of the pronunciation. But he made smeary messes in his draftsmanship in descriptive geometry. Again he failed to understand the fundamental and the not too difficult principles of projection of simple figures onto different planes, he who had been a whiz in plane and solid geometry. Geometry, his guardian angel subject, the course that had preserved his sanity. What the hell was wrong with him? Only in Philosophy 1 did he experience anything like the intellectual pleasure he had anticipated so fondly those hours before registration when he had trampled outdoors on the fallen leaves on Convent Avenue. It was in the engrossing, informal, sprightly lectures of Professor Overstreet that he did sense those pleasures of the intellect—in the lectures, spiced with wit, animated descriptions and personal experience: Professor Overstreet illustrating the general nature of assumptions by acting out how the French picked their teeth openly after dinner while Americans hid the toothpick behind their hand or a napkin. His lectures were a joy, and so too was reading the multigraphed brochure of selections from various philosophers the professor distributed to the class. Far and away the most stirring excerpts were from Bertrand Russell's audaciously contemporary statement of the faith of an atheist, the eloquent statement of the awareness of man's insignificance in a blind, indifferent cosmos. Nothing in that first semester captivated Ira more.

But the seminars, oh, the seminars conducted by a young graduate student, seminars dealing with the central ideas of Plato, Socrates, Aristotle, Spinoza, Kant, and the other great names in philosophy. The words embodying the abstractions the philosophers sought to convey flowed by him like the tide by a channel post. Utterly nebulous his notions of what their ideas consisted of, their concepts a floating ephemera, maintaining their outlines and distinctions from one another no better than a cloud, patches of haze. He did try to understand; the more earnestly he tried, the more soporific his endeavors became, the more opiate the elucidations in the text.

The weeks passed. Indian summer gave way to full autumn. Classes became routine; college became routine, an unhappy routine divided into equal segments of time. His performance in his subjects varied erratically, without ostensible reason, without rational control. In chemistry he did A work—and scarcely understood why; in trigonometry his failure was already irreversible. In philosophy it was just necessary to coast along to pass. In French, after a laudable start, he was soon warned by the precise, pedantic head of department that his work was deteriorating. Sluggish, incompetent, discouraged was the way he felt most of the time, was the way life made him feel, as if a pall separated his mind from his studies. And it did: a pall that confined him within it, that he passively submitted to.

With a quarter in his pocket, he would leave the house on 119th Street and hike along Park Avenue in the shadow of the trestle of the New York Central to 125th Street. There, wait on the corner for the Third and Amsterdam Avenue trolley, board it, ride to 137th Street and Amsterdam, alight, walk east with fellow students past Lewisohn Stadium, cross the small campus-quadrangle surrounded by Gothic conformity of white and gray edifices, enter the main building—and if time permitted, lounge in the Class of '28 alcove until time for class. Once or twice, in the morning, experimentally, he wore his Mili Sci uniform from home to college. He thought he would save time that way, by eliminating the change from civilian to military attire. But he found it embarrassing, coming out of the tenement onto the stoop into the slummy street on a bright fall morning, and then marching along grubby Park Avenue to 125th Street—all in World War scratchy, horse-blanket khaki breeches, puttees (which he could never roll on with any degree of neatness), rough woolen shirt and jacket that chafed the back of his neck. He would have to wear it all the rest of the day, until classes were over, and still in military uniform he rode home again. It didn't pay.

Altogether that first semester constituted a formless, foggy time; how formless and foggy it was he scarcely realized, because he was too confused intellectually to realize. What little satisfactions he derived, whether of attainment, as in Chem 1, or of enjoyment in listening to Professor Overstreet, were riddled, infiltrated, by the ever-present, the obsessive yearning for the exultation, the exaltation of perpetrating an act of glorious abomination. What the hell were studies compared to that? All they did was contrast his mediocrity, his aimlessness and boredom, his inattention with his ferocious audacity, his resourceful assaults on Minnie. Contrast his passivity, his temporizing in his studies, in his flaccid pursuit of knowledge, with his ingeniousness in winning Minnie's surrender. Ah, that was what mattered, that minute or two when he pumped the cry out of her of incestuous consummation.

Such was the nature of his attendance at college. Instead of imbuing him with aspiration and hope as it did his classmates, more often than not, it simply contrasted the ugly tenement facade and smelly hallway and four-room dump on 119th Street in which he and

his family lived, his dingy little bedroom, transmogrified by evil reful-
gence that minute or two when Minnie lay athwart the bed, drawers
hanging from one foot, like a white flag hoisted in capitulation contrasted with the staid, aloof, academic atmosphere of the halls of instruction within the Gothic exteriors of CCNY. Oh, bullshit. He was
ruined, he was ruined, okay. So he was ruined. Fuck it. Yes, others endured even greater extremes between home and college than he did,
but they hadn't gotten snagged, snarled inextricably, the way he had.

Oh, sure, he was crazy; he knew it. He was crazy and he welcomed, he cultivated, the exacerbation of his craziness all the while.
He should have frequented the piers on the North River, pestered
the steamship chief steward or boatswain or mate for a job, any menial job that would take him away from home, deckhand, pot wal-
loper, oil wiper, anything. But if he had been capable of that, had
that necessary smidgeon of initiative, then he wouldn't have been the
one he was, wanted and didn't want to be. At least, he could have
gone with Billy to Cornell. . . .

Larry, meanwhile, in pursuance of the two-year academic prerequisite for entering dental school, his "predent," as he humorously referred to it, had enrolled in the Washington Square extension of
NYU. He had encountered no difficulty in registering for any course
he chose, and was enjoying all of them, interested in all, doing well in
all, and especially in his two courses in English, one in English composition, the other titled Outlines of English Literature. The former,
the class in composition, was conducted by a young New Englander,
a Mr. Vernon, who incidentally was a poet, a writer of free verse, and
had already published a book of poems at his own expense.

The latter, the course in English literature, was conducted by a
young woman, a native of New Mexico, a poet as well as a critic, with
a background, or second discipline, in anthropology. A very stimulating instructor, she had already published two volumes of verse trans-
lations of Navajo Indian religious chants. The respect for and
harmony with nature, which the white man continually disregarded,
when not destroying it, she had rendered with great sensitivity and
sympathy. The reviewers had all praised her for her skill and delicacy
as a poet, and especially for awakening in the white reader a new understanding of the Indians' unique reverence for all things in nature,

and their awareness of its beauty, and above all, their unsuspected eloquence in rendering their feelings about these things. Her name was Edith Welles.

Both were recent appointees at the university, and both ranked as instructors. It was his instructor in Outlines of English Literature who captivated Larry's fancy completely.

Edith Welles, as Larry described her, was extremely girlish in appearance, dainty and petite, with the tiniest hands and feet he had ever seen on a grown woman. No one looking at her would have guessed that she already had her doctorate—interdepartmentally, in two disciplines, as they were called, English and anthropology. She was so sensitive, so fine and discerning, it was really a shame, Larry said, that such an exceptional person should waste her energies lecturing on English literature to a bunch of premeds and predents, who didn't give a damn about literature and about poetry. All they cared about—the majority in both Vernon's class and Welles's class—was getting a passing grade so they could go on to what they were really interested in: mastering a profession that would assure them a comfortable living.

"You never saw such a bunch of thick-skinned, fat-headed guys. Jewish, I'm ashamed to say." Larry grimaced.

"Yeah?"

"Oh, there are some in the class, a few, really serious students of literature, who intend to go on to graduate school and get their doctorates, or are preparing themselves for a career in writing: you know, journalism, writing fiction, criticism, poetry too. Some already excel. Really. I've got to admit it. They're not all interested in middle-class values, you know, becoming a doctor or a dentist with a good practice. They're really aiming at becoming creative writers."

"Yeah? You mean write their own stuff? Already? And only freshmen? Jesus, we don't hear anything like that at CCNY."

"Oh, I don't mean there's a lot of it here. But they tell me there's a lot more than in that hoity-toity NYU up on the Hudson, where they hardly admit any Jews."

"Yeah? I'm sure they would have admitted you if you wanted to go there."

"I'm glad I'm not there. They say it's dull as dishwater up there."

"No kidding."

"Yes. Isn't that funny? We don't even have a campus down here. Unless you want to say Washington Square Park is our campus. That's where all the Greenwich Village bohemians hang out."

"Is that the place they hang out? Where the college is?"

"Well, really the college is where they hang out." Larry smiled. "They were there before NYU."

"Oh, yeah?"

"They live in those run-down old town houses you see all around there. Mostly small houses. Those old brownstones with a flight of stone steps in front. Cheap and run-down, you know what I mean? And that allows them to be free, free to do what they want. Live unconventionally with a woman. Not marry if they don't want to. Paint, write, loaf." Larry shrugged for humorous emphasis. "Anything not to hold down—be held down, I should say, by a regular job. That's the main thing. Some of 'em are just fakes."

"Gee!"

"The whole place is that way. Unconventional. But I like it."

"What d'you mean? NYU?"

"Oh, no. I mean Washington Square. It's not the stereotypical college atmoshmear."

"Atmoshmear," Ira repeated appreciatively.

"Yes, no atmoshmear." Larry relished Ira's appreciation. "There's none of that rah-rah college spirit. No raccoon coats. At least I don't see any. None of that Ivy League crap. Fraternities. Maybe there are. I don't know. It's right smack in the middle of all kinds of cheap manufacturing buildings. It was once the center of the garment industry, the ex-sweatshop area. It's down-to-earth."

"Gee, what a college. Sounds less than CCNY."

"Yes. The main building, the administration office, most of the classrooms, everything is in a remodeled loft building."

"You mean it?"

"It's a fact. Someone pointed out the building where that Triangle Shirtwaist fire took place. You must have remembered hearing about that when you were a kid?"

"No, I didn't. My father was a milkman when we lived on the Lower East Side. So I got kind of left out of all of that trade union stuff. I've read about it, though. It was awful. Women jumping from the tenth floor. Boy."

"Well, it's practically next door."

"No kidding." Ira shook his head. "So what d'you like about the place?"

"There's so much ferment going on. In the English department especially. It's so informal. You feel as if it's the real thing." Larry held up a large white finger. "That's it. You don't feel any distance between yourself and your instructor. You talk literature, you talk writing. Stuff you may be doing yourself. You talk modern poetry. You exchange opinions about anything, almost as equals."

"Yeah? I get it now. That's the last thing you feel in CCNY—although I like Professor Overstreet. I told you about him. But you don't get close to him or anything like that. It's just the way he lectures, that's all. But otherwise—" Ira left the rest unsaid. "You think it's because you pay tuition?"

"I don't think so. I think Columbia would be like CCNY. Stiff and formal. And you pay tuition there. The only complaint I have is that Miss Welles assumes in Outlines of English Lit that none of us has heard of Chaucer or Milton or the Romantic Movement. So the course tends to be a little too elementary. I mean, she has to explain a great many obvious points. Gets a little boring for a few people, you know."

"Boy, I never heard anybody complain about that in the '28 alcove. We're glad to get into an English course. I couldn't."

"Probably Miss Welles has to keep things simple because she has to cater to a bunch of predents and premeds."

"Yeah?" Ira felt perplexed, at a loss. What kind of expectations did Larry have? Or were they called standards? He was a predent himself, and yet he criticized the presentation of literature, and criticized with such assurance, such interest, yes, as if literature took precedence over dentistry, as if he were disassociating himself from the others with the same aims. It was confusing.

Larry went on. For the benefit of those undergraduates who were disposed to go more deeply into the subject of writing, writing their own poems and short stories, Edith Welles and her colleague, John Vernon, had just instituted a new kind of student society: an Arts

Club. All those students who were seriously interested in the writing of fiction, criticism, poetry, in creative writing in short, could fore-gather, and read their own work, and listen to that of others. Members of the faculty could do the same. Also, professional writers, or those of established reputations, would be invited to give readings of their poems, stories, or essays. Larry himself had submitted some of his lyrics for Miss Welles to appraise. She thought them very promising. Very promising indeed. And for someone taking a pre-dent course, quite remarkable. "I certainly felt good." Larry's fea-tures seemed enlarged by separate glow of modest pride. "You know, hearing praise from her."

"Boy. I would, too."

"She suggested I join the Arts Club, that I become a member."

"Yeah? You going to?"

"Of course. I wouldn't miss this chance for anything. It's a real honor. And an opportunity. It's an incentive, you know what I mean? There are a lot of juniors and seniors in the club. I guess I'd be about the only freshman."

Rapt, avid auditor of marvelous tidings, Ira could feel longing whet his appetite. How free, how intimate, how awake and fulfilling NYU seemed compared to antiquated, drab, regulated CCNY. Con-temporaneous and vital the one, lusterless the other, except for that glint of life once a week—Professor Overstreet's lectures. NYU was what he thought college would be when he trod on the fallen leaves on Convent Avenue. College would be responsive to his needs, would mean an expansion of his mind, would challenge with all kinds of ex-ploration and discovery. Oh, to be on a par with English instructors, the way Larry described he felt, to listen to and meet writers and poets who actually had published books. What a privilege, as if a new empyrean had opened up. And he himself still without even a com-position course or an English literature course to provide the kind of leavening that raised his spirits most: the wonders of language, the felicity—he could already recognize it as if recognition were second nature—the appositeness of word and phrase to connotation. A kind of bleary fragmentation seemed to imbue studies and courses at CCNY, a sense of futility. On the basis of his A's in chemistry, in a kind of despairing search for a new purpose, or career, Ira asked genial

Professor Esterbrook, head of the chemistry department, whether he approved of Ira's majoring in chemistry. "I'm sorry to tell you," was the professor's reply, "there's not much future for your people in chemistry."

For your people. In a way, Ira was relieved, secretly, relieved of striving, relieved of purpose. Go the rounds, phlegmatically, get by somehow, shrug at your mediocrity, and—sink into her on Sunday mornings as fast as she'd let you, ram it into her ravishing crimson passage in fiendish need and savage turpitude, in her, who seconds after it was over would be just Minnie his sister. So what. A nickel a day kept the baby away. A nickel a day from his twenty-five-cent allowance, when he had stopped hustling at sports events, meant a quarter a week, meant a tin of two Trojan rubbers. So he swiped a ten-cent ham sandwich on white bread in the CCNY lunchroom. Fuck 'em. The sandwich wasn't worth a dime anyway.

And she was strange, Jesus, Minnie, she was strange, changeable. Sometimes she was wide awake by the time Mom left, not only awake, but waiting, peremptory, damn near, calling on him to hurry into the kitchen and snap the lock right after Mom left. He would have liked a few minutes of gloating, a few minutes of pawing, petting—he knew they could afford a few minutes of anticipation. But nothing doing. And he didn't have a dime to his name to offer her, but it didn't make any difference—as though he had partly perverted her. She had her thighs raised to him in her own folding cot, even while venting her displeasure at him for being dilatory. Lucky for him those times. "All right, all right, you can do it to me here. Hurry up. Put the rubber on. Just make sure it's a good one. I don't want that white stuff in me."

"I know. I know. It's brand-new. Jesus, don't rush me. Gimme a chance."

At other times she behaved quite the opposite, penitent perhaps, reverting to "O-oh, are you a louse! Why don't you leave me alone? I'm your sister."

And he, offended to the point of losing his chance, "So I'm a louse. If you're my sister, I'm your brother. So what're you?"

"Shut up. Sometimes I wish Mama would come home and catch us."

"Yeah? What d'ye think I locked the door for?"

"You don't think she'd know? You saw her look at us a couple of times funny. You didn't see because you got your head in a book."

"All right, so who would she blame?"

"You, you louse. Who would she blame? He asks yet."

"You don't get a thrill, too?"

"You're older, that's why it's your fault. Who started it?"

"All right, let me in, will ye?"

"The rubber's all right?"

"Of course."

"O-o-h, o-oh, my poor brother, my poor dear brother. Oh, that's good."

"Yeah? Ah."

"Don't kiss me."

III

The fall term at CCNY went by—routine and dull. Only through Larry could he share in the excitement of his freshman year at NYU, hear his account of the activities of the Arts Club, of the bohemian setting of their evening meetings in one or another of the restaurants in the college environs, the Pirates' Den, the Romany Inn, and listen to his entertaining descriptions of the eccentrics one might meet crossing Washington Square Park. With Larry, Ira went on an excursion to Greenwich Village, trying not to gawk at long-haired, freakish individuals, posturing in poetic disregard of conventional clothes and behavior. Ira's own vista was flat and uninspired in retrospect—punctuated by a few hectic minutes on a Sunday morning, or frenzied windfall on a rare weekday afternoon, when the two were alone, those unforeseen, wild pouncings of furor, snatching gratification out of baleful contingency—and the fears it spawned. . . .

He dropped trigonometry, hopelessly incapable of making headway against his utter confusions. The dropping of the course would mean a dangerous insufficiency of credit. It would bring a warning from the dean that Ira risked flunking out of college. As against the debacle in trig was the anomaly of an A in chemistry. A grade of D in phys ed—he who had been a sturdy plumber's helper only a few months before, and could swim the length of the college pool underwater. Mili Sci, with its marching around Jasper Oval in fair weather and in foul weather, rehearsing the manual of arms down in the "tunnel" between buildings, singing, "The Infantry, the Infantry, with the dirt behind their ears," in time to the beat set by the portly paterfamilias of a colonel (while the blond-haired sergeant could scarcely refrain from squirming in embarrassment).

> *"The infantry, the infantry,*
> *With the dirt behind their ears,*
> *The infantry, the infantry,*
> *That never, never fears . . ."*

For some unaccountable reason he received an A in the course.

Baba died in the fall of that first semester, only about half a year after Lenin had died early in the winter. She died a lingering death of "pernicious anemia." She lay at Montefiore Hospital in the Bronx, dying, but aware. Out of affection for his old grandmother, Ira accompanied Mom there: he entered a warm, sunny, bright room, joined his other relatives standing or sitting about the bed. Baba's face above the smooth, white bedspread looking as shriveled as a weathered husk, weazened, her skin corrugated and as if pigmented by the tiny shadows cast by a myriad of minute wrinkles. It was dinnertime; the nurse served Baba her meal. It looked so fetching on the platter: a thick juicy tidbit of rib steak under a sprig of parsley next to a mound of mashed potatoes banked by bright green peas. Ira drooled at the sight; in imagination, he sank his teeth into the succulent, rosy beef. Even Zaida's mouth must have watered, for his Adam's apple bobbed visibly as he importuned Baba to eat. "*Ess, ess, Minkeh,*" he urged, swallowing. Then he chided her for declining, exhorted with ever growing impatience, "*Ess, ess, Minkeh.* How can you live unless you eat?"

She refused, feebly; she wasn't hungry: "*Ikh vil nisht, ikh ken nisht.*"

"Goodbye, Baba." Ira went over to Baba's bedside, after he heard Max offer to take Mom home in his new car. "I hope you get better." He bent down and kissed the dark, shrunken brow of the head that rested in the center of uncropped, mousy hair diverging on the white pillow.

"May God watch over you, my child. Be a good son to your mother." Barely audible, her murmured blessing.

"Yes, Baba." He straightened up.

"*Gey gezunt.*"

"Thanks, Baba. Goodbye."

Amid prayers for speedy recovery, Ira bade farewell to his dying grandmother, forever after enshrined in his memory, lying in a white bed and refusing all importuning to eat a morsel of a juicy piece of beefsteak he could have devoured in two bites, and without an urging.

For another year or a little longer, Zaida lived with his last two unmarried sons, Max and Harry, in the apartment on 115th Street. And when Max married, two years after his mother's death, Harry went to live with Max and his new wife, Rosy, in the new house Max bought in Flushing, Long Island, while Zaida went to live with his daughter Mamie. She, in partnership with Saul, Ira's shifty and conniving uncle, had acquired from the local bank, marginally, two large adjoining apartment houses on 112th Street between Fifth and Lenox avenues, two squat blocks of dwellings of gray stone and gray brick, two matched six-story buildings with four apartments on each floor above the ground floor. Mamie managed the two places, for which she was recompensed with an apartment of her choice rent-free. She chose a spacious apartment only a flight up from the street. The apartment consisted of six rooms, more than enough to accommodate herself, her spouse, Jonas, her two young daughters, Hannah and Stella, and, eventually, Zaida, whenever he was ready to move in, which he did as soon as the lease of the apartment on 115th Street expired. A *sine qua non* for Zaida to board anywhere required the household to be strictly kosher, and, of course, Mamie kept a strictly kosher home.

Thus a new configuration now obtained among the family Farb. Ella and her husband, Meyer, still a kosher butcher, and their two infant children lived in an apartment house on Fifth Avenue and 116th Street. All the other siblings, except Harry, were married; all were in the restaurant business, as partners, except Sadie's husband, Max S, who preferred to remain a waiter and avoid the "headaches" of ownership. Mamie's husband, Jonas, at Mamie's insistence, had given up his trade of years' standing as a ladies' tailor in order to join his brothers-in-law in partnership. Moe and Saul, Max, and soon Harry purchased or shared in the purchase of newly built two-story frame houses in Flushing, adjacent to each other and not far from their place of business, a large cafeteria on Sutphin Boulevard in Jamaica.

The year 1924 waned into the Christmas holidays. In the Farb family a *bris* was to be celebrated on a Sunday during the Christmas holidays. A son had been born to Saul and his wife, Ida, the second Ida in the family. Of course, all the relatives had been invited to the circumcision, and the festivities to follow.

"At least show yourself," Mom pleaded. "You're so estranged from the family, they hardly know you. Show them I have a college son. Your father won't attend any occasion: always at odds with everyone. Escort me. I have no one."

"There's Minnie. What d'you mean, nobody to escort you?" Ira countered.

"That afternoon she has a date."

"A what?"

"A dance. A Christmas revelry, don't you know how the *goyim* celebrate? At Julia Richmond High School, with the young men from the *commoysheh* high school. *Commoysheh* high school has many Jewish students, as you know. Perhaps she'll find a good Jewish youth for a suitor."

"Oh, yeah?"

"Believe me, they'll admire you at the *bris*. My handsome son, and a college student, who won't admire you?" Mom wheedled. "And food and drink they'll proffer without end. They're all in the restaurant business, no?"

"And Minnie is going to be gone all afternoon?" Ira brushed aside the lure, at the same time as he probed for possibilities of another sort. "When is she coming home?" he probed.

"Not until late evening. I'm telling you. Not till your father is home from the benket in Coonyiland. Maybe not till we return," Mom affirmed. "Come. Be a kind and considerate son. Escort me this once."

"I don't see why. You can go with Mamie."

"I know. I know that. But this one time, favor me. What else does a mother wish but to display her admirable son?"

"Oh, yeah. That's just what I want."

"My sisters are bringing their children. Only I am without. Forlorn. Neither husband nor son. Public school graduation, not. High school graduation, not. I don't deserve anything? Is it so much?" She sat there so patiently, heavy hands in her lap, bobbed hair speckled gray, deep, sorrowful brown eyes pleading.

"Oh, well," Ira grudgingly consented.

"Indeed a precious son!"

"Okay, okay, I said I'd go," he quenched sentiment abruptly. "Holy mackerel. Sit there, and do what?" He wagged his head in distaste. "*Chibeggeh, chibeggeh, chibeggeh,* as Pop says. Boy, how to ruin a Sunday." He felt especially out of sorts, frustrated. Minnie had refused him this morning. She was having her period. "Anh, nuts."

"My darling child."

After a long ride to Flushing, and a walk of several blocks from the Sutphin Boulevard station, they came to Saul's brand-new frame house, full of relatives. As Zaida's oldest grandson, first of a new generation of cousins, and a "collitch" boy besides, Ira was greeted effusively and with admiration by all the guests. Complimented for her distinguished offspring by everyone there, Mom flushed with pride, glowed with pleasure. Laconic in defense, Ira, as he had anticipated, had embarrassingly little to discuss with his restaurateur uncles, a perfunctory minimum which he made no effort to expand. Nor could he interest himself, on the other hand, in the seemingly limitless differences of points of view they exchanged among themselves. As bored as he had ever been in his life, he sat inertly and with unfeigned listlessness amid the flow of opinions about aspects and prospects of the cafeteria business between naively boastful Max and slinking Saul, between tactless Harry and robust and candid Moe. Only Moe took time to make a few inquiries about Ira's collegiate activities, inquiries crossing the Yiddish and Yinglish hubbub of domestic and business activities. How did college appeal to Ira? And how many years more would he have to attend? And what had he chosen as a career? "Poor Leah, your mother, will finally have something to be happy about."

Replied to by Ira with remarks that were shallow and truncated, even in response to Moe's inquiries, perfunctory acknowledgments of kinship that had long since lost whatever living interactions it once had. Two worlds drifting further and further apart from their original cluster. "How is the restaurant *gesheft?*" Ira asked in humorous deference.

And received the expected stereotypical reply, "*M'makht a lebn.*"

Neither had anywhere to go in the other's domain. Ira could scarcely mask his utter indifference to, if not disdain for, their various observations on making a living in the cafeteria business. It was difficult for him to feign interest—out of politeness, out of minimal consideration for the occasion, or what? A celebration, birth of his uncle's firstborn son. Boyoboy, talk about tedium, about being bored stiff. What would life have been, relations have been in the close-packed Orthodoxy of the stagnant Galitzianer hamlet they came from? Something more meaningful, surely, more interwoven, shared and dynamic, even if seemingly insignificant when viewed by the outside world.

How far apart they had traveled since they had crossed the ocean—the thought repeatedly rolled through Ira's mind. Was it—he found himself mulling amid the cry and flurry of festivity—that he had preceded them to America by a few years, or was just an infant when he arrived? Trailed no residue of Europe? Or what? It seemed to him he was forever capturing the answer, and losing it again. Minnie was a damn sight closer to them than he was, and Minnie had been born here. You had to search somewhere else, search somewhere else for an answer. That move to Harlem from 9th Street on the Lower East Side—again the cause: "It is the cause, my soul," said Othello. That crazy impulse to drink of that rill of rainwater trickling down the hillside in Central Park. Or the reading, all the reading he did about the gentile world. But Minnie seemed to read as much as he did. She had spent whole afternoons in the library, when the Great War forced a curtailment in classes to half a day, to mornings only for her—and was he ever furious with her for not staying home, for not coming home early from the library. What chances she deprived him of, again and again. Jesus Christ, right away, the skull throbbed. He had no barriers, not even tissue-paper barriers to hold impulse within bounds—

Zaida didn't come to the *bris*. Ira thought he heard someone say he was still in mourning. And not all the uncles were there at one and the same time either. They had to take turns tending to the cafeteria, especially the cash register. Nor was Ida there, the "first" Ida, the flamboyant Ida Link, Morris's wife, who lived upstairs in the same house. She had had a falling-out with Sam, Mom whispered to Ira, adding, "And a *geferlikhe gemblerke ist* she too," referring to Ida's passion for cards.

With the assembled guests, Ira watched the shrill infant's foreskin slit by the *mohel*, thrown on the floor, and stamped on—to Hebrew invective. Then followed the feast: the *gefilte* fish, and the fricassee and the *kreplakh*, the *kishka*, siphons of seltzer, the wine and whiskey, and desserts fruity and desserts baked—all consumed amid ritual Jewish din. Mamie, already in girth like a barrel, ate until her eyes bulged. As for Ira, he not only gorged but tippled, first whiskey, with bravado, then copious drafts of sweet wine along with the ample viands, and by the end of the repast, he reached the end of his capacity. Loaded, bloated, in lethargic haze, reacting to his orgy of gluttony, he sprawled on one side of the twin love seat in the sunroom off the living room, wishing to hell he had never acceded to Mom's appeal. What the hell had he come here for? To cram his gut? Goddamn tun-belly.

It was evening. The sunroom lay in deep shadow. The living room was deserted. Most of the guests had eaten and gone their various ways, perfunctorily bidden farewell by Ira. And now, yawning dormantly, he waited for Mom to announce that she was ready to leave—before he would have to remind her that *he* was ready to leave. More than ready. After the departure of so many people, the place seemed to have subsided, become semideserted. From the brightly lit doorway of the kitchen on the other side of the unlit living room came the splash and clink of dishwashing and chatter of the women, interspersed by the voices of Mamie's younger and loquacious daughter, Hannah, and the treble voices of Sadie's kids, while their mothers—and Mom—helped the second Ida clean up in the aftermath of the banquet. Stuffed, reclining on his half of the love seat in lassitude of gourmandizing, Ira bided his time, lulled by the hum issuing from the kitchen, hebetating to the verge of somnolence . . . about to doze off—

The kitchen doorway opened brightly. . . .

Casting her shadow into the living room, the kitchen doorway darkened with her short, unhurried presence, and a moment later, framed her deliberate, casual exit from the others in the kitchen . . . darkening behind her as she shut it, stepping into the penumbra of the living room: Stella. For Chrissake. How old was she? Fourteen? Was he crazy or was he right? She was coming nearer. He could feel himself inflame: willing prey? Knowing prey? What? He marked something in her dim, wavering step. Innocent approach? No, innocuous approach, that was it, a possibility, a potential, feasible and farfetched at the same time: Mamie's older daughter, fourteen years old now, for Chrissake, short, plump, blond, blue-eyed, simple, but for all that, pudgy, tubby, unformed as she was, already wafting carnal tiding, diffusing nubile compliance. If he could only get her alone. Boy, she was like a lascivious cordial to his gluttony, cordial to satiation. Wow. Why the hell was she dawdling? Why didn't she come over to where he was? Oh, no, she was clever, dissembling; she knew what she was doing. Aimlessly arriving, on oblique tack, yes, yes. And here she was. Oh, he was right, he was right. All ploy, all surreptitious, like a noncommittal complement to her dissembling. He smiled cautiously without incentive.

She was very blond as she passed from penumbra into the deeper shadow of the withdrawn sunroom, drawled something banal, banal utterance of the obvious. "It's dark, and you're sitting alone."

And standing tubby, standing in front of him, in front of Ira, burning now in predatory rut, in lecherous fury that he felt would kill him, if he didn't gratify it on her. "Why don'tcha sit down." He beckoned innocently at the twin seat at his back. "It's nice here. Quiet."

And in vapid collusion she complied.

Sitting opposite, his eyes fixed watchfully on the kitchen door, he tilted his head sideways, sought her mouth. She converged. She parted her lips for his tongue to delve—to plumb. Oh, yes, Jesus Christ, no doubt, discreet, ready, expectant. Where could he try? Boyoboy, his blazing passion could kill this little, oh, fat little heifer, supine, submissive, inviting murderous sacrifice. Jesus. But where? Where freedom for rut to erupt, where a minute of privacy, innocent-seeming privacy? Think. Upstairs. Possibly. Try.

The signaling tip of his head when he stood up was superfluous. She followed, tractable as if on a leash. "Let's look at the rooms upstairs."

"Upstairs is Uncle Morris's and Ida's," she meshed with him in dissembling. "Uncle Morris is by the cash register tonight."

"Yeah?" Preceding her, he had climbed to the landing on top of the stairs. "And Ida? Do you know?"

"I don't know. Mama said she went to play cards."

He tried the doorknob. Fixed. Locked. "They're not home." But no good. Christ, get caught here on the landing as obvious as a placard, their ploy. What the hell would he be doing up here but to screw her? They came down again.

Throbbing, he felt as if he were treading on a surface without a floor beneath him in fierce, foiled quest. Chrissake, where? They went outdoors: stood a few seconds inspecting the narrow lane between duplicate houses. Cold the dark, and betraying. No good. Locked anyway. By Max who lived there. They'd be in the doorway, should anybody come along. And where were they, should Mom or Mamie ask? No good, no good, no good. Jesus, he'd go crazy. He led the way back into the house: kitchen light under the closed doorway, sound of utensils, voices. They'd be finished in another few minutes, probably, putting away the last of the dishes, silverware. Finished they. And so would he be. Somebody would pop out the door, and then. Goddamn. Ever hear of such a goddamn . . . such a goddamn . . . Here she was at his elbow, waiting—simpering, her blond head at his shoulder—

Hey, wait a minute. The cellar!

The cellar! The new concrete-floored, concrete-walled cellar that Saul had showed off so proudly to his guests—when Max had bragged about his. . . . Should he lead her there, to Max's darkened house, search for an entrance across the narrow lane? Go out again? Nah. Jesus, no time. Right here. Take a goddamn chance.

Ira beckoned with his head. She followed, as if bereft of independence, a puppet utterly guided by the sovereign depravity of will. Dummy. Hell, no. She wore a dummy disguise. Boy, that made it a lot safer. No blabbing. . . .

This way, yes, to the cellar. Fitting they should make exploratory excursion toward the cellar door, plausible to swing it ajar, tip switch up, and peer down into blank whiteness, emphasize surprise. Close door behind, descend . . . half-dozen wooden steps to the glaring new cement floor under the stark, unshaded light bulb. Sharp and solid shadow of furnace, hot water heater, laundry tub, displacing the glare of wall.

"Quick." Ira lifted her dress.

She pulled aside the skimpy sling of her teddy to reveal elemental, adolescent fuzz. Already out with it, his charger, ready, brute in the van, hauling creature after it, mind and body. "Ever do it before?" he asked.

She hesitated a moment, reluctant to confess, and yet not to forgo, to miss by being remiss: "The painter."

"The painter?" he approached.

"After we moved in. The new rooms." Her shallow blue eyes glazed—"Oh!"—glazed, unblinking . . . at his penetration, unblinking, shallow blue eyes accomplice of his perpetration. Minnie closed her hazel eyes, but not Stella, shallow, blue stare, gone vacuous, gone void. It was working, working, it was working, working. Look at her eyes, shallow, blue, stupefied: stultified inanity fixed on him, his prey, accessory to his violation, Jesus Christ, intrinsic to his spraddling her. Destroy her, ah-h, straddling him—slump, mum larva, squash her dumbstruck trance with guy-geyser brutish he—fucking her. Ai-i. Get out! Get away! Aoh, just when—

It was over.

"Upstairs," he commanded. And as she climbed back up the wooden steps, "You think you look all right?"

Her juvenile blond head nodded.

"Sure? Good. All right. Out."

He watched her juvenile round butt pause a second longer above him at the door, pause, her hands smoothing skirt. She went out, left the door a crack ajar. He loitered . . . to break nexus, quietly smearing ejaculate underfoot, as Jews smeared phlegm underfoot in synagogue, as the *mohel* had mashed the infant's foreskin underfoot after stamping on it. Dry up soon. Then tiptoed up the stairs, switched off the light as he eased out of the cellar door, sneaked back to the love seat, dropped quietly down, and sitting back, surrendered to last, vestigial panting.

—So you did it.

Yes, I did. And relived it too. Many a time.

—Why?

To alert the world to the menace of housepainters.

—Dispense with the levity. Why?

Good question, Ecclesias. I don't know why. Not at the moment. The answer may suggest itself later on, take shape into coherence, but for the moment I'm at a loss. *Certes,* I'm not engaged in a sociological tract, but a rendering, excuse me, or attempt at holistic rendering of my lamentable past. But even so, I suppose I'm open to the charge of appealing to the prurient interest. On the other hand, Ecclesias, I feel bound not to mitigate the behavior of this literary scamp, bound to present him as despicable as he was. Of course, as I say, I could have done so—in general terms, clinically.

—And chose not to. Why is the reliving so important to you, an old man edging closer to eighty this mid-August than seventy-nine?

Tough again. I mean to find an answer. Have I overstepped the boundary from the erotic into the pornographic? Is this the fumarole manifestation of the well-nigh extinct libido? Likely as not. Let the psychiatric specialist decide. There will be more of the same, by the way, and I must admit that I come to life, so to speak, leap into an orbit of higher energy, when in the grip of the sexual escapade or episode. Again why? Animal impetus, elemental instinct of an individual, alas, in whom the seismic wrench of sexuality brought libido into abnormal salience above reason.

—You think so?

Yes, and I can think only, if you call it that, I can think only figuratively, or subjectively: how the event, the episode, feels. Probably all of this is interconnected: my subjectivity, my weakness in objective analysis, my paucity of ideology—

—And of ideas.

And of ideas. Granted. It's all one zone, one ever-changing, ever-recurring zodiac: personality, proclivity, vicissitude, act, character, rearing, perpetual zodiac.

—Do you know what you're talking about?

Quite frankly, no.

—I think I have an inkling, though, one that breaks through the wall of your verbiage.

What?

—Unpremeditated too in this case. I do think that you wrote as explicitly as you did because you still are what you were. That the hold on you of what you were is, so to speak, still in force. Though your hard-won wisdom, or perhaps foresight, restraint, together with your depleted appetite, might make you, if not immune to those same temptations, at least resistant, more resistant than you were. Perhaps even to the point of distancing yourself from them, taking to your heels, the way that Saint Anthony did, who left his cloak in the harlot's clutch. Who knows, you cannot, never will, recover, have not shaken, cannot shake, the brand you seared into yourself.

That's why the explicitness?

—I think so. I'm almost sure of it.

Well. And what do you advise, Ecclesias?

—You might as well accommodate it.

It?

—What you were. Be it again you never can be.

You mean the danger of my being it again?

—Yes. And you already see that resisting it was to no avail. You set out in a first draft without a sibling. Ineluctably your sister forced her way into your narrative, strange, even bizarre though it may be for one to commit sibling incest without mentioning a sister, at least in the beginning. You see what a fix you're in now that the truth has made its way to the fore. You've lopped off the beginning of your yarn; you'll have to make amends some way. So powerful a shaping force in your life simply would not drown.

I had hoped when I was through, when all this sordidness was over, to introduce her, portray her as another character . . .

—As it was, you were left with a lopsided tale. Anyway, to conclude, it would be folly to repeat the error again. So make a clean breast of what you are. It's perfectly evident you can't do otherwise, because you're no other than you were, though you're other than you were—

All right. All right. All right.

—Or dangle in some surrealist limbo.

All right. All right. So now I maneuver in double jeopardy, double-furtive, double-scurvy, through incest-and-a-half. *Soror. Sobrina.*

—Yes. Doubly fecund and doubly fertile. Also doubly liable to indict-ment for statutory rape.

I do thank you, Ecclesias.

—Never mind. Incest *cum suror*—can you supply the ablative?

And so it came to pass that he had really screwed her. And no one had noticed, no one had guessed. She had gone back inside the kitchen to rejoin the others. Oh, she knew, she had wanted it, she feigned dummy-blandness. She'd never tell. Nearly hadn't told him about the painter, except—as if he'd back off, constrained in deflow-ering her. But that sonofabitch of a house painter. . . . Nobody home, and the plump pullet waggling her tail around. Down with his over-alls, let the walls wait. Balls for the walls, and pop goes the cherry-o over his overalls. . . . All right. Ira tried to put his thoughts in order. Jesus, only fourteen years old, but down went your kasha-colored sec-ondhand knickers. So what? Minnie was younger, just tickled sand-wich-style—till that time once suddenly, oooh! So when could he go there again to visit Mamie? After Zaida went there to live; that would be praiseworthy. Laudable pretext, boy, keep the old codger com-pany, hearken to his Talmudic disquisitions, commiserate with him in his widowerhood, in his hypochondriac ills.

But until then: let's see.

IV

With the resumption of classes in the new year, the year 1925, Larry
read a short story he had just written, with considerable help in plot
from Ira, at the next scheduled session of the Arts Club, but he came
away bitterly resentful at the contemptuous treatment his work had
received at the hands of his fellow undergraduate members of the
club. "The dumb bastards!" he stormed. "They never even saw the
underlying significance of the story. The dumb futzes! Always preening themselves on being in the vanguard. It's sheer empty bragging.
They're blind. Everything has to be so esoteric nobody knows what
it's about, and I'll bet they don't either. Just plain show-offs. Make a
big impression by running down an honest piece of work."

"Boy, I can't believe it." Ira listened sympathetically. "The parts
you read to me sounded great." He had never seen Larry so wrought
up.

"Oh, no, they're much too highfalutin for a straightforward
piece of writing, a genuine short story."

"I'll be damned."

"And do you want to know something? There's an undergraduate in the club, Schneider—swell-headed. Upperclassman. Senior,
you know the kind. A self-styled penetrating literary critic." Larry's
wrath took the form of an unblinking stare. "You know what he did?
He actually plagiarized an essay on Ezra Pound, and read it at the
Arts Club as if it were his own."

"Who?"

"Schneider! Snider! However he spells it," Larry snapped.

"Oh. Snider. He must be a good poet."

"No, Schneider's the plagiarist. Ezra Pound, *he's* the poet."

"I think I remember the name now."

"Schneider copied the whole thing word for word out of a small
out-of-the-way magazine that he thought nobody else would read.
Well, somebody did. Boris G. I told you about him. He's in love with
Edith. And the bloke was caught. Edith said he cried all over the
place about it."

"Wow. Sorry he was caught."

"Yes. And he had the nerve to get up and say that my story was just an old wives' tale. He plagiarizes an article, and he sneers at an honest short story."

Ira felt he had to wait a few seconds to let Larry subside. "What'd the others say?"

"Snide. Like Schneider. Snotty. Anything to show off. Oh, they said the story shed no light on the modern condition, modern quandaries. Quandaries!" Larry repeated, deliberately theatrical. "It didn't reflect contemporary attitudes. It could have been written in the nineteenth century. As if it wasn't expressing anything universal. Hadn't any value. What bull!" He slapped a phonograph cover. "*And* it had a plot! Sin of sins. Can you imagine? Even though I explained at the beginning I was trying to do a tightly knit short story."

"Yeah?"

"I read the whole thing to the family. They thought it was great. All right, say they're not the foremost literary critics in the world. Edith read it. She thought it was good. She saw I was working with a symbol about past and present. But to these superintellectuals—as they think they are—the story was trivial. They couldn't write one as good. That's the truth of the matter."

Again, as that day when he hustled soda at the Polo Grounds, Larry seemed prone to, seemed prepared to, dismiss adverse criticism. Was it because the critics belittled his ego, or wounded his vanity? Didn't recognize his distinction, maybe. Ira couldn't say. Unlike Larry, Ira realized, he had come to absorb humiliation almost as if it were his due.

"It was just a raw, a rotten exhibition of plain jealousy, that's all it was. It was mean," Larry inveighed.

"Yeah?"

"Especially that Percy-on-the-half-Shelley Markowitz, with his experimental poems about the sea-green sea and the hoar-gray hoar-frost. All kinds of Gertrude Steinish stuff. He—"

With his large, white hands flowing in front of him, Larry mimicked prissiness. "'The writer of the short story has not read T. S. Eliot. He has evidently been unaffected by the depletion of meaning, the erosion of consensus.' What a pose! Even John Vernon said they were being gratuitously unkind, ignoring the well-sustained mood, the local color, the genuinely fresh imagery. They weren't giving any credit to style and allusion. And touches of humor too."

Ira felt guilty, guilty in a curiously ambivalent way: for having not only suggested but also acquainted Larry with Mom's twice-told tale. He had dangled the lure before Larry—and thereby instigated his discomfiture—over which Ira now felt a secret satisfaction. Why? *Schadenfreude?* How could he be that way? He was an ingrate, perfidious ingrate. All unconsciously, so it seemed, he had sacrificed Larry, as one read about miners in coal mines sacrificing a canary to warn them of the seepage of insidious gas, that the air was no longer safe to breathe. So the sophisticated intellectuals didn't like formal, old-fashioned plots. What did they like? What *was* modern? What shed light on the modern psyche? Inevitably the thought led him to an awareness of the heaving magma of his own being. Was he feeling again that same hermetic superiority he had felt before, on the El ride that first time he went to Larry's home? That sense of possessing something deeper, deeper awareness, a greater span of sensibility, more startling fusions of fancy, even if maybe wild, uncontrolled. The notion troubled him at the same time as it elated, disturbed him with welcome contrarieties.

He wasn't supposed to be competing with Larry. He was supposed to go into biology, not English, study organisms, not write stories. But there was Larry himself: supposed to go into dentistry, and yet he was so painfully wounded about his failure to win sought-for praise for literary work. Jesus, what kind of aberrations were taking place? He could feel them in Larry, could feel them within himself. They had been imperceptible until now, but with Larry's vexed recital of the scornful reception of his story at the Arts Club, they were no longer imperceptible; they were appreciable; they were like a deliberate veering away from announced goal, not accidental but deliberate.

Ira had fostered the deviation. Jesus. From dentistry to writing, a careening of career, of aims and values. And if it came to the possibility of the same thing happening to him, of a drastic switch in aspiration, analogous to Larry's, from biology to writing, God, what would *he* have done? There was no comparison between himself and

Larry. What *he* had done and was capable of imagining: Minnie, Stella, violation and torment, frenzy and predicament—all in a sardonic ambience, wasn't it? Like a herring in tomato sauce. Knocked up his sister, or thought he had, in a murderous afternoon of plane geometry. Wow. Who the hell knew, as he knew, his private amalgam of vileness and caprice? And the jobs he had held, and the diurnal squalor of surroundings, yes, squalor and sordidness all stored in that glob that he was, amorphous glob, slowly revolving in his mind as Larry spoke. "Jesus, I'm sorry, Larry." Ira lowered his eyes.

"Nothing to be sorry about, Ira. If they're such egotistic show-offs, it didn't affect Edith. She just laughed. She thought the imagery was beautiful: that rind of moon above the graveyard—I told you about it. I knew she'd like it. It was genuine."

"Oh, she'd read it before?"

"New Year's Eve. Saturday. Before Boris came to take her to a party."

"That's why I couldn't get you on the phone?"

"I just *had* to show it to her."

Ira tried to trace one of the fiddlehead spirals in the carpet's design while he retraced the events of that same Saturday evening. Ironic. Or what? Because he hadn't been able to get Larry on the phone, Ira had strolled over to Mamie's house. So at maybe the same minute when Larry was reading to Miss Welles, reading his retelling of Mom's yarn, reading Ira's relayed tale—that was funny, how that word kept cropping up—Ira was wangling his chubby little coz into the precarious privacy of the cellar. Jesus, taken separately, one episode was almost holy, like an adoration, a votive offering that Larry was making to Edith with his version of Ira's version of Mom's yarn. The other episode was just as unholy as the first was sacrosanct; the second was wholly unholy, impaling plump little Stella on his stalk sitting down. First time he had ever tried it, and it had worked: it was good: bounce her up and down like a piledriver—boy! But the two things, his doings and Larry's, didn't occur separately in his mind. They occurred together, as if fused. They were more—what? More wicked together? No. More vicious together? No. They were more sardonic, that was it. When the hell did he get that way? When did he begin to recognize and enjoy that—that blend of pure and . . .

and nasty? Yeah, yeah, instead of the one or maybe the other by itself. Like a dissonance in music maybe that repelled him at first, a perverse dissonance, like Wagner, like *The Meistersinger* when he first heard Mischa Elman play it in Izzy's house, and was so fond of it afterward. So when? When did he begin to relish the sardonic mixture? Ira hung on to rumination another moment: after the East Side, that was when. Jewish living, feeling went poof. Well ... But wasn't it something, Jesus, wild, when you joined the two together: sardonics? Sardonics meant discovery: like that Saturday night way back—

"My grandfather gave me black Greek olives in the synagogue on Saturday night," Ira said, grinning. "*Havdalah,* they call it. Half-a-dollah. First time I ever tasted 'em, wow! I didn't know which way they oughta go: spit out or swallowed."

"What?" Larry was disconcerted.

"Nah. I was just trying to take your mind off your disappointment."

"Oh, I'm all right. You don't think I'd let their snooty pretense get me down, do you?"

Larry shook his head, ever so slightly, sighed and locked his hands. "I'm really not interested in coming up to their expectations." He swiveled about in his seat. "I wanted to do at least one rounded short story, conventional, yes, free of smut too, but with an underlying meaning. It's family-type reading." Larry tossed his head. "Somebody there—I think it was Reuben Mistetsky—very subtly wisecracked: 'It's decent, family-type fiction.' Well, I don't regret it. I just don't have to please them. And what the hell." He stood up, went to the phonograph, pushed the crank down. "If I'd done another kind of short story, I know just what they'd say—that I was imitating Sherwood Anderson or whomever. And yet I don't want to imitate anyone. That wasn't my intention. So to hell with 'em. It pleased Edith."

"You keep calling her Edith."

"Not before the other students, of course."

"No."

"It's just easier. Less formal. It gets a little artificial to keep calling her Miss Welles, and Iola Reid, the woman she shares the apartment with on St. Mark's Place—also an English instructor—Miss Reid. We were making out postcards for the last meeting of the Arts Club. We had coffee and cookies. She asked me herself to call her by her first name. All working together around the table. It was just natural."

"I get it."

"It's a chore, you know."

"What?"

"The postcards. We have to send out about a hundred of them. To faculty. Students. Guests. It's too much. Vernon never helps. The club needs an executive secretary. There are all kinds of arrangements to make. The tearoom to hire for the evening. Refreshments to order. Cookies. That sort of thing."

"Oh, yeah." Ira listened, contented and passive again.

"I've volunteered for the position," Larry said.

"You have?"

"Yes. I'll have to be nominated and elected at the next meeting, of course, and all that. But you can be sure nobody else wants the job."

"Holy smoke. You just got yourself in for a lot."

"That's true."

"Boyoboy."

"It's only once a month." Larry's countenance, so pensive, so level in response to Ira's exuberance, crinkled into a playful and enticing smile. "I know somebody I can count on to help when the time comes to send out postcards."

"What d'ye mean?"

"Don't tell me you'll let me down?"

"Oh. When?"

"Next term."

"Gee. Me? Where?"

"Right here."

"Oh. Okay. I was afraid for a minute." Ira plainly showed his relief.

"Why?"

"I thought it was—" He gesticulated.

"I thought that's what you meant. Edith wants to meet you anyway. She knows about you now."

"What for?" Ira felt abashed at the very thought. "I'm CCNY."

"Wouldn't you like to meet her?"

"I don't know. Jesus, I'm in biology."

"Doesn't make any difference. Come on, I'm a predent. It's for anyone interested in creative writing. You can come as my guest to the next Arts Club meeting."

"Nah. I don't belong there. I'll help you get the postcards off, but—" He grimaced extravagantly. "Leave me in pieces, will ye?"

"We're having an important poet there next time. She's giving a reading. Hortense L. You'll enjoy it. She's a very good lyric poet. What are you afraid of?" Larry changed tone of voice and mien. "Oh, come on, Ira! Honest, it's an experience. And *I* want you to meet Edith."

"Oh, God!" Ira cringed.

"She knows you're shy. She's a very fine, very sensitive and considerate person. All you have to do is say hello."

"Yeah?"

"All right?"

"Why the hell do you want me there?" Ira was close to flaring up. "Seriously. I mean it. For Chrissake, I'm nobody. Jesus, you know how painful that goddamn thing is. You know how awkward I am. Why don'tcha leave me out of it? I'm happy."

"Yes, but she'll think it's so strange—a close friend of mine, one I talk about all the time. I repeat your remarks. She says you sound very entertaining. So does Iola." Larry's voice rose to hold its own against Ira's strenuous note. "Ira, you're being childish."

"All right, I'm childish."

"Yes, but you're not childish!"

"Then I'm Jewish."

"Oh, cut it out! Listen, Ira. You've got to get over this business of—" The fingers of Larry's large white hand splayed out. "This business of being Jewish. I just think you're shy about meeting people."

"All right, the one after this one. The next Arts Club meeting. Okay? I'll earn my admission by helping you write postcards."

Larry was about to turn away impatiently, but then in midmovement, to and fro abruptly, he said, "I'll make a deal with you."

"Yeah?" More worried than wary, Ira watched him.

"You know that English jacket I have, the one you call kasha-colored?"

"Yeah. Like those knickers I have."

"Wait a minute." In three strides Larry crossed the living room and entered the hallway. "I'll be right back."

Ira sat waiting. He became aware of an indistinct contralto voice humming in one of the rooms down the hall: the Hungarian maid's voice? When had she come in, or had she been in her room all this time? There she went again, humming. Chrissake, that sounded like an American song: Titina, my Titina. Was it Larry's sister? It must be. He had said the whole family had gone to Bermuda. Boy! Ira expelled despairing breath: sure, she was about three or four years older. What of it? Just imagine Mom and Pop going off for a week, and leaving him with Minnie. The prospect made his temples bulge.

"This isn't fair." Larry's voice preceded him as he came back.

"What isn't? Say, I heard somebody in the other end."

"It was Irma." Larry came in, bearing his oat-colored English jacket—so distinguished, with leather elbow patches. "She works for a designer. You know. They were just too busy. She was sleeping. Reading in her room. Sewing maybe."

"Oh." It was terrible, it was just terrible, that was all. "So what isn't fair?"

"This isn't fair," Larry repeated. "But what the hell, all's fair in love and war. You go to the next meeting of the Arts Club, it's yours. It's yours anyway." A flush invaded his dappled cheek. "Try it on."

Ira stood up. "Jesus, Larry."

"All right, take yours off. Let's see how it fits. It ought to. The sleeves have always been too short for me." He slipped the garment up and over Ira's arms to his shoulders. "Say, that's—look at yourself. That's better than I expected. Isn't that good?"

The two surveyed Ira in the wall mirror.

"Boy, an English jacket," Ira breathed, swelled with elation. "Boy, it really fits." He bent his elbows toward the glass, hissed in pleasure at their reflection. "Real leather."

"It's yours. I was just kidding about the deal." Larry's brown eyes were soft; affection played over his entire countenance. "I'm glad it fits as well as it does. Just a little bit shorter sleeves—be perfect."

"It doesn't matter. Boy, you sure you want to—to part with it?"

"I thought of keeping it till spring before I gave it to you," said

Larry. "You don't have to wear it until you like. I mean, let's forget the whole deal. It's yours."

"Oh, no. I'll go." Ira's gaze traveled from the dark, buckwheat-colored tweed on his arm to the dark, buckwheat-colored tweed in the mirror. "Wait till Mom sees this."

"Do you want to wear it home instead of yours?"

"Oh, no. Not till the Arts Club meeting. No, sir." He was about to slip out of the jacket.

"Wait a minute," Larry advised. "Hold it a second. . . . Irma?" he called down the hallway. "I know she's up. Irma?" He waited for a reply. "Will you come here a minute? Please. . . . You don't mind if she sees you in it?" He turned to Ira.

"No, I don't care. I'll bet she yells, 'Robber, give it back!' "

A young woman with a full feminine figure, brunette, Irma shared a similarity of features with Larry, enough to make them easily recognizable as brother and sister. But Irma's features lacked the almost perfect regularity of her brother's, and her complexion was quite dark, while his was dappled and fair. Temperamentally, she was also far more matter-of-fact than Larry, prosaic and bored, in a sultry kind of way. She always made Ira think of the Yiddish word *bukher*, a guy, a suitor. There was never one in evidence, and maybe that was the trouble. But he was always on some tack or other like that, so he couldn't trust his impressions. But what if he had a sister three or four years older than he was? Would she consider making shift with him for a while? You never knew; the funny thing was, sultry as she seemed—maybe she was too sultry, maybe too demanding; now that she stood right in front of him, he wasn't sure how he would feel. He'd much rather have a go at Stella—of that he was sure. Minnie next.

"My, don't we look grand." Irma's praise was tempered; still in her surprise at the sight of Ira in Larry's jacket, she forgot to curl inward her very full, round lips. "Don't we look *distingué*?"

"Doesn't he?"

"*Hic* jacket," Ira quoted uncomfortably.

"What?"

"I was just trying to remember something by Sir Walter Raleigh. Nothing."

"It certainly does something for you." Irma rested two fingers on her cheek, as if she were seeing Ira for the first time. "It makes you look much more assured."

"Yeah?"

"And very successful. All you need is a million dollars to go with it."

Ira met her brown-eyed gaze unsteadily. She was so like Larry, and yet not like him in so many ways. Looked almost straitlaced, straitlaced and smoldering: the word *bukher* came to mind again.

"Well." Ira pulled at his ear. "I am now your brother's keeper."

"He may need one. Is that what you mean?"

"Well, no. I just said it. Instead of thanks. I mean, I owe him loyalty. Protection, I guess."

"I think I know one very good way of showing it." Irma directed a look at Larry. "Protection is something he may need. I'm glad to hear you're conscious of it."

"No, I just meant I owe him so much, that's all." Ira felt some sort of adverse pressure mounting.

"Irma, I don't see why you have to bring *that* up." Larry addressed his sister with uncommon curtness. "I didn't call you in here for that. All I wanted you to do was look at the jacket."

"Well, I've looked at it. He's very handsome in it."

"My sister sometimes behaves as if I'm not quite able to take care of myself." Larry's tone of voice was so elaborately equable that Ira couldn't miss the satiric overtone. "You don't have a big sister—or big sisters. You don't know what you're missing."

Irma ignored her brother's remark. She was not one to be deflected. Humorless, tough. "Are you an only child?" she asked.

"Me? No, I have a younger sister."

"You do? I never heard you mention her. Is she very much younger?"

"No, about two years or so. But you know how it is." Fecklessness served for pretext to obviate further explanation.

"Younger sisters don't count, is that it?"

"Oh, no. They count. But a couple of years' difference right now. . . . she goes to high school, I go to college. There's a big separation between us. You know what I mean?" Boy, she made him work, forced him to tread warily.

"Where is she in high school? What high school?"

"Julia Richmond High. She's aiming to attend Hunter College, the normal school." He offered more than asked to forestall further inquiry.

"Irma, do me a favor. I just called you to look at the jacket," Larry reminded.

"I told you. It's very nice, very becoming, Ira."

"Thanks."

"I'm glad to hear him say he feels he owes you protection for the gift. That's reassuring. That means he's a very good friend. And good friends keep each other out of trouble."

"That's not what he meant," Larry contradicted sharply.

"No, it isn't, and I know it."

Larry bridled at his sister's provocative smile. "I wish I had the luxury of having just one younger sister, instead of all of them being older, all three of them, and all talking down to me in their superior wisdom. Talk about sisters not counting." He turned to Ira. "My sisters have counted every day in my life, every day since I was born."

"Fortunately for you," Irma managed to comment.

The uncommon heat engendered by the two siblings finally began to stir perception in Ira's mind: Larry was reconsidering dentistry and had alarmed his entire family. At last, the dispute had come to a head at home. So . . . pleasing Miss Welles, Larry had said that before. Calling her Edith. That peculiar, sanguine look on Larry's face when Ira said, with mock consternation, as if a joke: you just joined the Arts Club. Something like that. What d'ye know? What did Larry's family suspect? They were becoming worried, that's what it all meant. He never would have guessed. That veering away from preset goals, a specific veering away. And not only in Larry; Ira felt it taking place within himself, a wavering anyway.

Undoing the leather buttons of the English jacket, Ira saw his reflection again in the mirror, smiled back at himself in satisfaction at the annealing of conjecture. So that was it—

"You needn't look so smug!" Irma snapped at him.

"Me?" Startled, he gaped in the mirror at her dark, taut face. She had never spoken to him that cuttingly before. No one in Larry's family had ever done so.

"You needn't pretend. You're enjoying it all!"

"Enjoying it?" Ira turned around. "I was enjoying the jacket." What a way of breaking the truce, the truce he tried to keep in his mind about her. It was as though she had caught him thinking of what he tried not to think about—she was so stormy and accusing. Chrissake. He felt like insulting her. Hurling some epithet out of his neighborhood at her. What the hell did she bring him into it for? What had he done? Maybe they thought he had; maybe they thought his friendship with Larry had influenced Larry, altered him in some devious, obscure fashion, tainted, marred Larry's nature. Who the hell knew? Maybe it had. Larry had in fact changed *him*. Ira could feel his own wrath rising to contend with her stormy looks. So goddamn protective. Smut, obscenities arose in his mind: 119th Street invectives. Suddenly, involuntarily, she became naked, she walked like a mare on all fours, a mare with a human visage, curling her lips in. There she was, sucking them in. Made her look so goddamn prim. Back-scuttle her, since he didn't want to face her, he was too angry; she had humiliated him for nothing. Do to her what the guys said on 119th Street: she had just the right chin to rest his balls on. And the way she sucked her lips in. Just right. Blow me, you bitch. Jesus Christ, he had never thought of her that way before. Jesus Christ, he was crazy. That was the middle-class manner that Larry spoke about, the middle-class manner that he himself didn't know a thing about. It had all kinds of foreboding gloom about it, flowed over him, like an impalpable sable surf. What the hell was going to happen here? *Hic* jacket, he had said. A joke. It was no joke: here lies. But then he was always getting scared for no reason. "What d'you mean? I was just looking at, ad—admiring the jacket," Ira insisted stubbornly.

"You were not. You know very well what I'm talking about, too."

"Would you mind cutting out the accusations?" an irate Larry lashed out at his sister. "You're officious!" he flung at her. "Officious, insulting. Please get out."

"And you're—I hate to tell you!"

"Don't bother."

"A silly romantic adolescent!" Irma was in a manifest huff. "If you don't think I haven't heard some of your remarks."

"When?"

"Oh, your tone of voice." Irma tried to portray a state of beatitude. Her eyes rolled up. She rested her cheeks on the fingertips of the two hands she held beneath it. "It touched my heart."

"Will you please get out! Before I start using stronger language. Get out! I'm sorry I ever asked you in here."

"I'm not only going to get out of here, I'm going to get out of the apartment."

"That's fine with me."

Tense, irritated, Larry waited for his sister to leave the living room, then held up his hand in signal of silence until they heard the house door open and close, denoting her departure. "You get an idea of what's going on—the acrimony," Larry said heatedly. "That's Irma, my own sister. Ever hear anything so mean? God, it's a crisis. I should have known better than ask her in. I'm sorry. I'm sorry you had to be dragged into this, sorry she dragged you into it."

"That's all right." Ira doffed the jacket, stood holding it silently a moment. "You know something? I got an uneasy feeling. Something like dread."

"Oh, no. They're all worked up—over an imaginary something. And even if it was, I'm legally responsible for my acts. They've no right to harass me."

"I didn't do anything wrong, did I?"

"Of course not. My God." Larry lifted his shoulders. "You can see—they can see the black coming out all over my wool. I feel like a black sleep. Any tiny deviation, they magnify it—into something horrendous. Ruin! On all sides. What I wished to be in high school, I don't necessarily have to wish to be in college. You're lucky. Your relatives don't—" He gestured vehemently. "Your parents, your sister, certainly don't crush you with all kinds of preconceived ideas about your welfare, do they? God, crush you with their concern. Talk about the weight on that diving bell meant to go down into the—Oh, I don't know what the name of that ocean trench is. Mariana?"

"I don't know. All I can say is my mother—I mean, I'm the whole world to Mom."

"Yes, but supposing she knew you were becoming deeply, deeply interested in an older woman? Irma has already told you. I'm just telling you what you heard."

"If she was a *shiksa*, maybe. A little." Ira felt a little breathless because of the sudden rush of feeling, Larry's and his own by proximity. "But only a little. Mom wouldn't worry. I mean, I know she'd *care*. But as long as I got my degree, my B.S. Bullshit," he said, trying to ease intensities. "That's the main thing with her. You know what she'd worry about? She'd worry about my grandfather—if I were to marry a *shiksa*. The old guy would go into a tailspin.

"That worries them less. Hardly. Victor, my dentist brother-in-law, is only half Jewish. I've already mentioned that. No, it's profession. That's their chief concern. You know? Profession. Convention. Assured respectability. Assured income. More important, Victor already told me he'd want me as a partner. And he has a fine practice." Larry seemed harassed indeed. "Trouble is, you see, we're such a tight family—I don't know what it is—everyone intertwines—do something out of the way, and everyone is affected. Do the unconventional, and everyone is"—he shook his head—"hurt, moaning, oh my God!"

The wooden bell tower on top of Mt. Morris Park hill, an indelible landmark from Ira's early teens, reared up with new, with momentous prominence. For a moment for Ira, the very timbers, the massive wooden beams, color and construction, loomed distinctly, near at hand, and within them the iron bell gleaming as it tolled. "So how'd they know about this? You tell 'em?"

"Oh, no. They didn't have to be told. They've begun to watch every move I make, and draw conclusions from every move. I'm sure I'm the subject of endless discussions. And you know, they're pretty sophisticated. My mother, my three sisters. My older brother. And there's my brother-in-law, Victor, you know, the dentist. And Sam, a lawyer. The whole family keeps tabs. I'm really the baby."

"Yeah? Wonder why I feel so funny afraid." Ira began folding the jacket absently. "Guilty collywobbles."

"Oh, that's my sister Irma. She'd worry anybody. But don't let her get under your skin. Here. Let me show you how to fold a jacket. This way: grab the seam. Turn the shoulders inside out. See? That's what packing for steamship traveling does for you."

Ira studied him as he folded the garment: big-handed, white-handed, he always did everything with that flair of assurance. Self-confident, he gave one an impression of competence, and he *was* competent. He took charge. He betrayed none of Ira's uncertainty and awkwardness. On the contrary, he displayed a convincing capability, a ready facility. What a neat job he made of the jacket, pressing the folded garment into a compact parcel. "I know just where the right-sized shopping bag is. I'll get it." He left the living room.

And generous, Ira reflected. Never any condescension, but as if generosity were natural, the way his being functioned, the way he conducted himself. Boy, giving away that fine English jacket . . . Jesus, life was strange. Just sitting down beside Larry in Elocution 7, and look what had flowed from it: their friendship, and all that was happening now, happening and going to happen. Like destiny. Had his friendship with Larry affected *him,* molded Larry? Into what? Maybe a little like Ira himself, his nonbelonging, noncaring, ambitionless, haphazard self. Half outcast self, pariah-Jew in Harlem getting into cruel, crazy fixes, with Minnie, with Stella, cunning, remorseless bastard pratting a fourteen-year-old. Maybe Irma was right when she turned on him. Maybe he did bear a share of responsibility in Larry's reconsidering a career in dentistry, drifting toward writing, becoming attached to his English instructor. Jesus, what a change. Larry was an altogether different guy back then. Poetry was something you enjoyed, like a song, something like that. Dentistry was your serious aim in life. Yes. Schoolteachers didn't earn very much. Right? Now he was in hot water with his family. Altered. A different guy. No wonder Irma was peeved: her brother was rejecting respectable goals, like Ira himself, as if he'd given Larry the fillip to go that way: prefer to fetch words out of a deep trance, like a coral diver, risk his future to delight Miss Welles. Yeah, dread, no wonder. What was it he had seen? Not a flywheel, a weight at the end of a rod, swung around, swung the other end around. Well, he should have gone to Cornell. They both would have been better off maybe, both attuned to a conventional America as they thought of it, rewarded by America. Now what? Jesus, you follow those threads, they get finer and finer, get tangled among one another, come back to where you were. You could go crazy.

Larry returned with a white Macy's shopping bag. "Let's forget about all that unpleasantness. I'll put on a record." He laid the shopping bag down in an armchair. "Don't leave this when you go."

"Oh, no," Ira assured, then laughed—at a loss. "I don't know. Is it the jacket that scares me? I said, *Hic* jacket."

"I thought you never studied Latin."

"I didn't. Those two words just happened to stick."

"What would you like to hear?"

"You know my favorite. The *Unfinished*."

"The *Unfinished* it shall be." Larry sought the record in the oak cabinet beneath the turntable, found it, and as he brought it out with customary flourish—

"You know, we had a phonograph when I was just a kid in Brownsville, in Brooklyn, even before we went to the Lower East Side," Ira remarked. "It was a little phonograph; that's all I remember about it. And I took it apart. Did I ever get a shellacking."

"Do you remember anything it played? I better change this needle."

"I think it was 'Hatikvah.' "

" 'Hatikvah'?"

"I can't tell whether Mom sang 'Hatikvah' or the phonograph played it. You know how it goes?"

"No, I don't."

"No?" Ira essayed the melody, filling in the words with a tra-rea-la. "I don't have your ear. I wish I did."

"That sounds like the 'Moldau,' Smetana's 'Moldau.' " Larry repeated the tune.

"Yeah? That's funny. Mom couldn't have known the 'Moldau.' "

"He was a Bohemian. You're a Galitz. It's not very far away, is it?" Larry lowered the needle into the outer groove. "Hungary, Czechoslovakia, weren't they all part of the Austro-Hungarian empire?"

"You know more about it than I do; I don't know about Hungary. . . . Boyoboy, that's music."

Larry sat down on the leather armchair diagonally opposite. After the first few chords, he closed his eyes: eyelids blank, his lips parted, he sighed. Eyelids blank outwardly, a screen inwardly, Ira could well believe. Head tilted back, fine black hair above pale brow, his body motionless, he was transported by his envisaging. So that was love, or loving, in love, or what was it? What else could it be? Ira wondered. How ennobling it was: transfiguring. Could one ever, one like himself, with desire dismembered, severed from the kind of pure dream Larry was dreaming of now—severed from love, something like that—ever, ever? No. As if hacked away. Or Humpty-Dumpty. Well, witness it in Larry. Observe it. Best you could do. But Jesus, that's where the guilt came in; that's where the guilt came in that maybe Irma sensed. You could imagine guiding him by mental telepathy, by intangible, remote control, to do your bidding. That's where your vileness had got you—

Just where the familiar "You are the dream of love" had been stolen from it, plagiarized, the music changed pitch, faltered. "I'll do it." Ira stood up, went to the phonograph, cranked.

"I guess I didn't wind it enough," Larry said.

Oh, the man with his ten thousand, ten million synapses flickering, his billion combinations of bits of thought, shred and filament of idea. Oh, a million billion threads, motes, spirochetes—

All of which he had to sweep aside to resume, in acceptable prose, prose in some sense, the continuity of what he already knew, and knew only too well and grievously, to strive to nurture the masterpiece model he hoped to re-create.

V

The fall term ended, ignominiously for Ira, with a C-minus average. The average would have been even worse, positively gruesome, without the A in chemistry to buoy the other grades up. As it was, what with two D grades, which automatically deducted an eighth of a credit from the total, he was woefully short of the complement for a first-semester freshman. What was he gonna do, Ira asked himself in self-aware, ninny-rationalizing fashion, when he had to compete with so many quick, sharp, bright Jewish classmates who knew all the answers?

To Cornell he should have gone, congregating with the relaxed gentiles; he might have shone there by comparison. . . . One never knew, consorting with the easygoing *goyim.* Competition destroyed him. And besides, away from Minnie and Sunday-morning persuasions—and grim aftermaths—away from Stella, dawdling, chubby, and blankly ready, and a new set of grim aftermaths, away from promptings that found a frame on any textbook page, prompting him with: good chance tonight at Mamie's. Lucky night, maybe, so hike over. All that, all that, all that, and now Larry and his Edith—the time wasted withal spent in study might have earned a B average at Cornell. He might have found a bimbo out there, or been tipped off about one by fellow classmates, a bimbo whose favors he might have bought for a couple of bucks, which he earned busboying in the college calf-eat-here-ia or something like that. Been a *mensh,* instead of—himself.

It was one of those dull, dreary late afternoons, a Sunday in February, the weak daylight clinging to the windowpanes of the Gordon living room, an afternoon encompassed by the cold murk outdoors like a diving bell in the sea around it. He and Larry were alone, Irma and their parents visiting with kin and in-laws, Mary the maid away on her day off. Late, dim winter afternoon enclosing the comfortable apartment, the coziness of the overstuffed armchair accentuated by the radiators in the room hissing at the rawness at bay the other side of the windowpanes. Still, for all the lowering of the day, the scantiness of conversation, the grayness of the living room, with unlit electric sconces, Ira felt the imminence of something momentous, something in reserve. He had only to be patient. There was some reason that Larry was so pale and listless. Other times it was Larry who managed the needle arm over the records on the phonograph; this afternoon it was Ira, choosing his favorite disks, while Larry sat in the flat cushion of the tilting leather armchair, sat withdrawn, in a kind of ascetic reverie.

"They always sound like each one is showing the other guy he can sing as high or low as *he* can." Ira tried to divert Larry from the wan trance that sheathed him. "Caruso and Gigli: *Solenne in quest'ora—Lo juro, lo juro.* You know what I mean?"

A silence . . . unnatural . . . extensive.

"I have something to tell you," Larry finally said. "Something I— I very much want to tell you."

"You mean now?"

"Yes."

Ira lifted the arm from the disk, pushed the little lever that stopped the turntable. "Yeah?"

"Something I'd like kept in confidence."

"It's all right. I mean, if you don't want to tell me."

"I do."

Ira went to the green divan and sat down. "Who am I gonna tell it to, anyway?"

"You're the only one I can talk to about this." So solemn he seemed, his cheekbones without their wonted dapple, cheekbones so pale and prominent they deepened the sockets of his eyes. He looked peaked, too slender and too flat. He took a deep breath, held it, as though to reinforce it for the thing he had to say. "I stayed with Edith last night."

Ira could only remain motionless, say nothing. Show comprehension, betray nothing, or as little of the incredulity he felt as possible. What could you say to someone who told you he stayed all night with a college instructor, *his* English instructor, a Ph.D.? Say something like "You did?" When the incredible became true it became magic; it worked a spell on everything within reach of the senses: on the unlit sconces on the wall, the nude on her swing melting into the darkening blue among the towers, the Corot reproductions waning, the parquet floor and the pattern on the Turkish rug merging at the boundaries. But that still left nothing to say. It could happen only once. Once in all of a whole lifetime. Say nothing. Let the blood whirl around inside your cranium. What could be more incredible?

"I'm in love with her." Larry crossed one big white hand over the other. "I've been in love with her for some time. Now I know we love each other."

Ira listened, heard, comprehended: all of a great gray cloud: as if the winter twilight were speaking inside a familiar, *gemütlich* living room, forming words drifting toward him. Who was there? Jesus, he had just turned off the aria from *La Forza del Destino.*

"I love her. I want to marry her. I want to take care of her. I want her for my own. Mine!" he added suddenly. "When I see her teaching her heart out for that dumb bunch of premeds and predents in her class, I want to take her in my arms, hold her there, protect her. She's so tiny. She's so girlish, small, you have no idea. And the tiny thing has to work so hard—" His voice choked, he snuffed, his eyes became moist, glistening in the gloom. He stood up, tried to speak, fidgeted for self-control.

Ira had to look away.

Silence within the room, silence so utter it whined, like a sling. And then abruptly Larry resumed talking again, unburdening himself of a turmoil of words, plans and yearnings. In a medium of the marvelous it all came, thick and fast it all came, and tumbling about Ira's ears, now comprehensible, now incomprehensible, the multitude of things Larry and Edith had discussed, his impulses, her advice, his declarations about his future, her comments on the announcement of his drastic change of career: to hell with dentistry. Literature was his proper calling. Damn middle-class conventions. He ought to get out, leave the family, defy their crass, materialistic carpings—and so unsure was Ira of what he heard, and what he felt, that he dared not comment, too conscious of his own ignorance of that kind of interrelation, of that kind of committal. It was so beyond the scope of anything Ira had ever dreamed of, his chief concern as he listened was to guard against saying anything dumb, exposing the depth of his mawkishness, the flimsiness of his comprehension. In a situation like this, when you knew you lacked anything cogent to say—in a situation like this—and how could anyone aspire to a situation like this? A lofty liaison, a mythical affair! Nod cognizance was the best you could do, even when you had only the faintest notion of the reality of it. She was older; that went through Ira's mind; *that* was different; but it made no difference to Larry. Neither did the gap in rank or station. *He* was a freshman, she a Ph.D., a college instructor; she was a gentile, he was Jewish. Only the bulky contrasts stood out. All right, give up dentistry, major in English, then what? The

substance, the actuality, the practical functioning of romance, the
fact of romance, simply swept away things that would have flitted
through his mind; the romantic gave the prosaic no access, no purchase: swept away all the carnal curiosity, all the irrelevant needs, self-
indulgent fantasizing, and the where and the when and the . . .

"She said it would be folly if I didn't go on and get my degree,"
said Larry. "Get my B.A."

"But if you left home—didn't you say you'd leave home?"

"She'd help me."

"So where do you go live?"

"That would have to be worked out. I'd go live in the Village.
Somewhere near her. And if we married, I'd live with her, of course—"

"Married!" It just didn't sound in the realm of the possible. "Do
you have to marry? I mean—" Scratching frantically up and down his
skewed neck was the only way he could end his question. "That isn't
what I mean. I mean, how can you marry?"

"It might not be convenient right away. She ought to wait till she
had tenure. I ought to get my bachelor's first."

"Yeah? But Jesus, that's three years off for you! Or what?"

"That's nothing. I can easily earn enough to support myself, certainly to get by on while I'm taking courses. I can always sell. That I
know. What I'm saying is, I wouldn't be dependent on her to make a
living. She wouldn't have to support me, if that's what you're thinking. I wouldn't allow it anyway. I could pay my own way—and more.
That wouldn't stand in the way of marriage. I wouldn't have to—to
wait until I got my degree to get married. But tenure in her position,
that's something else. So until then, marriage might have to be *sub
rosa*. At the very beginning, in other words. I told her we could get
married at the end of the term, if she wanted to—secretly." He
pointed a large white finger at Ira. "I don't *have* to go to NYU."

"You don't? What d'you mean?"

"I don't have to go there any more than you do. I wouldn't go
there anyway if we were married."

"Then to Columbia, you mean?"

"No! CCNY. Like you!" Larry exclaimed. "Of course. I'd switch to
a free college. Get my bachelor's there. Major in English."

"Oh."

"Write in my free time. That's what I want to do most—write. That diploma, that damned silly piece of paper! God, didn't we talk about that for hours! Suddenly you want to break all connections, everything that ties you to family, *my* family. Might as well say to the middle class. To conventions, respectability, all that you and I have talked about. Even to getting a degree. That's where I differ from Edith. I don't need a degree to write. I could get a job aboard an ocean liner: a steward's job, an engine wiper, a deckhand, anything. Knock around. Jump ship. You know how many Americans—they call them expatriates now—are in France? I could be another one for a while. Why not? Once we were married, and we belonged to each other, I could feel free to separate for a while. Others have done it. Marriage doesn't mean you're both tied together in the same place. That's the conventional view. That's what I'm talking about. You ducked the Arts Club meeting last time. But if you go to the Arts Club meeting this Friday, you're going to see Marcia Meede. She's married to Luther. She went to Samoa to do her doctoral; he went to England on some kind of grant. For a year. You get it? Edith and I could marry, and I could do all that. Instead of being tied down, I'm—I'm practically released, freed from my middle-class conditioning, which is what I need. I have to slough it all off, all that I've been. You know what I was." He hitched his shoulders almost violently. "A member of the comfortable, the smug, middle class. Supported by my family. Given an allowance. Coddled. A predent. What else was I?"

At odds with himself, agitation besetting him, transmitted even through the deep dusk of the living room, he stirred in his chair restlessly, aimlessly, uttered uneasy, subdued exclamations of protest. "To tell you the truth—you wouldn't believe this—I think I could fall asleep right here right now. We slept almost not at all last night. But that isn't it. I'm just worn out mulling over the thing, stewing about it. What's the best thing to do, for me, for us? What's the best thing to do right now? Announce I'm leaving NYU? I'm leaving the family? Go get a job? Here in New York? Or the kind I was talking about: ship out on a tramp steamer. Or an ocean liner. I know I can talk my way into a steward's job. Do you follow me?" His harrowed eyes further darkened by quandary, in manifest crisis, he hunted for his pipe, found it, held it between both large hands in his lap. "I've really come to a significant crossroads in my life. It's obvious, isn't it?"

"It is, yeah. Jesus, I wish I could help you, Larry. But you know . . ." Ira projected his helplessness by gesture and grimace. "It just doesn't belong in my world. Or I don't belong in it. And you're so far ahead of me in what's happening to you. I mean, who'd ever have thought that kind of a thing would happen, could happen, to a friend of mine just out of DeWitt Clinton? I can't even find the words. Okay? So I'm no help."

"And of course, the ones I might turn to—those close to me. Can you imagine?" He allowed himself a curt, derisive laugh. "Ask Irma, right? Ask any of my sisters. Ask any of my family." He brooded, twiddled the pipe.

"I'll tell you, I don't know a thing about these things. I don't know her. But she's the one to ask."

"Edith?"

"Yeah. In my opinion. Who else? Who else is there?"

"She doesn't think I ought to do anything rash. I mean, you know, follow my impulses: cut all ties, cut loose."

"No?"

"No. She wants me to get my degree. I told you, she said it would be folly not to."

"Yeah?"

"Yes."

"So what're you gonna do?"

"Hm! We're back where we began. What am I going to do?"

"All I can say is it's up to you." Ira gazed at the intricate vacancy the dark had begun to spin. "And that's not saying much."

Larry too seemed in the thrall of the same kind of vacancy. "I'd pretty nearly destroy them."

"You mean your family?"

"Oh, yes, you can imagine if I tore up all ties. If I went on the bum. Disappeared. Something like that. Pampered baby of the family. Brought up in Bermuda. I allowed myself to be, I grant you. But they'd be distraught. And then too I want to be with her, with Edith. I'm really torn. Instinct tells me that right now a wild move, a wild plan, is the right one. What do you think?"

Ira held up his palms to fend off the question. He shook his head. "Don't ask me. Boy!"

Larry rested his lips on his fingers, sucked silently on an unlit pipe. "Yes." He seemed to be affirming that the moment was critical. He sighed. And after a few seconds shook his head in resignation. "I guess Edith is right."

"Yeah?"

"I'm being rash. Romantic."

"Yeah?"

"Okay."

"Okay, what?"

"I'll just stay put. I'm worn out thinking about it. Maybe I'll get a better idea later." He slumped slightly. "Status quo for the time being. That's all. *Status quo ante.* You know what that means?"

"Do the sensible thing. The practical thing."

"Sounds that way, but not quite. Continue what you've been doing."

"Oh."

"Carry on, the English say. What I want to do is much too soon. We ought to be with each other for a while. And of course I want to. I want nothing more than that. . . . And there are my folks. My parents. Sisters. They're fine people, you know. Kind, generous. Just that—well, right now, I feel a world apart, and I think, well, you've got to do the surgical thing. Act! Once and for all." He turned his head away, moaned, inarticulately frustrated, fidgeted again. "Well, we better switch the lights on, hadn't we? I'm probably, you know, as they say, ready to go off the deep end."

"Want me to do it? I mean turn on the lights." Ira felt silly.

"I'd appreciate it. Before it gets pitch-dark in here."

Ira stood up, found the wall switch. The sudden onset of light discovered a somber Larry on the green divan. Exhausted, limp with indecision, he was gnawing at his upper lip, and still toying with his pipe. The fine black shell briar contrasted with the pallor of his large hands. "Well, that's that." Again random movements of body and feature expressed altering patterns of lassitude. Resignation seemed to replace agitation—a dissatisfied resignation. "I'm lucky I had you here, Ira, to talk to." He overrode Ira's self-belittling protest. "No, that's all right. I know what you're going to say. But I've never been in such a stew in my life. I'm lucky you were here, that's all. It's—" Resignation tinged his voice with bleakness. He sighed. "Edith's right. See what develops? It's just too short notice. I adore her, but—I'm going to get out of NYU next year. That much I've made up my mind to do. Without question."

"CCNY?"

"Gradually lessen my dependence on my folks—without killing them, you might say. Transfer credits. Maybe get part-time work of some kind."

"Hey, you know something? I think I oughta give you a chance to get to bed. Early. You're worn out."

"I suppose Edith is too. Well, in a little while. . . . Let's rustle up a bite of supper. See what's in the larder. Soup. Leftovers. I know we always have some."

"Oh, sure. Anything."

"*Soupe du jour,*" Larry said mirthlessly. "Soup du Jew."

"Want any help?"

"No, no. I'll do it. Do me good. Help bring me back to the—everyday. Let's go into the kitchen."

Ira followed him, watched him empty a bowl into a pan. "It's Hungarian goulash. It would be." He set the pan on the stove, returned to the icebox, brought out a half head of lettuce. "We make our own French dressing. Vinegar and olive oil, okay?"

"Sure, I like it."

"Toast?"

"Great."

As he did everything else, Larry set the table with a flair, and despite weariness prepared the supper with a flourish. Ira watched him in silence. It was a welcome silence, a minute in which to try to think, to ponder in secret, laboriously probe, grope into the future that allowed only the shallowest of shallow speculation, grope through a haphazard labyrinth. Jesus, for Larry to ask *him* what to do? When he hardly knew what there was to do, just barely could name the options. Let's see: to further his, Larry's, love affair, his aim of marrying Edith, Larry said he was ready, he felt impelled, to leave home, to go on the bum, he said: to change himself, leave Edith for a while, leave

his family, and all that comfort, spending money—he called it allowance—fine clothes, his own room. And leave his friend, bosom
companion, Ira.

The thought traveled inward to himself, to the fateful choices he,
Ira, had made. He had relinquished the appropriate high school because of Farley, and then had renounced a future, maybe, for the
sake of Larry's friendship, but Ira didn't enter into Larry's considerations. Not that he felt hurt. It was a lesson, a sobering one. But it was
crazy. Crazy. Larry wasn't going to set out, give way to that kind of impulse, especially when Edith counseled him not to; he would do what
she counseled. Oh, it was confused, it was confused, but as before,
the shape in the hovering obscurity of his mind took on the same,
strangely auspicious lineaments: Larry would have to do the thing
that Ira prefigured, that Ira predestined was for his own ultimate
benefit. Wasn't that crazy too? Oh, it was, it was. The same thing, the
same thing. Had he ever been in love, Larry had asked him, somewhere in the course of talking, ever known puppy love. Jesus, what a
joke. He had burst through barriers beyond love, known the urge to
murder, known the quaking of green walls when Minnie said, "All
right." And pratting his fat, foolish little cousin in the cellar. When
did he have time for love? He didn't need time for love; just enough
time to tear off a piece of hide in a despicable, precarious snatch.
Wow! What the hell, nutt'n like it. The risk, peril, win the jackpot of
the transcendental abominable.

No, he was clinging to Larry, because therein lay his future; that's
all he could tell himself—a hundred times. It was a future whose nature he couldn't discern, but latent with . . . with fulfillment. He was
in its grip; he imagined at the same time as he disbelieved; he disbelieved at the same time as he adumbrated. Somehow the dim, formless aspiration within himself had to be coagulated, eventually, this
nameless essence of a fatal sense of human plight, his own, of aberrations, hideous, zany, and sad, far more than Larry had ever imagined. No, Larry could never apprehend the infernal torments of the
kind of suffering he, Ira, had inflicted on himself, not even by moving out of the house.

But there it was again: that awful twist in his sophomore year
in DeWitt Clinton that became a murderous warp that conferred

uniqueness, conferred election, even though others were brighter than he was, like Larry, had quicker minds, dexterity, had all the attributes of greater intelligence, taste, judgment, still—was it delusion?—his, yes, he knew it was shameful—would he admit incest to anybody? Or did his impressing his fourteen-year-old cousin to his lechery confer a destiny that would not be denied? What madness! He had willed Larry's choice, willed Larry to remain with his family. As though in Larry's wake, like those cyclists behind the pace-setting motorcycles in the Velodrome, Ira would be drawn along to a destiny that was still only cloudy aspiration, fantasy. Still, fantasy had prefigured reality, as Michelangelo said the statue was in the marble.

Ira had ridden the jolting, windy platform of the Eighth Avenue El, and had heard his new acquaintance preen, soon after he had quoted from Louis Untermeyer's anthology those clarion lines of modern poetry like a fanfare for a new world, preen that he was going to be a dentist . . . and that schoolteachers didn't earn very much money. And then he knew something was wrong, something didn't fit. And now Larry, privileged, romantic Larry had attempted, in the high frenzy of his new love affair with Edith, to make it fit, to sacrifice the one he was to become, *but he thought better of it*, yes, acceded to practicalities. There he was—handsome Larry adding salt and pepper to the French dressing, judiciously tasting the mixture—wanting to become what Ira already was, had been for so long, the feckless, impractical, suffering sap—incurable sap, and incurably self-aware. The model Larry wanted to fit into fit Ira better than it did him, and perhaps this was the basis of the great friendship. Ira felt that this had occurred, if that slosh and slap of insight that went on continually inside his head had any truth in it. He had the terrible stamina, he had the range. He had no bounds, no hobbles on his imagination. He had striven with madness, suffered the utmost wrenching of the mind. Kill her! Kill her. . . . Still, in the midst of madness, he solved problems in plane geometry, problems demanding reason—how was that?—he found solace in applying theorems about tangents and secants, apothems and chords.

It fit Ira better, yes; he saw as naturally as breathing the stodgy facades the El passed, with faces in the windows awaiting lackluster advents. Still, Larry's perceptions didn't have to be on that level; they could have been deprived out of his own milieu. Listen to him saying, listen to him repeating, "I know she's looking out for my welfare. But I ought to experience life. At the very least, I ought to get a place in the Village, a cheap room. Anything. I have a small bank account—my Aunt Lillian left me a small legacy. Break away. Be on my own. I ought to. I ought to. I have to feel the necessity of what I'm doing." And again the question: "What would *you* do?"

Around and around, over the same ground (it sounded like the "Ancient Mariner"). "For me it would be leaving a dump; what do you mean? You'd be leaving—well, look at the place."

"I'd be leaving a suffocating middle-class atmosphere!"

"A suffocating atmosphere?"

"Yes." Larry turned around in eagerness from slicing bread on the breadboard. "Is French bread okay? I can't stay here. My folks aren't bad. You know that. But I've got to break away. Break my dependency, my connections. All that family feeling. God, it's awful! I love my folks. Even Irma, though I may not sound that way. My brother Irving. My sisters. My niece. My brothers-in-law. The tears and the grief I'd cause. Do you realize the amount of pain this is going to cause everybody? And my father's heart isn't the best. Still, I think it's the thing I ought to do. God, it would be cruel!"

How much older sheer strain made him appear, thin and drawn. Who would have guessed he was just a college freshman? One saw snapshots sometimes of a high school athlete in the very crux of competition—high school kids looking old as an adult.

"Yeah?"

"Edith thinks I ought to wait till the end of the term. I don't. She thinks I ought to try to take everything possible into consideration. I can't. I have the feeling I'm the kind of person, if I want to be a writer, then I have to create the situation for myself. Do you understand? Now, right now. Not next semester, three years from now, get my degree. No, no, no! Now. Committed." He ladled out the rich brown goulash.

"Committed?" Ira's mouth watered. "Wow, that smells good, looks, oh, boy. What makes Hungarian goulash Hungarian?"

"Paprika. That's the national condiment."

"Oh, yeah? Mind if I begin *fressing?*"

"Go ahead. There's more."

"Committed. So what d'you mean, committed?" He heard the word echo within himself, reecho, as if it tried to extract meaning from his noisy mouthfuls.

"Yes. Not follow Edith's advice. Follow my own instincts now! But then again, am I kidding myself? A few lyrics, a borrowed plot of a short story. What have I got to go on? I'm teetering on a knife edge. What if I'm wrong—" He reversed himself. "The Village wouldn't be far enough away from my folks. Irma would be down there, my sisters, my mother certainly, urging me back, coaxing, imploring, my brothers-in-law arguing—can't you just hear the pleas? I'd begin wavering. I couldn't stand it. That's the point I make. If I was going to break away, I'd have to go on the bum completely. Disappear like a hobo. Like a common seaman on a tramp steamer. And I can't. I can't break their hearts to that extent."

"No? Do you mind slipping over more of that French bread?"

"Here, help yourself. Should I slice some more?"

"I think there's enough. Boy, I like bread. We eat everything at home with bread. Sometimes even with Mom's compote."

"My family would go out of their minds if I disappeared," Larry added in gloomy aside. "Talk about causing pain." He lifted his fork with large trembling hand. "I can't do anything. I'm stymied. I'm just beginning to realize that. I'm just beginning to see those things. No wonder Edith kept insisting, 'Get your degree first.'"

"You better keep eating."

"Yes." He laid his fork down, pressed his eyelids shut, and when he opened them, reached for salad tongs. "I'll have some salad. You?"

"No. We always eat it afterward."

"Three years." He meditated, chewed a leaf of lettuce, disconsolately. "With a maximum schedule of summer courses—at NYU. She'd be in Silver City in the summer. Or Berkeley. One or the other. Her mother and sister are there. I think both divorced. The sister has ambitions to be a violinist—but she has no talent. And do you know something? Edith helps support—pays the life insurance I think, for her mother. Even helps out her father—he's a ruined politician—his health too. He drinks. I think I told you, the whole state of New Mexico went Republican in 1920. But it just breaks my heart. That tiny little thing, so generous, so devoted. I can't help but want to support her. I know I could, too. I could protect her—"

"Protect her? Jeez, she's got a job," Ira interrupted. "She's your instructor. I'm not trying to butt in," he apologized. "Can I have another spoonful of stew?"

"Oh, sure. Mind helping yourself out of the pan?"

"Oh, no." Ira arose to his feet. "I'm listening."

"She has so many obligations, so many demands on her. That's the point of my saying I want to help her. Make a financial contribution. To relieve the burden on her, the nervous strain. She's hardly able to bear up under it. The nervous strain alone is causing all kinds of digestive upsets."

"Yeah?"

"I could help guide her. I could contribute income. Commissions. Salary."

"Yeah? I don't see how, and get a degree in three years. I don't think it's possible." He sat down again. His mind had already begun its unhearing contemplation. His eyes drifted away and back, to provide a semblance of listening while he ate. Protect her. Was that part of love? He had never wanted to protect anybody—only himself. Protect Minnie? Jesus, the only protection he offered was on his own behalf: spare himself the anxiety, no longer the same anguish now, but the anxiety, of thinking maybe he'd knocked her up. And the same thing with Stella. Hell, tell her to say somebody else laid her. He was wise to that subterfuge now. Some big guy—some big *goy* stuck it into her. Maybe forced her. Give her advice. But protect, protect? He just wanted to get in and get out.

So that was one thing that was wrong with him. And what did *that* mean—even if Larry was being foolish on the subject? You weren't old enough, was that it? Yeah, that was it. Jesus, you could see the whole thing in a panorama: screwing your kid sister, Minnie, out of habit now—she wasn't such a kid anymore—screwing your cousin Stella. It made a self-enclosed entity: you were checked, your development was arrested; you weren't interested in adult problems, adult considerations. Boy, what a picture: of something clawing at an im-palpable net—clawing and squalling, and never really trying to get out of it. And how the hell were you going to get out of it? O-o-oh, Sunday morning, o-o-h, get Stella straddling him on weekdays. Jesus, if he could ever get her alone. He was dying to back-scuttle the little bitch. Get it way up in her. So there you were. Almost at a rage with yourself, listening. "You know, you're saying the same thing over." Ira tried to keep the irritation out of his voice.

"I am?" Larry was taken aback.

"Not exactly." Ira hastened to mitigate. "More or less round and round."

"I wouldn't be surprised." Larry became dejected

"No, no. Go ahead, go ahead. I just happened to think about something else. I get into these—I don't know whatcha call 'em: reveries."

"I've noticed. Do you want me to stop?"

"No, no. Go ahead. I'm—I'm beset, I guess."

"By what?"

He had to get out of that corner—fast: "All kinds of doubts—I mean about you, your fix," Ira said. "Gee, you do a nice job with salad." He helped himself.

"I don't go in for that bought dressing. What you were saying is putting things mildly."

"What d'you mean? Hey, have a little more to eat. You'll fall away to a ton."

"I mean the simplest solution is for Edith and me to get married. That would—" he brought his cutlery to a halt—"that would justify everything. My moving out. Transferring to CCNY. Be completely in-dependent. I have to cause them pain. But that would be the least. Don't you think so?"

"Maybe."

"And married, well—there's the fact, that's all: my parents, fam-ily, they'd have to face it, they'd have to take it, that's all. That was my point with her." Larry turned aside in negation. "She said I was very dear, very tender, and sweet. All right, maybe I am. But that doesn't help, doesn't solve anything. I could marry her now. Nobody has to know. My folks, yes, well, they'd be aghast. That's the sickening part of it. I'm eighteen, say, almost nineteen, and she's thirty. It's okay the other way around. I'm thirty. She's nineteen. Ask Father Time to draw us closer together. There's a poem about that in our Outlines of English Lit. I can't remember—Cartwright, I think, Cartwright. More or less on the same theme: difference in age." He began hunting for his pipe.

"Hey, eat something, will you? Christ, you'll have me turning into a Jewish mama: *Ess, ess, mayn kind.* SOS."

"No. I've had all I want right now. You can finish everything."

"Yeah? Thanks. There's still some goulash left."

"My mother'll be glad to see it gone."

"Yeah, you know why? She'll think you ate it. Anyway, I'm glad to help out. I'm glad I'm not in love either." Ira made another trip to the stove. "Sure?"

"Absolutely. She doesn't earn enough on an instructor's salary. She doesn't earn enough to do all the things she feels she has to do—mostly for others. She canvasses the *Times,* the *New York Trib, The Nation, The New Republic,* for book reviews. It breaks my heart to see her driving herself so—for others. And I'm beginning to understand what a disadvantage the women in the department are under, in the English department—and in the other departments too. She's already entitled to an assistant professorship. A doctorate and two books out on Navajo Indian religious chants. And praised by poets *and* anthropologists. Some man, just because he wears pants, will get there ahead of her. It makes her so mad. It makes me sore too."

"Yeah?" Ira had to suppress his disgruntlement with having to attend to the same thing, the same subject. Boy, to be able to say, the way Jews said: all right already. Well, *fress* instead. His gluttony would go unnoticed.

Annoyed, Ira locked fingers below the keyboard. That was not in the text; he was diverging from the text, diverging from the yellow typescript, from the first draft. He was bored with it. *He* was bored with it, rather than his character; he was bored with it in advance of his character—in fact, he was projecting his boredom onto his character. Why? Because there was so goddamn much information still to be presented, still to be introduced. Oh, Jesus, what tricks of the trade, new devices, to employ? He had used about every stratagem he could think of. He was fresh out, as the storekeepers said in Maine: we're fresh out of bacon.

It was John Vernon, Ira remembered, the homosexually inclined instructor, who had set the ball rolling—with his advances toward Larry. His advances toward Larry had aroused, so it would have seemed, Edith's competitiveness. Speaking of wearing pants as a reason for getting ahead of women! She had not wanted Larry to fall into the toils of a homosexual—at least before he had experienced normal love. Okay. You've said it, Ira told himself irritably. Delete all the rest, goddamn it.

Yes, as novelist practitioner, he had recourse to any number of different stratagems. True. Somebody entered the apartment, say, Irma again, and put an end to the intimacy of disclosure. Or Ira had deliberately thrown the narration off track, asked one of his typical obtuse questions. Or better yet—look, man—what was the legal lingo?—appeal to the prurient urge, postpone matters by writing that he had got an idea that maybe he might be lucky tonight. Tear off two pieces of ass in one day. And said: "You know, I owe my Aunt Mamie a visit. I haven't been there in an age." Or should he have said that his grandfather intended to move there soon? Or that Zaida was living there already? Christ, no. He had to keep something straight, and something in reserve too. He intended to use that ploy later. It was a thought, though. He always got horny a few hours after his connubial-type intercourse with Minnie in the morning. Usually, he pulled off that same night, and that held him for the rest of the week—or if he was lucky, the rest of the midweek, when a nocturnal call at Mamie's paid off. But actually, there was only one thing that was of value, quite apart from the information, one narrative detail that was interesting in itself, that had a touch of encounter about it, that mix of the absurd, the youthful, the silly yet erotic. Ira scrolled up the amber text on the monitor.

"There's somebody else lives there, isn't that right?" Ira felt impelled to assure Larry that he had an audience. "Somebody else shares her apartment with her, I thought you told me."

"Iola Reid. You know, they're both instructors in the English department. They have separate bedrooms and a common living room."

"Oh, that's how it is."

That wasn't bad, Ira encouraged himself. He felt better, now that he had released his pent-up impatience.

Larry began clearing the dishes from the kitchen table.

"Want some help with the dishes?"

"They're only a few. I'll stack them. I'll leave the pan for Mary. I don't mean, well, you know, that he's the cause of it all, but that's how it all began. I was telling her about John Vernon. He's a nice guy, but he's a homo."

"Huh?"

"He's been trying to make me."

"Yeah?"

"Oh, yes. I never bothered telling you all the details. But Edith knew."

"Jesus. In the college too. I know you told me about homos. But I have to get used to the idea."

"Oh, yes. It's nothing unusual anymore. He writes free verse. He read some of his work at the first meeting of the Arts Club I attended." Larry grimaced, tilted his head. "He had it privately printed."

"A book?"

"Yes. You pay for the printing and binding yourself. I don't see that it's worthwhile. Especially *his* stuff. Either I'm crazy, or it's—it's just prose broken up into different lengths. Edith thinks so, too. He has an idea it'll come into its own someday."

"You mean be—" Ira gesticulated. "Be recognized? Win applause?"

"He's convinced it will."

"Yeah?"

"He invited me up to his apartment. Turns the lights down. We smoke. His hand's on my thigh."

"When was that?"

"Oh, about a week ago. I thought to myself: you make for my fly, I'm going to tip that burning cigarette end down on the back of your hand."

"Did he?"

"No. He must have guessed."

"Jesus." Ira tried to grin. "What the—" He paused in semiperplexity. "The—er—the thing gives me half a dozen different notions: what a girl must feel like if a guy she doesn't like makes passes at her. What the hell makes guys that way? I can't imagine it, ye know. Getting worked up about another man?"

"Well, that was what worried Edith." He scraped the uneaten goulash on his plate into the metal garbage can, replaced the lid. "I told her about it."

"About him? Vernon?"

"She said that she was very much afraid. That he would succeed in seducing me before I had a chance to experience a normal love relationship with a woman."

Ira chortled in derision. "You already did. Aboard ship. Right?"

"Well, nevertheless, we all have that tendency," Larry assured him.

"What d'ye mean? In us?"

"In us, yes; we're partly feminine, partly masculine. One dominates over the other, usually. But it's true in all of us, no matter how masculine the fellow is. Sometimes he'll fool you. He acts like a bruiser, looks like one, and likes guys. Cowboys often were homos, Edith said."

"A cowboy!" He snickered. "Goodbye, old Paint. I'm a-leavin' Cheyenne. Yeah? I'm a-leavin' all men. Amen. Sorry."

"There's Vernon himself," said Larry. "He was brought up on a New England farm. He was married to a Russian noblewoman; she ran from the Revolution—you know, the Bolsheviks. He was married. He has a son. He's divorced now. He's bisexual."

"*Bi*sexual," Ira stressed. "Bi. Both ways? Did he tell you that?"

"No. Edith did. She said she was dreadfully afraid of my getting caught in the toils of homosexuality, as I told you. She had seen too many promising young men ruined that way. She didn't want to see me ruined. Homosexuality was not a normal way of life. It was a distorted one."

"But this is bisexual. He gets the best of both." Ira grinned. "But I still don't know what's good about the other half. Anh!"

"I told her there was very little chance of Vernon seducing me." Larry stood up a rinsed plate between the rubber-lined arches of the drainer.

"Gee, my mother oughta get one o' those," Ira observed.

"I told her I was too much in love with her to be interested in anyone else, man or woman. Certainly not a man. I want *her* love. I adore *her*. I want to marry her." He turned from the sink.

Why did he feel a pulse of embarrassment, hearing the reiterated declaration of that kind of ardor? "You told me."

"I was very mature for my age, she said. I was poised and serious; I had far more assurance in dealing with people and social situations than she had at that age. And she loved me very much. But I was still a lad—that's the word she used: lad. I ought not to be burdened with marriage, even secretly, before I got my degree. I ought to get my degree, and then decide. We'd both be in a better position to decide."

Jesus, wouldn't this be just about the right time, or say in another minute, to dig up a pretext for leaving? Be just about right to grab the subway downtown to the 110th Street and Lenox Avenue station. He'd get to Mamie's just about the right time, after supper. Mamie at the dishes. Oh, frig this love business. But he had to stall awhile, not make it look as if he were fed up and ducking out. The right time, the right time. Boy. Love. Dove. Shove.

"Shall we go back to the living room? Like to hear a record? 'Chanson Arab'?" Larry dried his hands on the dish towel.

"Not this time, thanks. I think you oughta get some rest. After all you've been through."

"I'm all right. Recovered." Larry seemed to hold his breath a moment, expelled it.

"I really think you should get some rest. A guy who told me he was ready to fall asleep talking. You've got big circles under your eyes."

"That was because of the crisis I've been through. It's over now. Not resolved. Just over the worst of it."

"Yeah? I'm glad to hear it. Anyway, I ought to shove off."

"Got anything on this evening?"

"No. But you oughta hit the sack."

"I will. I'm all right, though. Easier in the mind."

"Yeah. That's good. Thanks for the grub."

"It was nothing. Nothing compared to your being here."

"Glad I was. Some goulash, *amico fidato,*" Ira said, trying to render the oft-heard aria from *La Forza del Destino.* "Where's that second-hand rug of mine?"

"You left it in my room. Have you worn your—the one you call kasha-colored?" Larry followed him down the hall. "The English jacket?"

"Oh, no. I told you, that's for the big splurge," Ira answered over his shoulder, as he made for Larry's room.

He could hear Larry's chuckle. "It's just a poetry reading. You don't have to make a splurge. And Edith knows all about you."

"Yeah."

Well, he was only Ira Stigman, he thought; the more he did the more he was aware, alas, of his formidable deficiencies, his multifarious shortcomings. Then why do what he was doing, why make the attempt? He had asked himself that many times before, and would again, no doubt. It was something, this craving, innate—perhaps chronic would be the right word—craving of the octogenarian, or nearly. He could hear the intonation of old days, speech of recently arrived Jewish immigrants—"What do you want from me?" Yesterday, in making the longest walk he had made in many and many a month, some six or eight city blocks from the optometrist's to the Presbyterian Medical building, he was moved to compose something akin to a poem in prose, revealing the individual he was, the same one now seated before his word processor, tapping keys that invoked yellow letters on the screen.

But there is nothing . . .

Just the old man lurching across Central Avenue, thrusting his cane behind him, like a boatman his pole, to propel his hulk a foot or two nearer the curb before the traffic light changes from WALK to red.

And his lips writhe with effort, and he remembers the kid he was, so spry and jaunty, how he could have bounded across the street with exuberant, elastic stride. . . .

And the tear welling up is not his own, but one the kid sheds for him. . . .

VI

Where the hell was he? Where had he left off? After all these days and weeks spent in the Presbyterian Hospital where he had undergone removal of his gallbladder, days and weeks running up a hospital bill of over six thousand dollars, not to mention the surgeon's and other doctors' bills, the anesthetist's, his assistant's, the internist's. Jumpin' Jesus—he hoped his auxiliary insurance would pay the difference between fee and Medicare. He had been away so long from his yarn. Once, during the whole medical ordeal, he thought of Zaida, who, through one connection or another, probably via a fellow congregant in the synagogue, had been referred to a fine denture maker: a Dr. Veinig. He had made Zaida a *wunderbar* double set of dentures, and at an exceptionally reasonable fee. Naturally, he would repair Ira's teeth at the same reasonable rate, and thus end, once and for all, the misery of the toothaches Ira suffered from, sometimes sobbing and moaning all night long—in a home destitute of even an aspirin—gnawing at the corner of his pillow in vain attempt to ease his pain. Zaida introduced Ira to the dentist, who agreed to fill his patient's three dental cavities for a total of ten dollars.

Work began, work accomplished chiefly by means of an engine that Mr.-Dr. Veinig had in his office, a contraption with a foot treadle, like a Singer sewing machine, and while Mr.-Dr. Veinig puffed on his curved pipe, he pumped away at the treadle that spun the drill that ground away the decay in Ira's dental cavity. The rhythm of words, Ira thought as he wrote, reminded him of the Passover liturgy: *Khad gadyo,* one kid, one kid that my father bought for two *zuzim*. The door to the dentist's apartment was always locked, locked and further secured by a heavy chain that enabled Mr.-Dr. Veinig to scrutinize every caller before admitting him—or her—to the premises. From some source, perhaps from Mom, Ira learned that though Mr.-Dr. Veinig was without a license to practice dentistry, his illicit practice earned the funds necessary to pay his wife's tuition in dental school—she, in turn, taught him the latest in dental techniques.

Weeks and weeks went by before the cavities were filled, weeks of drilling and drilling, until at last the nerve was probed for and withdrawn from the squirming moaning patient, until at last the cavity was filled. Each session lasted at most ten minutes: in and out of the Mr.-Dr.'s "office," with the taste of tobacco-laden hands still lingering during the nighttime walk from 113th Street near Lexington all the way home. What did the mopey kid dream of then? The mopey kid who recalled in old age the Mr.-Dr., the humorless Litvak visage with a tobacco pipe in it, scrutinizing his patient above the heavy chain across the kitchen door before admitting him. Wraith of sixty-five years ago, the setting: the kitchen reception room, the ancient dental apparatus in the bedroom. . . .

Not many years later, when Ira was attending DeWitt Clinton, one, then another, and finally the third of the filled teeth began to ache unbearably. Each in turn had to be extracted, and each one, beyond the taste of blood of the torn gum, emitted a foul, putrescent stench in his mouth.

It was in early winter, in the old brick building that housed the DeWitt Clinton swimming pool across the street from the high school, when he came away from his frolicking in the winter, that the last of the three teeth began to ache. Peculiar associations, but inseparably bound together. With what indignation another white-jacketed dentist extracted the molar: would Ira tell him the name and address of the practitioner? Who had done his dental work? Ira no longer remembered. And after that, in the years to come, whether because of the gap left between teeth so early in life or not, all the other teeth loosened, abscessed and then loosened, and had to be extracted. So that at an age even earlier than Zaida's, Ira first acquired *his* dentures. Ira acquired his, though not at quite such a bargain price as his grandfather.

But he had to get back to Ira Stigman, before he disintegrated under the impact of so many collateral concerns.

It was a weekend evening in the kitchen of Larry's home, his parents and Irma away, perhaps the Hungarian domestic home, and only Larry and Ira there. Between them on the table was a stack of fifty penny postcards and several sheets of paper on which were typed and handwritten the names and addresses of the invitees to the next poetry recital. Site of the occasion would be as usual, the Village Inn Teahouse on MacDougal Street in Greenwich Village, and the time 8:00 P.M. this coming Saturday. As secretary of the Arts Club, Larry had undertaken the task of sending out the notices, thus relieving Edith of doing so. And Ira was only too glad to be coopted as assistant.

"It's a helluva bore." Larry slipped the elastic off the pack of postcards. "I'll write the addresses; you write the notices on the other side. Here's the model form: Time. Date of meeting. Place. Name of poet reading: Margaret Larkin. Get it? Soon as I'm finished addressing, I'll help with the notices. Maybe that'll speed things up, instead of each of us turning out one apiece."

"*Takeh. Takeh.* What d'ye call it, conveyor-belt production?"

"What's *takeh?*" As usual, Larry was amused at hearing a Yiddish expression new to him, and eager to learn it too.

"Tick-tockin'," Ira quipped, applying fountain-pen scrawl to the first postcard. "Actually, it means 'indeed.' "

"*Takeh,*" Larry repeated.

"*Takeh emes,* they say, Indeed the truth, though they might be lying like hell." Ira enjoyed Larry's grin. "Who's this Margaret Larkin?"

"She writes an easy-to-read, almost light verse. Charming most of the time. Feminine. I've met her at Edith's. Handsome, still fairly young. I think she's also a Westerner." He handed Ira a newly addressed postcard. "Kind of verse I like. She writes her name backward in her poems sometimes: Nikral."

"Yeah?"

"She has one about standing cigarettes up like candles in front of her lover's portrait. Clever."

"Hmm," Ira sighed for no reason: bohemian fancy. It was so whimsical. Ah, to have experienced that kind of life, at least once.

"When they get too cerebral, like T. S. Eliot, or obscure—well, just like *The Waste Land*—count me out. There's no pleasure in reading it." Larry slid a postcard over toward Ira. "Don't turn it over right away. The ink's still wet."

"No. T. S. Eliot is obscure?"

"Deliberately so. I resent it, too. I think I'm fairly sensitive to imagery, someone else's imagery in a poem. But when they get so highfalutin symbolic, I don't feel I need to dig and scratch around for all the allusions. To hell with 'em!" Larry's demeanor left no doubt about his distaste.

"Yeah?"

"You'd agree if you read him. There's no—" Larry raised his fountain pen in disapproval, circled his hands. "There's no connection that I can see between one part and another. And sometimes between one line and another. The whole thing's a disjointed collection of lines, some fine, some—well . . ."

"Where do you read T. S. Eliot?"

"At Edith's. She has about the best collection of modern verse in town."

"Yeah?"

"Wallace Stevens, Millay, Genevieve Taggard, Ezra Pound, Robinson Jeffers, A. E. Robinson, Léonie Adams, William Carlos Williams, Cummings, Frost, Elinor Wylie—"

"Wow!"

"She never hesitates to buy a new book of poems she thinks is good. Wilfred Owen, Yeats, Sassoon, Sitwell—some of them she doesn't think are so hot, either. But she needs them for her course."

"Oh."

"Everyone who's taken the course says it's great."

"Oh, yeah?"

"One of the things I'll regret about leaving the place. . . . Let's see." Larry reached over the table to look at the last card he had given Ira: "I don't want to send two of these to the same person: Berry Burgoign." he consulted the chart. "Next is Madge Thomson—she's in the English department too. Specializes in early English: *Beowulf,* and that kind of thing. Very homely, but nice. Fluttery. Giggles. She's like an adolescent."

"Yeah? You met all of 'em?"

"I think so. Not Professor Watt."

"Who's he?"

"Head of the English department."

"Oh." Ira waved a postcard to dry the ink. "Jesus, I haven't met a soul at CCNY. All I know is Mr. Dickson, the guy I'm taking English Composition with—English 1." He turned over another postcard. "I just know him in class," Ira added dejectedly. "What about the folks? Any more trouble?"

"No. I think they've decided to let things ride. We're sort of playing a cat-and-mouse game. Each one waiting for the other to make the next move."

"Yeah? And you?"

"Oh, I'll stay out the term, of course. That satisfies *them*. And what I do next—well, it all depends. I think I know what I'm going to do—CCNY. But there's no use my talking about it any further until—well, things jell a little more."

"Yeah." Ira watched Larry tighten the cap on the barrel of his fountain pen. It was a new substantial Waterman, not like his own bleary, old one. He could say: you know, a fountain pen got me into trouble once. Yeah, he could say. He could say . . . He suddenly saw Minnie's face brighten with pleasure when he dangled a stolen fountain pen in front of her—for bait. He could say, yeah, he had a cousin Stella—he looked for the next name on the list. It was the very one Larry had been talking about, the one who laughed like an adolescent. To Larry, she laughed like an adolescent. Not worth bothering about. To Ira, that spurred the predator. "Homely?" Ira turned the yellow card over, read the name. "This Dr. Madge Thomson?"

"Homely as a hedge fence." Larry smiled indulgently. "That's what Edith says. Cute expression, isn't it?"

"Hedge fence? Yeah. Gee," Ira said regretfully. "You know, you live somewhere in a different part of the world. You're really brought up differently. You say, 'Homely as a hedge fence.' Why the hell a hedge fence?" They both stopped writing, as Larry waited for Ira to finish. "To me it could be beautiful. A hedge fence. A hedge. The country, the—" He gesticulated, held his hands apart. "Wide, trimmed, you know, with little green leaves. Homely as a hedge fence. It's attractive."

Larry chuckled, his handsome face indulgent as he gazed at Ira. It was almost as if he wasn't sure whether Ira was serious or spoofing. "She's not pretty. Believe me." He shook his head for emphasis. "How would you say it? I mean 'homely.'"

"Me? You know what I'd say. What I heard." Ira shrugged. "Where I was brought up. You know the old gag. She had a puss that could stop an eight-day clock. On 119th Street that would be considered polite," he amended.

"Then that's what you say."

"Oh, no. Jesus, no." Ira paused to marshal distinctions. "It's different, Larry, it's different. Bejeezis, it ain't only—it's not only that one expression, it's the whole goddamn world that goes with it. What the hell am I doing here, will you tell me?" He confronted Larry more abruptly than he meant to. "Here I am, I'm helping you write out these postcards—to a poetry recital. Writing invitations in your house, your kitchen—" He checked himself; it would be folly to go on further.

"What about it?" Larry asked. "What's so strange about that? You're in college, it's a natural thing for a college man to do."

"Well, that's what I mean. It doesn't feel natural."

He could never tell him. There were times he felt as if he were levitated, as if completely in someone else's power. Tell that to Larry. "Nothing. Just—I don't know."

"I *do* know I'm going to take you to meet Edith."

"Yeah?"

"Of course." Larry was about to bend over the next card. "What are you shaking your head for?"

"You know what a palimpsest is?"

"Of course—it's a parchment with the writing scraped off," Larry replied.

"That's what I see, when I look at one of these blank cards. I don't see the writing. I see what's been scraped off."

"Oh, come on. Wait till Edith meets you."

"All right, all right. *Lo juro, lo juro.*"

A few seconds of silence ensued, while Larry amusedly addressed the next card. "How're you makin' oot?" he said, mimicking Scots dialect.

"Are these all right?" Ira held up a few postcards. "My hen tracks? Not much better than that."

"Oh, no, that's fine," Larry commended. "Perfectly legible."

Another span of silence. Ira felt he'd talked too much already.

"You wouldn't believe she had so much spunk," Larry said.

"Who?" Ira could guess, but asked anyway.

"Edith."

"Oh, yeah."

Larry smiled reminiscently. "She's really competitive, you know. You wouldn't expect it: somebody as small and gentle as she is. But look out if you make a joke about it, belittle the fact that women don't get the same treatment as men. About the kind of deal women get living in a man's world. *I* did."

"You did?" Ira rejoined incredulously.

"Yes, I was foolish enough to."

"So what'd you say?"

"I said, 'Oh, well, what's the hurry? You'll get there.'"

"Get where?"

"An assistant professorship."

"Yeah? So what happened?"

"Sparks. All over the place. 'If you were a woman you wouldn't say that. I'm sick and tired of men dominating the world, and stupid men at that.' She was right too, and I said so, I apologized. It's true, can't deny it. How're you coming?"

"All right—I think."

"Keep it up. You don't know how grateful I am for your giving up your time to pitch in. So will she be when she hears about it." Larry eyed the stack of finished cards. "Say, we're really gaining on it. I've got a few more to address, and then I'll join you writing notices. A Camel? Mustafa Kemal for this job."

"Sure. But the way it's going, it's not bad."

The two lit their cigarettes. . . . The invitations he scrivened on the yellow surface of the postcards, practically memorized by now, swam under Ira's gaze. Palimpsest, as he told Larry, parchment whose writing was scraped off and written over. What strange mirages shimmered beneath the words he wrote, beckonings: his course lay athwart those postcards into the world that they presaged. As though he were putting his seal on the new direction each time he wrote on one, as though he were opening a casement on scenes of a future that could be his if he wished, really wished from the depths of his being, shadowy imaginings waiting for him to realize, guerdon of his folly and guerdon of his dolor.

It was not a gift; it was more like a fate. A fate whose first intimation he recalled yet again when riding with Larry that day on the Eighth Avenue El in the open air between the sad, nondescript tenements, and his peculiar awareness, his awareness of his unique perception of them. That was it. But unique perception of what? Their intrinsic nature: the blacks on the stoop laughing as Larry went by singing. Things. No, it wasn't a gift. It was a specter over your plane geometry problem that you had invoked. Think of the way the catapult's cords were twisted, intolerably, to the limit of integrity, at the risk of snapping—and then twist further—his price in exchange for murder: that twist. . . .

He felt like just puffing on his cigarette, with pen in hand inertly on his thigh. Tell the guy that. What world were you in? Whose world were you in, were you caught in? *"O-o-h, I needed it more last night"* was her way of thanking him this morning. *"Did I have hot pants? Did I need a big one after the dance?"* Poetry recital: did I have hot pants? Did I need a big one after the dance? "Jaizis," Ira said aloud.

"What's up?" Larry inquired.

"Poetry recital." Ira snickered. "If I could only write a little faster, the way you do, with a real free movement—you move your arm, I wriggle my fingers."

"You never got used to doing it the other way?"

"No." Ira allowed himself to smirk. "Didn't I ever tell you?"

"You'll get a vote of thanks from Edith anyway. Wait. Just one more address, and I'm coming to the rescue."

"I guess I can use some help."

"You're doing just great," Larry assured him, teased sportively. "Quit complaining."

"I get so distracted. Honest."

"Here I come."

VII

... Mythical, like the myths read in boyhood, like the engravings of classic figures in Bulfinch's *Age of Fable,* loveliness in repose, rapture in repose, passion verging on the immaculate—that was how Larry's love affair with Edith Welles seemed to Ira. What a contrast to his own sordid and stealthy snatchings, his cynical maneuverings at Mamie's, his Sunday-morning ritual with Minnie.

"When are you gonna *shenk* me a dollar, my *koptsn briderl?*"

As long as you watched yourself, that's what happened to abominations when they became customary. Only on a rare afternoon, rare as could be, when they were taking one hell of a chance, not knowing when Mom or Pop might come home—boy, that was when furor made the green walls flap. Boy, the danger! Contagious. It infected Minnie too, as if snapping up the little brass nipple of the lock inflamed her. She was already standing in the doorway to his bedroom watching him pull the rubber on his hard-on. Jesus, if Pop ever came home and found his son boring it into his daughter crosswise on the bed. Wow . . . But the hell with him. Funny the kind of gags that came to mind: *it was all in the family.* And when Mamie told him they were going to form a Veljisher Family Circle, he laughed outright. Mamie thought it was out of pleasure at the idea; *he* saw himself hitting the bull's-eye, the ten-ring. What the hell. He hated pulling off—kept postponing. One more day maybe: tomorrow wouldn't be too soon to drop in at Mamie's. Oh, the hell with it. Hang on. Don't be like that rusty pervert bastard in Fort Tryon Park. . . .

As long as he got away with it, that was what counted—except for that wisp of fear that something might have gone wrong—and that corrosive revulsion he couldn't dispel, couldn't shake: nagging conscience, damn it.

So why shouldn't Larry's love affair be as beautiful as a romance conjured out of legend? It was pure—was that the right word? Sounded priggish; that wasn't what he meant. Seemly, oh, hell, just decent, without peril, without guile or guilt, unharried, unhurried. Not like his—copulations, that's all they were, depraved and abominable.

And the guy was so handsome, gifted, poised, charming, no sense of smirch about him, as Ira felt about himself, no sense of anything devious, ulterior. No wonder Larry's parents beamed and laughed at the sight of their son. Ira himself stared, so captivated was he by Larry's seraphic luster.

Oh, well, there could be no competition between them, no thought of competition in Ira's mind (except in the chaotic writhings of wishful imagination). They inhabited different spheres of breeding, of outlook. Ira couldn't name them yet, but he knew they were so different that Larry's love affair with Edith was beyond coveting—or nearly beyond coveting—because beyond comparing, on the only level Ira knew: behaving with Edith as with Minnie, or Stella. It was unthinkable!

Nevertheless, still too awestruck to overcome his reluctance to attend the Arts Club poetry recital for which he had helped Larry write the notices, Ira reneged again on his promise to attend—and stayed away. He received a pained, vehement exhortation from Larry when they next met. He wanted Ira there, damn it! He was *his* guest, a guest of the secretary of the Arts Club. Ira even had a certain claim to being there: for services he had rendered writing the invitations.

"You promise to come, cross your heart?" Larry demanded a month later, at the next session of writing notices.

"Cross my fingers, I will."

"No, none of that! I'm serious."

"Okay, okay, okay."

So wearing the English tweed jacket of Larry's beneficence, a garment "that never grew on your soil," as Mom reminded her son, wearing it a little self-consciously, with his secondhand chesterfield overcoat above, Ira set out to find the meeting place of the Arts Club. It was already dark. He followed the trolley tracks, as Larry had instructed him, from the Christopher Street subway kiosk through Eighth Street, splotchy with snow. Once past the lowering Sixth Avenue El, Eighth Street became active: animate with people, show window lights, delicatessens, bookstores, small art galleries. He turned right, to Waverly Place, and then along the west boundary of glimmering, snowy Washington Square Park, with its view of the Washington Square arch on Fifth Avenue, and the equestrian general himself, halfway toward the scattered lights of NYU's converted loft building, and walked to MacDougal Street. The neighborhood was largely Italian, to all appearances—and sounds—typically ill-lit and grubby. But near the corner, the illuminated sign proclaimed in large letters: VILLAGE INN TEAHOUSE.

Helpless, dubious, Ira waited for someone else to enter, someone whom he could follow. And soon a small group of youthful coeds, bright plaid scarves showing, and jolly as they approached the tearoom, made their way in. Ira trailed them through the door, tarried near it inside while the newcomers paid their contribution for the evening's entertainment, dropping their coins into the lidless cigar box on the counter. Behind the counter, in charge of proceedings, stood Larry—handsome, glowing, filling the part perfectly—exchanging mirthful greetings with the newly arrived guests. Ira had just time enough to glance about the large dining room, well filled with a murmuring audience sitting at round tables, each one softly lit by a candle in the center, the candle set in a dark bottle laced with wax drippings, the candle flames fluttering at each opening of the door, the unsteady light shedding bewitching gleam on the faces of the seated audience. Magic atmosphere, cigarette-smoke-filled, droning, shadowy ambience. So that was a poetry recital, that was how poets foregathered—

Larry's cry of pleasure broke through Ira's hesitant appraisals. In another moment, Larry strode from behind the counter, came face to face with the newcomer. "Ira! Am I glad to see you! You didn't let me down after all. I was beginning to wonder." He took hold of Ira's arm.

"I'm kinda leery." Ira grinned, tried to shrink comically within himself.

"What for?"

"What for? Hey."

"I told you there's nothing to be afraid of."

"Yeah, I know."

"They're just undergraduates, most of them. Some seniors, some juniors. You helped me write the notices. What's there to it? You sit and listen like the rest. Say, you're wearing the tweed jacket."

"Yeah. Hey, what's that *you're* wearing?" Ira pointed at the wide colored sash around Larry's boyish waist.

"That's called a cummerbund."

"A what?"

"A cummerbund. I bought it in Bermuda. The English wear it in the evening. Like it? Elegant, isn't it?"

"I guess so. Okay I sneak over there to that empty chair by the corner?"

"Oh, no. You've got to meet Edith first."

"Oh, Jesus, Larry!" Grimacing fiercely to shake his friend's resolve, Ira rubbed damp palms on the front of his chesterfield. "Why not afterward?"

"You'll meet her afterward too. She's been wanting to meet you for a long time. No excuses. Come on." He feigned an adamant frown. "Follow me."

"Ow, I knew it." Hangdog, struggling stonily within himself, Ira trailed Larry amid tobacco smoke and hum of voices in candle-lit murk toward the further end of the tearoom. A low dais had been set at that end, in front of the audience, next to the rear wall. A lectern reared up on the dais. An unoccupied table stood close by, a tablet on it marked RESERVED. Close to the table, a woman seemed to be introducing another woman: to older people, faculty members maybe. And as she turned away, leaving the other woman engaged in conversation with the new acquaintances, Ira, in the self-conscious numbness of approach, even before Larry addressed her, recognized her.

By some kind of inevitability, he knew, knew that the petite olive-skinned woman, turning away with winning and receptive mien, smiling countenance, like a dark-hued source for rays of generosity, sympathy, smiling countenance with prominent, sad eyes, the woman with small earrings, bunching a minute handkerchief, toying with a thin gold necklace, was Edith Welles. Larry spoke her name, spoke Ira's. She greeted him, fixed on him through the blur of his acute embarrassment her steady, large-brown-eyed and solicitous gaze. She gave him her dainty hand to hold—and of course he would drop his hat in his acute embarrassment. Was there a hint in her eyes of something appeasing—appeasing just in general, or because he knew about her affair with Larry? He couldn't say. Something stirred the notion in his mind that because she imposed her trust in him, it was like an immediate, implicit bond between them, a bond which, at the same time as she appealed to it, was intended to reassure him. It did nothing, though, to dispel his abashed inarticulateness. Larry left them to go back to the counter when a party of young guests came in.

"Larry says you're remarkably sensitive to literature, but you've made up your mind to be a biologist." Her face brightened with encouragement. "Of course, there's nothing mutually exclusive between the two."

"No, ma'am. Yeah, I'll be a biologist if I ever get a biology course. It's so crowded."

"So Larry told me. I think that's a great pity."

"Yeah . . ."

"Larry has gotten a great deal from you."

"I don't know. I got a lot from Larry."

"When did you develop your interest in literature?"

"I didn't know it was literature. I mean, it was just plain books."

She smiled, and yet her eyes remained solemn, never leaving his, studying him—unwavering. He wished he too could maintain so comprehensive and at the same time unoffending a gaze as hers. He had to steal glances at people—something like Pop.

"Have you tried writing anything?"

"Me? No, ma'am. I mean, only assignments." Small, pert nose she had, dark hair, not black, in a bun back of her head. She was built like a girl still, yet she was an instructor in English . . . in a university . . . with a Ph.D. And as his eyes lowered before her frank survey: what tiny feet she had. In shiny black pumps. Trim ankles. Trim calves . . . gave an inkling he wasn't supposed to think about. How could Larry think about it? A girl, but a college teacher girl. Another world: such sheer daintiness, delicate refinement. Gee . . .

Deep brown orbs peered into his, sympathetically. "I hope you'll be able to accompany Larry when he calls on us—at our place, Iola Reid's and mine. On St. Mark's Place."

"In the Bowery? I know. I couldn't believe it."

"Why?"

"In New York? In the Bowery? I mean, it's a tough place."

She dimpled. "We seem to be in some kind of haven there. I suppose you'd call it a respectable haven."

"Yeah? Everyone behaves?"

She laughed, candidly, freely amused by his unintended witticism. "You've been very kind to undertake so much of the drudgery of getting off the notices. I hope Larry has made known my appreciation. It's one of those unavoidable boring bits of drudgery."

"Well, we—we gab a lot, ye know, when we do 'em. Makes the time go. Doesn't feel so bad."

"I'm happy you don't mind—"

"Nah. I mean, no, ma'am."

"Before I forget I'd like to invite you to a party of my modern poetry class. Larry will be there. Other undergraduates, too. I'm sure he'll ask you to accompany him. I'd like to do it in person. You'd be very welcome."

Ira swallowed. "Me? Thanks. That's at night." He wished his voice didn't sound so rough.

"Yes. The first Friday in April. I hope you're free that evening. Are you?"

He scratched his head. "Yes, ma'am. I think so. That far ahead I must be. Friday. Oh, sure."

"I'm having my poetry class over for tea and cookies." She smiled fetchingly. "I'd be delighted to have you attend."

"Tea and cookies?" He giggled foolishly. "Yes, ma'am." Did he dare try to be funny? "Cookies even without tea. Thanks. But I don't know anything about poetry."

She found fresh cause for merriment in what he said. "You're not alone, by any means. A surprising number of people don't."

"They don't? So who does?"

Again she was stirred to merriment. "They're poets, or would-be poets. In large part."

"Oh, now I know."

"I find that hard to believe in your case."

"Yeah? Mostly I know what Larry told me. I mean about the modern poets."

Her solemn eyes that had been regarding him so fixedly swerved away. She let the fine gold necklace slip through her tiny fingers. "I'm so glad I finally met you, Ira. Will you excuse me? I've got to meet these people."

"Oh, yeah, yeah." He backed away.

She patted his arm.

He watched her move with gracious cordiality toward two people who had just come in, two women, whom Larry, lambent with the privilege, was escorting toward Edith. They both carried themselves with the polite air of inner distinction. The one was gray-haired, stately, slender, with a curiously veiled look, at the same time knowing and modest. The other was stockily built, decisive and public in manner, homely-bright, with restless, glittering eyeglasses on her snub nose, and mouth vigorously engaged in speech.

Ira sidled away, heard salutations exchanged, names and welcomes: "Marcia, Anne, so glad you could come."

And the gray, taller woman: "We wouldn't miss Léonie reading her poems for the world. Her voice is exactly suited to them."

"Contrasting, don't you think?"

"True," Edith seconded. "A huskiness against such mellow syllables."

"And yet so unaffected," said the stocky woman. "There she is."

And Larry, elated with office, a blooming, blushing Ganymede, "I've reserved the table in front. And guests."

Pleased by the very perfection of his presence, the very essence of his youth—one could see—the woman named Marcia bustled, "Oh, that's just fine! Thank you. . . . Léonie! How are you, dear? Anne, do sit down. So you plan to stay on in the Village? We get all the intellectual stimulation we need in the Columbia area. Don't you think, Anne? Perhaps not the same kind of artistic ferment . . ."

Boy, they were smart, smart, confident, quick, deft, so sure—Ira felt as if he were slinking away, seeking the chair in the far corner: smart, gee, and they were women too. Boyoboy. Made him feel like a—what? He didn't know what. Like a *grobyan*, as they said in Yiddish: a boor, a dolt. And he was, wasn't he? He knew he shouldn't be here, didn't belong here. They just seemed to drive him down with their, their manners, education, yeah, drive him down to street level, to the hoi polloi, to what he was. What the hell. Home was a slum, a bleary tenement, a railroad flat a flight up, with Mom and Pop in it, sometimes leaning out the window in balmy weather, as he did too watching the Pullman trains go by in summer. And . . . what strange brutality coursed through him at the thought of it, yeah, and Minnie, too.

So what the hell was he doing here? He searched for a likely seat in the most obscure corner. It made less sense than his friendship with Farley. At least the guy was his speed—as far as his mind moved, he was—however fast his legs flew otherwise. And yet, there it was again: who here had his reckless imagination? Nothing but *dreck* to work with, nothing but smithereens to feed the fire, splinters he made out of an apple box he jumped on that he had swiped from in front of the grocery—and he kept the spud baking in the can, like Weasel that night. He didn't know how to be polite, but he knew words; he was rich in words, a millionaire that way, a gentleman of great estate: words unbounded. That was indeed what crippled Mr. Sullivan discerned in class that day when he accused Ira of making a boob of himself for others' entertainment. That's what Ira felt Edith Welles was probing for when she looked into his eyes with her round, unwavering, solemn ones: words. Words, tameless and teeming, headlong. Apollo's steeds that ran away—not Icarus, fathead.

He couldn't deceive her, even in those few minutes they spoke to-gether—the realization grew to conviction—he couldn't hide his chaotic hoard from her—his fumbling, his disquiet, his crudities, traits that he himself recognized—and could do nothing about—his Jewishness that he was so conscious of, his ingratiating, silly grin, she saw it all, but not a reverberation of any of that returned, not a one; all that was mute as a bell ringing in a vacuum as it did way back in General Science—of only one thing did she make him aware, only one thing pulsed back to him: her appraisal of what she had found hidden in his mind, as if that above all was important to her. . . .

"There's a coat rack behind you," the young mustached under-graduate at the table suggested.

"Oh, yeah!" Ira stripped off his chesterfield hurriedly. "I'll just hold it." He draped the coat across his knees, and on top of it he rested his gray fedora. Now, exposed for all to see, conspicuous for this time of year, as Larry had said, because of its light color, Larry's kasha tweed conferred unwanted prominence on its wearer. Ira tried to look nonchalant.

"I haven't seen you before," the young undergraduate made overture.

"No."

"I'm Nathan. That's Tamara. That's Leonard. That's Wilma."

"I'm Ira." He nodded his head gauchely. "Ira Stigman."

"English major?"

"No. Bio."

"Do you write?"

"No, I happen to be a friend of somebody here. I go to CCNY."

"Oh. City College?"

"Yeah."

"How do you like CCNY? Any good courses?"

"You mean in English?"

"Yes. Or philosophy. The humanities."

He wasn't sure what they meant by the humanities, but he felt his benightedness too keenly to want to talk, to disclose his want of articulateness, his want of comprehension of more than elementary opinions. "I take English Composition 1. I'm just sittin' here," he said gruffly.

His reply had the effect he hoped for. After sharp surprise, they looked lingeringly askance, then divested themselves of interest in him. It was just as well. With nothing to communicate, he felt his isolation, and perversely preferred it intact: he was the obtuse and listless listener. Words crossed the table, and were crossed by others from nearby tables. Only a single time was his attention brought to a focus by what they were saying: when a spirited disagreement arose about a poet named Jeffers.

"He's crazy!" someone asserted.

"No, he's not."

"That *Tamar*. And now, *Roan Stallion*. You've read it?"

"Of course."

"What's next? Pasiphae giving birth to the Minotaur?"

"Pacify? Why pacify?"

"Oh, come on. You know what I mean. Animal sex and incest mean something else to him. Man is sick."

"*The* man is sick. Jeffers is sick."

"Oh, no, he's not. He's talking about man, introverted man."

"Well, aren't we all?"

"No. In general. And in general, I agree with him. Man is alien-ated from nature. Man is doomed."

"I don't think so. The further he gets away from nature, the bet-ter off he is. He became man only by getting away from nature. That's why I say Jeffers is crazy."

"That may sound clever—"

"It's been so all along. What else does it mean to be civilized?"

"At least he doesn't keep harping on the Jews, like Eliot," said one of the young women, Tamara. "Jeffers does use my name, which happens to be Hebrew."

"Oh, yes? Why? Any reason?"

"It means 'date,' the fruit, but it means something else—to Jef-fers. It's clear."

"What?"

"Tamar in the Bible is raped by her brother."

"I didn't get that connection at all. You Zionists have all the Bib-lical answers."

"You don't have to be a Zionist to know that. She was King David's daughter, and the whole thing fits into Jeffers's incest sym-bol."

Incest symbol. The way they used it, it didn't mean anything . . . a symbol? Putting a newspaper, *Der Tag,* under Minnie when she was bluggy, and then pitching it out the window down the airshaft, and scaring the rats scurrying. Now *that* was the real thing. Didn't Mom look all over hell for it afterward, though, for the *roman* she hadn't read yet to Mrs. Shapiro? Symbol, so all right, symbol. Symbol re-ferred to something else. Referred to alienation—that fellow there said it—alienation?—getting away from everybody else . . . sick intro-spection. . . . Maybe. So what're you gonna do? You're alienated. Yeah. "Where's *Der Tag?*" Mom kept hollering, accusing: "Did you see Friday's *Tag?*"

"Me? No. Not me. What do I want with *Der Tag?*"

Ira tried not to steal glances at Edith, but couldn't help it, and from time to time she caught his gaze before he could shift away, and she smiled at him, sympathetically, reassuringly.

Smiling winningly to gain attention, Edith, who, together with her guest, had seated herself on the dais a few minutes before, stood up. The poet they were privileged to hear this evening, she informed her audience, was undoubtedly familiar to the majority of them. She ranked as one of the most distinguished writers of lyric poetry in the country, rich and distinguished in her imagery, in her superb use of the poetic medium, her poetic meanings wonderfully compressed, and yet losing none of their singing quality thereby. Léonie Adams. And without more ado, she would turn the platform over to her. Edith expressed certainty all would find the evening a memorable one.

Followed scattered applause. The recital began. Léonie Adams arose from her chair, and with two slender volumes in hand, stepped up to the lectern; she opened the first of the volumes, a thin blue one, turned pages, pressed down the page selected, and yet without consulting it at all, she began reciting. Larry had praised her lyrics highly when he and Ira were engaged in writing the announcements of the recital—"Her poems really sing. You rarely come across such beautiful, really original imagery! She's tops. I wish I had one of her books of poems here to show you. She's way ahead of Edna Millay."

And now she stood there, in front of everyone, a real poet, a poet in the flesh, reading her poems. Ira listened intently, lost and recovered meanings, lost them again, never truly grasping the intent of the whole. Nevertheless, however sporadic, he was moved. Even the fragments had a richness that made him wonder whether, given the book in front of him, poring over it and returning, he would grasp the meaning of a separate poem in something like its entirety, something like the way he grasped James Stephens's "What Tomas Said in a Pub" in the Untermeyer anthology. Or trying to discover the essence of Walter de la Mare's "Here lies a most beautiful lady," or John Masefield's cargos, nearly any poem there, like Sandburg's "Fog"—oh, wasn't that beautiful fancy Adams read just now: "The dream of flying would lift a marble bird."

In the intervals while auditory attention lapsed, the visual replaced it. He studied the reader. She was pretty, short in stature, mature yet young, a short figure with a small head, small features contained in dark, bobbed hair. She was curiously built, though, almost as if her figure were at odds with itself. From the waist down, as her lower body appeared when she first stood up and from time to time when she stepped away from the lectern, her hips were chunky. Her face and torso were delicate, seraphic and delicate, but rested on a stocky base, strong, chunky hips, piano legs, as they were called. With her blue eyes set wide apart, and seemingly focused on an ethereal yonder, and with her soft, clinging, husky voice, she looked and sounded like a true poet, otherworldly and inspired—above the waist—and down below like any housekeeper. Could it be, Ira ruminated, the poet sort of borrowed from the centaur?

Murmurs of approval greeted the end of each poem. Though Ira failed to understand anything but lovely fragments, out of courtesy to his host, Larry, and in case Edith looked his way, he manifested appreciation, conveyed an immobilized rapture. He was slow, he was inveterately slow of mind—Ira palliated disappointment with himself at his failure to comprehend. He had to mull things over and over, he told himself—consoled himself once again—and then perhaps he might be able to fathom the meaning, or fuse the separate wonderful metaphors into a unity. Listen to her: "Since the salt terror swept us from our course"—that applied to him. Striking and unique juxtapositions of words, musical, labyrinthian in their evocation, if only he could encompass the significance of the whole. No, not the message. Whatever it was. The allusion. Yeah, yeah. When he read the Robert Frost poem about stopping by the woods in winter, he caught the central allusion of death and duty, he felt it within the context of the words themselves. Not this. Well, dummy that he was, what the hell could he do?

Afterward—when the reading was over—to sustained applause—cookies and coffee were served by young students, volunteer waitresses. Colloquy hummed anew. Cross-table talk set the dwindling candle flames fluttering, corresponding to utterance like tiny yellow tongues. And while the refreshments were being consumed, Larry sauntered over, bent down, and with lips close to Ira's ear, whispered, his words brimming with import. "I'm seeing Edith home tonight. Okay?"

"Sure. Sure. I get it." Ira nodded.

And audibly, "How'd you like it?" Larry asked.

"The cookies?"

"C'mon, Ira, I'm talking about art."

Larry patted his friend's shoulder, and again speaking *sotto voce:* "Someone likes you. Thinks you're very genuine."

"Yeah?"

"I'll tell you more later."

"Thanks." So easy to come out with a self-conscious, and discontented, "Tanks, tanks to dee, my wordy friend" (to parody Longfellow); but he didn't, and was glad he didn't.

Larry bent down again, murmured, "Come over and say good night."

Ira winced, shut both eyes. "Can't *you* do it for me?"

Larry glared a long, mock-menacing glare—and not until Ira nodded in grudging acquiescence did Larry leave.

"Know him a long time?" The question was put to Ira by Nathan, the undergraduate who had previously introduced himself and the others, the one who sported the brown mustache.

"Yars'n yars." Ira enjoyed his riposte. There was such a little difference between a fool and a foil, it just occurred to him.

"You don't sound like City College, much more like Columbia." Nathan was apparently glossing over with amenity his misjudgment of Ira's newly revealed status.

"I don't know what City College sounds like."

But the other was quick in riposte, quicker than Ira, as usual. "I know you've got to have at least a B average to matriculate."

"Yeah? I musta got in on a rain check." Again, without his intending, gruffness rasped in his voice. *Matriculate. Jesus. Highfalutin.* He cleared his throat. "What does NYU sound like?"

"You heard us tonight."

"I sure did. You mean you, right?" He felt surly. But hell, this wasn't the place to display ill will; he was Larry's friend. Ira simply lowered his head.

"Do you know Miss Welles, too?"

Pumping him. "Not very." He noticed that the others at the table were paying close attention, especially the rather svelte, sleek Jewish beauty toying with the earring. The earring slipped from her fingers, rolled toward Ira on the floor. He stooped, recovered it, and handed

it to her. She said not a word, just looked at him, loftily. Goddamn
her, where did she get off with that haughty crap? Next time he'd let
the goddamn thing stay where it fell. But a next time there would
never be. "Thanks," he said pointedly, animosity swelling within him,
his ears kindling. "You're Tamara?"

"Yes," she conceded.

"What happened to the guy?"

"I don't understand. What guy?"

"You might be Tamar yourself," Ira said. "I mean the real one. In
the Bible." He was being uncouth. Cut it out, he counseled himself.

"I don't see the point of that. What makes you say that?"

"She musta been real good-lookin', no?"

And this Tamara was too: svelte, sleek, basking in the glow of her
warm, harmonious Jewish features. And smart. Too smart for him, Ira
already knew, with her scale of appraisal, secure and deeply delineated. No docile kid cousin this one, or sister yielding to need.

"Thank you," she said, with a formal blink of eyelids; she wasn't
going to let him take acquaintance too far.

"You mind if I ask you what happened to the guy?"

"What guy?"

The others around the candle-lit table stopped chatting and listened. He struggled with the boor inside him, unmanageable suddenly. "The guy who raped her. He was her brother, wasn't he?"

"He was her half brother, Amnon."

"Oh. He was only her half brother."

"Only?"

"Yeah. So that was only half so bad."

"For heaven's sake!" she said, after the slightest, but curiously
electric, throb of silence. "I didn't think when I came here this
evening I was going to discuss degrees of incest."

"This kind must be the third degree." He was strangely glib, even
with a young woman as attractive as she was, just so long as no
amorous notions interfered in his head. Then his heart stopped
beating. "No, I know. But what happened to him?"

"Absalom killed him."

"Who? Absalom?"

"Please!" Condescending and affronted, she clearly found the conversation distasteful. She looked away, toyed with the earring he had retrieved.

"You're asking the right person," the young man named Nathan complimented, slyly. "She's Sholem Aleichem's granddaughter."

"Yeah?"

"Please, Nathan, don't drop names. You know how much I hate that."

"That's all right. I don't know who he is."

A few seconds of silence. He had really messed up, messed up the vis-à-vis, but gotten a few licks in, though, in return for her haughtiness, halfway gotten even with all of them. Anh, wasn't he a bastard? Yeah. Might as well move his freight the hell outta here. He gathered up coat and hat in brusque hold, and stood up, turned his back on them. Let 'em think he was crazy.

Jesus Christ, he didn't seem to be at home anywhere, not here among these—these well-behaved, well-to-do students, like the kid, the grown-up guy by now, whose silver-filigreed fountain pen Ira had swiped. And he wasn't at home at CCNY either, all of them Jewish, trying desperately to assimilate. He should have "fit in" there, but he didn't. If his family had stayed on the East Side—at least till he was Bar Mitzva, maybe. Not at home on 119th Street in *goyish* Harlem, that went without saying. He wasn't at home anywhere. He was Larry's friend, that was all.

Now for this last minor ordeal. Only for him it wasn't minor. Ill at ease, worried, he approached the small group standing about the table nearest the podium. If his first meeting with Edith was trying, this leave-taking promised to be even more so. Damn Larry. She was speaking with someone else, undoubtedly a faculty member, a fairly tall man, smooth and regular-featured, with darkening blond hair (was that Mr. Vernon, the cosponsor of the Arts Club, whom Larry had mentioned, the homosexual?). And another, an eager-appearing short man with a quick, frequent laugh and a pockmarked face (was he the one Larry had said disparagingly was frantically in love with Edith?). And the poet, Léonie Adams. And the two distinguished women who had come in at the last. Nah, he'd better beat it. He rippled fingers at Larry, screwed up the side of his face in sign of farewell. But Miss Welles turned toward him, again with winning, solicitous mien. He had to say something:

"I came to say goodbye, Miss Welles."

"I hope not as finally as that."

"No, good night, I mean. But I told Larry I already said it."

"I don't mind hearing it again. Did you enjoy the evening?"

"Yeah. Parts of it." Agitated, he jerked his head nervously. "Maybe I don't hear right, ye know? I mean fast enough."

She met his troubled frown with consoling smile. "That's true for most of us. Only we're too polite to say so. I hope you haven't been discouraged from coming again—"

"Well, I'm outta place, ma'am—Miss Welles. I'm glad to help with the postcards. But more than that . . ." He looked away hopelessly, tried to prevent the hitch of his shrug from exceeding polite limits, or what he thought were.

"Oh, no, please don't feel that way. You may enjoy the next one more. I'm sure you will. The students will read some of their own work then. Graduates and a few of the faculty," she corrected herself. "We'll mix prose and poetry next time."

"Yeah? Maybe it's a better idea. It's just that in poetry I don't get it right away. Larry does. Boy. He's talented.."

"Probably because he writes poetry. As I said before. You didn't miss all of it?"

"No. The words, I mean, ma'am, the words. When she says something about questioning my idol, wasn't it? 'What strange and barbarous fancy it may keep.' Boy, do I love that."

"You do?" She studied him anew, steadily appraising, appraising. "Are you taking English courses at your college?"

"Me? I finally got into English Composition 1." He spoke with a kind of glum irony, meant to amuse her.

But she wasn't amused; she shook her head, kinked the slim gold necklace over her tiny forefinger. "I expect you to come over with Larry.."

"You mean that party next month?"

"No. Before that. Some evening."

"Thanks."

"You mustn't be so shy, child."

"Me? Well . . . you know."

She extended her hand. "Good night, Ira."

How small and dainty were the fingers he held for a moment.
"Good night, Miss Welles."

"Thanks for coming this evening."

"Oh, yeah. Thanks too," he nodded, as he left the room and
headed into the chill air on MacDougal Street.

VIII

College, the world within CCNY's Gothic gray-white facade, was already shrunken from a place of blooming, nebulous expectations to
one in which Ira merely hoped to get a passing grade—a C for a
recitation, for a quiz—any passing grade. College was a loom on
which it would take four years to weave a diploma. The 125th Street
trolley was its shuttle, thrown between the mean cold-water flat on
119th Street and the trodden and scuffed alcoves and lecture halls
within the Gothic walls on Convent Avenue; between—should he call
it the adulterated *Yiddishkeit* at home?—and between that and the
Americanism presided over by the sometimes kind, sometimes sympathetic, sometimes aloof, but so far always gentile professors.

For Ira, college was dwarfed in significance by the world outside:
not only by the cruel encroachments of his relentless and degrading
appetites, but by their very opposite: the beautiful, the wondrous intrusion of Larry's world into his own. . . . College became a satellite,
no, a yo-yo, controlled by both the base and the lovely at the same
time: to sordid eroticism and seemingly celestial romance. In Ira's
myth-laden mind, Edith Welles could easily be the Elfin Queen who
had claimed Tom Rimer for her own: she imparted that sense of delicacy and remove: an Elfin Queen with a Ph.D., or despite her Ph.D.,
who had claimed her freshman student for her own. Wasn't that like
a fairy tale?

College became a place to go through paces while destiny unfolded. If it wasn't a loom, then it was a four-year holding pen. Good grades elated him—a little; elated him wryly; about as much as poor grades dejected him: with a shrug, because of the inconvenience they would cause him. He would have to take summer courses. Grades didn't make much difference one way or another, so long as he passed. And why were they of so little import? Because he felt in his innermost self, and couldn't reveal, that there was some kind of a design at work; that the passing of listless college days, academic weeks and months, was meant to ripen some kind of cloudy promise. If Larry sometimes had qualms about aborting his dental career in favor of an uncertain literary one, Ira, though he might chafe at the tedium, rarely felt misgivings in his fuzzy ruminations about the decay of his future as a zoologist or biology teacher. Everything seemed to play a role in his murky aspirations: even the things that beset him, that he did and couldn't stop doing, that he felt corroded him, besmirched him, all fitted into the design: the way he had felt on the flat diving rock on the Hudson River, after stealing the silver-filigreed fountain pen, it was part of a design. Fatalistic, was that the right word for it?

Incorrigibly, in intervals of quiescent appetite, his mind infringed on college time, on time due his studies. . . . He reviewed—and meditated on—every bit of information Larry conveyed to him about Edith. He added to Larry's observations, added to them, and dwelled on those he had made about her himself, some of them gleaned much later on when he would know Edith much better. He cogitated about them, like a sleuth almost, seeking clues to Edith's character, seeking to reconstruct her, in order to familiarize himself with her, in order to know how she would be apt to respond, her likes and dislikes, to know what to expect, *to adapt himself to her tastes.* And why was he so intent on learning all that? In part, he was driven by a kind of unconscious urge toward self-improvement, according to the standards of one he regarded with such deference, such esteem. But to an even greater degree, he felt impelled to attune himself to her in order to prepare himself *for* her, a strange, subliminal will to conform to her expectations, to establish his dependability, his loyalty, his indispensability in an imaginary hour of need. He had moments of insight, as in a fairy tale, that brought home to him that his motives clashed with probability, tilted against common sense. Intermittent aspects of actuality, of the actual state of things, the unlikely fruition of his fantasies, often sobered him, checked him, toppled his insubstantial aspirations. And yet he continued to entertain them. They prevailed against all odds. They would prevail because they were an extension, an elaboration of something in which he was already well schooled—ever since age eight and a half, when his parents settled in 119th Street in Irish Harlem. They would prevail by dint of his well-nigh precociously developed ability to adapt, by his powers of ingratiation. The path he had set out on years ago, and had followed for years, had become a confirmed one, and confirmed in him. It seemed to bid him to follow it whither it was bound, and by the same means that had become inveterate: by earnest application to adapt to her nature, as he learned her traits, by studied ingratiation. Paradoxically, that mode which he once *had* to adopt for survival, because the original East Side Jewish self was imprisoned and choked off, became for him, however obscurely felt, a hope for more than self-preservation: a hope for self-realization, a hope for freedom.

She had come to New York from California, from Berkeley, Larry told him, where she had gotten her doctorate, and afterward she taught English literature there, that much Ira soon learned. She was not a native of California, though, but of New Mexico. She was born in Silver City, a very small city, scarcely worthy the name (to a New Yorker), in that sparsely inhabited territory, where gun duels still took place in the street in broad daylight. How laconic and amusing were her descriptions of her father, who never carried a gun, prudently dropping to the sidewalk while the bullets flew. He had won his law degree from the University of Pennsylvania, had migrated west, and was one of the few lawyers in Silver City. He was also a member of the Democratic Party, and shortly became active in politics. At the outset, he was very successful; he gave promise of becoming one of the leading political figures in the Southwest. When the territory was admitted into the Union as the state of New Mexico in 1912, it was Edith's father, William Welles, who was the first representative elected to the Congress of the United States. He was again reelected during Woodrow Wilson's term in 1916, and held the same office until 1920. But, alas, with the end of the Great War came a revulsion against the War, against Wilson's violation of his pledge not to involve the United States in the War, against the enormous, senseless slaughter of the common people—with the result that in the elections of 1920, the Democrats went down to defeat; the Republicans swept the elections in New Mexico. Edith's father, nominated by his party as candidate for the U.S. Senate, which in predominantly Democratic New Mexico was tantamount to election, lost his bid for the seat, and with it most of his personal fortune, which he had invested in the race. He never recovered from his defeat. He sank in political stature; he slipped into political obscurity; he took to drink.

His political career a failure, his marriage also became one, Ira would subsequently learn. His wife, whom Edith described as a prudish Christian Scientist, wept when he approached her sexually. Her parents already had three children—the third was Edith's brother—and they were frequently forced to listen to loud beratings by a demanding, inebriate father of his beseeching, sobbing wife. And then occurred the most incredible thing he had ever heard in his life: Edith's father took a prostitute out of one of the local brothels, and with scarcely any attempt at concealment, provided a residence for her and installed her in it as his mistress. With that, his wife left him, sued for divorce, and being granted it, together with custody of the children and some alimony, moved to Berkeley, where she established herself as a piano teacher. Meanwhile Edith's father's health began to fail. His law practice fell off; he sank toward indigence. Faithful to him, though, through all this, was Mildred, the woman he had reclaimed from the brothel.

Edith had a brother and sister, both younger than herself. The brother, William Welles, Jr., went to work for a firm dealing in prefabricated aluminum siding as soon as he graduated from high school. The sister, Lenora, of whom Edith had no high opinion, because so totally impractical in financial matters, so very conventional and a Christian Scientist as well, was described by Edith as "very large. Lenora is huge." She had been directed, by maternal decree, to apply herself to the violin—the instrument Edith wanted to play. But no, Mother thought Edith was better fitted for the piano (one had to keep these things, these antagonisms, well in mind). Edith thought her sister was insensitive musically, for all her practice; and that her sister's ambitions, fostered by her mother, to become a concert artist, one who would make her debut in New York, were absurd. Edith herself relinquished the piano, not because she wasn't musical, wasn't sensitive in the extreme to musical nuance. Rather, she gave up the long, arduous practice that would have prepared her for concertizing because she decided her hands were simply too small to cope with the demands of professional concert performance.

She gave up all hope of being a concert performer—but then used her training at the instrument to play after school in movie houses, in the days of silent movies. And later, in company with other musicians of varying skills, at something she named—with a smile— shivarees. What things they did out West! Ira fixed on the word: shivaree. . . . It sounded wild and cowboy, wild and woolly: a corruption of the French word *charivari*, his *Webster's Collegiate* informed him: a mock serenade of discordant noises. . . . From her earliest teens she had been self-supporting, Edith had disclosed, her determination unmistakable in the way she tilted her chin. Much to Ira's secret embarrassment, that a slight young girl in her teens was already self-supporting, and he, big oaf, *farleygt*, as they said in Yiddish, burdening his parents. Lenora already had a child, and had custody of it, after *her* divorce. Mother and child also lived in Berkeley—precariously, according to Edith's incisively stated opinion—on alimony that would have been sufficient, "if Lenora had any sense." But she didn't. She couldn't manage anything; she was always in debt; and Mother, or more often Edith herself, was called on to help get her sister out of her monetary difficulties, which Edith did, at some sacrifice to her own welfare, indignant at her "ninny of a sister," but coming to her aid for the sake of the child. . . .

Her musical career foreclosed, Edith had gotten her B.A. *summa cum laude*, Phi Beta Kappa, from Berkeley, which Ira took to be the name of the university, learning only later that it meant the University of California at Berkeley. Afterward, while supporting herself as before, she had gotten her doctorate there. It was the first interdisciplinary doctorate ever awarded by the university. Her doctorate linked the English department with that of anthropology. The

subject matter of her thesis was an analysis of the rhythms and structure of Navajo songs and religious chants, their transliterations into
Roman characters, with scrupulous indication of accent and syllabic
pattern, and finally their rendering into English verse, not verbatim
but by re-creation into English, faithfully equivalent to the spirit of
the original Navajo. Out of this material, imbued with Southwestern
light and sky, and evocative of the primeval bond between man and
nature, Edith published two books of poems. They were well received; they were praised by critics for their successful capturing of
the elevated moods and mystical communings of a tribal people
whose culture had long been ignored, long despised, by those who
had all but despoiled them of land and heritage.

The poems also came to the attention of another young anthro-
pologist, one with a keen interest in poetry, the brilliant Marcia
Meede—the same young woman with the energetic lip and restless
glitter of eyeglasses whom Ira had seen together with her older, enig-
matically smiling friend, ushered to their seats by a radiant Larry at
the poetry recital. A correspondence between the two women, Edith
and Marcia, had begun while Edith was still in Berkeley and became
a bridge to acquaintance and friendship when Edith took up residence in New York to teach at NYU.

Edith divulged so much, and so freely, first to Larry and then to
both of them, that for all his eagerness to imprint a composite of her
on his mind—and to steep himself within the ambience of her temperament—Ira was sometimes embarrassed, even as Larry obviously
was, by the frankness, the explicit particulars of her disclosures: that
her mother believed sex ought to be terminated after five years of
marriage; that Edith, out of sheer impulse of altruism, and in defiance of convention, had married one Kurt Finklepaugh (did anyone
ever hear such a ludicrous Heinie name?), in order to provide him
with time enough to stay in the country and obtain his doctorate. But
after wedlock, he wanted more than had been agreed upon: he
wanted her body, and this she had no inclination to yield.

"No inclination, no desire, no anything." She laughed, and
added by way of explanation that she had devoted herself so completely to her studies, she had not yet been "wakened." So their
matrimony came to a violent and disgraceful end: with mutual

recrimination, and books—oh so academic—thrown at each other. Since consummation had never taken place, the marriage was legally annulled. Still, her account of their brief conjugal relation revised the picture of her in Ira's mind, tinged it with plucky defiance and acrimony: like warning shadows cast over her apparent sweetness and gentleness. Dainty and petite person though she was, she didn't flee, with eyes streaming tears, flee and seek refuge from her pursuer among friends and relatives. Oh, no, she stood her ground and fought back. Those large, sad eyes took aim, that tiny hand swung and hurled—a tome maybe, a dictionary, at her adversary. One ought to impress that on oneself: underneath the goodness and kindness was something akin to a coiled spring; it could be released, given sufficient provocation, and a spirited retaliation loosed. Yes, that tone of competitiveness, when she spoke of others being given books of poetry to review, not because of superior literary judgment, but because they were men—or because they were favorites of the editor of the book review section of the *Tribune* or the *Times*—that too was a trait that one had to take note of and be aware of. Under Edith's winning generosity, under pleasing sufferance, lurked militance, feminine militance. Larry's account of Edith's censure of his levity with regard to her professional advancement within the English department took on new meaning. Be aware of that trait in her nature, and beware of ruffling her on that account. Be sympathetic. . . .

But Ira still wondered, why did she reveal these intimate details? Her purpose seemed to be to edify her young lover, and his young friend with him, to inculcate in them the ways of the world, its griefs and malice and aberrations. And yet, her telling, which was always understated, had another effect—on Ira, at least. She was like someone acting a part, modestly implying a part: a tragic part, a tragic heroine enmeshed in misfortune, innocent victim of the cruelty and callousness of others—or victim of her own benevolence, a trait that would indeed manifest itself throughout her whole life. Her first marriage, begun as a magnanimous gesture, ended in ugliness and annulment. Her sexual awakening was by force, by someone she trusted.

Afterward, at Berkeley, she formed a liaison with a much-harassed Jew, one Shmuel Hamberg, a Zionist agronomist studying arid-land farming at the university. A man oppressed and tormented, an outcast, a frenetic ideologue—a Socialist, so stridently outspoken in his views that he was tarred and feathered by a gang of patriotic fellow students. She had befriended him, and he had turned to her for comfort and refuge. Attending Berkeley so that he could learn scientific principles of large-scale irrigation, which he was then expected to bring back to the Zionist cooperative farmers who had sent him to America to study, and thus help restore the ancient homeland from its present barrenness to its Biblical plenty, he never did return. Irrigating the deserts of California provided opportunities for private enrichment so great that his idealism folded before them. Large-scale irrigation of the arid regions around Los Banos was a novel idea at the time, and obtaining loans from the neighboring banks to finance his schemes was no easy task; but Shmuel's visionary zeal and powers of persuasion were equal to it. Even hardheaded and certainly non-Judeophile bankers succumbed to his rhapsodic proposals—and advanced loans. He was shortly in charge of farming great tracts of land, heretofore desert and worthless, but as soon as they were provided with water (brought up from artesian wells by means of huge pumps), they became immensely fertile, capable of producing huge crops of cotton, melons, vegetables, grain.

Edith liked to describe him: he was devoid of elementary courtesy. A Russian Jew, probably a Litvak, Ira surmised, he was tender, compassionate, and endlessly stimulating intellectually. At the same time, he seemed totally devoid of tact, without self-control in argument. Excited, he sputtered and spluttered, sprayed his auditors with saliva when he disputed with them. And such was his impoliteness that when company bored him, or he deemed it was time for them to go, he unceremoniously picked up the alarm clock and began winding it, shaking it, adjusting and setting off the alarm.

Still, Edith had become very attached to him; she would have married him, she said, for all his boorishness and craziness, but for one thing. He wouldn't consider marrying any woman not Jewish. He couldn't stand the thought of marrying a woman who was not Jewish! With that stunning rejection, Edith determined it was high time to leave Berkeley. Only by leaving Berkeley could she break his hold upon her, separate herself from his intellectual and emotional domination. She applied for a position at NYU, and fortunately for her, Professor Watt, head of the English department, although stuffy in many ways, rigidly decorous, believed firmly in as heterogeneous an English department as possible. Rumor had it he was even considering hiring a native Korean, author of a book about life in Korea. Nor was anyone sure that Professor Watt didn't know that Boris G, a fellow instructor in the English department, was Jewish. Professor Watt seemed bent on ignoring, though still under cover of propriety, the accepted standards of the parent institution on the banks of the Hudson River. And with enrollment in the English department downtown increasing dramatically, while that of the properly academic university uptown dwindled, his superiors could not help but acquiesce in his conduct of the department.

Edith was offered an instructorship to begin in the fall of 1924. It was the same year Larry enrolled in her freshman English class.

Hmm . . .

He'd have to think about that, Ira told himself: about her having an affair, as she called it, with Shmuel Hamberg, of his sleeping with her, as the euphemism went. Why did she accept that? Why was *that* okay? She must have realized that she was no whit less a *shiksa* in his eyes for all that. Then what did she expect? He'd have to muse on that, construe all the queer quirks impinging and overlapping within her nature. The things she welcomed, the things she couldn't abide. She refused to convert to Judaism to please her lover, if conversion would have been sufficient. That was her independent-mindedness coming to the fore. Hmm . . . Never mind the chemistry text, or the chemistry quiz coming up. Old Avogadro and gram-mass; you can get through. You're not heading that way anyway. Think of it: the guy was Jewish. But she had no objection to marrying him. He did, though, *he* did: to marrying her. A Zionist. A Socialist, too. Christ, for all his freethinking, he was as bad as Zaida in that respect. Or was that an excuse? Maybe it was; it just possibly might be. But notice, marriage was important to her. Aha. Then what was going to happen to this love affair with Larry? He was ten, eleven years younger than she was. How could anything come of it? He said he wanted to marry her. But three years from now when he got his degree, he'd be twenty-two; she'd be thirty-three. So . . . so you were a liberated, vanguard bohemian; you sneered at the Babbitts and the big butter-and-egg men, you despised the middle class. But what the hell, you had to get down to earth, and Larry especially, used to the best of everything—come on, for Chrissake, do a few of the chem exercises, balance a few of the tougher equations.

Not now. . . . But she could ride a saddle horse, she said. She was quite an expert horsewoman. She rode all over those Western trails, by the Indian reservations, the hogans, she called them, into the mountains that she said changed color all the time, the shadows slipping on and off them. And she showed her two friends a poem of hers in *Poetry* magazine that Larry understood and Ira didn't. Dunce. Why didn't they write like, oh, lots, lots he understood: Aiken and A. E. Robinson and Robinson Jeffers, and Teasdale and Millay, though he wasn't crazy about them; he liked A. E. Housman better. Why did they have to hide the meaning out of sight, as if behind a screen or a hill? Once in a while he got the idea; whose poem was it like that he got the idea from long after he read it, and enjoyed his discovery? It was Robert Frost again: "I have had too much of applepicking: I am overtired of the great harvest I myself desired." And even that time Edith helped a little. She didn't know it, but she helped when she said, "You'll notice there's always a compression in rhythm at the high point of his meaning." Boy, she could tell right away.

Well. . . . It's in 2.24 liters of solution. . . . What's the normality of a phosphoric acid solution containing 270 g of H_3PO_4? . . . And Edith could—oh, no, you're given moles, moles, you donkey. So just multiply 1.3 moles by the gram weight of Na_2SO_4. . . .

IX

Edith would not be denied Ira's company, not even so she could be alone with Larry, so for yet another time, while Iola was out, the three, Edith, her young lover, and a bewildered Ira, sat in the shared living room, white-painted, airy, and spacious, its windows on the street in one direction, and in the other on the churchyard of St. Mark's-in-the-Bouwerie. So light and unencumbered the apartment was! As unobtrusively as he could, Ira tried to sort out of his surroundings those specific elements from the composite that gave an airy charm to the whole. He had never seen sheer white walls like that before. So simple, plain, with just three pictures on them, reproductions, one of crude golden flowers almost leaping out of the frame. And another of a blue farm wagon. Whose were they? And the other adornments Navajo rugs, gray, white, and black, with thick, primitive designs on them, arrowheads some seemed to be.

Over her cup of tea, held with daintiest of fingers, Edith related that there was a certain Indian tribe that had apparently vanished entirely from its abode among the forests of California. No one knew its language, no one had bothered to learn it, or study the anthropological relics of the tribe's former existence, no one except a Dr. Wasserman, professor of anthropology, under whom Edith studied at Berkeley. But lo and behold, Edith told an enthralled Larry and Ira: one member of the tribe had survived into their century. His name was Zaru. In wretched state, emaciated and dying of starvation, he had given himself up, the last wild Indian in California. He was sure the white men were going to kill him, as they had killed the other members of his tribe. He begged his astonished "captors" to slay him at once, not to torture him. But no one understood his entreaties, no one understood anything of what he was saying, laymen and trained anthropologists alike, until Dr. Wasserman was called upon. He had acquired some rudiments of the language, acquired from fragmented though still extant remnants of California Indians. From these he had compiled an elementary dictionary. Aided by it, he succeeded in communicating with the terrified, miserable aborigine (who had refused all nourishment while in the county jail, in the belief he was held there to be fattened for sacrifice). Dr. Wasserman assured Zaru that no one was going to kill him—and by persistence and by slow degrees, he won the Indian's trust, prevailed on him to take food and drink, take medications, learn something of white man's customs with regard to sanitation, wear white man's garments, and won him back a semblance of well-being, a modicum of confidence.

How had he managed to survive in such close proximity to civilized settlements? How had he succeeded in eluding detection in an area that was scarcely more than an enclave in the midst of the dreaded white man's habitations? Edith enthralled her small audience, intentionally retarding the action of her story. Hunters in search of game traversed the terrain that was Zaru's refuge, sportsmen, fishermen, campers, and forest rangers. Zaru and his sister, while she was alive, using all the ancient lore of their forefathers, had subsisted on fish and wild animals, by spearing fish, by trapping small animals, hunting wildfowl with snare and bow. Ever vigilant, ever on the alert to the presence of the white man, depending on every device of stealth and concealment that tribal childhood had inculcated in them, the two siblings had managed to evade detection and survive. Zaru had lost track of the moons and the years that had passed during his and his sister's long, furtive, unobserved existence. . . .

Time, Ira thought, to break this exposition. Yes. He pressed the F7 key. Better try it out first, the change or insertion, try out whether it was appropriate, whether it blended with material before and afterward, and then if the interpolation appealed to him, he could move it into its proper place. If not, just delete. However, the insertion about Zaru, the new departure, did appeal to him. Such were the wonders of the age of computers. Ira pressed the F7 key again. In trying to describe the many advantages the device presented its user, he had said to others, without knowing exactly what he meant—just a general notion, or perhaps because it was a handy cliché— that the word processor added a new dimension to his writing. It summoned to the writer's side a faithful and supportive friend, Ecclesias, for example. Ira smiled. Fact was, and again he invoked a semi-cliché, the device vouchsafed the writer a quantum leap in means of communication, in versatility. It enabled him to do things he could not have done otherwise, operations too formidable otherwise, beyond his skills, his patience, though he regarded himself as patient where writing was concerned, to accomplish things beyond his stamina.

Even when he was young—writing his first and only novel—he could not have done now, so reduced in vitality, what he could do then, without the assistance of this marvel of electronic technology. Panegyric was furthest from his mind when he set out to make his remarks, but if anything ever came of this long, long opus, anything worthwhile, it would be owing in large part to the work of multitudes of men and women who, without fanfare, matter-of-factly, had perfected and assembled this instrument (and continued to improve it). They were liberators of the mind. . . .

"It's really true?" Larry asked. "It seems utterly fantastic."

"Oh, no." Edith smiled fondly at her young lover. "It really did happen. In 1912. Wasserman wrote a book about it later—called *Zaru*. I think the NYU library may have a copy. It ought to, anyway."

"How long did they live that way?"

"The brother and sister? Years, I imagine. As I told you, Zaru told Wasserman he lost track of the moons. The only way he could have counted them would have been to make a mark on a stick, or something of the sort, and I don't think he was interested. Survival was the main thing."

"I was thinking," Larry said diffidently. "They call them Indians, and they're not Indians."

"No, of course not." Edith regarded him indulgently. "Anthropologists have tried many other names. 'Aborigine' is one. But there's been an objection to that. On the part of the Indians themselves in some cases, yes. It makes them feel as if they were considered some kind of wild creature. And of course they're anything but that. They have—or had—a highly developed culture. 'Native' is a good term, probably the best, certainly the most legitimate. But our one hundred percent Americans, fourth- or fifth-generation superpatriots, object. They consider themselves the only native Americans. Which is absurd. 'Amerind' is one term that's been tried."

"Tamarind," Larry chuckled. "Tamarind is a tree, isn't it?"

"Yes. I think so. I don't know what kind."

"A wooden Indian," Larry quipped.

"And about as awkward as 'Amerind,'" said Edith. "I don't believe the name will last. Do you have a name to suggest, Ira?"

"No," he said, with lingering bashfulness. "But I was thinking of 'Indigen.'"

"'Indigenous' or 'indigent'?" Larry bantered.

"It could be both."

"As in fact most Indians are," Edith commented. "It's not a bad term. Is there such a word, Ira?"

"'Indigen'? Oh, I doubt it. 'Injun.' 'Aborigine.' Something like that." With the same finger that he pointed, Ira scratched his temple.

Larry smiled at him. "Ira is like a pack rat with words. I read once how they stow away every shiny trinket in their nests."

"I'm sorry." Ira grinned in abnegation. "It happens to be true about me and words. It's a habit."

"It's not a bad one. Your feeling for words is remarkable. I've noticed that," Edith said.

"If I could only remember important things the same way that I remember words. You know, practical things, useful matters, the way Larry does. But I don't."

"His sister died," Larry prompted. "I suppose it was sheer loneliness that drove him out of hiding."

"And hunger. Imagine the terrible ordeal of trying to survive, survive and hide, in a constantly shrinking living space. Oh, I'm sure he wanted to die."

"I wonder how long he had been alone."

"Many moons. Again many moons. Just as he said he and his sister had been together."

"Is that so."

Many moons, Ira meditated. Zaru and his sister had apparently lived a number of years together evading the white man. . . .

And at night, with Minnie beside him, the listening Ira became grim with fantasy, fantasy so close to his reality—and who knew, similar to that of the primitive siblings—they wouldn't dare build a campfire in their woodland covert, but he would have reached out and felt for her cunt. And she would have understood. It was the only pleasure they had. What else were they going to do? He'd slap her if she didn't submit. To whom was she going to complain? The white man? Besides, that was *her* only pleasure, too. Maybe she'd ask for it, the way Minnie did sometimes when she was younger: stick out her round white ass from under the covers—only Zaru's sister's would be brown. But what if he knocked her up? Jesus, you couldn't just leave the kid bawling in the woods. Poor naked little bastard. Who the hell would have had the heart to abandon the newborn infant? And somebody might find it, too. Then you'd have to kill it, bury it? Jesus, no. Maybe they knew native contraceptives, native scumbags. Or just get out a second before you came, left some of that "white stuff," Minnie called it, semen, and gave her a kid. Still, the goddamn Canaanites killed their kids, their firstborn. Lucky Edith and Larry didn't know what he was thinking about; how could they? Every night a chance to fuck your sister. Would you ever get tired of it? Among the trees in the forest, all quiet and bosky, only "O-o-h, o-o-h," beneath the green boughs, "I'm getting that good feeling! W-o-o-h!" crescendoing the first time she got it. And ear cocked, always cocked for that sonofabitch white man tramping through the woods, maybe just when you were coming—or she was. Jesus Christ, it wouldn't be so different, would it? As when he humped Minnie, always in dread of Mom or Pop; or if the airshaft window was open, afraid the two might be heard upstairs or downstairs? Yes. Or panic of Mamie in the kitchen, Mamie just around the hall when he was dandling Stella on his dick—oh, poor Mom; telling Uncle Louis she yearned and burned at three o'clock in the morning for Moe, Moe and his pillar of meat—"Look what I've got here, Leah"—alone with him, while Pop was making his rounds delivering milk. Husky Moe snoring, Mom yearning, *Es hot mir gefelte libe,* while little Pop, all by himself, crossed the low walls between tenement roofs at night, low walls topped by brown, glazed ceramic hoods. Oh, Ira knew rooftops well. . . . Sacrifice a newborn infant, but you can't screw your sister. Sinful, sinful. But he had broken through that barrier, broken through religion or taboo, or whatever it was. Before he knew it, he had broken through it. And paid, and paid, and—cut it out. Listen to what she was telling them, listen attentively, the way Larry did. Get everything else out of your mind. Ask her if Zaru and his sister ever cooked anything. . . .

When a lowered window shade happened spontaneously to snap free and roll itself up, the way window shades sometimes did, as if on a hair trigger, Zaru had averred, "Great magic."

Nothing else in the white man's world impressed Zaru. But he was awed by the skittish window shade. "Great magic!" Dr. Wasserman had gained international fame by publishing an account of Zaru's adjustment to twentieth-century civilization. Edith herself was so intrigued that she decided to take a course in anthropology with him. Then followed the most personal revelation of any she had made so far or as yet. One evening, during a field trip under the guidance of the same Professor Wasserman, she had been invited by him to stroll away from the campfire where the rest of his students were taking their ease, and as soon as they had walked beyond earshot of the others, he had virtually raped her. "I fought him off," Edith said. "But he knew just what to do to make me surrender. . . ." And poor Larry flinched at her explicitness.

Edith spoke with the two young men so intimately, with so little hesitation, it made Ira shrink. If he were to confess so about his family, what would be *their* reaction? But he listened, continuing to compose his portrait of her, of the life and its struggles this girlish Ph.D. had endured.

X

What a glorious silver ring Larry sported!

Edith had written her aunt in Silver City describing the kind of ring she wanted, and the finger size—large—and asked her aunt to buy the ring and send it to New York. Made by a Navajo craftsman from a silver dollar, an erstwhile "cartwheel" as silver dollars were called, it formed the setting for a chunk of glossy, mottled turquoise. Bold and solid, the ring just fit on the pinkie of Larry's big hand, and because it was on his pinkie, the ring seemed even bolder and more solid. And boy, was it beautiful!

Ira had never before seen anything so distinguished, so rare. What was gold, what were diamonds in comparison? Even platinum seemed a platitude. Anybody who hoarded up enough money could buy items of that kind; every jewelry store sold them. But this—Ira was bewitched. Not envious, though full of longing. Ah, to be the object of such affection, to be worthy of such a gift! It spoke of New Mexico, that far-off place from which Edith came. It spoke of open spaces, amplitude, of leisurely stances, of solitudes, of generous feelings—it called for rare perceptions that appreciated silver fashioned by an Indian artisan, perceptions that prized the unique artisanship more than standardized gems of gold, that esteemed the modest, elusive color of turquoise more than glittering diamonds. You had to change, you had to change and try to come close to her—her values: to learn to recognize artistry cultivated in the most unlikely places, adapting to the humblest materials. You had to learn to feel the aura of the created artifact. What a beautiful ring!

But what a *tummel,* a tumult, it stirred up in Larry's family when they saw the ring on his finger. They tried to dissemble their worry and disapproval when Ira was present, though he knew they were convinced he was in league. He could feel their dissatisfaction with him, their unhappy reproach. He secretly supported Larry, yes, but he was just a follower, an acolyte of sorts. He hadn't connived with Larry; he hadn't inveigled him to give up dentistry and enter upon a literary career. What did he have to do with Larry's falling in love with Edith? He was just a bystander, at most a confidant, willing, yes, but hardly more than that.

Sure, he was secretly happy Larry had made up his mind to switch from NYU to CCNY in the fall of 1925—who wouldn't want his pal to be in the same college? But Larry wasn't going to CCNY so the two would be together; he was going to CCNY in order to become more independent of his parents. He no longer would need to turn to them to pay his tuition to college. CCNY required no tuition. All he asked of them, at present, so it seemed, was just to furnish him with room and board. He could get enough money for the year, spending money, and cash for incidental expenses, and supply himself with a few clothes too, by drawing on his small legacy, and by working during the summer vacation. Avoid working for his brother Irving as housedress salesman, avoid practically all dependency on his family. His best bet this coming summer, better than being a counselor at a boys' camp, was to do something that paid a great deal more, and suited his temperament and talents to a tee: become an entertainer on the staff of a large borscht-circuit summer resort.

That would really be the most congenial job he could think of. He had a natural flair for acting, for thinking up skits, for the role of a stand-up raconteur—cracking jokes, hamming it up. Failing that, he might even earn as much in pay and tips as a singing waiter. The tips were good, and he had a good voice. He could hold a tune. He could read music. Not only would he come home with a tidy sum, but a singing waiter's job would provide an excellent avenue to the summer resort entertainment world. Perhaps more than that. With a little experience, versatility garnered on the borscht circuit, he could make the next step—to the world of the stage, to the world of entertainment in general, the theater. No question: that was his best bet for loosening his ties with his family, for gaining the kind of freedom he needed for a new career. He had friends and connections in the resort business, in the entertainment business. All he needed to do was to cultivate a few whom he had more or less avoided in the past. He had already told Ira about them. They would welcome overtures, welcome his initiatives of cordial relations. They were bores, but what the hell. Exploit them. Spend a little time with them. He could stand it for the sake of achieving a larger goal, promoting his future. Make a few phone calls, accept a few dinner invitations, take the daughter of somebody he knew who owned a famous Jewish resort to a dance. And if all his finagling failed, then, as he said before, he could certainly get a singing waiter's job. Not first choice, but a sure way of getting the next-best returns out of the summer. Anyway, he'd better begin action at once, make inquiries, follow up leads, land some kind of a well-paying job.

Ira approved. Although an entertainer's job or a singing waiter's job would not have been the kind he would have sought, that was only because he didn't have Larry's gifts. A more menial job, a *shlepper's* job, was more in keeping with his aptitudes—and his inclinations too, for that matter. He had no talent. But the type of job or position that Larry secured wasn't the important thing right now; the important thing was that Larry was going to use it to break his dependence on his family, break the mutually sentimental hold of family, widen the cleavage between them.

That was exactly how his family perceived his actions. When he announced his intention to get a job that would keep him away from home for most of the summer, the Gordons were deeply disturbed. Under other circumstances, without their son's obvious infatuation with a woman ten or eleven years his senior, and a gentile at that, without his apparent determination to carry the love affair, the liaison, all the way to marriage, they would have reacted altogether differently. They were accustomed to Larry's absence for long periods of time with his Bermuda uncle. But now they interpreted Larry's effort as exactly what it was: a definite signal of his decision to sever connections with his family. Perhaps leave them, quit the household, when he returned. And horrors, perhaps marry Edith when he returned. Assure them to the contrary though he might, that he wasn't planning anything so drastic at present, they were convinced that was his purpose, to enter on a preliminary stage of a road that would ultimately lead to his perdition. Such a handsome, gifted nineteen-year-old youth married to someone bound to become an old crone in a few years, bound to look like one in a few years: in her forties when he was still in his twenties. (*An alte klyafte,* an old virago, Mom would have said, but the Gordons didn't know any Yiddish.) He could have had young heiresses at his beck and call, a worldly, polished youth like Larry, exceedingly handsome, and with a bit of English accent to enhance his charm—so Larry reported them as saying—young heiresses, daughters of elite German Jewish families, millionaires, leading merchants and financiers. Even if they weren't heiresses, no, even if they weren't Jewish, at least someone near his own age; they didn't have to be beauties. At least young. Madness, his father burst out, sheer madness, what Larry planned to do. And she, meaning Edith, was to blame too, his mother accused, and the sisters concurred.

"At which I got hot under the collar," Larry added. "Especially when my officious sister Irma suggested that maybe Sam, being a lawyer, ought to go see Edith and talk things over with her. I told them flatly it was none of their business."

Edith, Larry had already let it be known emphatically, Edith would be gone for most of the summer. She had already made arrangements to travel to Europe, so his getting a job as entertainer

or singing waiter was no subterfuge for going to live with her, or elop-
ing, or whatever lurid imaginings they might have (and they did indeed seem to have them, if Larry's report of their behavior was any
indication: they sometimes seemed beside themselves, especially his
father). It was just a summer job, he kept insisting, a job, not an overture to disaster.

Much to his surprise, Sam agreed with him. Intensifying their opposition to the youth's love affair might only drive the two lovers together, so Larry gathered from hints dropped by Irma, and from
pumping their Hungarian serving woman, with whom he was a favorite. Getting a B.A. from CCNY was not the worst thing that could
happen to Larry, was the gist of Sam's argument. Sam had gotten his
B.A. there too, and gone on to be a lawyer. And who knew what
would happen in three years, the changes that might take place in
the youth—and in her, Edith? After all, she was an intelligent
woman; she could foresee the consequences of the disparity in their
ages a few years hence. Larry might even recognize the wisdom of
eventually getting his degree in dentistry. Their best policy, Sam
urged, would be a sort of truce. Let Larry have his way. He was head
over heels in love at the present. In time he might come to his senses.
Or *she* might. There were always those possibilities. *Laissez-faire.* . . .

They adopted Sam's counsel, but with little grace. They continued to simmer beneath the surface, barely suppressing their opposition to the course Larry was committed to taking. And worst of all, as
far as Ira was concerned, a by-product of their resentment of Larry's
flouting of their convictions of what was in his best interest, they believed Ira had a hand in his friend's disastrous design. They believed
he had helped Larry concoct the scheme. Or if not that, then by his
own pauperish example, his indifference to commercial and financial matters, his lack of ambition, he had undermined Larry's healthy
practicality concerning things material, led Larry astray. Ira no
longer felt welcome at the home of the Gordons. In his reluctance to
meet Larry there, unless Larry's relatives were absent, he declined
supper invitations, frankly proposed meetings elsewhere, sometimes
in a cafeteria, sometimes in Washington Square Park.

And when Larry, after his very first interview—with the manager
of Copake Lodge in the Catskill Mountains—was informed that the

management had already filled its quota of entertainers, but was offered a singing waiter job, even though, as the manager remarked, Larry was bumping someone else more or less assured of the same job, he accepted the offer immediately. At Larry's earnest importuning, Ira attended a sort of farewell reunion for his friend before he departed for the resort. Cordiality toward him had vanished almost entirely from the Gordons' reception. Mere recognition, something akin to sufferance, was all they vouchsafed.

And yet, oddly enough, though Ira could protest with good semblance of faith that he had nothing to do with Larry's change of career, Ira still felt a recurring sense of guilt, a fuzzy culpability that told him he deserved the ill-disguised censure emanating toward him from Larry's close relatives. He felt that in some obscure way he was influencing Larry, subverting his will. It went even further than that in Ira's untrammeled imagination: he deserved the censure of Larry's folks for helping mislead one they doted on, because he not only approved all Larry did but, like an understudy, conned all Larry did. It was all very strange. And confused. Yes, he felt guilty. No, he had nothing to do with it. Yes, he was taking advantage of his friend—he had always taken advantage of his friend, using him. But how the hell could it be otherwise? His friend had wanted him involved.

Long were the dialogues he audited in Edith's apartment. (And again, why should he have been there? Why did they both want him there?) They were dialogues he rarely entered into, not at the beginning certainly. They were dialogues he barely understood at first, he only slowly, slowly grasped their import, their abstract assumptions, which he could only do by filling them with specific references and examples: the Middle Class. Their values. The Middle Class, their materialism, their emphasis on acquisition, their striving for material things: for mink coats, for the latest in Grand Rapids furniture, for prestigious addresses. (Jesus, didn't they know what 119th Street was all about? Didn't everybody want to climb out of those cold-water slums?) The Middle Class, their abject subservience to convention, to keeping up with the Joneses. The Middle Class and their stifling of the Artist, or even the Artiste. Ah, that was their worst offense: in their demand for conformity they allowed the Artist no latitude; they condemned him to mediocrity. The Artist had to be free to express himself, and especially to give vent to his disillusionment with hollow Middle-Class standards, Middle-Class pretensions to morality, Middle-Class hypocrisy, shams, crassness. And ever and again, these faults and woeful shortcomings, these constraints and impediments were exemplified by the Gordons—Edith continually warned about the dangers inherent in Larry's family for him, the snares and temptations they would place in his way, their appeals to family loyalty, to his natural tenderness. On and on.

But what should he do? Larry asked. He had already taken the first step to oppose them. Next fall: CCNY. What else, what next? It was up to him, Edith said: it would depend on how provoked his family might become by the new direction he had taken, and how unpleasant their opposition to the change might be: the pressure of disapprobation on him personally, as well as the enticements they would put in his way. They had already shown their hand by their offer to send him to Bermuda to stay with his uncle till the next academic year, and afterward attend Columbia University. But she was always ready to help, should he decide to sever all ties: to pay rent for a room, to see that he had enough to eat, subsidize his attendance at CCNY—

Oh, no, he could take care of that, Larry immediately assured her. He had the salesman's knack, he could sell, after school. He could get a part-time job anytime. Action on so drastic a break with his folks could be deferred. Transition could and should be more gradual. He had to consider his father's condition, especially. After all, his folks did have his welfare at heart, however mistakenly they perceived that welfare. He owed them a gradual transition. Let them see that he could get a bachelor's degree at CCNY (as she too had recommended), even though in preparation not for the profession of dentistry, but for a writing career. And first and foremost he meant to accustom them to his attending CCNY while he lived at home; that would appease their anxiety. Another year, he might take the next step, move into a small apartment, and they might be reconciled to it. Edith agreed. It would be unnecessarily cruel to his parents to quit NYU, renounce a professional career, and leave home all at one and the same time; it would cause unnecessary distress, to his parents and to his close kin.

It was all very stirring, full of dark assessments and pending adventure, prediction and suspense. Intriguing, engrossing promises of exhilarating future that had the power in a moment to preempt for Ira any assignment in any subject—and even classroom instruction. "You began the term by doing A work." Pedantic, precise Dr. Laine, professor of French, raised his fine, delicately pastel features from his recitation grade book and cautioned Ira with chiseled words. "You've slipped very badly of late."

XI

Edith had been instrumental in securing an instructor's position at NYU for Iola Reid. She was taller than Edith, and because she was so slender and willowy, she looked quite statuesque. Just turned thirty, like Edith, Scandinavian in origin and appearance, Iola had straw-colored blond hair, which she wore in a tightly bound braid around her head. Her face was thin, her nose too, and barely saved from prominence by the general air of cultivation her countenance conveyed. And she wore, almost invariably, a green costume or green accessory (as against Edith's wide spectrum of colors); green dress, green earrings, green pendants.

All kinds of fascinating flecks of information pertained to her past, in one case sensational. All of them were divulged by Edith in matter-of-fact tones to her young lover and his friend (to their great wonder every now and then). Iola had been brought up with her brothers and sisters on a potato farm in Idaho. She was the oldest of the siblings, and after her mother died, the widowed father, either in fury or sexual furor, chased his daughter with an ax over the fields. Iola still dreamt of the terrible episode, and awoke at night screaming.

She was to all intents and purposes engaged to a Rhodes scholar, Richard Scofield, presently studying for his master's degree in English literature at Oxford. Oxford, hoary with tradition, epitome of cloistered scholarship, fraught with awesome prestige! Oxford! Could anything sound more utterly entrancing? Olympian, Jesus. Maybe that's what he had once dreamed CCNY would be like. Edith described Richard as extraordinarily polished, charming, and handsome. While on a visit to Paris, he had been raped by a homosexual friend in a taxicab. Raped by a homosexual in a taxicab? A grown man? Not the nine- or ten-year-old urchin *he* was when that rusty sonofabitch had lured him to Fort Tryon Park. And as if in answer to Ira's thoughts, Edith implied that perhaps the episode had not been altogether a rape—that Richard, she had reason to believe, leaned, ever so slightly, in that direction. "Bisexual" was the term she used. "Bisexual," that new term for Ira. John Vernon, her faculty cosponsor of the Arts Club, and an avowed homosexual (though he had been married), was "licking his chops," said Edith, waiting for Richard to return. And the whole affair, John Vernon's interest in Richard, and the episode in Paris, had naturally given Iola grave misgivings, distressed her with incertitude as to whether she could truly count on Richard to go through with his pledge of marriage.

What tiny, tiny inflections of tone entered Edith's recital of all this, so barely perceptible that Ira could imagine afterward that he had only heard his own suspicions, hearkened to his own suspect promptings. No, Edith couldn't possibly allow even a word of her account to dip into envy; she was too good, too kind; she was above finding relish in the possibility of Iola's hopes going astray. Maybe they *were* going astray; who knew? Why did he get the idea that Iola was deliberately fostering some kind of symmetry with regard to himself, symmetry, vis-à-vis Edith, to counterbalance Edith's affair with Larry? Ira felt a tug of enticement, albeit discreet, a tug of rivalry, a cool inducement to be her squire. And those private, faint signals, hints of incipient archness, that enlisted him into alliance, not of derision for the other couple, but of calm detachment, maybe imperceptible gravitation in the direction of her orbit. . . . Perhaps if he weren't so obtuse, and mistrustful of himself, he might have seen through Edith's sangfroid, accorded due significance to those millimicron signals, as Ivan, the physics whiz, would have called them, that she transmitted. But boy, would he make a dumbo of himself if he was wrong. And wrong he surely was. What else? And do what, anyway? Edith had already told him and Larry that after Iola's father had chased her, she became frigid, lost all interest in sex. So what did he think? That she was like Stella, ready to yield at a touch? Or like Minnie, with a little wheedling, lewd arousing—flap his hard-on with a rubber on it, ready to go? Or was Edith just getting back at Iola, because Iola envied Edith's growing reputation at the university, as Edith claimed, because Dr. Watt was very favorably impressed with the syllabus of her modern poetry course, and with the large body of students who attended her lectures? Or worse: Iola, Edith said, was jealous of her love affair, her infatuation, as Iola egregiously referred to it, with her freshman lover.

Look at that: Ph.D.s both, and they behaved almost like anybody else when they envied or were jealous of each other. Almost like everybody else, except their grudges were honed so fine, they hurt without lacerating, unlike the way Jews volleyed their grudges about, as did other tenement denizens on 119th Street. No, the edges of polite grudges were so fine, you had to be warned they could wound, you had to be told afterward they *had* wounded. Ira could hardly recognize the edges himself. Would he ever? Or was he wrong? All he felt sometimes in the exchanges between the two women was just a kind of—a faint rumor. . . . Was that the way you knew? It might have come out of your own head—

No, he had gone astray. . . .

Ira had poked about for causes all that afternoon and evening, dully, spiritlessly, like a blind man rummaging, only worse, hopelessly, as though the bottom had dropped out of his purpose, left him without any élan, any direction.

"I've suddenly lost all my zing," he confessed to M, his steadfast M, always so quick to console.

Oh, he recognized the symptoms of his malaise, although that did little good, symptoms of the sudden onset of acute depression. Old story. And yet, he wasn't quite sure, wasn't quite sure he hadn't brought the condition on himself. He had locked himself out, or rather in, painted himself into a corner, as they said: the corner of solipsism. He had oversimplified himself, for one thing; he wasn't that much of a simpleton—and moreover, he would be repeating that obtuseness leitmotif later on. But mostly the fault was, the blockade was, solipsism: it wasn't what *he* felt at this junction that was of primary consideration; it was what Larry felt or did, and was going through. Ira had lost sight of that. He knew he had to continue the tale, but in his need to portray his own sensations and emotions, he had almost forgotten those sharp, those acrid moments of quarrel that broke out between Larry and his family: over his staying out late or his staying out overnight, over his losing weight, his emaciation. All this, even before he announced that he intended to abort his career as dentist, devote himself to poetry and to writing. Those were the important things, those sudden and embarrassing eruptions of scolding and upbraiding by his parents or sisters—all three sisters—at family gatherings—and Larry's own irate and desperate rejoinders.

For it was true that to such a pitch had differences reached between Larry and his immediate kin that for a while Ira feared that *their* passionate concern for *Larry's* welfare, their furious resentment of Edith, might lead to *her* undoing. They might complain about her behavior to the head of the English department, Dr. Watt. They might excoriate her disgraceful carrying-on with a freshman. Exposing her love affair with Larry might lead to her termination from NYU, might ruin her chances for college teaching positions elsewhere. That Larry's family never did any of these things was to their credit. They also probably reasoned that there were other approaches to the problem, that time might be on their side, just as Sam advised.

He had quit. He was stuporous, and he slept; the miserable day had passed. Something else he had wanted to interpolate, but it had been forgotten, and the omission irked him now. Where was that goddamn ballpoint, or his alertness now to satisfy the need for making a memo of these volatile ideas, if such they could be called? He slept, awoke, went for a two-block walk along Manhattan Street, north of the mobile home court. Two blocks in one direction marked the limit of his present pedestrian boundary; retracing his steps made four blocks in all.

He mused about Israel, his people of Israel. Their almost forty years of statehood had forged them into a nation; they would never give up being one, even if it took atomic weapons to defend—and if possibly they would be destroyed in retaliation. And yet that was the world problem that had to be resolved, the problem on which the future of humanity pivoted. They had built a society with their own hands. The Israelis were different from the Crusaders, he mused. And his gloomy certainties were reinforced later, when he and M read their nightly paragraph or two from their Hebrew reader recounting the adventures and mishaps of one Shulim making *aliyah,* his privations and travails even getting to Eretz Israel, and once there the blood and sweat expended, the monsoons endured, the skin cracked by the heat, and the lives taken by malaria. Surrender it? Nothing doing. And then to read in the evening a Xerox out of the *New York Times* sent them by Barney B, about the movie Claude Lanzmann had made, monumental in scope—nine and a half hours in duration!—of the Holocaust, *ha-Sho'ah.* Never, never, never! And before bedtime, adjusting electronic watches, his and M's, from daylight saving to standard time, listening to the last of his tapes. Life without purpose, without writing, without re-creating toward some end or design, was simply unbearable. (Oh, and perhaps that was what he had had in mind and forgotten: today's frustration made for tomorrow's resolution. But at the moment the adage was devoid of comfort.)

So . . . proceed. He had said enough of his failure. He must reenter the stream, and with something merry, at last. . . .

That evening Larry and he had gotten rid of the crowd of Edith's modern poetry students, whom she had invited to attend the cookie and coffee soirée, by pulling a ruse, one right out of Robert Louis Stevenson, whimsical and daring. After winking at Ira to follow his lead, and with a great flourish that called the attention of all the young guests, Larry announced with just the right tone of authority that the hour had come when propriety called for departure. With apologies for having overstayed their welcome, he and Ira wriggled into their topcoats, waved their hats—and shamed the others into following their example and taking their leave. The trick was as old as the dawn of urban life, no doubt, but it worked. It terminated Percey's spouting about e.e. cummings and lured everyone out of the apartment into the dark, cool street. Larry declined the sensible route of the others, in the direction of the subway, but chose an incomprehensible one, on pretext of a belated engagement, and bade

the others a resolute farewell. Thereupon the two conspirators circled the block—and back to the apartment, which they reentered
with great laughter and gaiety. Ah, what a master stratagem!

And afterward, when he finally parted company with Larry, who
took the 42nd Street shuttle to the West Side, parted with such camaraderie and joy, the ride home was nothing short of rapturous: to
Lexington and 116th Street, and then treading on air to the stoop
steps of dismal tenement, up the ill-lit, bleary stairs, into the bleak
kitchen. And Mom and Pop in bed and . . . in her folding cot beside
them, Minnie asleep too, asleep, unapproachable, out of reach . . .
just as well, despite regret and flicker of craving. Gave him a chance
to meditate on True Love. He, alone, sitting at the round table with
the green oilcloth on it, in the silent, empty kitchen, to feel the transfiguring power of True Love! True Love that swamped Ira with glamour, hovered above the eyes in a rare twilight of tender ardor,
through which the roach crept over the scuffed linoleum for refuge
under the rosy apron that hung about the sink, crept on an oblique
mission on a strange geodesic.

But it's all screwed up for you, pal: the right words, screwed up—and how
to keep solipsism at bay, Ecclesias, when the snail of tomorrow, of Sunday
morning, left his tacky track on tonight's glorious reverie? Heh?

Yeah . . . It sat there like a rock . . . with its mind vitiated, like the mind
of a rock, if it had one, in the silent, bleak kitchen with the tired-white window blind drawn. . . .

How could he re-create it all? Ira mused. How could he re-create it,
limited by his own modest gifts and talents?—there would have had to
have been talents as inexhaustible as Shakespeare's to do justice to the re-
creation. Endowed with something more finite, such a one as he must
speak or write.

Finals in a month and May drawing to a close; Larry's departure for
Copake Lodge as soon as finals were over; Edith's Pullman tickets al-

ready bought for her imminent trip to California and New Mexico. The imminence of summer of 1925.

XII

Dulcet the air, and youth expansive. Expectations chromatic. Even in slum squalor, even in academic disaster, even in woeful gratifications, haunting depravity—despite all that, the waning weeks of spring could still infuse the nineteen-year-old with the preciousness of being alive, summon up, single out, enshrine the euphoria of the moment.

It was on a Sunday morning in late May. Yes, a Sunday morning just after dawn, before Mom went shopping on Park Avenue, and the provisions for the occasion already bought the night before, Edith and Iola and their two escorts, Larry and Ira, took the Hudson River excursion steamer to Bear Mountain. Amid the eager crowd of other excursionists, the four boarded the broad-beamed white paddle-wheeler, the *Henry Hudson*, and found four deck chairs on the open, agreeably breezy upper deck. Fair and lightsome the springtime zephyr met them as the boat churned away from its pier, a nimble breeze that brought the hands of the two women to the throats of their open collars, to the brims of their rakish straw hats. Edith's was edged with a black stuff of some kind, Iola's with jade velveteen. It was something to take note of, Ira impressed on himself again, that blond ladies favored green. Stella, too? He hadn't noticed. Forget it.

They sat facing the Palisades, the New Jersey side of the river broadening away in ripples beyond the railings. Quickened by the fresh, free-roving air, by the innocent, the safe novelty of the journey, one and all reveled at the sight of ever-changing, gliding, tree-lined shores. Meanwhile the vessel made headway against current upstream, leaving a creamy wake in the green water, the bow sending a never-ending small surf before it. It was all so lovely in weather that was flawless, under a sky without a cloud. Ira had never been so conscious of the sheer bliss of a perfect day. Smoothly the steamer traveled on, from tidal to fresh water, from banks that had been a mile apart to banks separated by only a few hundred rods. Euphoria savored both time and distance, would have extended both indefinitely, interchanged them both within the steady churning of paddle wheels impelling the excursion boat up the river.

After a sail of over two hours, they reached Bear Mountain, the other terminus. They disembarked, climbed up the slope until they found a shady place by themselves under a cluster of trees. They spread the blanket Larry had brought along, brought the sandwiches and the thermos bottle of iced tea out of the basket, and picnicked. The day was full of gladness and regret, gladness that sharpened regret, regret that thrust gladness into greater relief. For Ira, gladness at being there, being privileged to participate in traditional, innocent, untroubled diversion, to practice refinement, to spend a day in the company of two cultivated women, to share rare contentment with them, and note how they enjoyed nature, the outdoors, the warm, balmy air, sunlight and leafy shade, lolling, serving sandwiches, pouring tea from the quart thermos bottle. And regret at his naïveté, his nineteen-year-old bashfulness, his nineteen-year-old assessment of propriety, his callow assessment of what others would like or dislike—of what risks he ran in their opinion of him in his expressions of opinion, his reactions. . . .

I become mute here, Ecclesias, I become inert, suspended and still. For I am transported backward in time a total of sixty years. And though I now think I know what to do, what to expect, to recognize signal and interpret message, in a word, how to behave, time has long since embalmed the one who would have profited by all this.

—You bear within you a sort of edified mummy, is that what you're saying? Aren't all your memories that? Even those of a quarter of an hour ago?

I suppose so. Some I bear within me, blithely, some few. This is one of them.

—Most, it would seem, rather than bear within you, you have to bear. True. In this instance it would seem we chose the right place to picnic. —My felicitations.

Mom had prepared sandwiches early that morning for Ira to take along as his contribution to the spread—sandwiches, by the way, that in a flush of boldness—or rashness—of audacious gustatory sortie, he had himself asked Mom to buy the ingredients for the previous night, and to make early the next morning: fine Jewish salami, thickly sliced, to be sandwiched between fresh bulkies. She had obliged; she understood, and was impressed, as was Minnie, by how splendid and special the occasion was. Mom had everything in readiness even before Ira was awake. She packed the sandwiches in a brown paper bag while he had breakfast; they were waiting for him on the oilcloth-covered washtub lids when he kissed Mom goodbye and took his leave. With four bulkies, sandwiches in a brown paper bag, he skipped down the shabby stairs, spryly traversed the drab hallway, past the dented letter boxes, to the stoop. Into the quiet, grubby street. And with resilient, youthful stride, he hurried to the subway.

Redolence of salami, garlic redolence, in the subway train, garlic redolence trailing downtown from station to station, until he got off, got off, climbed up, with nascent dubiety, to the street. Redolence of salami, garlic redolence, environed him as he walked west to the Hudson River. And stronger and stronger, as the morning grew warmer—or he imagined—the nearer he approached the rendezvous, garlic redolence. The more he sniffed the paper bag, the more worried he became, the more the contents assaulted and alarmed his nostrils. Jewish immigrant boor, he was certain to be judged, slum, Jewish boor. He had blatantly violated the most elementary rules of etiquette: no one but a gross numskull, an ignorant chump, would outrage the delicate palates of two such well-bred ladies by offering them food that reeked of garlic to high heaven. Fortunately, he arrived at the dockside before the others.

That gave him his chance, his one and only chance. As swiftly as he could, he hurried toward one side of the pier, found open water between pier and bow of the excursion steamer, and tossed bag and contents into the river. Gone was the garlic, gone the redolence. What a relief!

Tell me, is this the place for regrets, Ecclesias?

—You might say it's the place for everything: regrets, confessions, confusions, despondence, and elation.

Because it occurred to me, Ecclesias, and not for the first time, occurred to me in my pusillanimity, that as Larry lay outstretched beside his love, why should not the incipient symmetry prevail, and I lie at ease likewise beside Iola?

—In the first place, it doesn't work that way. And in the second place, even if the example of your chum and Edith transmitted the same kind of prompting for Iola as it did for you, say, to the level of acquiescence, what then? You were already disabled.

It's very kind of you to be so explicit.

—No trouble at all, old chap. You were already incapacitated as far as passing encounters with mature women were concerned. Is that the truth or not? With women like Iola, for example. You lived, or comported yourself, in a fantasy world with respect to them, and were incapable of realizing your fantasies. And why? Because you were incapacitated, as I say: frightened, timid, puerile. I venture to surmise that your imaginary scenario, as they term it today, might indeed have had some basis in fact: that, acting on the incentive Iola seemed to proffer, the hints of inducement she seemed to waft your way, in all likelihood because of your puerility, had you not been so disabled, had you been another type of individual—masculine, virile, self-confident—your guess would have proved right, fancy might have materialized into event. Offer to stroll with her along the path through the woods round about (a velleity that guttered in your mind, and guttered out, all but stillborn). I imagine that because as she perceived you, you offered no threat, she would have accepted your invitation. It's a matter of intuition, of course, of surmise.

Nevertheless it coincides with yours. And not so farfetched, considering she was a woman, a human being, who had taken no vows of celibacy, a young woman of thirty, who had foregone sex for over a year, if not much longer, and was living with a woman who was enjoying its pleasures, or seeming to. Pretend you had the courage you lacked; summon up lost directness, conceive of yourself as the young Steve V, of later acquaintance: "Iola, let's leave these two lovers to themselves, and stroll among the leafy groves."

—So what if the other two had guessed your motives? There was nothing unnatural about them; nor would the guess necessarily have predicted the outcome: an innocent stroll was all that might have eventuated. . . . But, say that while strolling you took her hand. That was enough to tell you. And what would you have done had she returned the pressure of your hand in kind? What should you have done? Oh, you know now, you know now, decades and generations later. What would she have done with that narrow straw hat with the jade lining, uncovering the flaxen braids? Your jacket, the oaten one that had been Larry's, worn so much now, the creases on the inner side of the arm, creases opposite the elbow, had become permanent—Larry's jacket your improvised couch. But you didn't do anything of the sort, did you?

No, I didn't. I didn't come back from the walk, with the reverse of the well-known limerick, of the lady inside the tiger, that is, I having been inside the lady, come back with the leaves and weeds brushed from my kasha jacket, and looking bland and introspective, as if I had encountered only the vines and brambles of a hillside. No, I did not.

—Impeccable, slum Prufrock, conforming outwardly, and so faultlessly, to the correct, the virtuous paragon.

The conformation was pathetic; it was all that was left me, and you know it.

—Well, granted. So you're marooned on barren strands of fancy: desiring this man's gift and that man's scope. Too bad: Your *de rigueur* was *mortis*.

Indeed. How often I've thought, had it been Stella, had it been Minnie, the merest suggestion, an unspoken sign, had been sufficient. I did the same thing with another woman later. . . .

—We waste our time. You cast the salami and bulkies into the river, and they come back to you, not after many days, but in a few hours. During picnic time, still remorseful at the enormity of your throwing away good food, compounded by a new sense of how wrong, how distorted, was your view of refinement, as if politeness were shorn of naturalness, shorn of appetite, eschewed variety, piquancy, you confessed to the deed. And how roundly you were reproved by the others, were you not? By Iola in particular. She was terribly fond of Jewish salami, she said. She loved the savor and the consistency; it was so pungent and substantial. Oh, why had you done it!

Yes, why?

—Unkind of me to say so, I suppose, but sometimes your yearning to undo the done becomes very wearing. What it all amounts to is that had you been a man, you might have copulated with her—

Copulated, hell! Had I been a man I would have fucked her. Fucked her, else what's a word processor for? Fucked her, though the quasars at the utter bourne of the universe blushed twice their red shift; fornicated avidly, extemporaneously and ignobly. Do you know what "ignoble" sounds like in Yiddish? Its kindred sound is *knubl,* Yiddish for garlic, that I pitched into the river of my life, together with all the earthiness that was my birthright—

—Let's not go off the deep end, let's not storm, advert to coarseness, teeter over the brink of coherence. The fact is: had you been a man you would not have been there.

More than a little astonished with himself, Ira sat with fingers clasped, gazing at the vase-shaped base of the lamp on top of his computer. The "vase" was metal, brass-coated, imitation brass in other words, but it served its purpose, illuminated his keyboard. In the excitement of the fable, of attempting to produce a literary clone of reality, he noticed that he had neglected to set his small electronic timer (which he always set at 33:33) that warned him it was time to SAVE. He pressed none too soon the rubbery buttons that summoned the usual digits into place. "But now that I have become a man," the words of Saint Paul intruded without preface, "I have put away childish things." Aye, and wasn't it time?

Ah, such a perfect day! For Larry, it must have been felicity itself. And whatever regrets Ira may have felt, for him too it would remain a day full of light and tranquillity. At the warning hoot of the excursion steamer's boat whistle, they gathered their belongings. They sighed in agreement at Edith's remark, that the enjoyment of time was at the cost of time, and Iola adding that fortunately that was also true of misery, they walked down the hill to where the paddle wheeler was moored, where they embarked. They watched the river become wider as they returned to New York, passed the little dock of the boathouse, Ira reminiscing about days paddling the canoe with Billy Green.

When at length the excursion was over, and the steamer moored once more at its pier in Manhattan, Larry and Ira escorted the two women by crosstown trolley and subway to their apartment on St. Mark's Place. Daylight still held sway. The two youths were invited in. Once settled, everyone was ready for a snack again. The two women served them coffee and raisin toast. Coffee and raisin toast. Raisin toast. Bread with raisins in it, not cake, just bread. And because the weather was too warm for cream to keep on the window ledge—and there was no canned milk in the cupboard—for the first time in his life Ira drank black coffee. How strange it tasted without simmered milk, as at home, often with the skim on it, esoteric and yet not unpleasant. And for the first time in his life he ate raisin toast, sprinkled with brown sugar and cinnamon. It was good. Last of afternoon daylight still shone on the white walls of Iola's half of the apartment, daylight that illuminated Edith's olive skin and dark hair with its elusive glint of copper.

Discussion arose whether, as some scholar asserted, Navajo poetry rhymed—an assertion Edith indignantly refuted. After getting her doctor's thesis out of her room, she read several lines of a Navajo chant. "Why, there isn't any more rhyme to this than—" She paused, searching for suitable analogy.

"Than reason," Ira blurted.

To everyone's amusement, but chiefly Iola's.

The late-afternoon snack over, Iola took down a volume of Rudyard Kipling's poems from the shelf. And with an indulgent, deprecating air, the waning light on her tightly bound blond tresses and pale bony face, she read aloud several of her favorite poems . . . interspersed with amused comment.

Daylight ebbed from the white-walled living room, warm, golden, hallowed by its perfection; ineffable, the rare benison of untroubled hours, guerdon of respite from self, from self, but not from time drawing the day to a close.

With the coming of evening, swain and companion took their leave. Larry embraced Edith; they kissed. The two friends bade the two women farewell, closed the door between them, and walked down the muted stairs into the quiet street. Still inviolate, the twilight lingered at street's end, as if the rosy stain would never fade from the stone crater in the distance.

XIII

As the last week approached, the final week of freshman year, Ira ruminated more and more on Larry's romantic ties with Edith. The once miraculous affair appeared to breed new recognitions: a kind of strictness slowly encompassed it. Or was he himself, Ira wondered, beginning for the first time in his life to exercise something new to him—or exercise it consciously: his critical faculties? Not that he avoided doing so before, but rather, previously his attempts to exercise them became lost, became a fitful wandering in the mind's labyrinth. He now recognized the critical function as a distinct mental process. He had read and heard the terms associated with critical analysis before: in English class, in Philosophy 1. An addled smattering. But it was in Edith's company that concepts, like so many other abstractions he learned to identify there, became defined, braced with connotation and example. Ideas had begun to quicken in him, as something demarcated, independent. In "Little Black Sambo," which had beguiled him long ago, the tigers in their hot pursuit in a circle lost identity, were rendered into a mass of butter. Critical inquiry restored the rendered butter into distinct tigers again, arrested their motion, permitted contemplation of amorphous impressions, so that one could draw conclusions, reach judgments. Critical inquiry was something like that.

With a new sense of objectivity, an enhanced grasp of implication, Ira found himself isolating the significance of Larry's behavior, trying to infer the consequences of Larry's character, his nature—in relation to Edith. Was Larry's incipient tendency to prolong and elaborate an anecdote to the point where Ira began to feel he was foisting it on Edith, rather than entertaining her, was Larry doing that in order to dramatize himself? And something Ira could as yet scarcely name, for all his growing attentiveness to the effect of Larry's behavior on Edith, Larry didn't seek; Larry didn't probe for dilemma, didn't brood about sadness and loss. Curious, but that would never do for someone like Edith, would never satisfy the deep disenchantment Ira had already discerned in her, something akin to a kind of reconciliation with defeat, a tolerance of despair. She was given to insoluble quandary, temperamentally sad. Larry was disposed to optimism and well-being. Something was inherently dissonant here. And strangely, the suffering he had imposed on himself, and continued to do, sufferings, disenchanting and depraved lusts that robbed him of youthful joy, at the same time brought him closer to Edith's nature than was Larry. What an odd conclusion. Was it valid, or just an extract of a wish?

Also—and this too Ira began to examine, as something discreet, an element with its own consequences, that would determine the future of the relationship between the two lovers—she had prevailed on Larry to yield to discretion, to remain at home, though she offered to help in his support if he didn't. And it was his staying at home that already, even in that short time, seemed to hint at the possibility of the divergence of their temperaments. Because for all of their agonized disapproval of the course of Larry's affair, his family members still doted on him. He was the youngest and most gifted, the most charming and diverting. The set joke and the humorous trivia, it was clear to Ira as the bystander, Edith had no taste for. Larry's family flattered him with their adulation, rewarded him with their mirth, made him the cynosure of their admiration, and he enjoyed their unstinted appreciation in turn. His surpassing physical beauty wouldn't be enough to hold her indefinitely. (Ira wasn't sure whether he guessed that or he wished it.) And considering future developments from Larry's side, even though it was hard to believe, still it was almost impossible to discount entirely the effect that Larry's family brought to bear so heavily in opposition to his commitment to marry Edith, to believe that this same effect wouldn't, in fact, actually prevail in time, even against Larry's own buoyant, ardent self.

On the one hand, Ira envisaged Edith turning into Baba, his deceased grandmother, stooped, tottering, and tremulous, and Larry eleven years younger, resilient, handsome, energetic, attractive. Wouldn't that be true? And for Edith, granted she had grown old and wrinkled, wouldn't the classic young Endymion with whom she was so smitten have vanished? He would. "Beauty passes," Walter de la Mare wrote in the Untermeyer anthology, "Beauty vanishes, however rare, rare it be"; that applied to Larry as well. Then what? Abiding interest for Edith had to withstand her disillusionment, her confirmed gravity, her preoccupation with loss and loneliness, with aging and mortality. Any enduring relationship with her demanded a temperament, however acquired, full of misgivings, hurt, and affliction. Larry's temperament was anything but that: a happy one, a stable one. He gave the impression that the future would continue to be the same, a joyous extension of today. He sure wasn't used to grief, misgiving, lasting hurt, adversity, deprivation. Boy.

His loose-leaf notebook paper, fountain pen, pencil, scratch pad on the glass-topped table of the elegant walnut "set" in the front room, Ira sat looking at Pop's collection of bric-a-brac on the mantelpiece above the embossed metal shield of the chimney flue. The collection consisted of a little Dresden sheep dog, two sheep, a picturesque shepherdess. They reminded the old boy of the old country, Ira supposed. Nostalgic. Touching. Ira wasn't sure whether the little group would be considered in good taste by someone like Edith or not. But what the hell, though he never was sure of things of that kind, they were cute little things, fetching, innocent, so winsome in color. Up above, on the wall, were the two portraits of Pop's departed parents:

severe, if ever two faces were, severe in sepia: Grandma in her *sheytl*, her wig, Grandpa with beard and *peyot*, his earlocks. Mom had told Ira they were in fact as severe as their portraits, unsmiling and distant, the year or so she lived with them, after he was born. That was before Pop had accumulated enough dough to buy steerage passage for wife and kid to join him in America. So Ira had known them, seen and heard them with his own eyes and ears, as they had known him, but he didn't remember a thing about them—any more than they did about him in their graves in Galitzia where they lay buried. A year and a half old he was when Mom left for America with her baby son in her arms. Two strict sepia faces in ebony frames on the wall were all his paternal grandparents were now. Mom loved to repeat how the old man, Saul the Schaffer, whom everyone addressed out of respect as Saul the Overseer, had leaned on his walking stick the night before his daughter-in-law and grandson left for America. "And you danced so prettily that night, the tears came to the old man's eyes." And Ira had lately quipped in reply, "Oh, I did? Is that why I'm bowlegged?"

Oh, he had a term paper to do, term paper in his first term in English Composition, term paper for Mr. Dickson, the instructor of the course. And as usual he was addressing himself to the task at the very last minute. It had taken until the second term before Ira could get into a class in English Composition 1, a prerequisite for a B.S. or a B.A. degree. There was a class in English Composition 1 open, and it stayed open until he had it safely registered in his name. On that disastrous first night of registering for courses the previous fall, practically every freshman course had been closed, but between terms most of them were open, except Biology 1 still, because his class had access to them ahead of the influx of new freshmen.

Composition 1. The course was under the aegis of Mr. Dickson, a tall, angular Ichabod Crane sort of character, academically sedulous, academically sere. Mr. Dickson, evidently in pursuit of his doctorate, was in his late twenties, a man with curly, rusty hair, and with the funniest damn habit of screwing up his face into a quizzical gnarl, at the same time reaching over the top of his head with his long arm in order to scratch the opposite ear. As usual, Ira was acquitting himself with no better than a C for the course. Tomorrow, Monday, was the last day the term paper would be accepted. Its evaluation would determine fifty percent of the final grade. So . . . he'd better get to work.

Outside, through the open windows, spring on 119th Street was in full cry, full yippee. Balmy air wafting in through the open windows swelled the bellows of the long, lacy white curtains, curtains that would soon be taken down and stored for the summer. Urchins' yells down below scored the city's placid drone.

Sunday afternoon. Everyone was away: Mom was visiting her sister, Ella Darmer. She had married Meyer, and with their two kids they now lived on 116th Street and Fifth Avenue. Pop was working an "extra jopp," another "benket" in "Kunyilant." And . . . oh, Minnie had gone out with Lucy Goldberg across the street on a date. She was growing up now: having real dates. She could have all she wanted as long as he got his. But what if the right guy came along? Meant serious business, proposed, produced an engagement ring. Well, Stella was growing up, too.

Wasn't that the goddamnedest thing any photographer ever did? Musing, Ira eyed the portrait of his own sad three- or four-year-old self on the wall. Why the hell did the guy do that? Pose him that way? Ira shook his head. For all he knew, now that he had acquired a smidgeon of Freud, that might have planted the seed of his fixation, nutty fixation with and about sex—that might have got him into this, yes, abomination in the first place. These abominations, you should say. Man, wouldn't you have gotten stoned for that in days of yore? And not so long ago at that. Hanged, drawn and quartered, torn apart by horses or boiled in oil—*vey iz mir.* And as if that wasn't enough, how old was Stella now? About fifteen. Yeah, abominations you can call them now, now that you're cooled off with Sunday morning's abomination . . . not much of a one either . . . wonder how many scumbags the rats were treading on down at the bottom of the airshaft? But if you weren't, if you didn't get it, you'd be trotting over to Mamie's. Right? Right. *Hic jacet . . .*

Yeah, hic jack it . . . phooey.

But the goddamn fool behind the black camera box had set him on a chair—look at it—round-backed chair with upright spindles, but in the center, the main, ornamental spindle was truncated. It didn't reach from curved back all the way to the seat of the chair. Instead it hung exactly between the kid's legs, hung down like a gelding's slack hard-on after pissing. How terrified Ira had been as a child whenever he looked at the portrait. The photographer's camera had revealed the horrendous guilt that only Ira discerned, only he and no one else.

Silly phobia; no time to waste. Tomorrow, Monday, was the deadline for handing in the term papers. They were to be essays based on the general theme or topic of how to construct something of a fairly complex nature. How to carry out an elaborate scientific experiment. How to assemble a scientific exhibit. Or an account of the operation of some fairly complicated mechanism. Nothing simple, like fixing a bicycle, changing a tire. No, sir. To meet requirements, the piece of writing had to be at least a half-dozen pages long, which implied that the device or process be fairly complicated, and consequently test the student's ability to present the subject in clear, orderly, comprehensible exposition. Ira doodled contemplatively. Tic-tac-toe. A profile. A seagull.

His choice of topic had narrowed down to two subjects. He was familiar with both. First was the rifle cage of his high school days as a member of the rifle team, still remembered so clearly: the tiny target corresponding to the regulation-size target across the gym floor, the needle-pointer corresponding with the actual sighting of the mock firearm, the trigger mechanism, and all the do's and don't's of proper aiming, breathing, trigger-squeezing, types of gunsights, of leather slings . . . all so warmly entwined with memories of Billy, and days when another course, another career, another America seemed to beckon. . . .

He sought the next line on the typescript: no, the hell with it, true or not, he would delete it: Mrs. Goldberg, Lucy's divorced mother, across the street in her grayish, unbleached cotton shift again leaning disconsolately on her broom—what a graphic symbol!

Oh, he could work up another hard-on, given the incentive. After all, it was this morning early, his Sunday abomo—say, would that be an abomo or an abumo? If he walked across the street, nobody home here, nobody home there, nobody homeo, Romeo. Ask: was his sister there? He thought maybe she was. He wanted to ask her if she'd type something for him. Ask Mrs. Goldberg sadly leaning on a broom. See what she would do, or say. Leo Dugonicz, Hungarian pal, came to mind, and his account of the two cups of strong black coffee served him by his mother's acquaintance who then stroked his shoulder. So . . . one cup of black coffee, no cups of black coffee—no abumo.

Delete. Delete. There. "'Tis here, 'tis here. 'Tis gone!" said the guard in Hamlet, whacking away with his halberd. Not bad, though. That epitomized life: 'Tis here. 'Tis here. 'Tis gone. . . .

Say, don't tell me you don't know that jerk you see reflected in the thick plate glass on the glass-top table. Look at him, the dope, scowling back at you through steel spectacles, under a low half-moon brow topped by a mop of kinky black hair. That goddamn photographer posing the kid, the familiar child, in black armor, with a baton pendant between his legs. Look at you, fretting three different ways. No, that rifle-cage business was lifeless, lifeless as your high school hopes, separate from you—separate as you from Billy Green today.

The other choice of topic appealed to him more, was incomparably more stimulating. Alive. Just last summer. All summer. His eighteenth year. In the strong, burning sunshine, on practically rural land, just being parceled out by real estate developers. He'd have to be game to do it, though. Why not? He wasn't asking himself to sneak across the street, knock on Mrs. Goldberg's door, say hello. And just she, her, him. What the hell was the proper grammatical case? Object of a prepo—his heart was beginning to pound already. . . . No, it was just between him and the paper. You could flunk though, stupid. But why? Why should he flunk? It was how to build something, wasn't it?

Not how to abumo at sister's friend's home. Or how to finesse and fi-
nagle kid cousin Stella through Auntie Mamie's intangible household maze. No, it was how to build something. That was legitimate:
how to put up new plumbing in a new frame house. What was wrong
with that? Bold, huh? Original. Daring . . . as much as you like, yeah.
Between you and the paper. He pushed the scratch pad over the features leering back at him from the plate glass—the devil grinning at
him from the table could still have his due. Minnie would type it for
him—if there was time. But there was no time. He hadn't even written it, begun to write it. What if he typed it himself afterward? He
had a smidgeon of touch typing left from Mr. Hoffman's class in junior high. It didn't have to be in ink; he could write the first draft in
pencil. Let's go. On top of the page, capitalizing each first letter of
the title, he wrote: "Impressions Of A Plumber."

And then he took stock, he reconsidered. Impressions? Something was wrong here. That wasn't what Mr. Dickson had directed the
class to do. No impressions, but a process, a method, something sys-
tematic and factual. Otherwise, if he were to do an impression, why
then, the alarm clock would go off; he'd be getting up in the morning; he'd be riding on the subway with the other strap-hangers. That
wasn't a "how to." Oh, nuts. Still, he ought to be able to put enough
"how to" into it, enough specifics, to satisfy Mr. Dickson, right? How
to raise the cast-iron soil stacks up to the roof for toilet vents, how to
cut and thread nipples, how to tighten chrome-plated faucets without marring them, attach valves, wipe sink drain joints with molten
lead, oh, lots and lots of "how to" stuff. And there were all the fittings
to call attention to as well—what they were for: an elbow, a union, a
coupling, a tee. And the tools of the trade: a monkey wrench, a strap
wrench, and a Stillson wrench, the dye stocks for cutting thread on
pipe. Oh, lots and lots of implements. But he had to do it his own
way: *as a whole.* Mr. Dickson would understand. Sure he would.
Wouldn't he?

Doubt still gnawed at Ira. But if he made the process interesting,
colorful, if he awoke in Mr. Dickson the same kind of—of verve that
he himself felt when he recalled being a plumber's helper, Mr. Dickson would overlook small deviations from instructions, small liberties
taken with permission. Sure he would. Hope so.

"The alarm rings with frightened intensity," Ira began writing. "It is half past six. I wake reluctantly, shut off the alarm, and yawn. It is chilly even on a summer morning, and my bed is very warm. . . ."

Words flowed easily when he was writing about his own sensations and experiences that way. The evidence of his subject matter was at hand: no research was necessary, scarcely even exactitude of memory was needed. He had only to recall the approximate environment, the activities, recall the mood of the event, and then apply things to himself, not only to exemplify them, but to unify them in the course of an ordinary day's work. He had to choose from the variety that came to mind. He had to judge which element was most effective in capturing the flow of a day's work. He chose those elements that pleased him.

It was easy. He was the hub from which all else radiated, the center of perception to which everything and everyone was attached, everything and everybody, the tradesmen, the carpenters, the electricians, the roofers, the glaziers. So that was how it was done? He paused to reflect. No, that was how *he* could do it. If he tried to do it from another's point of view, from the inside of the mason who was laying the brick for the outdoor chimney, or the plasterer, he might as well give up, go back to describing rifle practice inside the rifle cage in the DeWitt Clinton gym. The others talked about wages, the comparatively low wages for the skilled work they were doing, no paid holidays, no time and a half for overtime and Saturdays. They talked about the high price of everything they had to buy, from pork chops to workshoes. And they talked about unions, unions, even the Italian bricklayer: oonion. No oonion, no good. Hymie, who had palmed himself off as a full-fledged journeyman plumber, was glad to get a job, and he never would have gotten one if the contractor had been hiring only union labor. Neither would Ira have gotten a job as a plumber's helper.

But Ira wasn't interested in subjects of that sort; he hardly even cared listening to opinions about them: where these guys went home, what kind of homes they lived in, what subjects were closest to them, how they amused themselves—bluefish or flounder fishing in the bay, the Saturday-night show—or how much the dues were in the metal lathers' union. No, there was no color to it, no place for him.

His way was the spectator's; his preferences were for the individual, not the collective: his getting up in the morning, his riding on the El as the sun came up, riding among the crowd of loudly yawning, grousing workers to the job. And once arrived at the work site, listening to the wisecracks on the job that only he could appreciate how funny they were: the parquet-floor layer cursing, "My goddamn rule lied to me!" And he himself, with eighteen-year-old exuberance, cutting three-quarter-inch galvanized pipe, threading it, lugging lengths of crusty, rough cast-iron pipe from the pile where the truck had dumped it to the frame house under construction: how hot the goddamn pipe was from lying for hours under the blazing sun. Wow! Right on his shoulder, unless he had a rag to buffer it. The images, as he scribbled, teemed within his mind so thickly he had to jot down a word or a phrase on the side to keep them in memory's reserve, until he was ready to use them. Watch out for comma-sentences. Didn't Dickson hate them. Look at that: five handwritten pages already. . . .

Mom came home: in dark street dress, her bearing portly and dignified, as always when she faced the public, her form squeezed rigidly into corseted shape, a silver fox fur over her shoulder. Was he hungry? she asked.

"No."

"If you'll eat something now, I'll fix it for you. I'm going out again."

"Oh, yeah?"

"We're going out to Baba's grave in New Jersey. It will soon be a year since she died."

"Oh, yeah?"

"I'll fry you some lox and eggs."

"I don't want any lox and eggs. I want to finish my term paper."

"Then what else?"

"Nothing."

"I'll leave you some bulkies in the same bag with the rye bread. The lox is between two saucers in the icebox." She opened her handbag, made sure she had her key. "If you should get hungry."

"Who's going?"

"All four sisters. *Ai,* where our mother lies, there in the earth of New Jersey. It's a good thing we contributed for a burial plot for all of us when we did. Jewish burial sites grow costlier all the time." She paused at the door. "I'll be home for supper. But you don't have to wait until then. Eat when it suits you."

"Okay. Mamie going too?"

"Of course. All four of us, I said. A drife," Mom said, trying the word in English. "A loffly drife through the country efter we cross the river. We'll enjoyet ourselves," she said, in English again. "While our mother molders in the earth, we go riding over it in Moe's *katerenke.* But so it is with the dead and the living."

A *katerenke* was a hand organ. Mom called Moe's automobile that because of the starting crank in front of the vehicle. Her unspoiled perceptions were something to admire, the way she shunted the macabre into the comic: a *katerenke.* Probably a Polish or Russian word the ever-accretive Yiddish had absorbed.

"Very well, I'm going," she said.

"Zaida, too?"

"Oh, no!" Her voice contained reproach—at his ignorance. "He's a *koyen.* A *koyen* in a cemetery? A priest? He would be defiled walking among the dead. Ask him next time when you go visit Mamie's."

"What do you mean, ask him? I can figure that out. A *koyen* must be a Cohen. Isn't that right?" He checked himself abruptly. "What do you mean, ask him when I go to Mamie's?"

"He's already moved away from the old place on 115th Street. He spent the Sabbath at Mamie's already. I told you. You and Minnie, your father. Ach." She moved her heavy hand in impatient gesture. "Your head's in the ground today. I told you he moved because he didn't trust the woman who cooked for him. She wasn't kosher enough for him, he thought. It heppens she's a loyal Jewess. But he has cataracts on both eyes. He sees scarcely anything clearly. So he suspects everything. Mamie he knows keeps a kosher home."

"But what about that lease on 115th Street?"

"Harry will finish it out. I'm going."

"So he's there now."

"Where else? Visit him. You'll learn something of *Yiddishkeit.*"

"That's all I need."

"Indeed. You know less of *Yiddishkeit* than those already lying in hellowed ground."

"Yeah? Okay."

"Goodbye, my hentsome son. Eat a morsel."

He watched the heavy, dark figure leave, heard the kitchen door swing shut. Solitude. So Mamie would be gone. But Zaida would be there now. Would Stella be home, too? Sunday? Nah. Maybe yes, with Hannah and a bunch of Charleston-jigging swains. Would Zaida allow it? Boy, what a gauntlet to run *that* would be now. All for a fat, oozy, surplus straddle, while the dance-band music barely seeped out of the Stromberg Carlson radio: couldn't turn it on too high: you had to hear every creak on the floor from the kitchen. Lucky for him again he'd lowered his peccary-pressure this morning. What the hell was a peccary? A sort of wild pig, wasn't it? Wild pig was right. Nonkosher. Oh, pecker, peccary, *peccavi.*

Ah, he bent over his scrawl. You scrawled a world out of words, and in turn the world you scrawled brought you to life. You glowed, rereading it, something the same way you glowed after you solved a geometry problem. You had to rise to a glow in order to solve it. Afterward, after the glow faded, you wondered, what the hell was all this about? How did you solve it?

He stood up, went into the kitchen, more in order to prolong his musing than in search of food; though when he found the bag with the bulkies and the "corn" bread in it, as Mom called it, the heavy rye bread, he cut off the heel of the loaf to gnaw on it. Funny, the bread didn't contain corn at all—that was maize—but this was made of rye flour: corn in the old, old sense, as grain was called. "The corn was orient"—Larry had called his attention to the beautiful lines by Thomas Traherne in his copy of *Highlights of English Literature:* "I thought it had stood from everlasting unto everlasting." Boyoboy, like himself that time he stood on a West Harlem street corner on a summer day: when he felt as if an aureate promise had been made him. "I thought it had stood from everlasting unto everlasting." An artist—was that the promise that strange aureate moment made? What an idea. Edith worshiped the artist, she said. Now don't get sidetracked. Don't let your flow of . . . of . . . whatever the hell it was that carried you along, like a scrap of paper—and that was a right figure—on a rain-rivulet by the curb. No, but it was true: you had to be able to hold the mood intact from beginning to end: hold it up in front of you, more than even you would in front of a mirror—because it had so many sides—and look at each side, and not be afraid the others would lose their shape while you did.

Still gnawing on the tough brown crust, bark-brown boat, skiff of crust, brown bark of old with a gray, pitted deck, corn bread, he went back to the front room, and resumed writing. . . .

So Baba was living once, and Baba is dead now, Ecclesias. And I'm writing about being a plumber's helper in the first quarter of the twentieth century, I who am virtually living in the twenty-first, though I don't belong there, and not merely because I have so few years left of living.

—You spoke of sustaining a mood.

And so I did. But you know as well as I do that my mood is a cracked mirror, no longer entire, no longer continuous. Not altogether trustworthy, in short, and incapable of withstanding extreme strain; it's a good, a reasonable facsimile of the pristine one, but certainly no longer that.

—Why do you break the thought so, the flow, when it was sustained, so obviously under firm guidance? I suppose I can guess the answer.

Yes, I do so not merely out of perversity. Safety valve, Ecclesias, safety valve. My wife invited me for tea—tea and yogurt—an invitation which she extended while wearing a pink skirt and blue shirt, a color combination at which we both laughed this morning, and then I returned here to you, passing through the hallway between the kitchen and my study. And here I am again, Ecclesias, on the second day of November of the year 1985, writing again of the plumber's helper I was in the summer of 1924.

—Nevertheless, I fail to understand completely the reason for all your intrusive and irrelevant associations, when it seems to me you could conveniently dispense with them. You ask, knowing very well why. Very likely, with his grandmother interred in the grave, then a year later, her lusty freshman grandson leers to himself while he writes of his (selected) experiences as a plumber's helper in the context, should one say—hardly the right word, in the iniquitous context of possibly, possibly of screwing his deceased Baba's second-oldest granddaughter, Stella—

—Do you realize what you've done? What you did, I should say.

Not till this very moment, Ecclesias. It has a certain order to it, hasn't it? Well, the plumber's helper, and his perhaps unattended first cousin, next in line, having more or less slaked desire on his sibling earlier in the day. No, the whole thing, not to pun, springs from memory: of the nasty ditty about not being a plumber, nor a plumber's son. And the all-too-obvious, smutty conclusion. Bear with me.

It was midafternoon when he finished, an execrable draft, barely legible, even to himself, particularly the last two pages, scribbled in the furious haste of completion. He sat quietly relaxing, exultant with consummation, whose fervor he could now afford to let drain away. It *had* to be typed—not only for the sake of legibility; it deserved typing. He felt so oddly proud of it, elated by it, complete justice could only be done to it by having it typed—typed rather than merely rewritten in ink. Minnie was the only one he could have turned to for the favor, and of course she would agree: but where was she? Beyond appeal. He could have dictated it to her. Too late even for that by the time she came home. He might as well do it in ink, in his best penmanship, which was lousy anyway, but would have to do. Or beg Dickson for another day. Lose a few credits maybe, as penalty. He was willing to accept that, God, yes, but the manuscript had to be legible. Typewritten it might mollify Dickson to some extent, which was another reason for typing it. It would make the reading easy; and that way he might get by his not adhering strictly to all the letters of the law, his small deviations from the strict confines of the cut-and-dried "how-to." His work had taken a few skips out of bounds. Small ones. And if he missed the deadline besides—ouch! Type it, type it. Make a

few amends. Time? Ten minutes to three. He stood up. Type it yourself, goddamn it. Walk over to Mamie's and type it on that ancient
gummy Underwood, weighing half a ton, that Stella employed making out dispossess notices for her mother, or new bills of fare which
the partners of the restaurant in Jamaica then mimeographed. Move
your ass. Hoof it over there. You can do it before it gets too late.

Should he include it, delete it? Ira studied his typescript. Written when?
When committed to the familiar yellow second sheets? He raised his eyes
to the umber, grainy piece of cloth M had attached to the curtain rod from
which the regular white curtain hung, in order to minimize the brightness
of the sunlight coming from behind the monitor and directly into his eyes.
Yes, when had he written the typescript? Ira retraced the years: evidently
when he could still type on a manual typewriter, however ineptly, when his
now weak and arthritic hands and fingers could then still abide the impact
of the keys of the large manual Olivetti portable he had used in those days.
   And when did *that* become too much for him? At . . . about . . . 1980
or '81. So he was still able to pound away at the keys—until M insisted he
buy an Olivetti electronic. (And that was only a halfway measure.) Anyway,
he was still typing manually in 1980; that was five years ago. And he was
then seventy-four years of age. What the hell was the odds, as his fifty-year-
old Irish crony, back in the thirties, Frank Green, would have said. What's
the odds? Why do it? Well, just to see what difference there was between
the Ira Stigman of five years ago and the Ira Stigman of today, the tone of
his literary difference. Why not? And one would have to consider the role
of Ecclesias too, credit him for any maturing of ideas, improvement in
prose—and Ira believed there was—again in good part thanks to Ecclesias.
He was so benign usually, caustic rarely, ever disposed to condone. "*Tolle
lege,*" Saint Augustine in spiritual crisis heard the voices of children crying:
"*Tolle lege,*" take up and read. That was in the days long before floppy
disks.
   It was important, this five-year-old prose that Ira was about to tran-
scribe, it was important for another reason, now that he had made mention of Saint Augustine. It was important because he had divested himself
of a formidable inhibition: he had admitted a sister into his narrative,

something he hadn't done in the draft on the desk beside him. He had been compelled, reluctantly, painfully, to make the inclusion; he had done so belatedly, in spite of himself, but eventually he had done so. And surely, prior to that, how different must have been the rationale of the narrative—"rationale" was a polite understatement, as Ira knew only too well. Once Minnie was admitted into the story, everything was different, drastically different, nay, it would be nearer the truth to say flagrantly different, self-revealing in approach, in treatment, in the contour of the narrative. How long it had taken him to square with the truth; how long he had clung to subterfuge!

"Homer, Virgil, Dante, Milton [the original typescript began], and at least several score of other lesser bards invoked the Muse at the outset of their grand epics, that she might vouchsafe the poet the power of imagination, the poetic stamina to sustain his lofty envisaging all the way to its successful conclusion. Invoking the muse has gone out of fashion these days: Dante's 'O Musa, O alto ingegno,' or 'm'aiutate.' Milton's 'Sing, Heavenly Muse,' Homer's 'aeide, thea,' are no longer heard. We don't believe in the Muse any longer. Still I feel the need to advert to some source of spiritual replenishment that will enable me to carry forward the account of this nasty, muddled, contradictory, and confused life of mine. In one of the cantos of the *Inferno*, Dante describes with the horrible vividness of his genius the gruesome transformation that takes place between man and serpent, both of them two aspects of damned souls (for committing what sin I've forgotten). As the one stings the other, the two exchange roles, the two exchange form and function, the erstwhile viper now assumes human guise, pursued by the erstwhile human, now viper: a paradigm of the interaction between depravity of environment and the susceptible individual: *De me fabula narratur.*

"Instead of the Muse, I turn for inspiration and a sense of renewal to the Lower East Side—though God knows, I was already wayward enough there. Still, I felt at home there, shored and stayed by tenets I imagined inhered in the nature of things. I *belonged.* And therefore, everything I did, however wicked, was somehow endemic, indigenous, part of the general scheme, as was even Pop's insensate corrections. (It was as a prank, and by my own volition, I dropped the milk dipper down into the third rail of the trolley—though it is true I had been previously initiated into the performance of the act by a couple of *goyish* gamins.) To repeat, I belonged. Therefore, nothing I did destroyed common norms, though I may have been guilty of their infraction. Escapade and punishment pertained to each other, and both comported with the Lower East Side consensus. In a way, I couldn't do anything that vitiated my normalcy, and inclusion within normalcy equated to a kind of absolution. As robust an absolution as the ever renewing innocence that coursed like an ichor through my veins, and made me ready to accept any challenge.

"What scraps are these I evoke, gather, to give me fresh impetus for the long rueful journey ahead? Well. Trimmings, findings, in a word, remnants: vignettes and tableaux that for one reason or another I either overlooked or found no place for in my first novel about an immigrant childhood on the Lower East Side. Or perhaps, as so often happens, they ran contrary to my conception of the spirit of the whole: they didn't fit, proved fractious (and perhaps, also, had they been accorded their due weight, a more viable model of a Lower East Side childhood might have emerged: viable, in the sense that it might have assured the author a longer writing career, a professional future). But—the ancient adage about the ill will has its application here—the previous exclusions of scrap and remnant now rescue me from redundancy.

"As I recall, I sit with my little schoolmates in the darkened primary-school assembly room, the one I attended when we lived on 9th Street and Avenue D. I was about seven years old, the year 1913 (year between the disaster that befell the *Titanic* and the outbreak of the World War). In the lighted frame of a miniature stage on the assembly-hall platform, a Punch and Judy show is in progress. And while the darkened hall reverberates with the shrill laughter of the assembled kids at the spectacle of Punch belaboring clamorous Judy—who should give vent to heart-rending sobbing but me. I bawled so loudly, I had to be removed from the assembly room. I still recall one of the schoolteachers bending toward me at the end of the row of seats, and with kindly forebearance signaling to me to get up, and come to her. 'He's hitting her!' I blubbered as the teacher escorted me out of the assembly hall. 'He's hitting her!'

"I alone saw it in that light. I wonder why? I don't think it was pure compassion on my part that led to the anomalous outcry—I was an aggressive enough little tyke. Rather, it was that the belaboring of one puppet by another provided altogether too faithful a reproduction of Pop's often insane beatings of me. Provocations I must have afforded in plenty, without any doubt. But the little man, pathetic, deeply troubled little man, frustrated by his inadequacy, haunted by fear of ridicule, undoubtedly a rejected child himself, lost all self-control in administering chastisement. He went almost berserk, seized the first scourge within reach, stove poker, butt of horsewhip, wooden clothes hanger. Mom, in fact, always maintained that the peculiar inward crook of the pinky of my left hand resulted from my trying to ward off some flailing blow. If nothing was at hand to flog me with, he yanked me up from the floor where I lay groveling under his blows, yanked me up by both ears, threw me down again, and trampled me. He himself—scared, resentful, unstable, little man! I have made mention before, in my novel, how I would stand in front of the long, black-framed pier glass, the same one we brought from the Lower East Side to Harlem, admiring the indigo-blue welts on my back. I am certain Mom must have saved me from being permanently maimed, or saved my life perhaps, on more than one occasion, by sheer physical intervention, grappling with Pop, for which she would have received blows herself. So I howled with terror when Punch battered Judy."

Thus he had written, the Ira of only five years ago. And he could have added that the assault by one puppet on another on the little stage might also have called to mind the sometimes violent quarrels between Mom and Pop, when they came to blows, when they threw the contents of coffee cups at each other—and when Ira and his little sister Minnie cowered under the table, and wept in fear. Punch walloping the vituperative Judy; Pop walloping Mom; Pop thrashing Ira. And so Ira sobbed at the fearsome verisimilitude. That was what he wrote, that was what he thought represented a valid reflection of childhood reality before, long before he ever dreamed he would or could bring himself to an honest admission of the true nature of his own adolescence, one which was undoubtedly shaped by much of the violence of his childhood.

It was that interpretation which underwent a change. It changed because of a reorganization of ethos that changed the former personality and viewpoint. The reason he blubbered at the sight of Punch beating Judy—Ira was now convinced—was not primarily that the act recalled his own savage chastisement at the hands of Pop, or those ugly, violent quarrels Pop sometimes had with Mom, especially in the cheerless penury of those earliest days on Essex Street and Henry Street. But rather that he was already deficient in the average child's ability to discriminate, to distinguish the virtual from the real. Surely other children were present in the assembly hall that day who must have been chastised as severely as he, or witnessed as harrowing scenes at home as those Ira had beheld; and yet they laughed noisily and unrestrainedly at the antics of the puppets. Was it because of lack of sensitivity that they didn't identify with the ludicrous little figures on the stage? Or because they were better able to distinguish the actual from the imaginary? Ira was certain of the truth now: it was because in the minds of the rest of the kids present, a fair balance between emotion and intellect had already been struck. Ira lacked just that: an equilibrium between his feeling about a perception and a rational appraisal of it, in a word, objectivity.

It was difficult for him, on account of that very lack, to undo, as it were, adequately gainsay, what he had written five years ago. But to have done otherwise, to have accepted what he had written, without making the effort to convey his altered view of self, would have meant that he still envisaged that self as unchanged from the child he had depicted in his novel, passive victim of malign forces about him, susceptible, innocent sufferer of the wounds and spiritual havoc inflicted on him by a neurotic father and by a callous and hostile environment. He was *not* innocent, and the environment was *not* callous and hostile; these were facts he no longer could conceal from himself. The difference between the Ira of five years ago and the Ira of today, who revised the view of his predecessor into a view he deemed more just, stemmed from that negation; and that negation in turn was accomplished by the slow, agonizing denial of a previously consummated *holistic* metaphor. The very travail that went into forging the plausibility and holism of the metaphor also forged the shackles on the spirit of the artisan himself. They had to be broken. By that and that alone: the breaking or repudiation of the approved and the applauded. The Marxist-Hegelian negation of negation. At all costs, because only thus could he win renewal of self. In his case—Ira thought grimly—revision and renewal were accomplished not by an accession of greater powers of analysis, an enhanced gift of abstraction, though with the passage of years something like that must have occurred to a moderate degree. Rather, he had learned to sublimate feeling into fine sensibility, until it became a more reliable, a keener, judge of reality than his dubious sagacity.

"And Pop [Ira reverted to the 1979 typescript]—memory harbors a few, tender recollections of Pop too, rare but precious. We climbed up to the roof of our house on 9th Street, he and I. We stepped through the roof door into the limpid vault of October sky. We located the chimney of our kitchen stove, spewing smoke from the woodfire Pop had kindled there. He had already bought a pair of calves' feet in the kosher butcher store, the small hooves still on them, and with a scrap of wire tied about them, he suspended the calves' feet within the chimney. They were to be smoked. For how long a time they were thus processed I no longer recall (until the small hooves came off, I think); nor how Mom prepared them afterward for the table. The entrée was called *pechah* in Yiddish: calves' feet in aspic, I daresay would be the equivalent in English, a quivering, amber mass savory with smoke and spice, and served on slices of toasted, stale *challah* impregnated with whole cloves of garlic rubbed into it. Much relished by all of us: *pechah,* savory Galitzianer token of rare paternal companionship.

"Again, though the recollection is almost too faint to descry, Pop and I are sitting on the barrier timber at the end of the dock jutting into the East River. In one sense, where we are sitting is a continuation of 9th Street into the East River. In another sense, it is where East 9th Street ends, and a cobblestone-paved, lopped-off block east of Avenue D begins. The day, a summer's day, has been scorching hot, and now at last, supper over, the first shadows of twilight fallen, a cooling breeze blows toward us from the river. Other residents, immigrants or less recent arrivals to the New World, residents of the immediate neighborhood, are sprawled there too, certainly. But I am aware only of being with Pop, of the unusual pleasure of sharing a pleasant interlude with Pop, a brief interlude of relaxed amiability: to sit side by side with him on the massive, splintery, weathered timbers and look out across the river at low-lying, smoky Brooklyn, to watch a hempen-mustached tugboat chug by, butting into green water, and driving undulating rollers toward us; with what sinister sound they lap among the piles beneath the dock. Sitting there, one could get a view of the gas company plant a few blocks uptown, its buff-colored storage tanks like huge bass drums at the foot of a smokestack against the darkening sky. Infrequently, but worth waiting for, as if it were a pyrotechnic display for our diversion, a lurid shaft of flame springs from the top of the smokestack into the twilight's dusty lapis lazuli, and flares, flares upward—'Look, Pop. Look!' . . ."

"One thinks that all this must vanish, the good and the bad, the treasured and detested, my heritage, my identity, must vanish with me, save for slight evocations, occasional distillation of eloquence preserved in print; all else must vanish. And eventually, even that too. From time immemorial, nay, ever since the universe became conscious of itself, in the form of *Homo sapiens,* the toll for that supreme 'privilege' has been consciousness of mortality—the toll, with all its overtones. The cry of every human has been: 'And when I crumble, who will remember?' Often have I imagined the rain leaching out memory, the wind making sport of it, the assiduous maggot consuming a recondite trope—or, for that matter, an elegant formula: $E = MC^2$; or e to the i pi $= -1$, ingested by happy helminthes. . . .

"All of these memories were a mere seventy years ago. That same summer, we flocked in droves out of our brick warrens into the street, shouting and pointing and craning up at the first squadron of aircraft we had ever seen, biplanes high above the rooftops. . . .

"Am I done? Am I sufficiently restored by my Antaean return to East Side origins to tackle what lies ahead?

"But there was still the matter of the tricycle. Mom and Moe—and I skipping in the van—stroll together to the store where 'tickets' are redeemed. By a combination of 'tickets,' a kind of trading coupon amassed by Moe as a result of his multitudinous candy-store purchases, 'tickets' plus a little cash, Moe was going to procure a tricycle—for me! Clearly remembered, as if fused together with the child's extreme eagerness to get to the premium depot, was the subliminal realization that the two adults leading the way through the crowded streets, chatting amiably as they walked, should be Mom and Pop. But they were not Mom and Pop, and because they were not, they called forth an awareness, like a well-defined after-image, the complementary realization, that *that* was the way Mom and Pop ought to behave together, easy and leisurely and pleasant—and did not. It wasn't the stolen tricycle, stolen the same day it was purchased, that mattered so much now, as once it had; it was the poignant awareness of how much he yearned for the untroubled companionship of his elders, how much he missed it, even as he was aware of the same thing later on, when Mom and Uncle Louis strolled together in the evening beside Mt. Morris Park.

"And there was Johnny-in-a-high-chair, as we called him, the driver of an old-fashioned hansom cab, leaping down from his elevated perch, and whip in hand, pursuing a pack of little gamins who had volleyed him with stones: furious, top-hatted cabby, whip in hand, chasing a covey of Jewish kids scampering away through 9th Street, leaving the patient, spotted white horse motionless in mid-street. . . . And my first near encounter with an automobile. Yes, I stepped off the curb into the path of the oncoming vehicle, and such was my frantic doubling back out of the way, my ribs ached for days afterward. And I would remember—even to this present— the amused profiles of driver and passenger as the motorcar rolled by. . . .

"Two eggs cost a nickel. Mom sent me down four flights of stairs to buy them; and an egg in each hand, I climbed back up four flights of stairs. Mom sent me down four flights of stairs to buy a pound of honey, bronze, crystallized honey, scooped up by the grocer out of a stubby wooden firkin in the little, untidy grocery store across the street. *Hunik-lekekh* was the Yiddish name of the cake that Mom concocted and baked from the crystallized honey, *hunik-lekekh,* a dark solid slab of cake, substantial enough to bolster up any Sabbath. . . .

"Oh, how lighthearted, light-footed, he who once was I, hopped down four flights of sandstone stairs, and up four flights of sandstone stairs.

"Yes, and do you remember how her father spanked Yettie, a girl of about twelve, for swinging a little kid between her legs, and thus exposing the crack between her legs through her torn drawers?

"I remember."

Alas, my friends—Ira scanned the lines of the typescript—the 1979 draft, the old one, just won't do. Oh, damn it, damn it: the subterfuges he had had to resort to, and the rectifications that supplanted, they made him feel like a juggler keeping aloft a number of incongruous objects, an orange, a skillet, a paintbrush. And there was another element too that would have to be reckoned with, and that he already foresaw would plague him with its consequences: to depart from the typescript meant departing from his general guide, demanding not only a different set of circumstances for the episode, but alterations in the treatment of it as well, a general reordering, in short. But if he was compelled to range too far abroad in the re-creation of the episode, when would he ever return to the comfortable mainstream of work largely accomplished? To his story? Ever? Discouraging, to say the least.

At one side of the typescript, the object that had lain there for days and days, with no particular significance, now asserted its significance: the paperweight (at least, he used it for that purpose), the bronze relief of Townsend Harris, the medal CCNY had given him for "Notable Achievement." (Notable achievement equal to a C-minus average in his scholastic work—but that wasn't the point.) The medal recalled the luncheon given in his honor by the then president of the college and members of the English faculty, and the account he gave them in the course of his address in acknowledgment of the honor the college bestowed on him: of the moment when he was lackadaisically listening to Mr. Dickson's comments on the quality of the term papers—and the sudden, the startling turn of events that ensued—none of which was on the original typescript, and which he now felt should be included. Why? Because those things he had subordinated before took on new prominence as a consequence of his new, his liberated, approach to his writing.

It was the last day of class. Mr. Dickson had read and graded all the term papers, and was about to return them to the various members of the class. They were surprisingly good, Mr. Dickson commented—and commended: some were exceptionally good. And one was of such unusual quality that in his capacity as faculty adviser to the staff of the magazine, he had recommended the inclusion of the piece, at the last minute, in the City College quarterly, *The Lavender.* Who was that whiz? Ira wondered idly at first, and then for some reason, listlessness gave way to an abrupt sharpening of attention. Was there, could there have been any substance to that zest he had felt, that lift, when he was writing the piece apart from Minnie's extravagant, though by her brother patronizingly discounted, praise of how "wonderful" it was when he accorded her the privilege of reading the typescript at breakfast in the morning? The term paper Mr. Dickson had recommended for inclusion in *The Lavender* was entitled "Impressions of a Plumber," and the author was Ira Stigman.

"Wow!" Ira had exclaimed.

Classmates turned to locate the recipient of the distinction.

"Is that you?" someone nearby asked, with gratifying incredulity. "He means you?" And another fellow student, "You mean to say *you* wrote it?"

Ira grinned, elated: he had fooled these wiseguys just as he had fooled the kids in Mr. Sullivan's class.

Mr. Dickson manifested his displeasure at this ruffling of classroom decorum. He grimaced in disapproval, and lest the grimace go unnoticed, he framed it by arching an arm over his leaf-brown poll and scratching the opposing ear. "You realize, don't you, Mr. Stigman, that for some reason you chose not to follow my very explicit instructions with regard to the treatment of subject matter?"

"Yes, sir."

"An impression of the subject, an impressionistic article, was precisely *not* what I asked you to write, but a straightforward work of exposition. You're a science major, aren't you?"

"Yes, sir."

"Then you'll have to be satisfied with the low mark you'll receive for your term paper. And, I'm afraid, in the course as well."

But no reproach, no matter what the magnitude, or potential penalty, could diminish the swell of exultation Ira felt. He was going to be in *The Lavender*! He! A nobody! Wow! What an exoneration of his nonentity! The years, the hours, the days enduring the sullen *shlemiel* who was himself. And worse than that: a *shlemiel* perpetrator. Reprieve. A rift of reprieve. Ah, wait till he told Mom, told the family—Mom's bosom would heave with joy. And what would Pop say? He'd have to admit that there was something more to his son than the *kalyikeh* he appeared to be. And Larry? And Edith and Iola? The magazine was due to appear during exam week, but he couldn't wait to tell them! Wow! Minnie would beam: my marvelous brother!

Exploit that adulation for what it was worth, of course. Oh, boy! And Stella—she was too dumb, malleable, to require extra incitement. Admire, go ahead and admire. And with vast, cynical gratitude, accept Mamie's proffered reward of a dollar afterward: "Here. Indigent collitch bhoy. Take." Jesus, wasn't the world wonderful!

He looked hopefully at the typescript at his elbow. Where was there an opening, an ingress in the block of prose? Or an unobtrusive place to justify end to beginning? There wasn't any really. So . . . grab the first convenient starting point:

Originally when Ira would tell the ¹story "The Impressions of a Plumber," he always treated the sequel as the climax. And what was the sequel? He received a D in the course. What a delicious contrast, he felt, between having won inclusion of his term paper in the college *Lavender*, received inclusion in the college literary quarterly because of its literary merits, or, at least, because of its narrative merit, and the ignominious D grade he received for the course in English Composition 1. That sequel no longer seemed now the climax, risible and paradoxical though the whole incident might be.

No. That, and all he envisaged—and which was realized too, for the most part—seemed, at this remove, anticlimax. The true climax was of a twofold nature. One, and perhaps the less important one, was Larry's barely concealed hurt, not resentment, hurt, expressed in the perceived attitude toward him. He was almost aloof, he was perfunctory in his compliments, in his congratulations. Larry was too kind and generous a person to be envious or discomfited; instead, he was hurt, he was reserved. His manner reminded Ira of that time in their senior year when they shared Elocution 8 together at DeWitt Clinton, and Ira had been excused from class for the balance of the period by Mr. Staip, as a reward for the excellence of his address on William E. Henley's "Invictus." Larry had seemed disconcerted, as much by Ira's unexpected infringement on purlieus he assumed were his, but more since he was doing so without credentials.

Oh, it was easy, Ecclesias—easy and unjust—for someone like me, fraught with guilt and self-hatred, to impute to Larry thoughts he may never have entertained: that I was some sort of apparition from the slums functioning ably in a cultural realm.

He should merely have said, the true result was of a twofold nature, one being Larry's reaction. The other—ah! Not Edith's flattering eagerness in reaching for the copy of *The Lavender,* when the sketch appeared in the last days of the college year. Nor the realization about Iola, awaiting her turn to read it, with a show of even greater eagerness—radiating pleasure and almost emphatic pride in this vindication of her judgment, as though the sketch were a disclosure of greater latency, developing under her implied aegis, in competition with Edith's sponsorship of Larry. No, nor Mom's flushed happiness, nor Pop's noncommittal raising of eyebrows— ah, no. The other result, to which everything else became peripheral external, became subsidiary, was the impetus to an internal change, an internal change wrought in him as a consequence of the publication of something he had written.

Difficult to formulate, other than badly, and perhaps there was no need to formulate it at all, but he now realized that if there was anything he could do in his life, there was only one thing he had a chance of doing well. If Ira was to have a career, a future, if he had a definite bent, he now had only one: it was in the art of letters, in the craft of writing. The publication of his sketch disclosed, at least to him, that in spite of the booby negligence of its author to follow clear instructions, which had yielded instead to an inner urge, he had nonetheless written something that compelled recognition. The piece had evidenced a nascent literary ability. The accolade, the seal of approval, was bestowed on a piece of prose written not in accordance with Mr. Dickson's directives, but on his own impulses. What was it those Spanish mariners shouted from the crow's nest high on the mast—or soldiers too, from some height, the conquistadores—when they spied the first trace of land? *"Albricias! Albricias!"* Bounty! So with Ira. *Albricias* for the inner discovery.

Moribund from then on became the subject of biology, the career of zoologist. So this was what he had been groping toward all these years? Ever since leaving the Lower East Side, surly and bewildered by what the years were making of him—or unmaking. Unmaking and making of him this, and he never knew it. This was all they could have formed or fashioned out of what was undone. So it seemed. When the core of decency, his self-esteem, was wrecked, what else could have arisen to win positive, approved fulfillment? Writing was all that could in some way gain rehabilitation—without his seeking pardon or absolution, but by employing what he was. Jesus. Because he had destroyed, or undermined irreversibly, the central strength of who he was, writing was all there was left to him as justification for being what he now was. God, it was a strange thing to have to discover for oneself. Because—shift the blame to chance, or to obscure, early influence—other strengths, other virtues, or fortes, he did not feel that he possessed. Ira had forfeited them, if he ever had them. It was a choice that was not a choice; it was a choice without alternative, without option. It was his sole recourse. And fortunately, there was even that, for without it, only crime and perversion would have been the consequence. He would have been another inmate in an institution.

So writing became a hope toward a career, not a true commitment, but an inchoate, befuddled aspiration. Nevertheless, however flimsy the aspiration, it afforded a kind of temporary haven for the maimed psyche, a holding pen (what a bilious pun!), until such time as opportunity for marshaling his inner turbulence into some order presented itself.

The literary path became thus his "choice," and as murky and confused a one as it was possible to be, not for any goal of material success, which certainly was a legitimate incentive, and a mark of professionalism, but out of that same blind intuition upon which he had come to depend as a better guide to survival than his intellect. And fortunate he was too that there already existed a road, a well-traveled highway in his psyche, one that he should have abandoned at a far earlier age than he did, but not having done so proved a boon: it was a road paved with ten thousand myths and legends, and the fairy tales he loved so well.

And the old man suddenly recalled Henley's lines from high school, so clearly across a fault line that seemed wider than the sixty years that sundered him from his boyhood—

> *And yet the menace of the years*
> *Finds and shall find me unafraid.*

GLOSSARY OF YIDDISH AND HEBREW WORDS AND PHRASES

Note: Some spellings reflect Galitzianer pronunciations and may seem unfamiliar to speakers of "standard" Yiddish; others, such as *cheder* rather than *kheder,* are the most common English spellings. Some words, such as *klyasses,* are adaptations of English words, and even Yiddish words, such as *fress,* often have English inflections: *fressing.*

abi gesint   as long as you're healthy
a bisl nakhes   a little satisfaction
a brukh af dir   a curse on you
af mayne playtses   on my shoulders
a gantser hunderter   a whole hundred
a gruber ying   a coarse lout
ai; ai, yi, yi   cry of surprise, alarm, etc.
aliyah   going up (as to the pulpit); back to Palestine, now Israel
an alte klyafte   an old virago
apikoros   heretic; lit. "Epicurean"
a veytik iz mir   woe is me
aza kup   what a head
aza lebn af dir   you should live so
az m'vayst nisht   if you don't know
azoy?   is that so?
Bar Mitzva   the initiation ceremony for young men into Judaism
bist takeh meshigeh   you're really crazy
briderl   little brother

bris Jewish ceremony of circumcision taking place eight days after birth

brukhe blessing

bukher fellow

challah egg bread made for the Sabbath

cheder traditional Hebrew school for young children

chibeggeh nonsense word meaning chattering

chompkeh chomp

chutzpa brass, nerve, gall

commoysheh commercial

daven pray

der viller iz mer vi der kenner he who aspires excels him who knows

dos tseyndl the little tooth

dreck dung; trash

dreidel a top marked with four Hebrew letters, used for games played during Hanukkah

Dummkopf blockhead, fool (German)

dybbuk evil spirit or demon

er funfet shoyn now he's speaking unclearly

es hot mir gefelte libe I lacked love

ess eat

Falasha Ethiopian Jew, isolated from mainstream Judaism

farbisener hint angry dog

farleygt displaced, out of place

farshtest? do you understand?; **ikh farshtey** I understand

Fraytik af der nakht is dokh yeder yid a maylekh on Friday night every Jew is a king

fress eat ravenously or loudly

gants geler quite yellow, ripe; acculturated

geferlikhe gemblerke awful gambler (female)

gefilte fish dish of chopped, poached fish

geharget zolst di veren may you be slain

gelt money

gemütlich cozy, comfortable, friendly; **Gemütlichkeit** friendliness (German)

gesheft business; pl. **gesheftn**

geshrey outcry

gevald havoc; **oy, gevald!** expression of alarm, concern, or amazement

gey gezunt farewell

gey mir in der erd go to hell, drop dead

git-oyg evil eye

glatt kosher strictly kosher

golem humanoid from Jewish mythology made of clay; dolt, monster
goniff thief
Gotinyoo dear God
Got's nar God's fool
goy gentile (noun); **goya** gentile woman; **goyim** gentiles; **goyish**
  gentile (adj.); **goyishkeit** the world of gentiles, gentile matters
grobyan gross, coarse fellow; boor
gurnisht it's nothing
Haggadah collection of stories and scripture for reading aloud on
  Passover
hamantashen stuffed pastries served at Purim, the festival commemo-
  rating the deliverance of Persian Jews from Haman's plan to kill
  them
ha-Sho'ah the Holocaust
Hatikvah "The Hope," Zionist hymn, now the Israeli national anthem
Havdalah prayers recited at the conclusion of the Sabbath
hint dog
hunik-lekekh honey cake
ikh vil nisht, ikh ken nisht I don't want to, I can't
Kaddish Hebrew prayer for the dead; **kaddish'l** son who will eventually say **Kaddish** for the parent
kalyikeh cripple
katerenke hand organ
keyn ayin-horeh [may there be] no evil eye
khad gadyo one kid; the name of a song sung at Passover
kinderlekh children
kishka stomach, or dish made of stuffed stomach
knubl garlic
komets-alef, "o"; komets-beys, "bo"; komets-giml, "go" Hebrew syllables combining the vowel **komets** ("o") with the consonants **alef,
  beys,** and **giml,** as recited by child learning to read
koptsn briderl poor little brother
koyen priest, descendant of priests of ancient Israel
kreplakh a stuffed pasta dish, similar to meat-filled ravioli
kugel casserole of noodles or potatoes
kup head, mind
kushenirke female shopper; haggler
landslayt fellow immigrants from the same hometown or region (German **Landsleute**)
lemekh lame, clumsy, awkward fool
leydn suffering
lokshn-treger noodle porter

makh gelt   make money
makh shnel   make haste
matzah   unleavened bread
mayn kind   my child
mazel   luck
mazel tovs   best wishes, congratulations
megillah   long story
megst takeh geyn in der erd   you can drop dead
melamed   Hebrew teacher
mensh   man; honorable or admirable man; a good-hearted person
meshigener   crazy person
minchah   daily afternoon prayers
minyan   assembly of ten men necessary for religious services; quorum
Mishnah   interpretations of Biblical texts forming the older part of the
   Talmud
mitzva   good deed or Biblical commandment
m'makht a lebn   I'm making a living
mohel   person who circumcises a child at a **bris**
nafke   whore
nar   fool
nekhtiger tog   lost hope; something impossible; lit. "yesterday's day"
noo   well, well now, so
nosh   snack
oukh   also
ousgeshtudiert   learned
oy   oh
pechah   calves' feet in aspic
peyot   earlocks (Hebrew; **peyes** in Yiddish)
pisher   one who urinates; insignificant person
potateh kugel   potato pudding
prust   simple, crude; **pruster arbeiter**   plain worker, worker on lowest
   level
roman   serial romance, novel
rugeleh   pastry
Schadenfreude   pleasure in other's misfortunes (German)
seykhl   intelligence, common sense
Shabbes   the Sabbath; **Shabbes bay nakht**   Sabbath evening (Saturday
   night)
shekheyooni   blessing said at beginning of holiday or other happy occasions, lit. "that He let us live"
shemevdik   timid, shy, shamefaced
shenk   give, donate

sheytl wig
shikker drunkard
shiksa gentile girl
shiva the seven-day period of mourning the dead
shlemiel bungler, fool
shlepper someone who fetches and carries at work; someone who drags one's feet; someone untidy
shlimazl unlucky person
shmaltzy fatty
shmattas rags that old women buy and wear; clothes
shmooze converse in friendly fashion
shmulyaris dollars
shoyn already; **shoyn farfallen** already lost; **shoyn genug** already enough
shtraml wide-brimmed black hat worn by orthodox Jewish men, especially in Galitzia and Poland
shul synagogue
s'iz azoy shver it is very heavy or hard
s'iz git kalt it's quite cold
s'iz takeh gold? it's really gold?
takeh indeed; **takeh emes** indeed true
tsimmes sweet dish of stewed fruit or side dish of vegetables and fruit; dessert
tsuris troubles
tsu velkhe klyasses to which classes
tukhis afn tish ass on the table
tummel commotion
vey sorrow; **vey iz mir** woe is me
vidder again
vi m'geyt un ven m'geyt tsu hern di professors how and when you go to listen to the professors
wunderbar wonderful (German)
yenems belonging to that other person; bummed cigarettes
yenta shrewish or gossipy woman
yeshiva rabbinical college; also an Orthodox Jewish high school for both secular and religious study
Yiddisher kup Jewish head; intelligent or wily person
Yiddishkeit Jewishness, Yiddish life or culture
Yisgadal, v'yiskadash, sh'mey rabo first lines of the **Kaddish:** "Magnified and sanctified be the name of the Lord"
yold fool
Yom Kippur Day of Atonement, most solemn Jewish fast day

zey hobn gemakht a gitn shiddekh   they've made a good match
zol er gehargert vern   may he be murdered
zolst gebentsht vern   may you be blessed
zolst shoyn nisht elter vern   may you not grow any older
zuzim   coins (archaic; occurs in song **khad gadyo**)

ABOUT THE AUTHOR

Henry Roth was born in the village of Tysmenitz, in the then Austro-Hungarian province of Galitzia, in 1906. Although his parents never agreed on the exact date of his arrival in the United States, it is most likely that he landed at Ellis Island and began his life in New York in 1909. He briefly lived in Brooklyn, and then on the Lower East Side, in the slums where his classic novel *Call It Sleep* is set. In 1914, the family moved to Harlem, first to the Jewish section on 114th Street east of Park Avenue; but because the three rooms there were "in the back" and the isolation reminded his mother of the sleepy hamlet of Veljish where she grew up, she became depressed, and the family moved to non-Jewish 119th Street. Roth lived there until 1927, when, as a junior at City College of New York, he moved in with Eda Lou Walton, a poet and New York University instructor. With Walton's support, he began *Call It Sleep* in about 1930. He completed the novel in the spring of 1934, and it was published in December 1934, to mixed reviews. He contracted for a second novel with the editor Maxwell Perkins, of Scribner's, and the first section of it appeared as a work in progress. But Roth's growing ideological frustration and personal confusion created a profound writer's block, which lasted until 1979, when he began *Mercy of a Rude Stream*.

In 1938, during an unproductive sojourn at the artists' colony Yaddo in Saratoga Springs, New York, Roth met Muriel Parker, a pianist and composer. They fell in love; Roth severed his relationship with Walton, moved out of her apartment on Morton Street, and married Parker in 1939, much to the disapproval of her family. With the onset of the war, Roth became a tool and gauge maker. The couple moved first to Boston with their two young sons, and then in 1946 to Maine. There Roth worked as a woodsman, a schoolteacher, a psychiatric attendant in the state mental hospital, a waterfowl farmer, and a Latin and math tutor.

With the paperback reprinting of *Call It Sleep* in 1964, the block slowly began to break. In 1968, after Muriel's retirement from the Maine state school system, the couple moved to Albuquerque, New Mexico. They had become acquainted with the environs during Roth's stay at the D. H. Lawrence ranch outside of Taos, where Roth was writer-in-residence. Muriel began composing music again, mostly for individual instruments, for which she received ample recognition. Since Muriel's death in 1990, Roth has occupied himself with revising the final volumes of the monumental *Mercy of a Rude Stream*. The first volume was published in 1994 by St. Martin's Press under the title *A Star Shines over Mt. Morris Park*. With the publication now of *A Diving Rock on the Hudson,* the first two volumes of *Mercy of a Rude Stream* have appeared. Roth has already completed the other four books of this six-volume work, and they will be scheduled for publication in successive years. St. Martin's has also reissued Roth's 1987 collection of short stories and interviews, *Shifting Landscape.*

In the spring of 1994, Henry Roth received two honorary doctorates, one from the University of New Mexico and one from the Hebrew Theological Institute in Cincinnati.